THE DEFIANT DEBUTANTE

Helen Dickson

MILLS & BOON®

First published in Great Britain 2006
Paperback edition 2007
Harlequin Mills & Boon Limited,
Eton House, 18-24 Paradise Road, Richmond, Surrey TW9 1SR

© Helen Dickson 2006

ISBN-13: 978 0 263 85153 3
ISBN-10:   0 263 85153 2

Set in Times Roman 10¼ on 12 pt.
04-0107-95833

Printed and bound in Spain
by Litografia Rosés S.A., Barcelona

He was rendered speechless as his eyes fastened on the young woman descending the stairs.

Angelina possessed the grace and beauty of a Grecian goddess and the regal bearing of a queen.

When she reached the bottom step Alex took her hand. A slow, appreciative smile worked its way across his face as his eyes leisurely roamed over her body. The unspoken compliment made her blood run warm.

'You look entrancing,' he said in a quiet voice. 'I'm delighted you were able to join us—if tardily.'

'I'm sorry. Am I late?' The look she gave him was one of unadulterated innocence.

'You know you are. What were you trying to do? Hold out to make a grand entrance?'

'What? Me? Really, Alex—you know me better than that,' she murmured meaningfully.

He glanced down at her with a hooded gaze. 'Do I?'

She smiled impishly. 'No one knows me better,' she breathed.

Helen Dickson was born and still lives in south Yorkshire, with her husband, on a busy arable farm where she combines writing with keeping a chaotic farmhouse. An incurable romantic, she writes for pleasure, owing much of her inspiration to the beauty of the surrounding countryside. She enjoys reading and music. History has always captivated her, and she likes travel and visiting ancient buildings.

Recent novels by the same author:

THE DEFIANT
DEBUTANTE

Chapter One

London, May 1812

Birds were stirring in the trees and dew was still on the grass as dawn began to spread its watery grey light over the deserted park. Two men shrouded in long black cloaks rode towards the seclusion of a group of trees and dismounted.

Cursing at his own folly, Alexander Montgomery, the seventh Earl of Arlington and taller of the two, glanced irritably at Sir Nathan Beresford. The two men were as close as friends could be, and as different as night and day. Nathan, with his ash-blond hair and blue eyes, was well liked, good natured and easy-going, and he lacked the aura of authority and power that seemed to surround Alex. Nathan was to act as Alex's second, when the other party deigned to arrive for the duel.

Three inches over six feet tall, Alex was a man diverse and complex, and could be utterly ruthless when the need arose. There was a hard set to his firm jaw, and his wide, well-shaped mouth was held in a stern line. His face was clean shaven and one of arrogant handsomeness, dark brows slashed his forehead and his hair was thick and ebony black. In the midst of so much darkness his eyes were dove grey, striking and piercing. Hidden deep in them was a cynicism, watchful, mocking, as though he found the world a dubious place to be.

He possessed a haughty reserve that was not inviting and set him apart from others in society. There was an aggressive confidence and strength of purpose in his features, and he had an air of a man who succeeds in all he sets out to achieve. From the arrogant lift of his dark head and casual stance, he was a man with many shades to his nature, a man with a sense of his own infallibility.

'You've tied yourself into some knots in your time, Alex, but this is by far the tightest,' Nathan remarked, tethering his horse to a branch and scanning the park for the arrival of Alex's opponent. 'I only hope you can extricate yourself from this mess with some modicum of honour.'

'I agree. It's a damned unfortunate business, Nathan, and I bear the entire weight of this incident on my own conscience.'

'Surely Amelia Fairhurst must shoulder some of the blame.'

'The responsibility is all mine,' Alex replied curtly, dismissing Nathan's well-meaning attempt to absolve him. 'But if ever I am stupid enough to fall prey to another pretty face, remind me to scrutinise her credentials for hidden husbands.'

'Knowing how assiduous you are to detail, I am surprised you·didn't vet her more carefully.'

'I must have taken leave of my senses,' Alex replied, contemplating the irony of the situation. Here he was, one of the most eligible bachelors in England, and yet he had made the fatal mistake of taking to bed a married woman. His stupidity galled him, and he cursed himself for being a dim-witted fool.

Nathan cast him an arch look. 'The delectable Amelia Fairhurst must be quite something for you to have overlooked the fact that she has an aging husband tucked conveniently out of the way in Yorkshire.'

Alex's firm lips curved in a slight smile when he remembered the stunningly vivacious brunette, who had taken no persuading to jump into his bed. 'She's certainly an interesting, unconventional female.'

Nathan chuckled, giving his friend a conspiratorial wink. 'And I seem to recall you saying on more than one occasion that unconventional women are always more exciting between the sheets.'

'Exactly,' Alex replied with a wry grin. 'Providing one doesn't happen to be married to one.'

His words were flippant, but Nathan heard an edge to his voice. Alex was a self-proclaimed single man. Past experiences had forged him into a hardened cynic, and he discarded all women as being dispensable and irrelevant. Age and experience had taught him that women couldn't be trusted, and the first lady to show him this had been his own mother. Her affairs had been notorious and had hurt him badly. They had also been the reason why his father had sought oblivion in alcohol before blowing out his brains. Alex's mother, the beautiful and immoral Margaret Montgomery, had married her Spanish lover soon after and had gone to live in Spain. Whether she lived or had died Alex neither knew nor cared.

'Thank God Fairhurst is in his dotage. With any luck his eyesight will be impaired and his brain addled. I am merely one in a long line of Amelia's lovers. Why the devil he's singled me out is quite beyond me.'

'Maybe it's because you're the only one he knows about.'

'I doubt it. But whatever the reason, remind me not to stray from Caroline from now on. She's more than enough to satisfy my needs.'

Alex was always careful to choose a mistress whose company he enjoyed. She had to be intelligent and sophisticated, who would not mistake lovemaking and desire with love, and, moreover, she had to be a woman who made no demands and expected no promises.

For these reasons she would be kept in the lap of luxury. She could expect a smart town house, a beautiful carriage and horses, servants, gowns, furs and jewels that would be the envy of every other woman.

'Does Caroline know about your affair with Amelia?'

'Yes, but she understands not to ask for an explanation. However, I must admit that I've been unfair to her.'

Nathan quirked a brow, his blue eyes twinkling with light mockery. 'What's this? Are you becoming sentimental?'

'I am never sentimental,' Alex snapped. 'But for the life of me I can't understand why someone as stunning as Amelia married old Fairhurst in the first place. It's disgraceful that so much beauty is wasted on such a pathetic old man.'

Nathan regarded his friend with mild cynicism. 'Yes, you can. You know the type of woman she is. She's a scheming fortune-hunter who likes to drink the finest champagne and wear the most expensive jewels. She openly and shamelessly admits she married Fairhurst for his title and wealth and flaunts it with aplomb.'

'So she does, but you must admit she is more pleasing than those simpering young misses, who swoon at the merest hint of a stolen kiss, their mamas hovering over them like hawks, ready to latch on to me if I show any sign of compromising their precious daughters.'

Alex was aware that he was a fantastic matrimonial prize—top of the list of every ambitious matchmaking mama, whom he treated with amused condescension. They were women whose only ambition in life was to form an alliance with the powerful and illustrious Montgomery family. His ancestors on his mother's side had been rewarded for their loyalty to the crown through the ages with estates and riches enough to make him one of the wealthiest men in England.

Alex's attitude to the female sex was highly critical, his opinion low, but his own popularity among them was high. He was unattached, unattainable, and he would stay that way.

'Perhaps if you were to give marriage some serious thought it might put a stop to the hunt.'

Alex threw Nathan a look that would have stopped a race-horse in its tracks. 'When I want some of your logic, Nathan,' he retorted tersely, 'I'll ask for it.'

'Nevertheless, it would solve the problem,' Nathan went on imperturbably, ignoring Alex's black look. Nathan was one of the few people who could argue with him and escape unscathed.

'Marriage and love are for fools,' Alex stated caustically.

'I never mentioned love. Besides, where you are concerned, since when has love anything to do with marriage or anything else for that matter?' Nathan proclaimed.

'You're right. I despise the romantic ideal of love. I've seen enough of it in the past to know of its destructive effects. Desire I understand. It's a more honest emotion. Passion and desire are easily appeased—fleeting—and easily doused.'

'It's a good thing we're not all as cynical as you are,' Nathan chuckled. 'Not every woman is as ambitious and devious as you seem to think they are. I am fortunate to be married to one, don't forget.'

That was true. Twelve months ago Nathan had found wedded bliss with the lovely Verity Fortesque, a woman with whom even Alex had been unable to find fault. Alex and Verity were cousins, Verity being the only daughter of his Aunt Patience, Uncle Henry's younger sister. Patience's husband had died after just a few short yet happy years of marriage. She had never re-married and still lived in the house they had shared at Richmond.

'Verity is a sweet thing, I grant you. But she is the exception. However, unlike you, I do not find marriage a desirable institution.'

Nathan shot him an exasperated look. 'I agree it can be heaven or hell. Thankfully I chose my wife wisely. Our marriage will be long lasting, based on caring—and love. And you may scoff at that all you like.'

Alex looked at his friend, suddenly serious. 'I'm not scoffing, Nathan. In a way I envy you.'

'You do?'

Alex nodded and looked away.

'You know, Alex, you Montgomerys have become thin on the ground; if you want to continue the line, you really should give some thought to producing an heir. You don't have to marry for love—but I suspect that one day you will fall prey to what you consider to be a debilitating emotion, and it will come as the greatest shock in your life.'

Alex favoured him with a look of absolute disdain, but Nathan ignored it. 'I don't think so,' he answered coldly, his tone suggesting that the subject was closed. But as he turned away he frowned, his thoughts reverting to the matter of an heir. Nathan was right. He was heir to his uncle, the Duke of Mowbray, and Alex knew how anxious his uncle was for him to marry. If he didn't produce a legitimate heir, the title would become extinct. It troubled him more than anyone realised, and he knew he couldn't go on ignoring the issue.

He had stayed a bachelor far longer than most of his contemporaries, and the truth of it was that he was beginning to tire of courtesans and mistresses, and all the jealousies and petty tantrums they brought with them. This latest affair with Amelia Fairhurst had made him see that he was susceptible to women of a certain type, and a wave of disgust swept over him. There had to be an easier way of satisfying his physical needs. Perhaps Nathan was right and a marriage of convenience was the answer after all. In fact, it might have much to offer, and, further, the ideal woman was waiting in the wings.

Lavinia Howard was the eldest daughter of Lord Howard of Springfield Hall in Kent. She was eminently suitable and available. He would dwell on the prospect and invite her—along with a party of friends—to Arlington, his estate in Hertfordshire. If he offered for her, marriage would be a comfortable arrangement that would suit them both. A union between two civilised people who knew what to expect from each other might be just what he needed. He could still enjoy pleasant intrigues, providing he had a compliant wife.

Cursing softly under his breath, impatiently he moved away and began pacing to and fro. 'Fairhurst's late. Where the devil is the man?' Annoyed, Alex thought of the impending duel with distaste. He hoped Fairhurst would achieve satisfaction by merely wounding him—or preferably missing him completely. Alex would fire into the air, and, in so doing, would be admitting his guilt—then the affair would be ended. This was how duels were usually settled between gentlemen. If a death should occur, it would draw the attention of the law, and neither of them wanted that.

'Tell me, Alex. Does your uncle know that Fairhurst has challenged you to a duel?'

Alex's mouth narrowed into a thin line of annoyance. 'No. At this very moment my uncle is en route to America.'

'Really?' Nathan expressed profound surprise. 'I say! That's a bit sudden—and reckless, considering the present situation. It's highly probably that America will declare war on us very soon.'

Alex knew this to be true and his irritation about the situation had increased considerably. 'I know it's only a matter of time before the situation ignites. His decision to go was all rather sudden. He has a cousin, Lydia Hamilton, in Boston who is dying. Her husband is dead and she's fallen on hard times. It appears she has appealed to my uncle to make her daughter his ward. The girl is a minor and Lydia wants him to bring her to England and offer her a home.'

'And you're not pleased, I can see that,' Nathan stated.

'No. When I returned to London from Arlington and read his note, my first impulse was to take the next ship and go after him to bring him back.'

'Thank God common sense prevailed. Do you think your uncle will bring the girl back with him?'

'Uncle Henry is far too sensible to do anything irrational, but from what I recall, his feelings for Lydia were far stronger than just cousinly fondness. Their mothers were sisters, and Henry and Lydia created a scandal that embroiled both families at the time. I believe she is the reason why my uncle never married. I don't know the gist of it, but what I do know makes me decidedly reluctant and uneasy about admitting that woman's daughter into our lives.'

'Why did she go to America?'

'Against her father's wishes, Lydia married an adventurer by the name of Richard Hamilton with undue haste and went with him to Boston. I believe they went west and settled in Ohio. Apparently, her father was outraged and cut her off without a penny. As far as I am aware, nothing has been heard of her since—until my uncle received a letter from her three weeks ago.'

'And no doubt you're afraid he'll be taken in.'

'Yes. He is not a man who shirks his responsibilities, and he obviously thinks of his cousin's daughter as just that, otherwise he would not have gone tearing halfway across the world without discussing the matter with me first. But why go at all? He could have written or sent someone to escort the girl to England.'

'It occurs to me that this grand gesture might be your uncle's way of telling Lydia Hamilton that where she is concerned his feelings are no different to what they were all those years ago.'

It was a possibility that Alex refused to dwell upon.

'Alex, your uncle may have a soft heart, but, contrary to what you believe, he is no fool.'

'You're right. But to saddle himself with a ward at his time of life could be disastrous.'

Nathan arched a sceptical brow. 'For whom? Him or you?'

Alex shot him an icy glance. 'All right, damn you. Me,' he answered curtly.

Nathan grinned, arching a brow at his grim-faced friend. 'It needn't be. I think it's rather touching. But is there no one in America who can look after the girl?'

'Apparently not. My uncle is Lydia Hamilton's next of kin, and I suspect she will take advantage of that. It's years since he last saw her and I'm afraid she might turn out to be a scheming opportunist.'

'Never having met the woman, don't you think you do her an injustice? Come, Alex. I doubt her daughter will bring any real changes to your life,' Nathan argued.

Alex's eyes were full of distaste when he looked at Nathan. 'I hope you're right. But a girl from the wilds of America will have no social skills and find it hard to adjust to the kind of world we inhabit. If so she'll be nothing but a damned nuisance and an embarrassment.'

'Good Lord, Alex! What are you expecting? An ill-bred barbarian? A girl who is half-savage, with brown skin and feathers in her hair?'

Alex shrugged. 'Why not? She could be anything. We know absolutely nothing about her.'

'Nevertheless, having met several colonists both on my travels and here in London, on the whole they are extremely civilised, pleasant people.'

'Several of my acquaintances are Americans, Nathan, so I would be grateful if you did not lecture me on their attributes,' Alex replied drily. 'If my uncle brings the girl to England, he will have legal control over her until she is twenty-one.'

'Are you afraid that she'll be a drain on your resources?'

'No. We can afford it,' Alex bit out.

'Not only will you have to feed her, but you will be faced with the enormous expense of clothing her and introducing her to society.'

'I don't need reminding.' His eyes like dagger thrusts, Alex glared with deadly menace at the amusement Nathan was unable to conceal in his eyes. 'Damn it, Nathan! I do believe you're enjoying my predicament,' he flared in exasperation.

Blithely ignoring his friend's ill humour, Nathan grinned good-naturedly. 'No, not really. I merely find it odd that a girl you have never met, a girl you know nothing about, is capable of rousing so much ire in you. It appears to me that you have already made up your mind not to like her, and have no intention of being charitable or accommodating.'

Alex's eyes impaled Nathan like sharp flints. 'I cannot be accused of being either uncharitable or unaccommodating in this instance. And contrary to what you may think, I have formed no opinion of her whatsoever.'

'I am glad to hear it. You may be pleasantly surprised. Why, she might be a pretty young thing with a sweet disposition and excellent manners.'

'Let us hope so—for all our sakes,' Alex drawled, scanning the park for Lord Fairhurst, his annoyance increasing by the minute the longer he was kept waiting.

'Nevertheless, try to imagine how she might feel,' Nathan persisted. 'Her mother is dying, you say, and she has no relatives in America. Maybe she doesn't want to come to England. My fear is that when she is faced with your formidable manner—a daunting prospect for any girl—it will alienate her from the start. Has it not entered that arrogant, stubborn head of yours that you might like her, Alex? And, if so, will it wound your pride to admit it?'

'Even for an arrogant, stubborn male like me it is not beyond the realms of possibility,' Alex conceded with sarcasm. 'I am protective of my uncle; as you are aware, he does not always enjoy the best of health. He is renowned for his generosity and I am naturally concerned that he is not taken advantage of.'

'Yes, I can understand that. How old is the girl?'

'I really have no idea, but it is my intention to marry her off to the first prospective suitor.'

Nathan watched an inexplicable smile trace its way across the other man's face. 'In which case, you do realise that you will have to provide a somewhat generous dowry?'

Alex regarded Nathan in casual, speculative silence, one dark brow lifted in amused mockery. 'If she turns out to be a wilful hoyden with outrageous manners,' he said drily, 'it will be worth it to get her off our hands.'

Alex had been trained to discipline as soon as he had drawn breath. Already the American girl had caused a rift in his routine—a disturbance that had brought a feeling of unease which had begun to trouble him. It was like a pebble breaking the calm surface of a pond. Once thrown there was nothing to prevent the ripple widening in ever-increasing circles.

The quiet of the park was interrupted. Hearing the measured thud of horses' hooves on the soft turf and the creaking of wheels, they turned to see a closed carriage bearing down on them. It came to a halt and they saw it had only one occupant, a man in middle age. He climbed out and calmly told an astonished Alex that Lord Fairhurst had died suddenly of a seizure during the night.

When Angelina and her mother, Lydia, had left Ohio, never in her life had Angelina known such grief. It broke her heart to think that as well as her father, all the people she had known in the settlement were dead, that whole families had been wiped out by the Shawnee.

Will Casper had accompanied them to Boston. He was a loner, a man of few words, who helped Angelina's father on the land when needed. Will had become a good and loyal friend to them over the years. He had found a doctor to tend to Lydia after she was badly wounded in the Shawnee attack, but he could give them little hope that she would live beyond the next few weeks.

With a horse and wagon, a few meagre possessions and a rifle, they had faced east, pushing themselves hard on well-worn trails. The months of trekking through Pennsylvania and across the mountains were a harsh and emotional time for Angelina, during which she was veiled in a curtain of shock. Her pain defied release. It hid itself in a hollow place inside her heart, beyond the reach of understanding.

Will silently watched her battle to be brave and grown up. He showed her she wasn't alone, and together they made it to the state of Massachusetts, making their home in a shack on the outskirts of Boston. The land round about was wild, and fast-flowing water cut its way through a steep rocky gorge beside the shack, moving north to the Charles River.

The night of the massacre and her own treatment at the hands of the Shawnee had scorched its memory on Angelina's soul. Even now, two years later, she felt defiled and beyond redemption. The terrible, haunting nightmares had pursued her all the way back east. At first they happened every night, but now they were less frequent. But no matter how much time passed, she could not swallow her feeling of outrage and pretend the incident had never happened. She would never be able to come to terms with it, never be able to speak of it. Her terrible secret would remain a burden she would never be able to put into more manageable proportions.

Angelina galloped so hard towards Henry Montgomery that he half-expected a troop of Amazons to materialise from the trees in her wake. Riding the forest pathways on a pony as energetic as herself, she was reckless, like an Indian, and as refreshing as a cool, invigorating wind. With long bouncing braids sticking out from beneath a battered old beaver hat with an eagle's feather stuck in its brim, she pulled her lathered pony to an abrupt halt in front of him, unconcerned by the clouds of dust that the restless animal sent into the air with its hooves, which covered his fine clothes.

Dressed in a worn brown jerkin, ill-fitting deerskin trousers and dull brown boots that no amount of rubbing would bring a shine to, Angelina levelled a steady dark gaze at the tall, silver-haired man. Silently they took stock of each other. She was guarded, wary, looking at him with a wordless resentment.

Henry Montgomery possessed a commanding presence. He had the poise and regal bearing of a man who has lived a thoroughly privileged life. With Angelina he aroused a curious inspection. He looked cool and contained in his immaculate charcoal grey suit and pristine white stock. He was the sort of gentleman her mother had told her about—his rather austere mien and noble bearing out of place here in the backwoods of New England.

Despite the unease and resentment his unexpected arrival caused her, knowing how much her mother was looking forward to meeting him, she had primed herself to be gracious.

'You're the Englishman,' she stated without preamble, her pronunciation clear and distinct. Taking note of this, Henry smiled inwardly. He would have expected nothing less from Lydia's daughter. Swinging her leg over her pony she jumped down like an Indian—lithe, supple and long limbed.

Henry inclined his silver head with amusement and quite without resentment on being confronted by the bold and forthright manner of the girl, who positively oozed energy and vitality. Somehow it came as no surprise to see the butt of a rifle sticking out of a saddle pouch on the side of her pony.

She held out a slim hand. 'It is most kind of you to come all this way.'

Taking her hand in both of his, Henry held it, gazing with complete absorption into the darkest eyes he had ever seen. Set in a face burnt golden by the sun, they slanted slightly and were fringed with sooty black lashes. Her cheekbones were high, her nose pert, and an attractive little cleft dented her delicately rounded chin. Dainty and fine though her features were, her face could possibly pass for a boy's, and with a baggy shirt and jerkin concealing her adolescent breasts, the same could be said of her body. But the mouth was much too soft and pink, too delicate, to belong to a boy. There was something inexpressibly dainty about her, which aroused vague feelings of chivalry.

'I am Henry Montgomery—the Duke of Mowbray. And you are Lydia's daughter.' The likeness almost cut his heart in two.

'My name is Angelina Hamilton,' she replied, withdrawing her hand, completely unfazed by the stranger's grand title and fancy clothes. 'You've come a long way.'

If Angelina did but know it, Henry would walk through hell fire and promise to live in eternal damnation if Lydia asked him to. Even though he was fifty-five and a veteran of hundreds of dispassionate affairs, this girl's mother was the only woman to have captivated his heart. He had loved her as much as it was possible to love another human being, but, because their parents had considered their relationship to be incestuous, he'd had to resign himself to letting her go. Yet, despite the distance, their hearts were still entwined, and neither separation nor time had lessened the pain or their love for each other.

'I came in response to your mother's letter.'

'I know.'

Her eyes were questioning and direct, and her voice was steady, but there was something in it of a frustrated, frightened child.

'How is she? In her letter she mentioned that she was ill—that she was wounded when Indians attacked your home.'

'My mother is dying, sir.'

Carefully Henry schooled his features as he took note of the pain showing naked on Angelina's young face upturned to his. A hint of tears brightened her translucent eyes, which were like windows laying bare the suffering and many hardships of her young life.

'I'm so very sorry, my dear. How dreadful this must be for you.'

'Mother knows she's dying, but she set her mind on not doing so until she heard from you. She didn't know if you would come in person. She didn't expect you to. She thought that perhaps you would write in response to her letter.'

'We used to be very close, your mother and I, before she married your father and came to live in America.' He averted his eyes when Angelina gave him a curious, questioning look. 'Come—walk with me back to the hotel. Mr Phipps, the proprietor, has kindly offered me the use of his buggy. You can take me to her.'

Mr Phipps was a man who liked to talk. All Henry had had to do was sit back and listen when he made it known that he was here to see Mrs Hamilton and her daughter, Angelina.

'Real nice is Miss Angelina,' Mr Phipps had told him. 'Shame about her ma an' pa, though—what the Indians did an' all. After the attack an' when she'd buried her pa, she brought her ma back here an' bought the old McKay place down by the gorge. It was a wreck of a place so it didn't cost much.'

'Did Angelina see what happened?' Henry had asked him.

'She saw all right—more than is right for a child to see. Done killed the Indian who killed her pa, she did. Stabbed him right through the heart, accordin' to Will.'

Unable to comprehend what Angelina must have suffered during the Indian attack, Henry's expression remained unchanged as he absorbed this shocking piece of information. 'Will?'

'Will Casper. He was out west at the time an' came back east with her and her ma. Been right good to them, too. Don't know what they'd 'ave done without him.'

'How do they manage?'

'Miss Angelina spends all her time huntin' an fishin' an' lookin' after her ma, while Will does all the work about the place—when he's not off trappin' beaver. They 'aven't much—but what they do 'ave they make the best of.'

Moving towards the door through which the Englishman had disappeared, Angelina stopped on the threshold, suddenly feeling like an outsider in her own home. Knowing her mother wanted to be alone with him, she would go no further, but before the bedroom door closed she saw the Englishman bend and pick her mother's limp hand up off the patchwork quilt and place it to his lips. At the same time her mother raised her free hand and gently placed it on his silver head, as if bestowing a title on the Duke of Mowbray. It was a scene that would remain indelibly printed on her mind for all time.

When he emerged from Lydia's room after what seemed like an eternity, Henry passed through the house to the veranda, welcoming the cool air after the heat of the sick room. Night had fallen and a languid breeze stirred the trees. The air carried a heavy fragrance of jasmine, wood smoke and cedar wood.

Henry had been taken aback at first to see how ill Lydia was, and he knew she wasn't long for this world. As fragile as a plucked wildflower, she lay still and as white as death against the pillows. But when he'd gazed once more into those glorious dark eyes, he had seen that the years had not quenched their glow.

Lydia had been his *grande passion,* the woman he had been prepared to relinquish his title and his family to marry. She had been part of his flesh and his spirit, and a large part of him had died when she left him. Without warning and without his knowledge she had married Richard Hamilton, sacrificing herself for his own sake, and gone to America. In a brooding silence he was conscious of the girl standing silently behind him, waiting for him to speak, her dog, Mr Boone, at her feet.

Henry turned and looked at her. The soft, silvery moonlight washed over her, touching the delicate, pensive features of her face. He saw the questioning black eyes in cheeks pale with apprehension, and it was only then, upon meeting that dark, misty gaze, that he realised the enormity of the responsibility Lydia had placed in his hands.

'You know why your mother wrote to me, Angelina,' Henry

said, sitting in one of two battered old wicker chairs. 'You also know that I am her cousin and closest kin. It is most unfortunate that on your late father's side there are no close relatives. It is your mother's wish that I take charge of you, and take you back with me to England. Would you like that?'

Angelina's reaction to say no was instinctive, but, realising that this gentleman had travelled a long way to help her mother and herself, she could not be so discourteous. It wasn't that she disliked the Englishman, but the question of being forced into something she had no control over that troubled her. Independence had become a part of everyday life, and she had no wish to renounce that.

'I don't know.'

'I have promised your mother that before we leave America I will legally make you my ward. When she is gone, as your next of kin your responsibility rests entirely with me.'

'Are you really my only living relative?'

Henry frowned. It was one question he had anticipated, and since he now knew what Lydia had told Angelina about her grandparents—that they were dead and nothing more—he was capable of answering. He would rather not, because it meant having to lie. However, he didn't see how it could be evaded if he was to abide by his promise to Lydia.

'Your grandparents on your mother's side were killed in a carriage accident some years ago,' he told her in a gentle, straightforward voice, praying she would never discover the truth.

'My grandparents never wrote to her, and she would never speak of them. Do you know why?'

He nodded, silently cursing Jonathan Adams, Lydia's father. Anne, his wife and Henry's own aunt, had been a gentle woman, who had lived in awe of her husband, and had been unable to stand against him when he had coldly cut Lydia out of their lives.

'When your mother married your father and left England,

Angelina, it was against your grandfather's wishes. He was a hard, unforgiving man and meant to punish her for disobeying him. He cut off all connection with her—and insisted that your grandmother did the same. You mother never forgave them.'

How true this was, Henry thought sadly. Lydia's lack of forgiveness was no temporary state of affairs. With great intensity she had insisted that there must be no connection between Angelina and her grandmother. Not wishing to distress her further, Henry had promised he would abide by her wishes.

Angelina sat on the top step of the veranda with her back propped against a wooden rail. 'Won't someone like me be a burden to you in England—a financial one?'

Henry was mildly amused at her words so innocently and frankly spoken. 'I can well afford it. It will be a pleasure. And you are far too lovely and independent to be a burden. You will learn to be a fine lady,' he told her, wanting to tell her not to change, that she was just perfect the way she was. But, if she was to live in the social world he inhabited, regretfully it was necessary.

'How should I address you? For me to call you "my Lord" every time I speak to you is too formal and quite ridiculous.'

'I couldn't agree more. Uncle Henry will be appropriate.'

She considered this for a moment and then nodded. 'Yes. Uncle Henry it is then.'

Angelina's new uncle had a warmth of manner that made her feel as if she had known him a long time. His physical impression might be one of age, yet his twinkling eyes and willing smile were the epitome of eternal youth. Over the distance they smiled at each other, comfortable together, sharing a moment of accord on the veranda that seemed to bind them together.

'It is obvious to me that your education seems to have been taken care of, so we'll have no trouble in that quarter,' Henry remarked at length. 'Your pronunciation of the English language is excellent.'

'Thank you. I am also conversant in French, Latin and some Greek, too,' Angelina confessed proudly. 'Despite the everyday hardships of living in Ohio, my mother saw to that.'

Henry's admiration for her was growing all the time.

'Do you have a wife?' Angelina asked suddenly, with the natural curiosity of a child.

'No,' he answered, startled by the abruptness of her question, but not offended by it. 'I never found a woman I wanted to spend the rest of my life with—except, perhaps, one,' he said softly, his eyes clouding with memory, wondering how Angelina would feel if she knew that her beloved father had been accepted by her mother as a hasty second best.

'But isn't it the custom for gentlemen of your standing to marry to beget an heir?'

'I had no intention of adhering to custom by chaining myself to any woman I might only have a passing fancy for, in order to beget an heir. Besides, I have a perfectly acceptable heir in my nephew, Alex—my brother's son.'

Angelina's eyes became alert. 'Alex?'

'Alexander Henry Frederick Montgomery, the seventh Earl of Arlington and Lord Montgomery—which are just two of his titles. His friends call him Alex.'

Angelina's eyes widened in awe. 'Gracious me! What an awesome responsibility it must be to have so many names. Doesn't he feel weighted down by so many titles?'

'Not in the least. He was born to them and learned to accept and ignore them from an early age. One day he will become the sixth Duke of Mowbray—following my demise, you understand. His title as the seventh Earl of Arlington he inherited from his mother's family. The sixth earl died several years ago, and as the estate is unentailed he left it directly to Alex—with provision made for his mother, who was an only child. He made representations to the King that Alex be given the title of seventh Earl on his demise. You'll meet him when we get to

England. He is the only son of my brother, who died when Alex was fifteen. Alex is now twenty-eight—and I swear that young man is the reason for my hair turning white,' he chuckled softly.

'Is he married?'

'Despite being one of the most eligible bachelors in England, I've all but despaired of ever seeing him suitably married.'

'Why? What's wrong with him?'

'Nothing. He hasn't got two heads or anything like that.' Henry chuckled aloud. 'It is his unequivocal wish to remain a bachelor and childless. I cannot hide the fact that he's an exacting man, who insists on the highest standards from all those he employs. However, he can be quite charming, when it suits him.'

'What does he do?' Angelina asked, already in awe of Alex Montgomery.

'Alex handles all my business and financial affairs—as well as his own. He has a brilliant mind and a head for figures that shames me. He drives himself hard, demanding too much of himself—and others. Ever since he took over he's increased all my holdings considerably. Now I'm in my dotage I'm perfectly content to sit back and let him handle everything. Oh, he consults me now and then, but business is not my forte.'

'And do you trust him?'

'Implicitly. Besides, my dear…' he chuckled softly, his grey eyes twinkling merrily '…if I didn't, I wouldn't dare tell him so.'

Angelina frowned. He sounds quite formidable. He's bound to resent me. How do you think he'll react?

Henry grinned. 'He'll be outraged when he finds out I have made myself your guardian—but he'll soon get used to having you around. Besides, there's not a lot he can do about it.' He relaxed, regarding her warmly. 'Don't worry, my dear. You'll soon get used to Alex.'

Just two days after Henry Montgomery had come to Boston, Lydia slipped quietly away in her sleep.

Angelina's heart was heavy with sadness, but she didn't give in to her grief. Her mother had suffered greatly, and now she was at peace. Henry gave no outward sign to Angelina of his own private emotions, but his face was lined, his eyes dull with a deep sorrow.

It was difficult for Will to stand on the bustling quayside and watch Angelina board the ship. Her leaving would leave a huge hole in his heart.

Feeling quite forlorn, a hard lump of tears formed in Angelina's throat as she looked into Will's rheumy eyes. He looked lost and torn and old. Although it broke her heart to do so, she had decided to leave Mr Boone behind, in the hope that he would help console Will and that it would ease their parting. Will had carved her a wonderful likeness of Mr Boone out of ebony. It was packed in her trunk and she would cherish it always.

'Goodbye, Will. I'll never forget you, you know that. I promise I'll write and let you know what it's like in England.'

'You go and make your ma proud,' Will said, his voice hoarse with emotion, wondering where she would send her letters to when he had disappeared into the backwoods of North America. 'You're going to do all those things she talked about. You'll dazzle all those English gents—you see if you don't. Remember it's what your ma wanted. She told you that.'

'I do remember, Will, and I'll never forget. Ever.'

Will's eyes met those of Henry Montgomery in mutual concern. Unbeknown to Angelina, Will had told the Englishman what had happened to her on the night of the Shawnee massacre, and how he had rescued her. He hoped that, in knowing, the English duke would have a deeper understanding of his ward.

Henry had listened to all Will had said with a sense of horror. Will had told him that there was still something about that night Angelina refused to speak of. It was like an inner wound that was bleeding. The secret lurked in her gaze. Was it the shock of the massacre and her father's death that caused it— or something else? Whatever it was might be eased when she reached England. A new country, a new home—a new life.

Chapter Two

The sky was overcast as the carriage ventured north towards Mayfair. Angelina devoured the sights and sounds of what her mother had told her was the most exciting city in the world. On reaching Brook Street she gaped in awe when the door of one of the impressive houses was opened by a servant meticulously garbed in white wig, mulberry coat edged in gold and white breeches. His face was impassive as he stepped aside to let them enter.

'Welcome to Brook Street,' Henry said, smiling as he watched his ward's reaction.

Angelina was completely overwhelmed by the beauty and wealth of the house. Standing in the centre of the white marble floor she looked dazedly about her, wondering if she had not been brought to some royal palace by mistake. She wasn't to know that compared to Mowbray Park, Henry's home in Sussex, this house on Brook Street was considered to be of moderate proportions. Craning her neck and looking upward, she was almost dazzled by the huge chandelier suspended from the ceiling, dripping with hundreds of tiny crystal pieces.

A superior-looking man with a dignified bearing and dressed

all in black stepped forward. 'Welcome back, your Grace. You are expected. I trust you had a pleasant crossing from America.'

'Yes, thank you, Bramwell. Is my nephew at home?'

The butler replied, 'No, your Grace. He's out of town for a few days, staying with Sir Nathan and his wife in Surrey.'

'I see.' Henry smiled at Angelina, who looked visibly relieved by the reprieve. 'Perhaps you would like to see your room and freshen up before dinner, my dear. Show Miss Hamilton to her room, will you, Bramwell.'

'Certainly, your Grace. The green room has been prepared. I'm certain it will meet with Miss Hamilton's approval. It's quiet and overlooks the garden,' he told Angelina, before leading her up the elegant staircase.

Entering a large room on the first floor, Angelina blinked at the extravagance and unaccustomed luxury. The walls were lined with mirrors and pictures depicting placid rural scenes, and the bed hangings were in the same pale green brocade embroidered with ivory silk as the windows.

'Oh, what a lovely room,' she gasped.

'I thought you'd like it.' Bramwell directed his gaze towards the dressing room when a fresh-faced young maid emerged, her arms full of linen. 'This is Miss Bates, Miss Hamilton. She has been appointed your personal maid.'

When Bramwell had departed Angelina smiled warmly at her maid, who bobbed a curtsy. Two or three years older than Angelina, she was quite pretty, small and rather plump, with the majority of her dark brown hair concealed beneath a modest white cap.

'I've never had a personal maid before,' Angelina confessed. 'What does it mean?' She saw surprise register on Miss Bates's face, which was replaced by an indulgent little smile. No doubt she had decided that, as she was from America, her new mistress's ignorance could be excused, that perhaps people over there weren't as civilised or refined as they were in England.

'Why—I see to all your personal needs—take care of your clothes—everything, really,' she explained cheerfully.

'Well, it seems you will have to teach me—and I have much to learn. Where I come from, unless you are very rich, one doesn't have personal maids.'

Miss Bates seemed to be lost for words at this candid admission. 'I'm sure you'll soon get used to having me do things for you.'

'Perhaps, but I simply refuse to call you Miss Bates. What is your Christian name?'

'Pauline, miss.'

'Then since we are to spend a good deal of time together, I shall address you as Pauline,' she said, as two footmen entered with her trunk.

The following afternoon while her uncle was resting, and feeling hemmed in and restless at having to remain indoors because of the rain that continued to pour down, Angelina wandered through the house. Her uneducated eye was unable to place a value on the things she saw, but she was able to appreciate and admire the quality of the beautifully furnished rooms.

The library, with its highly polished floor and vividly coloured oriental carpets, was like an Aladdin's cave—a treasure trove of precious leatherbound tomes. It was a room which, to Angelina, encapsulated every culture and civilisation of the universe, where bookshelves stretched from floor to ceiling, broken only by a huge white marble fireplace and long windows. Happily she browsed along the shelves, looking for a book to suit her mood, eventually finding just what she was looking for.

Unaccustomed to being indoors for such a long period, she placed her books on the desk and went to the window, leaning her shoulder against the window frame, gazing in a somewhat disconsolate manner at the garden, glad to see it had stopped raining and envying the gardener pottering about among the flower beds. Unable to resist the temptation to join him, but not wishing to dirty her dainty slippers, she dashed to her room and donned an old pair of stout boots she had brought with her.

She entered the garden by the long French windows in the library, and spent half an hour chatting to the gardener and helping him debud some of the sodden roses—which Jarvis thought highly irregular considering who she was. Then the rain came down again and the wind rose with a vengeance, so she made a dash for the house. On entering the library she was unable to prevent the sudden gust that sent some loose papers blowing off the desk all over the place and a tiny figurine from crashing to the floor.

'You stupid, reckless little fool. Do you have to enter the house like a bloody whirlwind?' a voice thundered.

Angelina's face was a frozen mask. In her struggle to keep the door from blowing off its hinges, she hadn't seen the man sitting at the desk with damp, unruly locks of raven black hair tumbling wildly over his head. Scraping his chair back, he stood up and strode towards her, his face livid.

Like an animal on the defensive, Angelina's eyes narrowed and flashed. 'You are just about the rudest man I have ever come across and you have a foul mouth for such a well-bred gentleman—I assume you are Lord Montgomery.'

'Precisely, and I know who you are—Miss Hamilton.' He seemed to lose control of his expression momentarily as his gaze passed over her, from the top of her shining head to her boots, where it froze.

Angelina followed his gaze and saw her mud-caked boots dirtying the parquet flooring. Soil clung to the front of her skirt, resisting all her efforts to brush it away. Despairing, she groaned inwardly with frustration. For two days dressed like a lady, she had waited for the master of the house to appear, and what good had it done her? Having no intention of apologising for the way she looked, ignoring the irate nobleman, she bent down and eased off her boots, placing them by the door. She then further astounded his lordship by going down on her knees and beginning to pick up the pieces of the broken figurine.

'Leave it,' he snapped. 'The servants will clean it up.'

'I made the mess so I will do it. I don't wish to put anyone to any trouble.'

'I said leave it. The servants are here for your convenience as well as mine.' When she took no notice he reached out and grasped her arm, his fingers biting into her flesh. There was a loud crack as Angelina slapped his hand away. Momentarily startled, he drew back. 'Why—you hot-headed little savage,' he barked. 'What the hell are you trying to do?'

His scowl bore into her as Angelina rubbed her smarting hand. 'That will teach you not to touch me,' she snapped, hotly irate. 'It's your own fault. Keep your hands to yourself in future.'

Alex's lean cheeks flexed tensely and his grey eyes narrowed. 'Do you have any idea how exasperating you are?' he gritted. 'And do you have to appear looking like a labourer?'

'I'm not afraid of hard work,' she snapped testily.

'I imagine you're not, but you will find that here you will do things differently.'

The pieces gathered up, Angelina got to her stockinged feet and placed them on the desk. 'I'm sorry I broke it,' she said, unaware of the streak of mud on her cheek as she faced him squarely, two fiercely indomitable wills meeting head on and each refusing to step aside to allow the other to pass. His face was as cold and hard as the stone from which his fine house was built. 'I didn't mean to. I suppose it was valuable.'

'Priceless.'

'If I had some money of my own I would offer to pay for it, but I don't.' Angelina recognised authority when she saw it. Everything about this illustrious lord bespoke power, control and command. The hard set of his darkly handsome face did not suggest much tolerance or forgiveness. 'No doubt you have already made up your mind where to bury me?'

'Not yet. But I dare say I will.' His voice was of a rich, deep timbre. He watched as she flexed her arm. 'Is anything wrong?'

'You hurt my arm,' she said crossly, her dark eyes narrowing and accusing.

'I apologise for that—if you will apologise for appearing like a field hand.' He waited, his grey eyes penetrating.

'I suppose so,' was all Angelina was prepared to relent.

Dressed in snug-fitting, calf-coloured trousers tucked into highly polished tan boots, and a fine white lawn shirt open at the throat, his body well honed and muscular, Angelina could see there was something purposeful and inaccessible about Alex Montgomery, and those grey eyes, which penetrated her own, were as cold and hard as newly forged steel. There was no warmth in them, no humour to soften those granite features.

She sensed his amazement that she had the effrontery to face him as an equal. Clearly this wasn't what he'd expected—and certainly not what she'd intended. She knew better than to be rude to a man in his own house, but after suffering the indignity of being spoken to so rudely and manhandled, she had mentally drawn the battle lines and moved her guns into position. They looked at each other hard, suspicion and mistrust on both sides.

His expression became suddenly thoughtful and he inspected her upturned face as if something puzzled him.

'Do you always subject people to such close scrutiny when you meet them for the first time?' she asked directly. 'I am not used to being looked at like that and find it extremely disagreeable. Is there something wrong with my face that makes you examine it so thoroughly?'

'When I look at you I think unaccountably of fairies and imps and things, and have half a mind to demand whether you have bewitched Uncle Henry and my servants—according to my uncle, every one of them seems to be under your spell.'

'I will not argue the point, but I assure you, Lord Montgomery, that it is not my intention to disrupt your household.'

With a look that betrayed a mild degree of surprise, he nodded. 'Thank you. I respect your frankness.' Thrusting his hands into his pockets, he walked to the window, standing with his back to her while he gazed out. His body was tense, his shoulders squared. 'I hope the servants are looking after you,' he said at length.

Angelina was uncomfortable, but she was relieved to hear civility in his tone. 'Yes—thank you,' she replied, imitating his politeness. 'Everyone is being very kind.'

'And you like the house?'

'Very much. But then, who wouldn't?' she said, warm in her admiration. 'Have you spoken to Uncle Henry since you arrived home?'

He turned and looked at her. 'Briefly.'

'And did he tell you anything about me?'

Alex nodded. 'He told me that when your mother died he did the Christian thing by making you his ward and giving you a home. He assures me you are a charming, delightful and remarkably intelligent young woman who, for the short time he has known you, has made him extremely happy. In short, you are an absolute treasure.'

Angelina was stung by the irony of his words. 'But you don't believe him.'

'Not if the past few minutes are anything to go by. I am more astute than my uncle. I prefer to reserve judgment.'

Lifting her chin proudly, Angelina met his gaze, not with defiance but a quiet resolve. 'You don't want me here, do you, Lord Montgomery?'

'I love and hold my uncle in the highest esteem, Miss Hamilton. I may not be happy about what he did, but whether I like it or not you are here now and a member of this family. As such, that is how you will be treated and how you will behave.'

'I realise that my presence in your house is an inconvenience, but taking everything into account, you must see that I have been more inconvenienced than you.'

'In which case, since we have no choice in the matter, the obvious solution is that we should both try to make the best of things and be cordial to each other. Don't you agree?'

'Yes. I have no wish to upset Uncle Henry,' she said.

Absently she tucked a stray lock of silky hair behind her ear that had dared escape her tight braid. The unconscious gesture caused Alex to study her properly for the first time, and he was amazed by what he saw. Her hair was the colour of rich mahogany with highlights of red and gold, making him think of harvest corn, chestnuts and autumn fires. Parted at the center, it was drawn back and woven together in one long thick braid that reached her waist. Accustomed to seeing women with neatly arranged curls and ringlets, he found this style unusual, but strangely attractive on this young woman. He had the absurd desire to reach out and set her hair free and let it spill about her shoulders, convinced it would glow with the glorious vibrancy of autumn leaves.

Her eyes, surrounded by thick, curling sooty lashes, were captivating. At first they looked so dark to be almost black, but on closer inspection they were seen to be not black at all, but the colour of two glorious purple velvet-soft pansies. Her skin was flushed with warmth like that of a ripe peach, and she had an enigmatic mouth, ripe and full of wonderful promise. The daffodil-yellow gown she wore revealed a female form that was faultless, slim and strong, with long legs and curves in all the right places. With angular cheekbones her face was alluring, interesting, and overall there was an innocence and vulnerability about her that would put a practised seducer like him beyond the realm of her experience.

'You are not at all what I expected.'

'What did you expect?' she retorted sharply. 'A creature

from the wilds who is half-savage, with brown skin and feathers in her hair?'

Alex smiled tightly. Nathan had said something along those lines. 'Heaven forbid! I certainly didn't expect to find someone with an interest in fine literature.'

'Education has reached America, you know. We are civilised.'

'Looking as you do just now, Miss Hamilton, I would say you have some way to go before you reach that status,' he said with an ironic curl of his lips. 'However, it's apparent to me that you are extremely clever.'

Angelina's eyes narrowed. She could feel her ire returning. 'Something tells me that it is not my interest in fine literature that you speak of,' she said, her smile deliberately cold and ungracious. 'It is plain to me that you are displeased about something

Alex crossed to his desk and perched his hip on the edge, crossing his arms with a casualness that aggravated Angelina's temper still further. His imperturbable gaze studied her stormy eyes. 'Miss Hamilton, when I read my uncle's letter informing me he had gone to America, everything about you displeased me at the time,' he told her firmly.

Angelina's temper flared at this open affront. 'I thought it might. And I sense your displeasure has increased since. Is it so very strange for people to look after relatives who find themselves destitute?'

'It is, when the parties concerned live on opposite sides of the world and there has been no contact between them for some time. I find it strange that after all these years, when not a word or a letter has passed between them, your mother should suddenly write to my uncle and beg him to make you his ward.'

'You're mistaken, Lord Montgomery,' Angelina answered, stung to the quick by his remark about her mother. 'My mother never begged for anything in her life. She wrote to Uncle Henry because he was her next of kin and she had no one else to turn to.'

Alex knew this not to be the case, but, having been warned

by his uncle of the need for secrecy relating to this young woman's grandmother, he respected the request for silence.

'If you must know, I opposed it,' Angelina went on. 'I had no wish to leave America, but it was my mother's wish.'

'A woman with colossal aspirations where her daughter is concerned,' Alex said coldly. 'Do not think me ignorant of your situation in Boston, Miss Hamilton, and that your mother sent you to my uncle as a poor relation, seeking to save you from poverty.'

Alex caught the flare of anger his words about her mother brought to her face, but he also saw something that resembled pain and hurt in the depths of her eyes. For a split second her young face looked defenceless and exposed, and already he was beginning to regret his unjustifiable and unpardonable attack.

His cutting remark directed at her mother erupted inside Angelina like a volcano and she longed to lash out at him. Feeling the nightmare of the Indian attack closing around her again, she could see her mother's face as she lay on the ground after the knife had ripped into her, digging deep, and the rich, proud colour of her blood as it had poured from her wound to be soaked up by the dry earth.

'You cold-hearted, overbearing, arrogant beast. How dare you? You insult my mother, and I will not allow anyone to besmirch her memory. She was the kindest, gentlest of women ever to draw breath, but that is something a man as conceited and disgustingly rude as yourself would never understand.' Furiously she turned and marched to the door, her fists clenched by her sides.

For a split second a flicker of amused respect replaced Alex's anger as he gazed after the young American girl. 'Have you nothing else to say?'

She turned and glowered at him, feeling tears prick the backs of her eyes. Furiously she blinked them away. If she broke down and cried, he would have the mastery over her. She would not grant him that. 'Not to you. Might I suggest that in future you mind your own business and I will mind mine.'

Alex's black brows snapped together and his eyes narrowed, but his voice was carefully controlled when he spoke. 'You may suggest anything you like, but since you have raised the matter, you ought to know that I have full control over all my uncle's affairs.'

His words were insulting and their meaning cut Angelina like a knife. 'His business affairs, not his personal affairs,' Angelina corrected acidly. She should have withered beneath his icy glare, but she was too enraged to be intimidated by him. 'I should tell you that I have a streak to my nature that fiercely rebels against being ordered what to do.'

'I have a formidable temper myself,' he told her with icy calm.

'I do not come under the category of property, Lord Montgomery, and I am not asking you for anything. In the eyes of the law Uncle Henry is my legal guardian, and if you wish to challenge that then you are free to do so.'

'I have no intention of doing any such thing.' His words were like a whiplash, his eyes glacial. 'My uncle has taken you in and does not need to justify his actions to me or anyone else. What matters is that you are in this house under his guardianship and a member of this family, and because I care a great deal for his happiness, I will do nothing about it. But in time I suspect you will show your true colours without any help from me—so I advise you to take care, unless you want to be shipped back to America, lock, stock and barrel.'

Angelina glared at him, two bright spots of colour burning on her cheeks. She refused to look away, but there was little she could say in her defence. This man had already made up his mind about her, and anything she might say would be futile. He was convinced she was a clever, scheming opportunist out to rid his uncle of his last shilling, and nothing she said was going to change his mind.

'Have you nothing to say for yourself?'

'What's the point? There is no argument against a closed

mind. You made up your mind about me before I set foot on English soil.'

Alex contemplated her with a half-smile. 'It may surprise you to learn that before I met you I was prepared to give you the benefit of the doubt.'

'And now?'

'That still applies. You accuse me of making up my mind about you before I met you. I accuse you of doing likewise. You also summed up your opinion of me,' Alex stated. 'From the moment you entered this house, no doubt you have listened to gossip from below stairs, but whatever you have heard, forget it. You don't know me.'

Angelina could not look away from him—in fact, unconsciously her feet took her slowly back to where he still perched on the edge of the desk, her rebellious eyes holding his. She stood close, her face on a level with his, her skirts brushing his tan boots.

'You're wrong. I may only have been in your presence a few minutes,' she countered, 'but I have made a very accurate assessment of your character.'

'Do you normally form an opinion of a person after so short a time?' he asked, trying to ignore the delectable attributes that stood just within his easy reach. Instantly, his whole body began to hum an ardent, familiar song that clashed with what he should be feeling.

'In your case it was not difficult,' she provided. 'You are rude, overbearing and dictatorial, and you have the manners of a barbarian.'

Alex arched his brows, faint amusement and a stirring of respect in the icy depths of his eyes. 'That bad?'

'Worse. You are cold and heartless and I cannot abide your superior male attitude—your insufferable arrogance and conceit.'

He looked at her with condescending amusement that in time she would come to detest. 'And you, madam, with a tongue on you that would put a viper to shame, can hardly be called a paragon of perfection.'

'Go to hell,' she blazed, which was most uncharacteristic of her. But at that moment she was sorely tempted to fling more than abuse at Alex Montgomery and inflict physical damage. No doubt this infuriating man was already telling himself that she was showing her 'true colours'. She cast a look of pure loathing at him, noting that her words had brought a satisfied smile to his arrogant mouth.

His dark brows rose and he gave her a lofty, superior look. 'I shall, but I shall go in my own way and in my own good time.'

'It cannot be too soon for me.'

Afraid that she was going to crack completely and make a fool of herself, Angelina raised her chin and turned. With all the dignity she could muster she picked up her boots and left the room, her slender hips swaying graciously. She didn't see the admiring light in Alex's eyes, or the indefinable smile lurking at the corner of his lips as he observed her less than dignified progress through the hall, for as she stormed towards the stairs she almost knocked over an elderly manservant who was carrying a silver platter.

The poor man halted in his progress and turned and watched her go halfway up the stairs, wondering what could have happened to wipe away her sweet expression and replace it with one of black thunder. His answer came when he glanced through the open door into the library and saw Lord Montgomery still perched on the edge of the desk. Shaking his head, he chuckled. His lordship was home, which explained everything.

Alex couldn't think of anyone, male or female, who would have stood up to him the way Angelina had just done, verbally attack him and walk away as regal as any queen. The girl had spirit, a fiery spirit that challenged him. Her arrogance was tantamount to disrespect, yet in spite of himself he admired her style. Nor was she afraid of him. That was the intriguing part about her.

He allowed himself to remember her face, an alluring face, captivating and expressive, he decided. Her chin was small and round, with an adorable, tiny little cleft in the centre. But it was her eyes he remembered most—enormous, liquid bright—the kind of eyes a man wanted to see looking up at him when he was about to make love.

Idly he picked up the books she had selected to read and left behind. On opening them he stared, so taken aback that he almost laughed out loud. Alex had a familiarity with the ways of the female sex, but nothing had prepared him for this.

Ornithology! Horses!

When all the women of his acquaintance read romantic poetry and cheap, insipid novelettes that had a deleterious effect on their impressionable minds, Angelina Hamilton preferred reading about birds and horses. He chuckled, shaking his head slowly in disbelief. The girl was a phenomenon.

Setting his jaw, with purposeful strides he left the library and climbed the stairs to her room, rapping sharply on the door. Angelina opened it herself, glowering when she saw who it was.

'Well? What do you want?' she snapped, fully prepared for another angry confrontation. 'Have you come to tell me that the war is over and I've won?'

'No. In view of my former rudeness, I've come to make amends,' he told her, standing in the doorway in a misleading, indolent manner.

Angelina eyed him warily. 'Have you? You seem unsure.'

Alex raised his eyebrows quizzically. Without being invited to do so he stepped past her, as bold as may be, his eyes settling like a winter chill on her terrified maid. 'Leave us.'

Pauline looked nervously at Angelina, who nodded. 'It's all right, Pauline. I don't think Lord Montgomery intends to ravish me,' she said, her voice dripping sarcasm, 'since the only emotion I seem to rouse in him is a desire to strangle me. Not wishing to be hanged for my murder, I think we can safely assume he will keep his hands to himself.'

Alex's face was set in an almost smiling challenge. 'Don't be so certain. I am sorely tempted. I could break you in half like a twig if I so wished and to hell with the consequences.'

'Lord Montgomery,' Angelina retorted sharply, dark eyes locking on grey ones, 'if you plan another battle, you can leave right this minute.'

'Nothing so dramatic—merely a mild skirmish.'

Pauline gaped, amazed at her mistress's courage. No one ever spoke to Lord Montgomery in that tone. Bobbing a hurried curtsy she scuttled out.

'Well?' said Angelina, feeling strangely threatened now the closed door separated her from Pauline.

'You left your books,' he said, holding them out to her.

Disarmed, she was completely taken aback. 'Oh! Thank you,' Taking them from him, she placed them on a chair. 'Why did you dismiss Pauline?'

'I do not like my conversations being listened to by servants.'

'And are we going to have a conversation, Lord Montgomery? Do you mean to tell me that you sought me out in my room for a reason other than to bring me the books I selected from the library—which I could have collected myself?'

'Miss Hamilton, in common agreement, can we not strive to portray ourselves as being both gracious and mannerly for our uncle's sake?'

'A truce, you mean?'

'Something like that.'

At first she seemed to consider his offer, but then her expression changed and she was on the defensive. 'No. There will be no concessions. In the first place, I don't like you.'

Alex arched his eyebrows at her frank admission. 'And the second?'

'Until I have an apology from you.'

'An apology? What are you talking about?' he asked with infuriating calm.

'You insulted and degraded my mother. I cannot let it pass. If I were a man, I'd demand satisfaction and call you out. Believe me, I'm sorely tempted to do that anyway, but since your demise would cause Uncle Henry extreme distress, I suppose I shall just have to make do with an apology.'

Alex looked at her with a mixture of amusement and disbelief. The chit truly was incredible. 'You? Shoot me?'

'Yes. And I never miss my target.'

'Then, faced with determination such as this, you leave me with little choice. Very well. I apologise. It was wrong of me to say what I did.'

Angelina was astonished. She hadn't expected it would be that easy to extricate an apology from him. 'You apologise?'

'Of course. And consider yourself fortunate. Apologies don't come easily to me.'

'I gathered that.'

'You accept it, then?'

'Providing it isn't lukewarm and you mean it, I will,' Angelina replied stonily.

'Thank you.'

'Now you may leave,' she told him firmly, her smile deliberately cold and ungracious.

Alex calmly ignored her and looked about him for a moment, his eyes caught by Will's skilful carving of Mr Boone, which Angelina had placed on a table beside the bed. Every night since leaving Boston it was the last thing she looked at, and as she closed her eyes and went to sleep it made her feel less wretched and alone. With genuine interest Alex moved towards it, looking at it with admiration and the eye of a connoisseur.

'This is a fine, interesting piece of craftsmanship—lovingly carved. Yours, I presume?' he asked, looking at her.

'Of course it's mine,' she snapped, annoyed because he showed no inclination to leave. 'I haven't stolen it, if that's what you mean.'

'That was not what I meant. I was asking you if the dog was yours—a pet, perhaps.'

Angelina felt foolish for having misunderstood his meaning. 'Yes. A very dear friend of mine carved his likeness. He carves animals and birds and sells them to make a living—along with his beaver pelts,' she explained, captivated by Lord Montgomery's strong, lean fingers as they caressed the wooden object. 'He presented me with it before I left Boston.'

'Do you miss him?'

'Who?'

'Your friend.'

'Why—yes. Very much.'

'What was the name of your friend?'

'Will. Will Casper.'

'And your dog?'

'Mr Boone.'

A lazy smile spread over his face, which seemed softer now. 'So named after Daniel Boone, the intrepid pioneer.'

Angelina was pleasantly surprised to learn that he knew something of America's history. 'Yes. You've heard of him.'

Alex nodded. 'I'm a businessman. I make a point of keeping abreast of world news. It proves advantageous where investments are concerned. And did your dog live up to his namesake?'

'Does. He's a brave little thing with a heart as big as a lion.'

'Is?' Alex's eyebrows snapped together as a sudden, decidedly unpleasant thought occurred to him. 'You are not going to tell me you brought him with you—that the animal is here, in this house?'

Alex looked so horrified at the prospect of Mr Boone capering through his stately rooms that Angelina's composure slipped a notch closer to laughter. She bit her lower lip to still the trembling as she caught his eyes. 'You needn't glower in that ferocious fashion, my lord. You will be relieved when I tell you that I left him in Boston with Will.'

His relief was evident. 'Thank the Lord for that. The last thing I need right now is a dog disrupting the routine of things.'

Angelina made a pretence of looking offended. 'I will have you know that Mr Boone is extremely well behaved and never disgraces himself. Have you an aversion to dogs, Lord Montgomery?'

'I keep several of my own at Arlington. But they are used for hunting and well disciplined by their handlers. They are also kept outside in kennels where they belong.'

'Yes, I expect they are,' Angelina replied, with a cheeky impudence that Alex found utterly exhilarating. The ghost of a smile flickered across his face as his eyes locked on to hers in silent, amused communication, and he was quite entranced by the idea of sharing her humour.

He walked towards the fire where he stood, hands behind his back, staring down at the glowing heat. 'How long did you live in Boston?'

'About two years. We left Ohio when the Shawnee raided our settlement. They—they killed everyone—including my father,' she told him softly, 'and wounding my mother.'

Alex moved closer, looking down into the sensitive face before him, but, unable to meet his gaze, she lowered her head.

'And you?' he asked, placing a finger gently under her chin and tipping her face up to his, his eyes searching, probing, seeing something flicker in those dark, appealing depths: a secret grief, perhaps.

'As you can see, I was more fortunate. I am alive and I'm grateful.'

Alex saw her eyes register an anguish and horror he couldn't begin to comprehend, and observed the gallant struggle she made to bring herself under control.

There was silence, inhabited by the living presence of the fire. In spite of herself Angelina found her eyes captured and held by Lord Montgomery's silver gaze. Then, aware of Lord Montgomery's finger still poised beneath her chin, she suddenly recollected herself and recoiled with an instinctive fear that he might get too close.

'Lord Montgomery,' she said, her voice tight, 'I have known you long enough to realise that you didn't consider your manner towards me earlier as warranting an apology. Will you please come to the point and tell me the real reason for coming to my room? I am not so dim-witted as to believe it was your interest in my dog or my life before coming to England. I may have accepted your apology, but it doesn't change anything, does it? You still don't approve of me and think I'm out to hurt your uncle in some way.'

His eyes became as hard as granite. 'Contrary to what you may think, I sought you out because I could see that some form of atonement for my earlier behaviour was in order. However, since you are determined to harp on about it, I will remind you I am concerned about Uncle Henry's happiness and well being. As you will know, having spent the past few weeks in his company, he does not always enjoy the best of health.'

'That I do know, having seen how he is often plagued with rheumatic pains.'

'Correct. So naturally I was concerned when I returned to London after an absence of several weeks in the country and discovered he'd taken off for America without discussing the matter with me first.'

'I cannot for the life of me see why he should. Your uncle is of an age to act without your permission.'

As he rested his hands on his hips and looking down into her stormy eyes, Alex's own were so cold that Angelina was sure they could annihilate a man.

'My uncle is the finest, most generous man I have ever

known, Miss Hamilton. What my opinions are concerning you has no bearing on the case, but because he and your mother were once close, and, as you correctly pointed out earlier, he is your next of kin, he will take his responsibilities where you are concerned seriously. If you hurt him in any way, I will personally make your life hell. Do you understand me?'

The look that passed between them crackled with hidden fire. Just for a moment Alex saw something savage and raw stir in the depths of Angelina's eyes, before they blazed with outrage.

'Perfectly,' she replied. With her fists clenched and her chin raised, she faced Alex like a raging hurricane, while he took a step back before the onslaught of her fury. 'Allow me to tell you a little about my background, Lord Montgomery. In Boston I was living with my mother in a two-roomed shack. Everything I owned I sold to pay for the doctor and her medicine. We had no money and the food we ate I provided. I do all manner of things a young lady ought not to do. I shoot, I fish, and I skin and gut whatever I kill. I dare say the properly reared young ladies of your acquaintance would be horrified and fall into a swoon at such behaviour and liken me to the savage you obviously think I am. I may seem gauche to you and lacking in social graces, but I am not ashamed of the way we lived.

'When your uncle came to Boston he was courtesy and kindness itself—and I give you my word that I shall not abuse his kindness. When my mother died it was a great comfort to me having him there. In the short time we have been together I have come to love him dearly and would sooner end my life than cause him pain. Despite what you believe, I haven't asked him for anything and I do not expect anything. I am simply grateful for a roof over my head wherever that happens to be. For this and his support at a time when I had nothing, I owe him much—much more than I can repay. Your uncle knows this and now you know it too, so if it's not a problem for him it needn't be a problem for you.'

Alex stared at the proud, tempestuous young woman in silent, icy composure. Her words reverberated round the room, ricocheting off the walls and hitting him with all the brutal impact of a battering ram, but it failed to pierce the armour of his wrath and not a flicker of emotion registered on his impassive features.

'That, Miss Hamilton, was quite an outburst. Have you finished?'

Pausing to take an infuriated breath, Angelina finally said, 'Far from it. You may have been born with blue blood in your veins and all the advantages that come with it, but you have a lot to learn. It isn't where a person comes from that matters. It's what a person is that counts. You are being vindictive without just cause, but if you want to carry on hating me then please do so. It does not matter one jot to me.'

Their minds and their eyes clashed in a battle of wills.

'I do not hate you.'

'No? Well, I hate you,' she told him, glaring at him wrathfully.

'I know you do,' he replied quietly. Not only had he heard, but also he sensed it. Cool and remote, Alex studied her for a moment, as though trying to discern something, and then crossed towards the door and went out.

Angelina stood looking blindly at the closed door for a long time, her heart palpitating with a raging fury. A whole array of confusing emotions washed over her—anger, humiliation, and a piercing, agonizing loneliness she had not felt since she was fifteen years old in Ohio.

Chapter Three

Henry and Alex were partaking of a glass of wine while they waited for Angelina to join them. Whenever Henry looked at his nephew, he was overwhelmed with pride.

At best, Alex was a fiercely private man, guarded and solitary, accountable to no one. At worst, he was a man with a wide streak of ruthlessness and an iron control that was almost chilling. To those who knew him he was clever, with an almost mystical ability to see what motivated others. To his business partners it was a gift beyond value, because it provided insight into the guarded ambitions of his adversaries. He could be cold, calculating and unemotional, which was how his rivals saw him.

'Angelina's a lovely young thing, don't you agree, Alex?'

Alex's look darkened. 'Lovely? She's certainly out of the ordinary. The girl's a hoyden. Good Lord, Uncle, what can you be thinking of? I've never seen you so taken with anyone as you are with this American girl.'

'You're quite right, but then I've never had a ward before, and so far I'm thoroughly enjoying the experience. Angelina's a delight. She's a thoroughly charming and engaging young woman with a remarkable intelligence. In the short time I've known her, I vow she's lopped ten years off my life.'

Alex's reply was a sardonic lift of his dark brows. 'You may find her charming, Uncle, but it is not the kind that passes for charm in the ladies of my acquaintance. Miss Hamilton's charm is more sinister and elusive than that. It is the kind that weaves spells and puts curses on people.'

An inexplicable smile traced its way across Henry's face. 'If that be the case, then take care she doesn't put a spell on you, dear boy.'

'I'm immune,' Alex said, bestowing the kind of lazy smile on his uncle that turned female hearts to water. 'Whatever she is, you're going to have your hands full.'

'Try and be more understanding towards her, Alex. Until she marries I am committed to her—and, as you know, I am not a man to shirk my duty. I've told you everything that I know of what happened to her in America—and the reasons why her grandmother's existence must be kept from her, so you will bear with her, won't you? I know how difficult you can be.'

Alex gave him a narrow look, deflecting his uncle's question by answering it with another. 'Did you tell her about me—listing all my transgressions?'

Henry chuckled, encouraged by his nephew's lack of argument. 'I did. I considered it wise to have her well prepared in every aspect of what her life would be like in England.'

'And?'

'When I told her I had all but despaired of seeing you suitably married, she asked me—with all the candid innocence of her youth—what was wrong with you.'

'Really.' Alex gave his uncle a mildly sardonic look. 'Evidently she regarded me as being way past the age of eligibility for marriage at twenty-eight.'

'No. I think she probably thought you were some fire-breathing monster with two horns and a tail. And when I told her you dealt with practically all my business affairs—'

'Let me guess,' Alex interrupted drolly. 'Did she by any chance ask if you trusted me?'

'She did.'

'I see,' he said drily, swearing that he'd not be bested by the dark-eyed witch.

'So you will try to curb your temper when you are together and be gentle with her, won't you?' Henry asked, casting his nephew an anxious look of appeal.

Alex hesitated for an endless moment and then nodded, a reluctant smile lurking at the corners of his mouth. 'Since I have no intention of laying a finger on her or being in her company for longer than I have to, I assure you, Uncle, that she will be perfectly safe from me. However, I feel I should warn you that I have already had a run-in with your ward; if that encounter is anything to go by, I cannot promise to be charm and graciousness personified where she is concerned. We may very well need a referee to keep us from murdering each other—which is where you will come in.'

Angelina swept into the dining room, intending to make a determined effort to be pleasant and agreeable to Lord Montgomery for Uncle Henry's sake. A chandelier suspended above the table filled the room with flickering light, reflecting on the large, ornate silver pieces set on the mahogany sideboard, next to where the two gentlemen stood drinking wine.

Breaking off his discussion with Alex, Henry placed his glass on the sideboard and came to meet her, his eyes twinkling in admiration. 'You look lovely, Angelina,' he said, taking her hand and drawing her towards his nephew. 'Alex tells me the two of you have already met.'

'Yes—and as you can see, Uncle…' she smiled with a hint of mischief dancing in her eyes '…I have survived the encounter without coming to grief.'

Henry lifted a brow to Angelina in a silent salute and smiled.

Angelina met Lord Montgomery's sardonically mocking

gaze. With his eyes as intense as a hunting falcon's locked on hers, he moved forward, bowing his head with a studied degree of politeness, which to Angelina was a masterpiece of gracious arrogance.

Alex looked down at the tempestuous young woman in her lilac gown. Her face, which arrested and compelled his eyes, was both delicate and vibrant, and her large amethyst eyes still stormy.

'Miss Hamilton was looking for something to read,' Alex told his uncle without taking his eyes from hers.

'Then I hope you found something to your liking, Angelina.'

'How could I not? There were so many interesting books to choose from. I had absolutely no idea that so much knowledge could exist in one place.'

'Alex must take the credit for that.'

'Yes, I thought he might,' she replied ironically.

Handing Angelina a glass of wine, Alex's lips curled with a hint of a smile. 'Miss Hamilton selected two illustrated editions—one on birds and the other on horses. Perhaps you prefer looking at pictures to reading, Miss Hamilton.'

Angelina's eyes narrowed when she took his meaning and bristled at the intended slight. 'I don't just look at the pictures, Lord Montgomery. Contrary to what you might think, I am not illiterate.'

Henry chuckled. 'Don't underestimate Angelina's intelligence, Alex. She reads anything you care to name and is conversant in French, Greek and Latin.'

'Perhaps if I had chosen Voltaire or Socrates you would have been more impressed. Usually I read for enlightenment, for knowledge, but yesterday I fancied something light. I cannot see why you should pour scorn on my choice of reading. It just so happens that I like birds and horses.'

'You speak French *and* Greek?' Alex asked incredulously, with surprise and doubt.

'You seem surprised,' said Angelina.

'I confess that I am. There are few ladies of my acquaintance who are familiar with the classics—and I am hard pressed to think of any one of them who is conversant in any language other than their own native English, and perhaps a smattering of French.'

Now it was Angelina's turn to be surprised. 'Then I can only assume that your experience with the female sex is somewhat limited, Lord Montgomery.'

A gleam of suppressed laughter lit Alex's eyes, and Angelina could only assume, correctly, that her remark about his inexperience with women had not been taken in the way she had intended.

'Angelina also plays an excellent game of chess,' Henry championed, giving Angelina a conspiratorial wink to remind her of all those times they had played together on board ship, when she had more often than not finished the victor. 'She can swim like a fish, outshoot most men, and handle a horse better than any female I've ever seen.'

Alex arched a sleek black brow in mock amusement when his gaze met Angelina's. 'I'm impressed! And to add to all these admirable attributes the cut and thrust of her tongue is sharper and deadlier than any rapier,' he drawled.

'I'm glad you've noticed,' Angelina replied with an impudent smile and a delicate lift to her brows, taking a sip of her wine.

Alex lost the battle to suppress his smile. The girl had spirit, he had to give her that. 'As you can see, Uncle, Miss Hamilton's opinion of me is far from favourable. Earlier she accused me of being rude, overbearing, dictatorial—and she told me that I have the manners of a barbarian.'

'And I fear I have to agree with her.'

'Really, Uncle! Where's your loyalty?' Alex demanded with mock severity.

'Forgive me, Alex. But that's a difficult dilemma.'

'I can't see why it should be.'

'I find my loyalties torn asunder. You see, they lie with you both. You are both family. Angelina is my ward—my cousin's daughter—and you are my nephew. Surely you can understand the pressure I am under.'

'Lord Montgomery is the other half of your family, Uncle Henry. Not mine,' Angelina pointed out forcefully.

'Noted for our obstinacy,' retorted Alex.

'Much good may it do you, my lord. I am no less obstinate, I assure you.' The smile Angelina turned on Henry was full of sweetness. 'It's a pity one can't be more selective with one's family as one can be with one's friends, don't you think?'

'I couldn't agree more, my dear. But I am going to ask you both to lower your swords as a favour to me—at least until after dinner so that we can do justice to Mrs Price's excellent cooking. It wouldn't do for all three of us to end up with indigestion, now, would it? However, I grant Alex can be a touch overbearing at times, Angelina.'

Angelina raised a sceptical brow, tempted to say that Lord Montgomery was a complete and total ass, but instead she said, 'Only a touch, Uncle Henry?'

'Well, perhaps a little more than a touch.'

Angelina caught Lord Montgomery's silver gaze that seemed to slice the air between them, warning her not to overstep the mark. She met his gaze calmly, with a defiant lift of her chin. 'And Lord Montgomery has no need of a sword, Uncle. He can accomplish as much with his eyes as he can with the point of a sword. I swear he could slay a man at twenty paces.'

'And you, my dear, have the unique distinction of putting his back up.'

Henry smiled indulgently and pulled out a chair for her at the table. Alex would sit opposite her and he would sit at the end—to act as referee if they were to continue sparring with each other. The air crackled and sparked between his nephew and his ward, and their looks and conversation were like daggers being hurled back and forth. It was better than he could have hoped for.

'But you must forgive Alex,' he continued. 'The ladies of his acquaintance are usually more languishing. He can be quite charming.'

Angelina favoured Lord Montgomery with a look of pure mockery as he took his seat across from her. 'Is that so?'

'Most ladies do find me charming and pleasant—and some actually enjoy my company.'

'And no doubt live to regret it,' she bit back.

With a mixture of languor and self-assurance, Alex started to relax and lounged back in his chair, absently fingering the stem of his wineglass as his gaze swept over her in an appraising, contemplative way.

His instinct detected untapped depths of passion in the alluring young woman across from him that sent silent signals instantly recognisable to a lusty, hot-blooded male like himself. The impact of these signals brought a smouldering glow to his eyes. So much innocence excited him, made him imagine those pleasures and sensations Miss Hamilton could never have experienced being aroused by him. The lazy, dazzling smile he bestowed on her transformed his face.

Angelina found herself staring at him, momentarily captivated by it, unaware of the lascivious thoughts that had induced it. It was the most wonderful smile she had ever seen and full of provocative charm. Oh, yes, she thought, feeling her heart do a little somersault, when he smiled like that and spoke in a soft-as-honey voice and looked at a woman from under those drooping lids, he could make a feral cat lie down and purr.

Angelina found hot colour washing her cheeks under his close scrutiny and she hated herself for that betrayal. Alex saw it and smiled infuriatingly. His strategy had worked. Little Angelina Hamilton was just like all the rest of her sex when it came to the matter of seduction. It would not be too difficult a task demolishing her pride and cold resentment and have her melting with desire in his arms, and the idea of conquering her appealed to his sardonic sense of humour—if that was what he had a mind to do, for he must remember that, for him, she was untouchable, being his uncle's ward.

'I'm sorry. Do I unsettle you, Miss Hamilton?' he asked with a slight lift to his sleek eyebrows.

'You don't unsettle me in the least.'

'Come now, you're blushing,' he taunted gently, being well schooled in the way women's minds worked.

'I am not.' Her unease was growing by the second, but she tried not to show it, attempting to maintain a façade of uninterest and indifference.

'Yes, you are. Your cheeks are as pink as those roses,' he said, indicating the lovely bowl of deep blush-coloured roses on the table between them.

'Good gracious.' Angelina laughed. 'If that's the kind of melodramatic rubbish you engage in with the ladies of your acquaintance, I'm surprised they don't vomit.'

'I assure you they don't.'

'No—well—perhaps if they're all vacuous peahens unable to see further than your impeccable credentials, they wouldn't, would they?'

Alex was so astounded by her reply that he almost threw back his head and burst out laughing. 'No,' he replied his smile widening. 'They wouldn't dare. Now,' he said when a footman came in carrying platters of food, 'shall we accede to our uncle's request by lowering our weapons and agree to a truce while we eat?'

'Very well—but only while we eat,' she agreed. 'I've never tasted such wonderful food as Mrs Price turns out and have no intention of letting you spoil it. However,' she murmured, looking at him from beneath the thick fringe of her lashes, 'my sword may be sheathed, Lord Montgomery, but please remember that it is still there and every bit as sharp and lethal.'

Alex's eyes narrowed. 'I do not doubt that for one moment,'

he replied—and, he thought with wry amusement, it will make the play between us all the more exciting.

Angelina bestowed a smile on him that was utterly devastating, and she was certain she glimpsed approval lurking in those inscrutable silver eyes.

A footman under the stern eye of Bramwell served the delicious meal. Angelina did full justice to the food and tried not to feel intimidated by Lord Montgomery when his eyes settled on her now and then, his lids hooded like those of a hawk. Just the cold pupils peered out from his closed face, but throughout the meal she could feel him tugging at her from across the table. It really was most unsettling.

From his vantage point at the head of the table Henry was more observant about what was passing between the two of them than either of them realised. He carefully noted the absorbed way Alex watched Angelina as she ate, recognising something in his expression that he hadn't seen in a long time, and he was utterly delighted and encouraged by it.

'You had a large complement of post while you were away, Uncle,' Alex commented while they waited for dessert to be served, tearing his gaze away from the tantalising creature sitting opposite. 'Was there anything of importance?'

'No, just the usual—most of it from Mowbray Park. Oh, and I've received a letter from Robert Boothroyd—Sir Robert is a very close friend of mine, Angelina, who resides in Cornwall,' he explained. 'As you know, Alex, I had planned to visit him before I went to America, but on receiving Lydia's letter it had to be postponed.'

Alex sensed his hesitation and threw him a questioning look. 'Is something wrong?'

'Robert has not been at all well. It's his heart, I'm afraid. He doesn't enjoy good health at the best of times, but this latest setback is causing both him and his family considerable concern. He has asked if I will go to Cornwall as soon as I am able—but of course I shall write and tell him it's impossible for me to leave London at this time. I couldn't possibly leave Angelina when she's only just arrived in England.'

'She could go and stay with Nathan and Verity at Hanover Square—when Verity returns from Surrey, that is. Failing that, she could go and stay with Aunt Patience at Richmond,' Alex suggested. 'Which she should do, anyway. It's most improper for her to be living alone in a house with two unmarried gentlemen.'

'Yes, I have considered that, but both Verity and Patience lead a hectic social life and Angelina would inevitably become drawn in. I would like to give her time to adjust—to settle into her new life gradually. I consider it too soon for her to go out into society just yet.'

Henry was not at all in agreement with Alex's solution, for he had no intention of removing Angelina from his nephew's immediate sphere. Before Lydia had died, he had promised her he would make the best possible match for her daughter, and he had known immediately who that would be. Angelina and Alex had much in common, both being wilful and spirited. Tragedy had touched them both at fifteen years old, and it was his hope that together they might find solace.

However, anyone listening to his ward and his nephew in verbal combat would say they were too much alike to ever come to a complete and harmonious understanding of one another. But Henry thought otherwise and was determined to bring them together. To achieve this it was important they spend some time alone away from London, and he had contrived for them to do just that.

'Of course,' he went on casually, taking a sip of his wine and deliberately avoiding his nephew's eyes and looking down at his dish as he began spooning his dessert, 'I suppose she could accompany you when you go to Arlington next week. And the country air will do her good.'

Alex's arm froze midway between his dish and his mouth as

he was about to eat his strawberry soufflé. He stared at Henry as if he'd taken leave of his senses, returning the spoon to the dish with a resounding clatter. 'You are not seriously suggesting—'

'I couldn't possibly,' Angelina objected in growing alarm, appalled at what her uncle suggested.

'What in God's name would I do with Miss Hamilton at Arlington? Really, Uncle, it's quite impossible.'

'I don't see why.'

'I do. It's out of the question. Besides, it would be most improper for her to stay with me without a chaperon.'

Angelina glared at him. 'Don't worry, Lord Montgomery. The prospect is as distasteful to me as it is to you.' Looking with concern at Henry's downcast face, she hated being the reason that prevented him visiting his sick friend. 'But, Uncle Henry, of course you must go to Cornwall. Perhaps I could accompany you?' she asked hopefully, finding the prospect of being alone with his nephew absolutely horrifying.

'Thank you, my dear,' Henry replied with a smile, reaching out and patting her hand in a fond gesture. 'But I won't hear of it.'

Alex was suddenly contrite, knowing how fond his uncle was of Robert Boothroyd. 'I'm sorry, Uncle. Of course you must go. Miss Hamilton will accompany me to Arlington. To still the gossip, I shall ask Aunt Patience to come and stay. With her and a house full of servants, that should be more than ample to uphold the proprieties.'

'To protect me, you mean,' Angelina couldn't help retorting.

Having suddenly lost his appetite, Alex threw his napkin on to the table. He scowled darkly across the table at her and their eyes met and held, irresistible force colliding with immovable object. 'Let me assure you that you do not need protecting from me,' he said with scathing contempt. 'By nature I am not a violent man, but if you inconvenience me in any way or disobey me, you may have good reason to seek protection from me. Is that understood?'

Angelina merely glowered at him.

Henry seemed to be torn two ways, but in the end he gave in to their persuasion to go to Cornwall—a little too easily, Alex thought, giving his uncle a narrow, suspicious look. Henry would join them both at Arlington at a later date. 'And don't worry, Angelina,' he said when he saw the worried look in her eyes. 'You will like Arlington—and, if you find Alex's presence irksome, the house is so large that you can go for weeks at a time without bumping into one another.'

'That sounds appealing,' she responded, throwing Lord Montgomery a glance like a poison dart. 'And after your visit to Cornwall, are we to return to London?'

'Yes. It is important that we return to prepare for the Season in April. You will have to master all manner of accomplishments so we must allow ourselves enough time. I shall employ a tutor to instruct you in social protocol, conduct, polite conversation and that sort of thing. You must also have dancing lessons and arrangements will have to be made for a complete wardrobe— a responsibility I shall be more than happy to place in my dear sister's capable hands. We must see that you are well prepared when you make your curtsy. I am convinced you will be a tremendous success and will be inundated with suitors. Eventually you will make a perfect match.'

Angelina felt a terrible, unexplained dread mounting inside her. The whole idea of the Season terrified her. 'Uncle Henry, I know you think that what you are doing is in my best interests— and please don't think I'm not grateful because I am. I—I do so want to be worthy of you, to make you proud of me, but…'

'But what, my dear?'

'It's just that I have no interest in being paraded in front of society merely to acquire a suitable husband. Besides, I cannot see the point of going to all that bother and expense when I have no intention of marrying.'

Stunned into silence, both men looked at her.

'If it's all the same to you, I'm quite happy as I am. I don't want to be married. I'm never going to get married.'

Henry was troubled by the intensity of her statement. It was said with deep conviction, and more than a little pain. Recalling what Will had told him about rescuing her from the Shawnee, he wondered what had happened to her that she refused to speak of. Whatever it was, she hid it well, and he was certain it had something to do with her decision not to marry.

'Don't be alarmed, Angelina,' he said gently. 'It is not my intention to make you do anything you have an aversion to. You need time to adjust to things. Perhaps, after a few weeks spent at Arlington, you will come to see everything in a different light.'

'No, Uncle Henry, I won't,' she told him with a quiet firmness.

'I do not believe you realise the seriousness of what you are refusing,' Alex commented, listening with a great deal of interest to what was being said.

Angelina looked across at him calmly. 'What are you saying?'

'The point I am trying to make is that, as the ward of the Duke of Mowbray, when you fail to make an appearance when the Season starts people will want to know why. You will leave yourself wide open to a great deal of gossip and speculation.'

'I have little interest in what people think.'

'No, but my uncle has. There is more to this than you seem to be concerned about. There are standards to be upheld. Of course you must marry some time.'

'No. I meant what I said.'

'I applaud your honesty. Have you no desire for a family of your own—children? Is that not an incentive to marry?'

'Not to me.'

'Then what is it you want from life?' he asked, his steady gaze locking on to hers.

'I don't know,' she whispered, the sheer desperation and pain of the look she gave him making Alex forget all his hostility towards her. He was made uneasy by it. Something reached out and touched him in half-forgotten obscure places.

'It would seem, Alex,' said Henry, sensing the distress signals coming from Angelina and rallying to her rescue, 'that someone else is of the same opinion as yourself regarding the honourable institution of marriage.'

'On the contrary, Uncle. I've decided to marry after all.'

Henry looked at his nephew sharply, surprise registering in his eyes, and more than a pang of disappointment settling on his heart. 'Really? Now that is a surprise. You have been busy while I've been in America.'

'I imagine you are pleased that I have decided to marry and provide you with the heir you are constantly plaguing me about.'

'That depends on the lady you intend to marry. Who is she?'

'Lavinia Howard.'

'Lord Howard's eldest daughter?'

'Yes,' Alex replied, watching his uncle closely.

Henry nodded slowly as he digested the information. 'I see. Well, she is eminently suitable, I grant you, and her father has been hankering after a match between the two of you for long enough. She is a fine young woman of excellent character. Have you spoken to her father?'

'Nothing has been decided. I'm giving a small weekend house party at Arlington in two weeks' time and I have invited her along with her parents and a party of friends. If I am still of the same mind, I will speak to Lord Howard then.'

'His daughter will certainly preside over Arlington with grace and poise and has been trained to manage the demanding responsibilities of such a large house. However, it is evident to me that you are thinking with your head and not your heart, Alex. I see you are considering marriage to Miss Howard with the same kind of dispassion and practised precision you employ when dealing with your business transactions.'

Alex shrugged. 'Did you expect anything else? I am no more

sentimental about marriage than anyone else. It's a contract like any other. Besides, considering my success in that area, the odds for our marriage being successful are highly favourable.'

'I think "excruciatingly boring" would be a more appropriate term to use. In this you are ill advised, Alex. Marriage is not a business transaction.'

Angelina met Lord Montgomery's gaze, amazed by his indifference to such an important matter. 'You are not in love with Miss Howard?'

Henry chuckled softly. 'Alex cast a blight on love a long time ago, my dear.'

'Why, those are my sentiments entirely, Lord Montgomery.'

'I'm glad we are agreed on one thing at least,' Alex responded.

For a moment they regarded one another in silence, finding it strange that they were in accord over something that to everyone else was the most important thing in their lives.

'Maybe we are. But I do feel that where something as important as marriage is concerned, then it is essential that the two people concerned love each other.'

Alex suddenly smiled. 'In my opinion, that is sentimental nonsense. Aren't you going to congratulate me on my forthcoming nuptials, Miss Hamilton?'

'No. You said yourself that as yet nothing has been decided. When it has and Miss Howard accepts your proposal of marriage, I feel the only sentiment I shall be able to offer will be my commiserations.'

The following morning Henry's widowed sister, Lady Patience Fortesque, arrived at Brook Street. She was eager to see her brother after his journey to America, and to meet his ward. Two years his junior, Patience resembled Henry in many ways. There was a fragile quality about her and she radiated a kindness and gentility that was immediately endearing to anyone who met her, but when she pleased she could be awe-inspiring.

Patience politely restrained herself from saying anything until Henry had finished telling her all about what had happened in America. The secret fears of what Angelina might have suffered at the hands of the Shawnee he kept to himself.

When he had completed his tale, he looked across at his sister who was calmly assessing what he had told her. 'Well, Patience? Am I a sentimental old fool? Was I behaving like a lovesick youth when I went tearing across the Atlantic the moment I received Lydia's letter? Should I have ignored it after all these years?'

'No, Henry,' Patience replied with gentle understanding. 'Lydia meant a great deal to you, I know that. Is Angelina aware how deeply you felt about her mother?'

'If you mean does she know I was in love with her, then the answer is no. Angelina is a remarkable young woman, Patience. When I first saw her and how proud she was, how resilient and brave after all she had been through, she stirred all my protective instincts. I find her such joy to be with. She is a rare jewel and with just a little polish she will outshine most of her sex. Lydia taught her well.'

'I am concerned about the matter of Angelina's grandmother. I know that since the death of her husband Lady Anne never comes to town. But there is the possibility that she will find out about her granddaughter coming to England when she makes her curtsy next year. It could be a major problem if she decides to see her.'

'I know, but we will deal with that *if* it arises.'

'What about Alex?'

The name seemed to hang in the air a moment before Henry replied. 'Ah—Alex!'

'Oh, dear! I take it from the tone of your voice that he does not welcome the intrusion of this American girl into his life.'

Henry chuckled. 'You've hit the nail right on the head. Battle lines were drawn and the artillery positioned the minute they set eyes on each other. Already they've had their first skirmish. Angelina refuses to be subdued and is unimpressed by both Alex and his title. At present I do not want her to go out into society—and nor does she wish to. She refuses to consider a Season, but I'm hoping that she can be persuaded. I feel some time spent in the country will be beneficial to her until she's had time to settle down—which is why I would like you to accompany her to Arlington.'

'Arlington? But why not to Mowbray Park?'

'Because I am to leave for Cornwall early next week to visit my good friend Robert Boothroyd. Besides,' he murmured, a mischievous twinkle in his eyes, which did not go unnoticed by his sister, 'Alex is to go to Arlington in a few days to check on the renovations he's having done to the house.'

Patience studied her brother carefully. 'Henry, are you matchmaking by any chance? If so, you must think very carefully and proceed with the utmost caution. Alex will not take kindly to your meddling.'

'Meddling?' Henry arched his brows in mock offence. 'I have no intention of meddling in anything. There is nothing I want more than for the two of them to wed,' he told her, taking her into his confidence. He needed his sister's unquestioning co-operation and willingness to comply with anything he suggested if he was to bring Alex and Angelina together.

Chapter Four

'Come here, my dear, and let me look at you,' said Patience with a gracious smile when Angelina entered. 'I've been so looking forward to meeting you.'

Angelina moved towards her and found herself enfolded in a sweet smelling embrace. 'I am happy to meet you, Lady Fortesque. Uncle Henry has told me so much about you that I feel I know you already.'

Patience stood back and smiled, approving of what she saw. Her features were delicate and pretty like Lydia's, but there was something untamed and quite unique about this lovely young woman.

'Your mother and I were close, Angelina. I was so distressed to hear of her death—and your father's, my dear. Come and sit by me, and please call me Aunt Patience. We are related, after all.'

At that moment the door opened and Alex strode in. He was dressed in riding clothes, his crop still clasped in his hand. Angelina noticed how fiercely elegant he was in his immaculate coat and polished brown boots, and the way his breeches fit his thighs like his coat fit the breadth of his shoulders, without a wrinkle—and, if they were inclined to do so, they wouldn't dare on so formidable an owner.

Closing the door and advancing into the room with ground-devouring strides, his cool gaze swept over the three occupants, pausing a little longer on Angelina before moving on to his aunt.

'Why, Alex, how lovely to see you,' said Patience, her face shining with adoration as she looked up at her handsome nephew.

Bending his tall frame, Alex lightly kissed her offered cheek, and as his head passed close to Angelina she caught the spicy aroma of his cologne mingled with leather and horses. As he was about to stand up straight he turned his head and looked at her, his eyes on a level with her own and no more than a foot away. Finding herself in such close proximity to him brought an indignant flush to her cheeks, which Alex observed and brought a slight smile to his lips, his silver eyes gleaming with knowing amusement.

Her contempt met him face to face until he straightened, looking down at her from his daunting height, seeing turbulent animosity burning in her dark eyes. She looked serene and almost coy, and yet he had the feeling that it was a charade, and that the environment forced upon her was too restricting for her ebullient nature. She made him feel alert and alive, and curiously stimulated.

'I really should scold you,' Patience went on, her eyes following her nephew as he strolled towards the fireplace, where he took up an infuriatingly arrogant stance beside Henry's chair, resting an arm on the marble mantelpiece and crossing one booted foot casually over the other, looking every inch the master of the house. 'You did promise to visit me at Richmond while Henry was away.'

'Forgive me, Aunt. I had pressing matters to take care of.'

'So I understand,' Patience replied with a note of reproof, having heard all about his affair with Amelia Fairhurst. 'I had hoped that with all your years of experience you would have learned to conduct your affairs with a little more discretion, Alex.'

'The pressing matters I spoke of were purely business, Aunt.

And if you are referring to my friendship with Lady Amelia Fairhurst, I assure you it was nothing more than a harmless flirtation and was blown out of all proportion. I did not think you paid any attention to gossip.'

'I don't, as a rule, and I'm certainly not going to become embroiled in your personal life. Next you will be telling me that you took pity on her and were trying to console her in her marital unhappiness. But what may seem amusing and harmless to you, dear boy, others may find offensive and insulting—which was the case with Lady Fairhurst's husband by all accounts, when he demanded satisfaction and challenged you to a duel.'

Chagrin and irritation flickered across Alex's face. 'And no doubt you heard that the old fool died of an apoplexy the night before. Amelia Fairhurst is a proficient flirt. You should know by now not to worry about my reputation, Aunt. You must know that most of what you hear is nothing but gossip and wishful exaggeration.'

'Are you telling us that you have been unfairly maligned, Lord Montgomery?' Angelina asked, gazing at him with an amazingly innocent smile on her lips, and an insolent light in her eyes. 'That what people say about you dishonouring every woman who is foolish enough to fall for your golden tongue is not true?'

Content to sit back and listen to the interchange in an amused silence, Henry met his sister's smiling, conspiratorial gaze, each admiring Angelina's courage for daring to speak out, while Alex favoured her with an icy stare that was meant to put her firmly in her place. But she merely held his gaze with open defiance, which told him that her proud nature knew nothing of compliance or submission.

'Not entirely,' he replied tersely, his jaw rigid. 'I see you have met our colonial cousin, Aunt.'

'Yes,' she said, smiling at Angelina and taking her hand in an affectionate clasp. 'I came just as soon as I received Henry's note telling me he had arrived back in London with Angelina.'

'And?'

'And what?'

'Is she all you expected her to be?'

'Yes, she is. Angelina is very much dear Lydia's daughter.'

'Tell me, Uncle Henry—was your nephew obnoxious as a boy, too?' Angelina asked boldly.

Her question earned her a broad smile of admiration from Henry. 'Why—I do believe he was.'

She frowned, feigning sympathy. 'How distressing for you all.'

'So distressing that both Uncle Henry and Aunt Patience have complained bitterly over the years and threatened to disown me,' Alex retaliated calmly, 'but as you see, Miss Hamilton, as a family we have a way of sticking together.'

Angelina sensed there was a hidden message for her in his words, which she prudently ignored. Looking at Patience, she smiled shyly. 'I can see Lord Montgomery's affairs both concern and embarrass you, Aunt Patience—so you must be relieved to know that he is considering marriage.'

'So Henry was telling me just before you came in. Is this true, Alex?'

'That is so, Aunt,' he replied, tapping his boot with his riding crop, sorely tempted to use it on the softest part of the chit's anatomy. 'I am considering it.'

'Lavinia Howard?'

'That is the young lady I have in mind.'

'A sensible choice. The title and position she will acquire if she marries you will delight her family—especially her mother,' she said with a faint trace of irony, 'for she has long been desiring a match between you. However, I'm glad to know you are thinking of settling down at last, Alex.'

'Thank you, Aunt,' he replied drily. His smile was sardonic. 'I shall endeavour to do my duty and produce an heir.'

'Nevertheless, it will hardly be a love match,' retorted his aunt with a note of disapproval in her tone.

'No, but I have a high regard for Lavinia.'

'Poor Miss Howard,' murmured Angelina. 'I doubt she knows what a cold and cruel fate awaits her if she takes you for a husband.'

Alex looked at her coldly. 'There are very few men who love their wives, Miss Hamilton.'

'Or women who love their husbands, it would seem. If Miss Howard will not be hurt by your indifference, she must be very unhappy or very cold.'

'She is neither,' Alex countered.

'Henry tells me you are to give a small weekend party at Arlington to which she is invited,' Patience put in quickly in an attempt to relieve the situation. 'I shall look forward to meeting her again. In the meantime, I am so looking forward to getting to know Angelina better—which is why I shall be staying here until it is time for us to leave for Arlington next week.'

'You are?' Alex asked with some surprise.

'Of course. Angelina cannot remain in this house with you and Henry alone. Her reputation would be beyond recall if it gets out.'

'Then the obvious solution to that is for you to take her to Richmond. The park is lovely at this time of year. I'm sure the air will be more conducive to Miss Hamilton's health and temper than it is here in town.'

'There is nothing wrong with my health or my temper that a distance away from you would not cure, my lord,' Angelina countered.

The bright silver eyes considered Angelina without a hint of expression, then with slow deliberation. Had it not been for the coldness that came into them, his reply might have passed as a flippant remark. 'Then I shall have to take that into consideration and adjust my affairs accordingly to assist you in your cure, Miss Hamilton.'

Patience looked from Angelina to Alex crossly. 'Good

heavens! What is this nonsense? Why so formal? You must address one another by your given names if you are to get on.'

Both Angelina and Alex disagreed. Formal address conveyed neither affection nor intimacy, which suited them both.

'Come, now, what do you say?' Patience persisted.

Unwillingly, Alex conceded. 'Very well, Aunt.'

'Thank you. Now, in answer to your question, I did consider taking Angelina to Richmond, until Henry told me he is to visit Lord Boothroyd in Cornwall shortly. He has been away so long that I would like to spend some time with him before he goes. Besides, I would like to take Angelina shopping before we leave for Arlington. The clothes Henry had you fitted out with in Boston were adequate for the voyage, my dear, but I shall see you have some more day dresses for Arlington. When we return to London my dressmaker will fit you out for a whole new wardrobe. However, I shall ask her to call before we leave for Arlington and take your measurements so she can make a start.'

Alarm bells began ringing in Angelina's head and she could see the excited gleam of future arrangements in the older woman's eyes. 'Oh! But I—I explained to Uncle Henry that I—'

'Have no wish to be introduced into society.' Patience smiled. 'I know. Henry told me,' she said, glancing meaningfully at her brother. 'Tell me, have you not considered having a Season just for the fun of it, Angelina?'

Angelina's expression became grave. 'It's a long time since I did anything for the fun of it, Aunt Patience.'

'Launching a young woman into society is a serious and expensive business, Aunt,' Alex stated sternly. 'I dare say it can be "fun", but one must not forget that all that time and effort is taken for the sole purpose of procuring a husband.'

Angelina glared at him. 'I know that, which is precisely why I told you yesterday that it would be a waste of both time and money.'

'Well—whether you have a Season or not is immaterial, my

dear,' said Patience lightly, attempting to defuse a situation that threatened to become explosive. 'As the ward of the Duke of Mowbray you cannot hide yourself away indefinitely. It is imperative that you have a fashionable wardrobe.'

'To pass her off in society, Aunt, she will need more than a fashionable wardrobe to be accepted,' Alex said curtly. 'She will also need instruction on manners and breeding, which, in my opinion, will take some considerable time.'

Patience studied her nephew's stony countenance with something akin to surprise. 'I disagree. Henry and I intend to employ a tutor to instruct her on all she needs to know. She is highly intelligent and cultured—which is more than can be said of some of the vain henwits who are turned out year after year for the Season, so it will take no time at all. What do you think, Angelina?'

Angelina knew Lord Montgomery was jeering at her, but refused to let him see how much the intended rudeness of his remark had hurt her. Glancing up at him, something in his look challenged her spirit and increased her courage in a surge of dislike. She managed to force her lips into a smile.

'I think that is an excellent idea, Aunt Patience. Perhaps your nephew would care to sit in on my lessons. Unfortunately, it may take him a good while longer since he has more to learn than I. He is a man of high birth but low manners.'

Alex's eyes narrowed and took on a most humorous glint, which Angelina took pains to ignore. She suddenly smiled radiantly, her soft lips parting to reveal her small, sparkling white teeth that dazzled her adversary. 'If you have an aversion to joining me at my lessons, you could take them by yourself,' she generously suggested, her expression serious but her dark eyes dancing with intended mischief, 'if you can find the time between your many amorous affairs and business commitments.'

Alex stared at her, caught somewhere between fury, astonishment and admiration for her defiant courage. It was the first time he had seen her really smile and the effect was startling. It started in her eyes, warming them, before drifting to her generous lips, stretching them, parting them, her teeth small, perfect and white. In danger of becoming entrapped by his baser instincts, he straightened abruptly from his stance by the fireplace and walked forward, ignoring Angelina as he glanced from his aunt to his uncle, who was enjoying himself immensely.

'Excuse me. I must go and change. I must also leave before I relinquish my carefully held temper and do something to your ward that will embarrass you both—something I would not regret, I might add,' he snapped, clenching his crop between both his hands and leaving Angelina in no doubt what he would like to do with it.

When he reached the door he turned and looked back at Angelina, fixing her with a hard stare. 'If there is anything I can do to make your stay in this house more pleasant, please don't ask. I should hate to show discourtesy by refusing. But if you want to win my approval, you are going to have to change your attitude and make yourself more agreeable to me. That should be your first concern.'

Angelina's ire at his condescending superiority was almost more than she could contain, but she gazed at him with a cool hauteur that belied her agitation and managed to speak calmly. 'Why on earth should I want your approval? And as for my attitude, no one else finds it a problem. Perhaps it is your own attitude that is at fault.'

Alex glared at her before turning to leave. 'I'll see you all at dinner.'

'Of course, my lord,' Angelina quipped.

He swung round in the open doorway, his face glacial. 'My name is Alex. We agreed to dispense with formalities.'

'No. You did,' she replied, turning her head away, having told him she did not want the intimacy of addressing him by his given name.

When the door had closed behind him she relaxed, feeling as if a great weight had been lifted from her shoulders. Looking from Henry to Patience, who were watching her calmly, not in the least put out by the heated interchange between her and their nephew, a little impish smile tugged at her lips. 'Oh, dear. I don't think your nephew likes me very much, does he?'

For most of the journey to Arlington, Angelina stared out of the window, uncomfortable beneath Lord Montgomery's watchful gaze. He sat across from her next to a sleeping Patience, with his long legs stretched out in the luxurious conveyance, studying her imperturbably.

He had discarded his coat and his pristine white shirt and neckcloth contrasted sharply with his black hair and dark countenance. His body, a perfect harmony of form and strength, was like a work of Grecian art and most unsettling to Angelina's virgin heart. To rid herself of his studied gaze she closed her eyes, but even then the vision persisted and she could see and feel those piercing eyes boring holes into her. Unable to endure his scrutiny a moment longer, she snapped her eyes open and locked them on his.

'Well? Have you had an edifying look?' she demanded irately.

Quite unexpectedly he smiled, a white, buccaneer smile, and his eyes danced with devilish humour. 'You don't have to look so angry to find yourself the object of my attention. As a matter of fact I was admiring you.'

Unaccustomed as she was to any kind of compliment from him, the unfamiliar warmth in his tone brought heat creeping into her cheeks. In fact, she decided that she liked this softer side she was seeing even less than the one she was accustomed to. This other Alex Montgomery was beyond her sphere and she didn't know how to deal with him.

'If you think to use flattery as a new tactic to subdue me, it won't work.'

'I was merely thinking that when you aren't scowling you really are quite pretty.'

'And how many women have you said that to?' Angelina asked, raising her nose to a lofty elevation.

'Several. And it's always the truth.'

'Oh dear,' Patience said, fighting a sneeze, which brought her back to awareness. 'I do hope the two of you aren't going to argue again. If so, kindly wait until we reach Arlington. I don't think my nerves will stand it.'

Angelina was concerned about Patience, who had been suffering a chill for the past twenty-four hours. Unfortunately it seemed to be getting worse. Her eyes were bright and feverish, her nose streaming.

'I'm sorry, Aunt, we didn't mean to wake you. As soon as we reach the house you must go straight to bed. Lord Montgomery will send for the doctor.' Leaning forward, she tucked the rug over her aunt's knees.

Wiping her streaming eyes Patience looked too poorly to argue. 'I shall not be sorry to get to bed. I do hope I am in my old room, Alex, and away from the noise of the workmen.'

Reaching out, Alex gently touched his aunt's cheek with long caressing fingers, causing Angelina to stare in astonishment at the smiling, tender expression on his face, which was not in keeping with the man she knew.

'You are,' he said in reply to his aunt's question. 'As yet work hasn't started on the west wing. And Angelina is right. You must go to bed the instant we arrive.'

'Where have you put Angelina?'

'I hope you have accorded me the same consideration and I'm away from the noise too,' Angelina retorted quickly.

'The carpenters and masons do not work around the clock. They go home at night, so you will not be disturbed—unless you are in the habit of sleeping through the day,' Alex said with a hint of sarcasm.

Angelina threw him a wrathful look, but refrained from answering when Patience gave way to another fit of sneezing.

Nothing had prepared Angelina for the exquisite splendour that was Arlington Hall in the heart of the Hertfordshire countryside. She saw it from a distance sitting like a grand old lady on the crest of a hill, timeless and brooding, its elegant beauty expressing power and pride.

'Oh, my,' she breathed, with a growing sense of unreality. Her mother had told her about the grand houses the English nobility lived in, but never had she envisaged anything as lovely as this. Arlington Hall was certainly not a house of modest proportions. 'Why—it's beautiful. Is it very old?'

Alex smiled at the dazed expression of disbelief on her face, well satisfied with her reaction. 'I'm afraid it is,' he replied, folding his arms across his chest, preferring to watch a myriad of expressions on Angelina's face rather than the approaching house. 'Built during Queen Elizabeth's reign about two hundred and fifty years ago, the main structure survives relatively unaltered.'

'It must have taken years to build.'

'Actually, it rose at amazing speed.'

'And all those windows,' she murmured, watching as the evening sun caught the three stories of huge windows, lighting them up like a wall of flame, contrasting beautifully with the green and yellow tints and fiery shades of the finest, early autumn foliage.

'People were enthusiastic for enormous windows in those days. Glass was very expensive, so it became a status symbol. People used it in large quantities to show how rich they were.'

Angelina looked at Alex with large eyes, her animosity forgotten for the moment. 'Your ancestors must have been very rich.'

'They were. The first Earl of Arlington was a powerful politician and a trusted adviser of Queen Elizabeth.'

'And did Queen Elizabeth ever come to Arlington?'

'Frequently. She liked living at her subjects' expense. I'm having considerable alterations and improvements made just now—woodwork has to be renewed, rooms redecorated, and I'm having the modern convenience of running water installed. It's being done in stages and at the moment it's the east wing that's being renovated. Needless to say there's an army of workmen tramping all over the place so you'll just have to bear with it.'

'Is Uncle Henry's house anything like Arlington Hall?'

'No. Mowbray Park was built at a later time and is quite different. It was designed on a much larger scale and is very grand. But you'll see it for yourself before too long.'

'And will you inherit Mowbray Park one day?'

'Yes.'

She gave him a puzzled look. 'Then—who will live at Arlington?' It was a simple question, one she regretted asking when she saw his jaw tense and his eyes cloud over. 'Will you sell it? After all, you can't very well live here and at Mowbray Park.'

Alex hesitated, and for a moment Angelina thought she saw pain in his eyes. 'No, I don't suppose I can,' he answered quietly. 'But I will never sell Arlington. If I marry, I will pass it on to my heirs.'

Angelina shook her head and sighed with sympathy for their mutual plight. 'So you don't have any family either—apart from Aunt Patience and Uncle Henry. You say your mother's ancestors built Arlington Hall. Does she still live here?' she asked, recalling Uncle Henry telling her that Lord Montgomery's father was dead. Immediately she sensed his withdrawal. It was as if a veil had come over his features. Her eyes saw the changing expression on his face, a look that at once seemed to warn her not to pry and to shut her out.

Again Alex hesitated. When he replied to her question his tone was harsher than he intended. 'I would prefer it if you did not mention my mother to me, Angelina. I cannot imagine that she would interest you.'

'I—I just wondered—'

'Then don't,' he said coldly. 'My parents are both dead.'

There was so much finality and suppressed anger and bitterness in his voice that she refrained from asking any further questions.

The four bay mounts pulling the crested coach at last danced to a stop in front of the house and Alex got out, gallantly extending his hand to help his aunt and Angelina. Just for a moment Angelina's fingers touched his, and she felt as if the warm grasp of his hand scorched her own. The two following coaches carrying staff and baggage drew to a halt.

Scarlet-and-gold-liveried footmen appeared out of the house and descended on the coaches to strip them of the mountain of baggage. In a hurry to be inside the house, Patience went ahead of them. Alex turned to Angelina.

'Welcome to Arlington Hall.'

Side by side they climbed the steps and entered the house.

At a glance Angelina became aware of the rich trappings of the interior, the sumptuous carpets and wainscoted panelled walls and great beams crossing the ceiling. An ornately carved oak staircase opposite the entrance cantilevered up to the floors above. The butler, Jenkins, a lean dignified man with dark brown hair and rather austere features, stood aside as they entered, keeping a keen eye on the footmen to remind them of their duties as their eyes kept straying with frank approval to the young woman who stood beside the Earl. Angelina turned when Patience patted her arm.

'Forgive me, Angelina, but I really must go to my room. Mrs Morrisey, who is the housekeeper at Arlington Hall, will show you to your room,' she said, looking quite distressed and turning to a middle-aged woman who came towards them with a rustle of stiff black skirts. 'Go and settle in and refresh yourself before dinner.'

'Angelina, wait,' Alex commanded brusquely when she was about to follow Mrs Morrisey across the hall to the stairs.

Angelina's spine stiffened and she turned to him. Taking her arm he drew her aside. Gazing up at him through the thick fringe of her lashes, she met his piercing eyes. Inwardly she shivered, seeing something ruthless in that controlled, hard silver gaze. She stood perfectly still and tense, waiting for him to speak.

'I will see you at dinner?'

'If you don't mind, I think I will eat with Aunt Patience in her room,' she replied stiffly, averting her eyes.

'I do mind,' he told her quietly. 'Your opinion of me matters not at all, but I refuse to have the servants see my guest has an aversion to me. I would appreciate it if you would try to practise a little courtesy while you are in my house. Is that too much to ask of you?'

Angelina heaved a heavy sigh. It would be difficult to do as he asked, but she saw no reason why they should not at least be cordial to one another. 'No, of course not,' she conceded.

'Thank you. Dinner is at half past seven.'

Abruptly he turned and strode away, leaving Angelina to follow Mrs Morrisey up the stairs. The opulence and elegance of the blue and white room into which she was shown took her breath away.

'Oh, what a lovely room,' she enthused with delight.

'Lord Montgomery instructed me to have this particular one prepared for you because it offers such a splendid view of the garden. It also faces south and has an abundant supply of sunshine—especially during the summer months.'

'How considerate of Lord Montgomery,' Angelina replied, strangely touched to discover he had spared the time to think of her comfort.

Later, she joined Lord Montgomery in a small candlelit dining room off the main hall. Presenting a pleasing appearance, having donned one of the gowns Patience had purchased for her in London—a violet silk which complemented her figure and her eyes—she managed to maintain an outward show of calm, despite the tumult raging inside her.

Lord Montgomery was standing by the sideboard, pouring red wine into two glasses. Angelina was struck by his stern profile outlined against the golden glow of the candles. She saw a kind of beauty in it, but quickly dismissed the thought. It was totally out of keeping with her opinion of him. He turned when she entered and moved towards her, his narrow gaze sweeping over her with approval.

'I hope I'm not late. I went to look in on Aunt Patience.'

'How is she?' Alex handed her a glass of wine. Having lost all desire to quarrel with her tonight, he was relieved to hear she sounded more calm than aggressive.

'Sleeping—but she really does look quite poorly.'

'Then you will be relieved to know the doctor has seen her and has left some medication that should help relieve her discomfort. Is your room to your liking?' he asked, pulling out her chair at the damask-covered table decorated with orchids.

'Yes, thank you,' Angelina replied, slipping into it and taking a sip of wine, hoping the meal would be over quickly so she could escape.

'I'm glad you decided to join me for dinner,' Alex said, seating himself across from her. 'I hoped you would.'

'I could hardly ignore a royal command, could I?' Angelina replied, unable to resist taking a gentle stab at him, the impish curve to her lips softening the tartness of her reply.

His glance darted across the table. 'It was not a royal command.'

'No? That's how it sounded.'

Reining in his mounting irritation, Alex stirred impatiently. 'Angelina, don't be aggressive,' he told her quietly. 'I am in no mood for a quarrel.'

Angelina laughed shortly, a mischievous light twinkling in her eyes. 'Why, what kind of miracle is this! To what do we owe it?' When he shot her an annoying look she sighed in capitulation, though in the light of his previous animosity towards her during their brief acquaintance, she remained suspicious of this softening to his attitude. 'No. Neither am I,' she answered, smiling at an aloof-looking footman who was standing to attention like a soldier close to a large dresser containing platters of food.

'Good. Now that is settled, perhaps we can enjoy our dinner in peace.'

'I shall endeavour to do so.'

'As long as you don't upset my cook by not eating. Mrs Hall is very efficient—and, being a woman, she is extremely temperamental and takes it as a personal criticism if anyone refuses to eat.'

'What! Even you?' Her eyes sparked with laughter.

'Even me.' He smiled in response, spreading a napkin over his knees.

It was a simple, lovely meal, excellently cooked and served by the aloof footman who came and went. Alex talked amiably about Arlington Hall and the surrounding countryside, giving Angelina a brief insight of the people who lived and worked in and around the village of Arlington, just one mile from the hall.

'Do you often go to London?' she asked, wondering how he could bear to leave such a lovely place for the hurly-burly of London.

'I have to take my seat in the House of Lords occasionally—more so at this present time with Europe in a state of turmoil and the war with the United States.' A faint smile touched his lips when he observed Angelina's expression of bewilderment, and realised that, coming from America, she would know very little about English politics.

'You are a politician?'

'No—at least not in the professional sense. It is simply that

I, and all peers of the realm, have been trained to regard it as our right and duty to participate in governing the country. We enter Parliament as we do university and gentlemen's clubs—such as White's or Brooks's.'

Angelina was impressed. 'It all sounds very grand to me. And what do you debate in the House of Lords?'

'The issues at this time are many and varied—and of an extremely serious nature. Fortunately we have managed to stand against Napoleon, despite his attempts to throttle our trade. The present economic crisis is foremost in the debates, and the textile trade, which is getting worse. Following two bad harvests, there is general unrest in this country—especially in the north and the Midlands. And on top of all this comes the need to pay out gold to support the war in Portugal and Spain and our naval battle with America.'

'Dear me. What a muddle it all is. I wonder at you having time to leave London and come to Arlington.'

'I'm not required to spend all my time in the House of Lords, and much of my business can be taken care of here.' He went on to explain the basics of British politics and the English Court, telling her that King George III had lapsed into incurable madness and his son, the Prince of Wales, had been made Regent the previous year. 'There are times when I have to go to Carlton House and other haunts of the Prince Regent and the *beau monde*. But I must point out that political exigencies take me there, rather than personal tastes.'

'Uncle Henry told me that George III and his Queen set a standard of decorum and domestic virtue, but that their court was a very dull place to be—much different to that of their son.'

Alex smiled broadly. 'Uncle Henry was right. As soon as the old King was struck down with madness and fastened into his strait-waistcoat, the Prince of Wales took to wearing corsets and the ladies to shedding their petticoats. There are those who say the country is falling into a decline in moral standards—if not the onset of national decadence.'

'I was of the opinion that the English aristocracy has always been a profligate lot, who has indulged in loose living and has never ceased to do what it likes and cares only for its own whims. Why—I know you enjoy a certain reputation yourself, my lord,' she said softly, glancing across at him obliquely.

Alex looked at her sharply. 'Correction,' he defended curtly. 'I may have acquired a certain reputation, but I did not look for it and certainly do not enjoy it.'

Angelina shrugged, swallowing a juicy baby carrot. 'Whatever the case, it is no secret that you are something of a womaniser and that you keep a mistress—a notorious beauty by all accounts.'

Alex's gaze narrowed and slid to her seemingly innocent face. 'Really,' he said drily. 'You are well informed, Angelina. Did Uncle Henry tell you that too?'

Her eyes opened wide. 'Of course not. Uncle Henry is too much of a gentleman to indulge in tittle-tattle. But I do have ears—and servants talk. What's she like?' Angelina asked, popping another baby carrot into her mouth whilst lowering her eyes to hide their mischievous intent, secretly delighting in his discomfort.

Alex's jaw tensed and a flash of annoyance darkened his eyes. 'Who?'

Calmly Angelina met his gaze. 'Your mistress.' As he arrogantly raised one brow a dangerous glitter entered his eyes, which warned her that his temper was not far from surfacing.

'She's very sweet, as a matter of fact,' he drawled.

'Then instead of marrying Miss Howard, why not marry your mistress?'

'Gentlemen do not marry their mistresses, Angelina.'

'Why—I cannot for the life of me see why not. If a man considers a woman suitable to take to his bed, why not marry her?'

Alex's grey eyes observed her with ill-concealed displeasure from beneath dark brows. 'I think we will drop this particular subject. It is pointless and leading nowhere.'

Restraining the urge to giggle, Angelina shrugged flippantly. 'As you like.'

When he turned the conversation back round to his home, she listened with a good deal of interest, and mostly in silence when she realised just how much Arlington and its people meant to him. It brought to mind her own home and all she had left behind. Memory clouded her eyes and Alex seemed to sense her despondency.

'Tell me, are you homesick for America?' he asked suddenly, correctly guessing the cause of her dejected attitude.

Angelina raised her eyes and looked at him sharply. His question was unexpected. 'Very much,' she admitted, unsure whether she wanted his sympathy, but comforted by it nevertheless.

'And you miss Mr Boone and your friend Will, I suppose.'

'Yes, I do miss Will. He was a part of my life for a long time.'

'And now? What do you think he is doing?'

'Trapping beaver somewhere among the Great Lakes of North America, I suppose,' she murmured, unable to conceal the yearning she still felt for her homeland.

'What made your father go out west?'

'He was bitten by the bug that bit everyone else. The lure of the west changed him and eventually he became hungry to see it for himself.'

'He wasn't the only man lured by the Promised Land.'

'It was a dream shared by many. Thousands of men all seeking a better life, a different life, to raise their children—all the time pushing further west in a valiant attempt to tame the land and carve themselves a niche. Hundreds perished in the migration, becoming victims of the elements or at the hands of the many tribes of hostile Indians.'

'And your mother? Did the lure of the west attract her also?'

'No, not really. She tried telling my father that homesteading was best left to those who know how to work the land, but Father was determined to go west.'

'And how did your father fare as a farmer?'

'Being unskilled in agriculture, he did not fare well. The weather became his mortal enemy—and then there were the Indian raids, when livestock would disappear overnight. Lack of money was a constant problem. The prosperity he'd dreamed of always eluded him. He possessed a grim determination to survive despite the odds stacked against him—but in the end he was defeated,' she finished quietly. 'The Shawnee saw to that.'

'Uncle Henry told me he was killed in an Indian raid, and that your mother was wounded,' Alex said gently.

The light in Angelina's eyes hardened. She seemed to withdraw into herself and her body tensed. 'Yes. Will looked after me and took me back to Boston with my mother—but I hate to remember. On the night of the raid I believe I faced the worst that could happen to me,' she whispered.

Having some comprehension and understanding of how desperate her plight must have been at that time, his own unhappy days as a child and the dreadful visions of his father's final moments returned to him vividly. Alex looked at her for a long moment, his eyes soft and filled with compassion. Whatever it was that had happened to her, she still saw her ghosts—just as he did. His voice when he spoke was kind, kinder than Angelina had ever heard him use in addressing her.

'Then we won't speak of it again. But if you truly believe you have faced the worst that can happen to you, nothing can really be that bad again.'

Angelina raised her pain-filled eyes to his, wanting so much to believe him. 'Do you really think so?'

He nodded. 'Yes, I do.'

The footman returned to serve them with a lemon pudding

and they continued to eat in silence until he left them alone once more. Alex watched Angelina's unconscious grace as she ate. She looked so prim in her violet gown. Apart from her face and slender hands not an inch of flesh was exposed, and not a single hair escaped that severe plait.

In the soft light her face was like a cameo, all hollows and shadows. There was a purity about her, something so endearingly young and innocent that reminded him of a sparrow. He tried to envisage what she would look like if the little sparrow changed her plumage and became a swan, and the image that took shape in his mind was pleasing. Feeling compelled and at liberty to look his fill, he felt his heart contract, not having grasped the full reality of her beauty until that moment. She must have sensed his perusal because she suddenly raised her eyes, hot, embarrassed colour staining her cheeks as he met her gaze with a querying, uplifted brow.

'I would be obliged if you would please stop looking at me in that way. Your critical eye pares and inspects me as if I was a body on a dissecting slab.'

'Does it?' Alex murmured absently, continuing to look at her, at the soft fullness of her mouth and glorious eyes.

Her flush deepened. 'I have imperfections enough without you looking for more. Please stop it,' she demanded quietly. 'You are being rude.'

'Am I?' he said, his attention momentarily diverted from her fascinating face.

'Yes. And if you persist I shall be forced to leave the table.'

Her words brought a slow, teasing smile to his lips and his strongly marked brows were slightly raised, his eyes suddenly glowing with humour. 'I apologise. You cannot leave before you've finished your dinner. But I cannot help looking at you when you are sitting directly in my sights.'

Hot faced and perplexed, Angelina almost retorted that she was not a rabbit in the sights of his gun, but she halted herself in time. She had never known a man to be so provoking. She was suddenly shy of him. There was something in his eyes tonight that made her feel it was impossible to look at him. There was also something in his voice that brought so many new and conflicting themes in her heart and mind that she did not know how to speak to him.

The effect was a combination of fright and excitement and she must put an end to it. She was in danger of becoming hypnotised by that silken voice and those mesmerising grey eyes; the fact that he knew it, that he was deliberately using his charm to dismantle her determination to stand against him, infuriated her. As soon as she had finished her dessert she stood up.

'Please excuse me,' she said stiffly, making a display of folding her napkin in order to avoid his eyes. 'I want to look in on Aunt Patience before I go to bed.'

'Of course,' Alex replied, rising and slowly walking round the table to stand beside her. 'Would you like some coffee before you leave? Or perhaps you would like to stay a while longer and play a game of cards—or chess, maybe? Uncle Henry did say you play a pretty mean game.'

Meeting his gaze, Angelina felt her flesh grow warm. His nearness and the look in his eyes, which had grown darker and was far too bold to allow even a small measure of comfort, washed away any feeling of confidence. The impact of his closeness and potent masculine virility was making her feel altogether too vulnerable.

'No—thank you. Perhaps another night.'

'As you wish.' Alex's voice was as soft as silk. There were the uncertainties of innocence about her, telling him that the sudden panic in her eyes was not in the least feigned. He accompanied her to the door, opening it for her. 'I hope you sleep well. I must warn you that the old timbers creak and groan, so don't be alarmed if you hear anything untoward during the night. Tomorrow I will ask Mrs Morrisey to show you the house.'

Angelina felt a sudden quiver run through her as she slipped away from him, a sudden quickening within as if something came to life, something that had been asleep before. She went up the stairs in awed bewilderment, feeling his eyes burning holes into her back as she went.

Chapter Five

During her first few days at Arlington, Angelina contrived to keep out of Alex's way as much as possible. She became a familiar and welcome sight at the stables. From Trimble, the head groom, she learned that horses were Lord Montgomery's abiding passion. Possessing some prime horseflesh, he was immensely proud of his large stable. He was also an expert horseman, who adored his gun dogs and was passionately interested in every kind of field sport.

Arlington Hall was a complex maze of rooms and arched passageways leading into each other. A billiard room and a music salon led off from the long gallery, and the smaller rooms had been made into private sitting and dining rooms and libraries, ornate with Italian marble and Venetian glass chandeliers.

Around mid-morning she invariably found herself in the domestic quarters to partake of a cup of Mrs Hall's delicious chocolate. Her charm and friendly, open manner had precipitated the admiration and devotion of the entire army of servants.

Angelina had never seen so much food in her life as the amount that existed in Mrs Hall's kitchen. 'Are all the animals eaten at the Hall reared on the estate, Mrs Hall?'

'Why, yes—at least most of them. As you will have noticed,

Lord Montgomery likes good, plain food when he's at Arlington—none of your fancy French cooking smothered with rich sauces and the like, which he says he gets more than enough of when he's in town. He prefers a roast or a game pie any day of the week.'

'What? Rabbit and partridge?'

'Aye, that's right—although it's a while since I made a rabbit pie. I have to wait until the gamekeepers bring me some, you see. The woods round here abound with all kind of game. I dare say it's the same where you come from.'

'Oh, yes. Although shooting isn't a pastime as it is here in England. It's a way of life and often the only means of survival.' Suddenly Angelina was struck by an idea and her lips stretched in a wide smile. 'I shall get something to fill your pie, Mrs Hall,' she said, leaving the kitchen with a jaunty stride.

Mrs Hall smiled indulgently after her and did not take her seriously, but she would have been astounded if she could have seen Angelina fifteen minutes later, striding towards the woods with her rifle.

Alex was returning home after visiting Mr Cathcart, one of his tenant farmers, who was concerned about the large band of gypsies encamped on his land and the recent outbreak of serious poaching in the area. Many a rabbit or a pheasant found its way into a family's pot, but the offence was more serious when deer were killed on a large scale, the ill-gotten gains sold further afield.

Alex was riding across open country when he heard the report of a gun. Frowning, he reined in his horse sharply and looked in the direction of the woods. Recalling Mr Cathcart's grievance and determined to get to the bottom of it, he whipped Lancer, his horse, into a burst of speed and set off in the direction of the shot.

In the process of reloading her rifle in the hope of bagging another rabbit, Angelina paused, distracted by the thundering approach of horse's hooves. Horse and rider emerged out of the trees and came towards her, and, much in the manner she associated with him, Lord Montgomery swung off his still-prancing, powerful black horse. With long, purposeful strides he swooped down on her like Satan in his entire frightening wrath. Angelina beheld a countenance of such black, terrifying menace that she trembled, fear coiling in the pit of her stomach. Never had she encountered such cold, purposeful rage. He took in the dead rabbit on the ground, and, with a look of cold revulsion, his eyes raked over her, riveting on the rifle in her hands.

'What the devil are you doing?' he demanded. 'If you don't mind, I will take that.' He held out his hand for the rifle, but Angelina had no intention of parting with her precious possession. Once it had been her only means of protection against hostile predators—both human and animal—when she had made the long trek from Ohio to Boston, and also the means of supplying her and her mother with many a tasty dinner.

'Mind! But of course I mind,' she retorted, losing control of her temper. Recklessly and without thinking what she was actually doing, taking a step back she levelled it at Alex's chest.

Alex's face darkened even more. 'Give it to me,' he said in that infuriatingly same awful voice.

Undismayed Angelina glared at him without removing her hand on the well-worn grip.

'Angelina, I repeat, give it to me.'

'No, I won't,' she said, trying to ignore the fury her defiance ignited in his features.

'You little hell cat,' he said quietly, watching her closely. Almost gently he warned, 'Before you consider pulling the trigger, pause to consider if killing me is worth hanging for.'

Angelina didn't flinch. 'I actually think it would be worth it,' she hissed, but, seeming to realise the absurdity of her action, she slowly lowered the gun.

'I'll break that rifle over your backside if you so much as raise it again.'

Highly incensed by his threat, a feral light gleamed in the depths of Angelina's eyes. She was like a kitten showing its claws to a full-grown panther. 'You lay one finger on me,' she ground out in a low husky voice, 'and I'll scratch your eyes out. I swear I will.'

In the face of this dire threat Alex moved towards her and leaned forward deliberately until grey eyes stared into amethyst from little more than a foot apart. His eyes grew hard and flint-like, yet when it came his voice was soft and slow. 'You dare me?' Seeing flagging courage and alarm flare in those dark orbs close to his own, reaching out he plucked the rifle from Angelina's grasp before she knew what he was about. 'I have never been an abuser of women,' he said, speaking carefully and distinctly, 'but if you tempt me enough, I might change my mind. I become very unreasonable when I'm angry.'

Stepping back, he scrutinised the lightweight rifle, with its fine engraved patch box and ripple-grained stock. He recognized it as a Kentucky flintlock rifle, one of the most popular small firearms of the American frontier. It was also ideal for hunting and, Alex thought with annoyance, for use against marauding Indians and irate lords. 'Yours, is it?'

Rather than let him see she was afraid and refusing to be humbled, she raised her chin and assumed an air of remote indifference. 'Yes.'

'Now why doesn't that surprise me.' Before Angelina could protest he quickly unfastened the cowhorn powder flask from her waist, which, he would see when he looked at it at greater length later, was attractively engraved with designs of maps and ships. He looked down at the rabbit on the ground and then back at her. The blood he saw on her hands repelled him. 'What a bloodthirsty little wench you are,' he said in a savage under-breath. 'I imagine there are other things you enjoy as much as killing rabbits—like cock fighting and badger baiting,' he accused with scathing sarcasm.

'I don't,' she responded angrily, smarting beneath his hard gaze. He was looking at her like some irritating but harmless insect he wanted to crush beneath the heel of his expensive, glossy black boots. 'They are cruel sports. Such useless bloodletting utterly repels me. It's a different matter to kill in order to eat.'

'I do realise that things are different in America—'

'Good. Then you must realise that you hunt to kill.'

'And you are not squeamish?'

'I was taught not to be. It was a necessary part of my life.'

'Do you realise I could have you arrested for threatening me at gunpoint—and have you hanged for poaching with a firearm on my land?'

'Poaching? What do you mean? Considering I was going to take the rabbit to Mrs Hall to put in a pie for your dinner, my lord, I don't understand what it is you're complaining about.'

Alex stared at her, anger emanating from every pore. With deliberate cruelty he carefully enunciated each vicious word. 'I don't want you killing rabbits for me, or anything else for that matter. If it were not for the fact that you are a foreigner and can plead ignorance, it would be necessary to reprimand you very severely.' Turning to his horse, he fastened her rifle and powder flask to the saddle. 'Come, walk with me back to the house.' When Angelina made a move to do just that he looked down at the rabbit and then at her. 'Aren't you forgetting something? Now you've killed the wretched animal you might as well bring it with you.'

He frowned when Angelina bent to pick it up and suddenly produced a thin-bladed knife from the top of her boot. His silver eyes glittered and his mouth curled up at the corners, those sleek black brows snapping together. 'Don't you dare attempt to gut or skin it,' he hissed, his voice icy and vibrating with anger.

'Why? What will you do?' she taunted, glowering at him.

He met the angry daggers that came hurtling at him from that glower. 'I'm liable to choke you to death with my bare hands. We have servants to do that.' He paused, holding out his hand palm up. 'I'll take that too.'

Tempted to inflict the same treatment on him as she would have inflicted on the rabbit, reluctantly Angelina handed him the knife. To her consternation and fury, all of a sudden she felt infuriatingly close to tears. 'I can always get another.'

'I forbid it,' he snapped.

'My skinning technique is excellent.'

'I don't doubt that for one moment—which is why I've confiscated your knife.' He examined the weapon. 'A nasty weapon for a young woman. I'd rather see it locked away than one day find it stuck in my back.'

'If I wanted to dispose of you I would not stab you in the back. I would find some other means.'

'Oh?'

'I'd poison your food.'

'Would you indeed? In that case I shall have to be very careful what I eat when you're around. Now come along. You'd best take the rabbit to Mrs Hall.' Turning his back, he took the horse's bridle and walked away.

Angelina was absolutely furious when she saw he had an infuriatingly smug and supremely confident expression on his face, as if he had won that particular round. In fact, she was so incensed that she was tempted to fly after him to do physical violence. Casting her eyes down at the rabbit and picking it up by its hind legs, through a silvery blur of angry tears she glared at his back as he set off through the trees. 'Wait,' she called out. Alex turned and looked back at her. Clamping her mouth shut, she stalked towards him, thrusting the rabbit into his hands and feeling a tremendous surge of satisfaction when blood spattered his light grey riding breeches and marked his immaculate black coat and kid gloves.

'What an arrogant, conceited beast you are, Alex Montgomery,' she spat, so angry that she didn't notice that she'd addressed him by his Christian name. '*You* take the rabbit to Mrs Hall—and I hope that when you eat it it chokes you. I'm going for a walk.'

Brushing past him, she marched back down the path to the edge of the wood, and Alex won a private battle not to smile at her retreating, indignant figure.

After returning Lancer to the stables and handing the rabbit to one of the stable lads, instructing him to take it to Mrs Hall with Miss Hamilton's compliments, Alex returned to the house and locked Angelina's crude weapons in a cabinet in the gun room. Then, after changing his blood-spattered clothes, he went into his office and tried immersing himself in his work, but his concentration wavered and he found his eyes constantly straying to the windows, looking for Angelina's slender form returning to the house.

When his fury had finally diminished to a safe level after an hour or more, and there was still no sign of her, making sure she had not slipped into the house by a back entrance, he went to look for her.

He was thoughtful when he walked in the direction Angelina had taken when she'd left him. He could hardly believe that she had gone out into the woods to shoot rabbits, or that she had aimed the rifle at him, but with that wilful, fiery temperament of hers, he imagined she did do things spontaneously. Only Angelina would have done such a thing and then dared to confront him so magnificently.

A reluctant smile touched his lips when he remembered her standing valiantly against him. She had looked so heartbreakingly young, with those mutinous dark eyes flashing fire and the dead rabbit at her feet, seeing nothing wrong in what she'd done—and, to be fair to her, she could not be blamed. Obviously no one had told her it was a crime to shoot rabbits in England.

She had told him she'd killed the animal for him, and to his surprise he found himself chuckling. She was truly amazing. Of all the women in the world, not one of them would have offered him such a simple, primitive gift, and he had spoiled it for her. He had seen the hurt in her eyes, and it had wrung his heart. If he hadn't been so damned furious he would have given her the applause she deserved for the clean and accurate shot that had killed the rabbit outright.

He had long considered her the most infuriatingly exasperating woman he had ever met, believing her to be a scheming little opportunist, driven by nothing but her own ambition. It seemed he was wrong about her—very wrong—and he bore the heavy load of self-recrimination for the accusations he had heaped on her. His loyalty to his uncle had clouded his judgement, and it had been wrong of him to condemn her out of hand.

Angelina was sitting beside a brook, her arms hugging her knees to her chest. Her hurt and humiliating sickness had not lessened.

'I can see,' drawled a deep, amused voice, 'that with an expression like that on your face you must be thinking of me.'

Angelina's head swung round in surprise. Her eyes and brain recognised his presence, but her emotions were bemused by anger and damaged pride and were slow to follow. Alex had crept up on her with the stealth of an Indian, and was idly leaning against a large oak, his arms folded across his chest watching her. Angry at the intrusion, she let her scowl deepen.

'You're right. I was.'

'Don't tell me. You are plotting some new way to antagonise me or how best to murder me.'

'Yes. And with as much pain as possible. Why don't you go

away and leave me alone? I don't want you anywhere near me. You are loathsome and I hate you.'

Unperturbed by her anger, Alex relinquished his stance by the tree and moved slowly towards her, an infuriating smile on his handsome mouth, his black hair curling attractively over his head and into his nape. 'Come now, you don't mean that.'

'Yes, I do. I never say anything I don't mean.' She glanced up at him towering over her, clutching her knees tighter. There was an uncompromising authority and arrogance in his bold look and set of his jaw that she didn't like. 'I told you to go away. Are you deaf?'

'No, and neither am I blind,' he answered, preoccupied with her cross little face and rosy mouth.

She looked at him sharply. 'What do you mean?'

'Only that you are lovely to look at—even when you are scowling.' He gazed down into her stormy eyes and proudly beautiful face. 'When I returned to the house I got to thinking about your unusual behaviour this afternoon.'

'Really? And what was your conclusion?' she scoffed, trying hard to ignore his compliment about her looks—if that's what it was, which she very much doubted.

'That you are hell bent on self-destruction or you are testing me.'

'It was neither.'

'No?' he replied in mock horror. 'Then this is more serious than I thought and needs further investigation.'

Lowering himself on to the grassy bank, he stretched out beside her. Bending his arm and propping his head on his hand, he lazily admired her profile as she continued to watch the water.

'Please go away. I know you dislike me as much as I dislike you.'

'You are mistaken. I don't dislike you,' he countered softly. Reaching out, he took the end of her plait in his fingers and began gently twisting it round his hand, idly contemplating its thickness, its softness.

'You don't? Then I can only assume that your opinion of me must be worse than I thought. You see, I always believe in first impressions, and your desire to offend me at the beginning of our acquaintance did nothing to endear you to me. So let us not pretend. In future we will strive to keep out of each other's way as much as possible.'

'We will?'

'Yes,' she answered, feeling the gentle tug on her hair. She turned slightly, and, seeing him twining her plait round his fingers, it dawned on her that he was far more interested in her at that moment than anything else. Considering what had happened between them earlier, she thought he seemed infuriatingly and disgustingly at ease. Casting him a sidelong glare, she yanked the plait out of his grasp. 'Please don't do that. Kindly leave my hair alone.'

Alex grinned leisurely as his perusal swept her face, watching as the crisp breeze flirted with tendrils of her hair, which had escaped their cruel confinement around her face. 'You have beautiful hair. It should not be restrained in a plait. You really ought to wear it loose.'

'I prefer to wear it like this,' she snapped, trying to ignore his virile body stretched beside her on the grass and the lean, hard muscles of his thighs flexing beneath the tight-fitting buckskin breeches that clung to him like a second skin.

Alex sighed. 'How can I defend myself when faced with so much determination and hostility?'

'You can't, so don't try. I'm sorry about what I did this afternoon,' she said, feeling the need to explain her actions to him.

'What—for threatening to shoot me or killing the rabbit?'

'Both—but I wouldn't have—shot you, I mean. Killing the rabbit was stupid, I realise that now, but—you see, I knew nothing about your laws governing poaching. Where I come from it is so very different. It's not because we are uncivilised, it's because some of us have to hunt to survive.'

'I know.'

'Do you?'

Alex nodded, his expression serious as he listened to her.

'That's how I was raised, you see—how it was for me and my mother when we left Ohio and returned to Massachusetts, and I can see nothing wrong with it. All I knew was hunting rabbits and wild turkeys and following fox. It was necessary. I make no apologies for that. However, I apologise if I offended you. When Mrs Hall told me your gamekeepers had not brought her any rabbits for some time, I thought I would oblige. Had I been told it was a criminal act to shoot rabbits, I would not have done it. Do you believe me?'

'Yes,' Alex replied, struggling to repress a smile, wanting to reach out and touch her fine-boned profile, tilted obstinately to betray her mutinous thoughts.

'And do you promise not to destroy my rifle? It once belonged to a frontiersman and Will gave it to me, you see.'

'I won't destroy it. I promise,' he answered, having some idea just how much that rifle meant to her. 'When I returned to the house I put it in the gunroom along with the rest. That is where it will remain. You may look at it whenever you wish, providing that's all you do—look.'

'Thank you. That rifle and I have travelled many miles together—and it saved my life on more than one occasion on the journey over the mountains. Without it the wolves or black bears would have made a meal out of me in no time.'

Alex stared at her, astounded. 'You shot bears and wolves?'

'Yes,' she replied, quite matter of fact, as if it were the most natural thing in the world to do. 'I had to. It was either them or me.'

'Good Lord!' Alex felt a stirring of admiration. He could not help but wonder at the grit of this young woman. She was truly remarkable. He had known no other like her, and the disturbing fact was that she seemed capable of disrupting his entire life, no matter what character she portrayed.

'So you can see why I've grown rather fond of it.' She glanced sideways at him. 'I suppose that, knowing all this about me, I've sunk even lower in your opinion.'

'Not at all. Quite the contrary, in fact. There isn't a man I know who would have the courage to go out and shoot a wild bear,' he replied, without a hint of mockery.

Angelina looked at him fully, probing the translucent depths of those clear grey eyes. 'I expect *you* would.'

'If I were confronted by one and I had a gun in my hand, yes, I would.'

She sighed. 'But it's not the sort of thing women do over here. You won't tell anyone, will you?'

Alex smiled, his eyes crinkling at the corners. 'Your secret is quite safe with me.'

'I can see I shall just have to try harder at being a lady.'

He grinned. 'You'll make it. Have you finished?'

She nodded.

'Then will you allow me to have my say?'

'If you must. But it will make no difference to how I feel.'

'And how do you feel, Angelina?' he asked softly.

'I will tell you.' She met his gaze coolly. 'I don't want anything from you. I don't belong here. I never will. I want to go home, back to America—but I can't go home. My mother saw to that when she made Uncle Henry my guardian.'

'You are right. Accept it. Your former life is over—permanently. And as much as you are against it, as the ward of the Duke of Mowbray you must face the fact that you will have to make your début into society.'

'I don't want a Season,' she cried explosively. 'I will not have you browbeating me into it.'

Her dark eyes sparkled with anger, and Alex thought what a

waste it would be for her to hide herself away, but then, better that than having to endure half the hot young bloods in London targeting her. He decided not to pursue that subject for the time being. 'What is it that has made you feel you don't belong here?'

She shrugged. 'I don't know. I just feel it.'

'I thought you liked Arlington.'

'I do—but—but I would like to return to London,' she said suddenly.

Alex took a deep breath. 'No.'

'Why not? After what happened between us earlier, I'd have thought you would be glad to see the back of me.'

'Uncle Henry gave you into my care and authority. Until he returns from Cornwall this is where you will remain. Besides, there is no one in London to take care of you.' When she continued to glare at him mutinously his face hardened. 'And, of course, you know I'll come after you if you spirit yourself away,' he told her, knowing she was capable of anything, even running away.

Scrambling to her feet in a huff, Angelina was tempted to call him names that would have set his ears on fire, but, realising it would serve no purpose, she refrained from doing so. 'Do you have contempt for women in general, or just me? Is it cruelty that makes you so obnoxious towards me, or are you naturally so?'

'I don't mean to be obnoxious and nor do I hold you in contempt,' he countered, getting to his feet. 'A moment ago I asked you to let me have my say. Please oblige me by doing so.'

'Very well,' she said primly.

'First of all, I apologise for any offence I caused you when we first met in London. My affection and loyalty to my uncle clouded my judgement and it was wrong of me to upset you. Please forgive me,' he said with disconcerting sincerity. 'I was rude and boorish in my behaviour towards you and now I heartily beg your pardon.'

Angelina was astonished. She stared into those clear eyes, searching for mockery, the veiled contempt, but found neither. 'You were rude and insulting,' she agreed.

'I know. I also know you would not have flouted the law so blatantly had you known it is a criminal offence to go around shooting rabbits—or any other animal unlucky enough to find itself within your sights, for that matter. I should have realised you had not been told and not reacted so furiously. I do not ask you to like me, Angelina, I only beg you to grant me some of your time so that I might present my case. In so doing I am sure you will reverse your opinion of me.'

'I won't,' she said adamantly.

'Nevertheless, it would be poor spirited of you to deny me that.'

Angelina stared at him, her eyes wide with astonishment. To be responsible for an offence, punished for it, to feel shame and bitter remorse and then be forgiven and absolved, was a succession of events beyond her experience. Rendered almost speechless by his apology and change of attitude, she welcomed it and yet she was suspicious, wondering why he was suddenly bent on charming her. She found him easier to deal with when they were engaged in open warfare than when he was being agreeable.

'What are you saying?'

Sensing that she was wavering a little and that he was close to victory, Alex pressed home his advantage. 'Only that a truce would not go amiss between us. That is the obvious solution, don't you think?'

Not knowing how to react, suspecting a truce between them would be more dangerous to her than when they were enemies, she opened her mouth to object, but closed it quickly.

'Come. What do you say?' He moved closer, touched by the innocence in her large, liquid eyes. 'Why do you hesitate? Are you afraid of what might happen if we become too close?'

'Of course not,' she replied, with a confidence she was far

from feeling. 'But a truce isn't friendship. It's only a halt in hostilities between enemies.'

Alex grinned. 'It's a start.'

'Perhaps it is, but I still don't trust you. And nothing will happen, so don't you dare think you can seduce me, because you'll be wasting your time.'

'Seduction is a time-honoured tradition in my family,' he told her, moving close like a hawk threatened to challenge. 'One that we're good at.' His wickedly smiling eyes captured hers and held them prisoner until she felt a warmth suffuse her cheeks.

Angelina took a step back. Her pride was taking a battering. He was deliberately manipulating her, forcing honesty into the battles between then. Oh, why did he have to look at her like that? The flush deepened in her cheeks. 'How many women have you said that to, Lord Montgomery?' she asked in an attempt to sound flippant in order to hide how she really felt.

A crooked smile accompanied his reply. 'Several. I am no saint. I enjoy the company of beautiful women, true, but is that such a crime? I would like to enjoy your company better, Angelina. I would like you to be more amiable towards me. I find you quite challenging.'

'Why? Because you want to bring me to heel, and when you have done so trample me under your foot?'

He arched a brow, amused. 'No, but I would like you to be less hostile towards me, less stubborn. Did anyone ever tell you that you have lovely eyes? You've got a lovely mouth as well.'

She looked away, staring fixedly at a point beyond the brook. 'Please don't say those things. I am not interested.'

'No?' Reaching out, he placed his forefinger gently on her cheek and turned her face back to his. He arched a questioning brow.

Angelina lifted her small chin and met his gaze unflinchingly, feeling his finger scorch her flesh. Firmly she removed it with her own. 'No. If it is your intention to gentle me, my lord, you will have to use brute force to subdue my rebellion rather than seducing me. Those are the only tactics I know.'

In spite of himself Alex threw back his head and exploded with laughter.

Wounded by his reaction, Angelina marched past him, yet her anger and resentment were considerably diminished. 'You brute. You're enjoying this, aren't you?'

'Every minute of it,' he confessed, laughing, his eyes dancing with merriment.

'Well, I don't know what you think you're doing, but I'm going back to the house.'

Alex matched her stride as they walked back across the park. Knowing exactly what he was doing and why, he smiled inwardly, enjoying the hunt and anticipating the kill with a good deal of pleasure.

Having no concept of his thoughts, after a moment Angelina turned and gave him a mischievous look.

'Tell me, Lord Montgomery—'

'Won't you call me Alex?'

After thinking it over for a moment, she smiled. 'Yes, all right,' she conceded to his immense surprise and satisfaction. 'Alex it is, then. Tell me,' she repeated, 'does all this belong to you?' Taking an energetic hop backwards better to see his face, she spread her arms wide to embrace the park and surrounding countryside.

'All of it,' he replied, utterly enchanted by her. Her dancing eyes and quick smile were sublime.

'So—if you wanted, you could grant permission to anyone who asked to shoot game on your land?'

The remnants of mirth still gleaming in his eyes, Alex shot her a warning look, seeing where her thoughts were travelling. 'Don't even think about it,' he growled.

Giving him an impish grin, with a laugh as clear as the purest water, Angelina left his side and skipped on ahead, releasing all her suppressed energy. Alex watched her go, her bright blue skirts dancing about her feet as she went, allowing him a tantalising glimpse of slim calves and ankles. He felt a surge of admiration. Her purity and the sweet wild essence of her shone like a rare jewel. She was innocence and youth, gentleness and laughter, a wood nymph surrounded by nature, and without warning he felt hot desire pulsating to life within him—not unexpected and certainly not unwelcome.

It was at dinner that same night when Angelina looked down at the succulent trout on her plate, then raised her eyes to the man sitting across from her in mock horror. 'What!' she exclaimed. 'No rabbit?'

Alex suppressed a grin. 'No. I've suddenly taken an aversion to that particular animal. I've instructed Mrs Hall to take it off the menu. Permanently.'

Angelina wasn't sorry. A softness entered her eyes and a haziness that suggested tears. Alex looked at her in disbelief, at a complete loss to know why his refusal to eat her rabbit should have brought her close to weeping.

'You're not going to tell me you're offended, are you?'

'No,' she whispered truthfully, humbled. 'I'm so sorry I killed the rabbit. I'll never shoot another as long as I live. I swear I won't.'

Alex stared at her. Those were not the words he had expected from her, but they were the ones he most wanted to hear. Somehow her regret for her foolish deed made him feel better. He grinned. 'Does that apply to fish, too?'

Angelina saw the humour lurking in his silver eyes and laughed. 'Oh, no. I'm good at fishing.'

'I'm glad to hear it. So am I. Now, eat your trout.'

Mrs Morrisey was busy supervising the housemaids as preparations for the weekend house party got under way. Angelina was not looking forward to it, finding the prospect of meeting strangers daunting. Aunt Patience was feeling much better and hopefully the doctor would permit her to leave her room by the weekend.

When Angelina left Alex to sit with their aunt after dinner each night, he had taken to accompanying her, where, under the ever-watchful eye of Aunt Patience, he would engage the young woman in cards or chess—and Uncle Henry had been right about her skill. At first he had doubted her talent, but he soon realised he had grossly underestimated her ability and that she was no novice.

They played in front of the fire, so engrossed in their game that they failed to notice Patience's expression of pure delight as she looked on from a roll-backed sofa, pretending to read a book. With a well-satisfied smile, she watched Alex as he relaxed in his high-backed chair with a decanter of brandy on the small carved table beside him. His eyes were fastened on the young woman across from him, and she strongly suspected his interest was not in the game.

While Angelina thought out her next move, the only sound in the room was the occasional crackle of the fire and the steady tick of the ormolu clock on the marble mantelpiece. Alex was fascinated by the way Angelina always vacated her chair and either perched on an embroidered footstool or knelt on the carpet, as she did now, as soon as they began to play. Her casual posture was not at all what he was used to among the proper ladies of his acquaintance, but he found it enchanting nevertheless. Sitting back on her heels and resting her elbows on the low chess table and cupping her face in her hands, her dark lashes curving against her cheek, she presented to him a captivating picture of bewitching innocence as she frowned in deep concentration over the board.

Every so often she would reach out and take a piece of pink Turkish delight, liberally sprinkled with powdered sugar, from a salver beside her and pop it into her mouth. Sipping at a glass of brandy, feeling the heat course down the back of his throat, Alex would watch from beneath half-lowered lids as she sucked the sugar from each sticky finger, her lips ripe, perfect, and so adorably kissable. It was almost impossible to believe that he could find such an ordinary act sublimely erotic, an act inflaming him beyond logic. As she was taking her time contemplating her next move, he looked down on the top of her head where the shining chestnut-coloured hair was drawn into an even parting, tempted to reach out and run his finger down the perfect line.

'Are you woolgathering or have you forgotten it's your move?' he said with a hint of gentle mockery.

Angelina shot him an indignant look. 'I am not woolgathering—whatever that means—and I know it's my move without you having to remind me. I just want to make quite certain that the move I make is the right one.'

'Who taught you to play?'

'My father. I used to beat him more often than not.'

'I am not your father, and you have not won yet, young lady. I have your knight.'

'And I have one of your bishops,' she countered.

'That makes no difference. It's the skill that matters. Now—are you going to move or not?' He flicked her a lazy grin. 'Of course, if you want to accept defeat, I'll accept your surrender.'

'I think not. The game is not over yet. And do you always talk as much as this when you play chess—or are you trying to put me off my game?'

'If you move your bishop, you will relieve my knight,' he suggested softly.

Angelina looked up, a deep furrow etched between her brows. 'Certainly not. If I were to do that, you would take great delight in capturing my queen,' she replied, giving his queen a scathing look where she lurked threateningly on the edge of the board ready to pounce.

Crossing one long leg over the other, Alex relaxed, content to wait until she was ready to make her move, fully prepared to wait all night if need be. He stared at her tight shoulders, at the taut, slim fingers moving her chess piece, each one exquisitely carved and depicting a character out of one or another of Shakespeare's plays. He watched her lift a finger to her lower lip and begin to nibble her nail in a characteristic gesture that made his blood run warm.

'That's a bad habit,' he chided softly.

She raised her eyes in surprise, the familiar, distant look of concentration in their dark depths. Her lips were slightly parted.

'What is?'

He smiled, looking down at her. 'Nail nibbling.'

'Oh—it helps me concentrate.' She flushed softly and quickly lowered her hand to her lap when his gaze lingered hot and hungry on her lips.

'Then try not to concentrate too hard, otherwise you will not have any nails left—and I will lose to you yet again.'

He sighed, beginning to enjoy himself as she took her time over her next strategic moves. It required every ounce of his self-control to concentrate on his own game. His pulse began to quicken as he dwelt on the graceful sweep of her neck and the mobile curve to her lips—so ripe, so soft, so kissable. Instantly his body began to hum a willing, familiar song and he wanted to toss the board and all those irritating little pieces aside and join her on the carpet right there in front of the fire and crush her against him.

'Check!' Angelina suddenly cried, cornering his black king with her white queen.

Alex grinned. 'Mate,' he responded, knocking his king over in final, willing defeat.

'That's two games to me to your one,' she told him.

The triumphant joy on her face was so startling, so captivating, that Alex was tempted to let her win every time. It would be well worth it to see her look like that. 'I admit defeat and consider myself well and truly trounced.'

'Will you not play another game to try to get even?'

Alex threw up his hands in mock despair. 'Alas, no. Don't you think I've been punished enough for one evening? We'll play again—perhaps tomorrow—and for your impudence I'm afraid I shall be forced to deal with you as you deserve,' he chuckled. He rose and went to his aunt, bending down and kissing her cheek. 'I will bid both you ladies goodnight and retire to my rooms to lick my wounds in private. As you know, Verity and Nathan will be arriving tomorrow—a day ahead of the other guests. I have business in St Albans in the morning so my secretary Hawkins and I will be away first thing. I should be back early afternoon.'

'Alex, wait,' said Angelina, scrambling to her feet and halting him as he was about to go out, remembering she had a request to make of him. With his hand on the door knob he turned and looked at her, waiting for her to speak.

'May I ride? You have so many fine horses in your stable. I've asked Trimble if I may ride one, but he told me to ask you first.'

'Of course. As long as you remain within the vicinity of the house you may. If you wish to ride further afield, a groom or myself must accompany you.'

'Why?'

'Because it is not done for young ladies to ride alone, that's why. There are also gypsies in the area, so I do not want you to venture too far.'

'Are they harmful?'

'As a rule, no. They have my permission to be on Arlington land just as they had from my predecessors—to come and go as they please, providing they behave themselves and abide by the law of the land while they are here. Unfortunately the gypsies encamped on the other side of the woods are strangers and therefore unpredictable. My bailiff has told them to move on. With luck they will have gone before the end of the week.'

Chapter Six

⟨⟨⟨⟨⟨∼⟩⟩⟩⟩⟩

'I'm glad to see the two of you are getting on,' Patience said when Alex had gone.

'Yes, we are, but he never talks about himself. Despite his self-assurance, I sense a deep sadness in him, something frozen and withdrawn. He gives of himself sparingly. The only thing I know about him is that both his parents are dead.'

'Gerald, his father, is—but Margaret—his mother, is very much alive,' Patience told her with uncharacteristic bitterness. 'After the death of her husband, Margaret married a Spanish count and went to live in Spain.'

Angelina was surprised. 'Oh, I see. Did Alex not approve of this? Is this the reason why he refuses to speak of his mother?'

'There's much more to it than that.'

'And I should not ask,' Angelina murmured sagely. 'I'm sorry, Aunt. I don't mean to pry.'

Patience smiled. 'It's only natural that you are curious—and maybe I should tell you. Alex wouldn't want us discussing something that he considers to be a purely personal and private matter, but, if you know something of his background perhaps it will help you understand him a little better and not judge him too harshly.'

'I don't judge him at all. What was his father like?'

Angelina listened avidly as Patience told her how Alex's mother had married Gerald, Henry's younger brother. Pampered and spoiled, she'd had her sights set on Henry, but Henry—who was deeply in love with someone else—didn't want her. To spite him, Margaret married Gerald, who loved her to distraction. Being lamentably weak, Gerald was forced to endure her many affairs, which she flaunted shamelessly.

For some malicious reason of her own—which Patience suspected was because Alex bore such a striking resemblance to Henry—she had hidden nothing from Alex. He was young and impressionable and adored his father. Gerald began drinking heavily to blot out what Margaret was doing, until it became too much. One day when he was in his cups he shot himself. Alex was fifteen at the time and witnessed the whole dreadful business.

Angelina listened in horror, seeing her aunt's eyes cloud with pain and bitter memory.

'Because he sensed it could destroy him, Alex refused to submit to the anger and anguish that raged inside him. In Henry he found warmth and understanding. But no one has been capable of unlocking that closed compartment inside his mind where he keeps his pain. Margaret distorted his mind, inflicting mental injuries on her son no mother should. She fostered in him a loathing and terrible bitterness against the female sex. It will take an exceptional woman to succeed where all others have failed. Alex needs someone to love—and someone to love him unconditionally in return.'

Angelina felt a lump of constricting sorrow in her chest, deeply moved by what Patience had revealed to her, which went a long way to helping her understand Alex. She also realised that the same demons that chased her were chasing Alex, and that it was as hard for him to talk about what had happened to him as it was for her.

* * *

The following day saw a deterioration in the weather, with rain fluctuating from a drizzle to a torrential downpour. Disappointed at being unable to ride, Angelina's spirits drooped. Undecided about what to do with her time, she decided to take a bath.

Unthinkingly Pauline sighed. 'It'll be a relief when the workmen have finished their work and water pipes have been laid throughout the house. Then we won't have to haul water up from the kitchens any more. No doubt they'll be starting on the west wing soon now work on his lordship's apartments is complete.'

'Trust him to take care of his own comforts before anyone else's.' Recalling Alex telling her that he would be away today, interest kindled in Angelina's eyes as a sudden thought occurred to her, and when she turned to her maid they were feverishly gay. 'Oh, Pauline!' she said, laughing, scrambling off the window seat. 'I've just had a rather splendid idea.'

There was such a look of excitement on her face and a familiar gleam in her eyes that made Pauline suspicious. It was a look she was beginning to recognise, one that boded trouble.

Five minutes later, when Angelina presented herself at the door of Alex's rooms armed with a large pink towel and bathing lotions, Wyatt, Alex's valet, was so astounded that all he could do was gape at her with a look of palsied shock. Bestowing on him her most brilliant of smiles, using her softest voice and being her most charming self, she eventually managed to cajole him into letting her use his lordship's bath tub.

Carried along under some kind of compulsion in which his responses were suspended, shaking his head in disbelief at what he had permitted, knowing the full force of his master's wrath would descend on him if he were to find out about this, Wyatt went to spend half an hour or more in the domestic quarters.

Angelina let her gaze roam over Alex's apartments in wonder. Even if she hadn't known to whom these rooms belonged she would have guessed, for the familiar spicy scent of Alex's cologne hung like an invisible intoxicant in the air. Essentially masculine and fit for a king, the room in which she stood was tastefully decorated in dark green and gold, with walnut dressers and bureaus and a large bed on a shallow dais.

Placing her towel on a chair, her curiosity getting the better of her, she went and peeked into another room, seeing a large desk and leather chairs, the walls lined with books. It was a busy room, a working room, with everything neatly in place. Crossing to the room that Mr Wyatt had told her was his lordship's bathing chamber and adjoining dressing room, gingerly she pushed open the door. Blinking at the extravagance and unaccustomed luxury, she felt as if she had suddenly been transported to a magical cave beneath a tropical sea and that Neptune would appear at any minute.

The ceiling was white, the walls pastel blue, green and white tiles interspaced with sparkling mirrors. In the centre of the tiled floor strewn with soft rugs was an enormous bath of white marble and gold taps. This fabulous object—the very height of luxury—beckoned her, and, unable to resist it a moment longer, she immediately turned on the taps and added her perfumed lotions before stripping off her clothes and stepping in.

Having concluded his business in St Albans sooner than he had expected, Alex and Hawkins returned to Arlington Hall, sodden after their long ride. With no sign of his valet and in a hurry to get out of his damp clothes, Alex stripped the garments from the upper part of his body and unfastened the top buttons of his trousers before crossing to the bathing chamber, picking up a towel as he went. Something about the towel made him pause and look at it in puzzlement. Pink? All his towels were either green or gold. Unable to work out what a pink towel was doing in his room, he shrugged and began to rub his wet hair.

On opening the door a wave of moist, perfumed air hit him

in the face. He stopped short, unable to believe the sight that met his eyes. An enormous cloud of fragrant steam was rising from the bath, and emerging from the steam was a head, a woman's head, crowned with a glorious wealth of chestnut- and copper-coloured curls. Stray tresses fell about her ears and clung to her nape in a saturated tangle, the rest of this adorable creature immersed in a mass of froth.

At first he was sorely tempted to ask her what the hell she thought she was doing in his tub, but it would have deprived him of the pleasure of watching her from his vantage point by the door. Until that moment he had never thought so much pleasure could be derived in simply watching a woman who was oblivious to being watched. The mere sight of her, with the soapy water lapping those twin orbs of femininity with infuriating, tantalising familiarity, was, for Alex, such a pleasurable experience that it made him ache.

It was the faint draught of cool air on her bare shoulders that alerted Angelina to the open door. With a gasp her head whipped round, and like a flame the powerful awareness of Alex's physical presence scorched through her. His unheralded appearance startled her to a sitting position, and Alex watched the soapy water sluicing off her satiny skin. The heat of his appreciative gaze ranged with deliberate slowness over her hair and face and down to her slender shoulders, pausing at length on the exposed, creamy swell of her breasts, leaving the frothy water to provide modest cover for the rest of her.

Alex's bold scrutiny caused Angelina's modesty to chafe. With her heart thumping in her breast and fighting to quell the shriek of panic that was rising in her throat, she cast a surreptitious glance about her. Her clothes lay in an untidy heap on the floor like a fallen barricade, and Alex was holding her towel.

Casually Alex relinquished his stance and, closing the door, moved further inside the room. Watching him, uncertain and silent, it was this action that caused panic and fear to course through Angelina. Suddenly she felt intimidated, vulnerable and alone. Memories she was unable to stifle paraded across her mind, and there was a haunting vision of her cowering, quivering and terrified beneath other eyes, with hysterical pleas tumbling from her trembling lips.

Having no concept of her thoughts, Alex crossed towards the bath where she cowered low in the water.

'Well, well,' he said, his voice low and mocking, his eyes burning into hers, the atmosphere inside the bathing chamber hot and sultry. 'Not content with poaching in my woods and threatening me at gunpoint, you now have to add trespassing in my private rooms to your crimes. It's a good thing I returned early—but—on second thoughts—perhaps I should have waited a while longer. Had I done so, your curiosity about my rooms might have extended to my bed.'

Angelina felt the colour drain from her face. Alex loomed large and menacing, his awesome presence filling the bathing chamber. With his hair a cluster of shining black moist curls, all she could do was stare with a bemused intensity. Compulsively and with a will of their own, her eyes travelled over his broad chest spread with a dark mat of hair, down over the hard leanness of his flat stomach, the pink of her cheeks returning when she saw a trail of black hair start beneath his navel and disappear into his trousers, where a bulge strained against the material.

Alex was watching her closely; her continued regard of that most private part of his anatomy increased the heat in his loins and he felt his tumescence grow. Good Lord, he thought. To his horror he realised his body was reacting to her without the least encouragement on her part.

With a jolt of mortification Angelina tore her eyes away when she realized that she was staring. She looked up at him in desperate appeal, terrified that her blatant intrusion into his private rooms and audacity to make use of his bath would have aroused his wrath to such a degree that it would bring some terrible dark vengeance down on her. She watched him with the terrified eye of a mouse watching a stalking cat.

'I—I didn't hear you come in,' she whispered, disturbed by the scorching heat of his perusal, and quite put out that he had been silently watching her and had made no effort to alert her to his presence. 'You should have made your presence known to me.'

'What! And deprive myself of the pleasure of watching you?' he murmured softly, desperately wanting her to look at him as she had a moment ago. 'If you don't get out this instant, you cannot depend on my ability to exercise restraint.'

'Why—what will you do?'

'Join you,' he said, casually lowering his hand to the few remaining buttons securing his trousers.

Horror registered in her eyes when she realised he intended removing that last vestige of decency and joining her in the bath, which was disgustingly large enough to accommodate the two of them. 'Please, Alex. Pass me my towel, I beg of you. I'll get out.'

Without revealing any more of her lovely form than was exposed to him already, she held out her hand, dripping water on to the floor. Alex saw it was trembling. Raising his eyes, he studied her as if he were truly trying to understand her. His gaze moved over her pale face, searching her dark eyes and discovering something in their agonised depths that brought a puzzled frown to his brow. Just when Angelina thought her time was up and no angel of deliverance would come to her aid, and that he would either scoop her out of the water or climb in with her, he handed her the towel and turned abruptly, actually scowling.

'Get dressed,' he ordered succinctly. 'I'll wait in the other room.'

His command penetrated Angelina's paralysed thoughts, and, when he had gone, she climbed out of the bath immediately, shaking in every limb. After drying herself and struggling into her clothes, she unpinned her hair from its fastening and shook it loose so that it cascaded just past her waist. Emerging from the bathroom into the lion's den, she drew a deep breath as she tried to steady her nerves. Having thrown on a shirt, Alex stood with his back to her looking out of the window, his whole body tensed into a rigid line, as if he fought some private battle within himself.

Sensing her presence, he turned, his jaw set. She was oblivious to the sight she presented to him. The pure, sweet bliss of having her close spurred his heart. She was too damned lovely to be true. Her cheeks were still rosy from her bath, and her hair—all the wonderful shades of autumn he'd imagined it to be—formed a torrent of brilliant silk tresses, with adorable damp tendrils clinging and curling around her face. The very sight of her here in his rooms wrenched his vitals in a painful knot, and the urge to go to her and pull her into his arms savaged his restraint. If she knew the full force of that emotion he held in check, she would tremble and seek the sanctuary of her room.

In a calm voice that nevertheless carried an unmistakable threat of command, he said, 'Come here.'

With the width of the room between them, clutching her towel and lotion bottles to her, Angelina could almost believe she was crossing an immeasurable abyss. As she slowly moved towards him, Alex's towering height increasing. Halfway there she paused.

Alex raised one black devil's eyebrow. 'Closer. That's not far enough.'

He looked like a dark, invincible god, forbidding, intimidating, and yet strangely compelling. When she stood close his hand reached out and touched her tumbling hair, taking one curling tress and winding it gently round his finger.

'You have beautiful hair, Angelina. It's a sin to restrain it the way you do.'

Frantically she began to think of things she could say, but all she could do was stare at him in mute appeal. Alex's suppressed energy and desire seemed to burn in that warm, elegant room, where all reality had been suspended. Angelina felt weak, unable to find the antagonism amid her confusion.

'You should not be here.'

'I know,' she whispered, finding her voice at last. Her pulse quickened when he stepped nearer. Feeling the bold look of his hungry gaze she trembled and instinctively took a step back, her only thought being to avoid any contact with him. 'I—I was not expecting to see you back so soon.'

'Evidently. I concluded my business in half the time and returned early—and it's as well that I did. The last thing I expected was to find you making use of my bathtub. I shall have a few choice words to say to Wyatt.'

Angelina's eyes flew to his, alarmed that he would vent his wrath on poor Wyatt when the fault was all hers. 'Oh, no. Please don't be angry with him. I am entirely to blame.'

'I believe you,' Alex replied drily, thrusting his hands into his pockets to keep from reaching out and dragging her into his arms.

'I—I didn't mean to intrude, but—I—'

'You wanted to sample my bathing chamber.'

'Yes.'

'Then don't you think it would have been common courtesy to ask me first? Why didn't you?'

'Because I didn't find out until this morning that you had one. Besides, you would have refused,' she said softly.

'On the contrary. I would gladly have given you my permission,' Alex said, finding that with the light from the window washing over her she was like a radiant sunburst and looked adorable.

Surprise etched Angelina's lovely features and her misty eyes widened. 'You would?'

'Yes,' he answered reasonably. 'Does that surprise you?'

'Yes, it does.'

'Why?'

'Because I—I don't understand you,' she murmured hesitantly. 'I never know what to expect from you. At the beginning you were hostile towards me. You were my judge, jury and executioner all wrapped into one.' Her luminescent eyes were large and desperate with confusion. 'And now—these last few days—you—you—'

'I told you not three days ago that I was wrong in my assessment of both you and your mother and I apologised. But you know, Angelina,' he said softly, seeing his reflection in the dark centres of her eyes, 'I seriously think you enjoy baiting me, and nobody does it as well as you. But shall I tell you what I think when I look at you now?'

'I—if you like,' Angelina said, trying to answer lightly, but her voice was low and husky.

'I see an extremely beautiful young woman with shining hair all the wonderful shades of autumn and the smile of an angel.' His heavy-lidded gaze dropped to the inviting fullness of her mouth, lingering there.

Angelina stepped back a little, but an answering quiver that was a combination of fright and excitement was tingling up her spine. 'Please don't look at me like that,' she whispered.

'Then I think you'd better go.'

Alex's desire for Angelina was hard driven, but he couldn't overstep the mark. But then, he thought, dwelling on a suspicion that had been forming in his mind since before he'd left London, would his uncle mind all that much if he made advances towards Angelina? Wasn't that what that wily old man had in mind when he'd insisted on her accompanying him to Arlington while he removed himself to Cornwall?

Clutching her towel and bottles to her chest, Angelina crossed the room and opened the door, only to find it slam shut when Alex came up behind her with the sure-footed skill of a panther. She stood there, frozen, anchored between his strong arms, the sleeves of his shirt rolled back to reveal their power.

Unable to turn, she could feel his closeness, the muscular hardness of him, the vibrant heat of his body pressed close against her back and his warm breath on her hair.

She trembled when he drew the heavy tresses to one side, feeling defeat, afraid, when she felt his mouth on the soft warm flesh on the back of her neck. On a gasp she sucked in her breath when he parted his lips and touched her skin with the fiery tip of his tongue. Her heart was pounding, and for a moment she knew a feeling of sheer terror when his voice spoke very quietly into her ear. 'I want you,' he murmured hoarsely. To his surprise she didn't fight him; in fact, as his lips began a slow, erotic seduction over her flesh, she didn't seem to know what he was doing to her.

'Please—don't do this,' she whispered, her heart thundering in her ears.

'Why? Don't fight me, Angel. What are you afraid of?'

You, her mind screamed. *You, and what you might do to me.*

'You are as much a victim of the overwhelming forces at work between us as I,' he murmured, his lips continuing their tender assault on her neck, the scent and living heat of her invading all his senses. 'You and I are one. The simple truth can no longer be denied.'

Lowering her head, a small knot in the wood of the door became the focal point of Angelina's concentration, a misshapen image tugging at the heart of her memory, conjuring indistinct, cloudy visions in her mind and blending them with a confused jumble of events that took her back to another time, another place, when other hands had touched her, when she had wanted to flee, but had been unable to escape the filthy, groping fingers. She fought a welter of unwelcome emotions that threatened to drag her down to a new depth of despair.

But she was not immune to Alex standing behind her, of the hard rack of his chest pressed against her back, making her feel things she had never felt before, things that were alien to her that she didn't want to feel. An alarming, treacherous warmth was creeping through her body, a melting sensation unlike anything she had known. She wanted to relax back against him, to feel his arms close around her, but because she could still feel those powerful emotions that seemed to have been drawn into her heart and soul from that night when she thought her life had ended, she could not bring herself to make that move.

With desire crashing over him in tidal waves, Alex looked down at Angelina's bent head, his lips brushing her shining hair. Slipping an arm about her waist he drew her tight against him, feeling a shimmering tremor in her slender body.

For a moment Angelina leaned into him, let his arm hold her, let him prevail in his hunger, his desire—but she didn't want it. Her confusion, her passion and her pain rose to a pinnacle as she stood trembling against him. To be this close to him felt like suffocating. She didn't think she could survive it. Terrified of making an overestimation of her ability to carry out the course she had chosen for herself, somehow she managed to place her trembling fingers on the doorknob and turn it.

'This is mistake,' she whispered, knowing that if she allowed some tenderness now between them she would be lost. 'I told you on the day we met that I do not want to be close to any man in the way you imply—and that includes you.'

Twisting herself out of his embrace, she opened the door and then she was gone, her feet driven by panic away from the east wing. Let him rant and rail, let him insult and chastise her to his heart's content—anything. Just let him never look at her as he had just then, or touch her with such tender intimacy. She would not let herself be at the mercy of a man like Alex Montgomery, who radiated sensual hunger in every glance, every move and every touch, but she could not deny that something had passed between them that would change their relationship for ever.

On reaching her room, she was struck by a desperate, impelling urge to get out of the house. In an act of rebellion and to bring some semblance of order back to her confused and troubled mind, she strode into the closet and rummaged in her trunk, finally finding what she was looking for—her old breeches and shirt. Removing her dress, she pulled them on, tucking the trouser legs inside her new pair of dark brown leather riding boots and lacing them up—incongruous against her shabby garb. After hastily plaiting her hair, she left the house by a back entrance without seeing a soul until she reached the stables.

When Angelina had left him, Alex stood in the centre of his room in deep reflection. Angrily he attacked his sentimental thoughts until they cowered in meek submission, but they refused to lie down. His attraction to Angelina was disquieting—in fact, it was damned annoying. If he wanted an affair or diversion of any kind, he had a string of some of the most beautiful women in the country to choose from—so why should he feel this insanely wild attraction for an eighteen-year-old girl who had hardly left the schoolroom?

He tried to put her from his mind, but failed miserably in his effort. The sweet fragrance of her perfume lingered everywhere, drifting through his senses, and the throbbing hunger began anew. He cursed with silent frustration, seized by a strong desire to go after her and cauterise his need by holding her close and clamping his lips on hers.

Instead he went into his study and attempted immersing himself in his work. Sitting at his desk, he set himself the task of going over the household accounts, subtracting and multiplying and adding long columns of figures. Under normal circumstances this was a simple matter for his keen, mathematical mind, but, slowly, a face with a pert, dimpled chin, a lovely and expressive mouth with soft, full lips, cheeks as flushed as a ripe peach, and thickly fringed amethyst, velvety eyes crept unbidden into his mind—

teasing him, tantalising him, laughing, beckoning him—fearing him.

At this thought Alex leaned his head back against the chair and set down his quill, giving in to his reluctant musings. Fear! Having marked Angelina's unexpected vulnerability when she'd cowered beneath the water, he now realised that that was what he'd seen in her eyes, but failed to recognize, when he'd threatened to join her in her bath. Then he remembered the words she had spoken before she'd left him and the pain in her voice—that she did not want to be close to any man, including him.

Why? He was both puzzled and curious. What had happened to her? Did it all stem from the time the Indians had attacked her home? Had they attacked her? Was the cause of her determination to close her heart and mind on marriage, on men, something to do with the relationship that had existed between her parents—or something else of an entirely different nature that she dared not reveal to anyone?

He directed his gaze to the window and his eye was caught by a mounted rider galloping across the park at breakneck pace. Frowning, he stood up, straining his eyes through the slightly distorted diamond panes better to recognise the person—which he did. Immediately. He was unable to believe his own eyes, as his gaze became impaled on the figure on the horse.

It was Angelina.

In the space of a heartbeat, fury had replaced Alex's calm composure. He was furious that Angelina worried him with her recklessness, furious that she was able to evoke any kind of emotion in him at all. Clenching his fists, he stood and watched her. Crouched low over her horse's neck with her face almost buried in the dancing mane, she rode as no lady should, in breeches and astride. There was simplicity and confidence as she soared over a hedge, at one with her mount, its tail floating behind like a bright defiant banner.

Her mount!

Alex's face was almost comical in its expression of disbelief when his eyes shifted from the breeches-clad girl to the horse. It was Forest Shadow, a high-spirited, excitable sorrel stallion he'd purchased two months ago at Newmarket to introduce into his hunters. Forest Shadow presented a challenge to even the most accomplished rider, who would be hard pressed to keep the high-stepping animal under control. White with rage, he felt his body go rigid.

'Of all the brazen, outrageous females,' he said in a savage underbreath. When she had shot the rabbit, he would have sworn he was incapable of feeling more furious than he had then, but the rage that exploded inside him at that moment surmounted even that.

Turning quickly, he strode to the door, jerking it open, the stallion bearing its young rider already a diminishing speck in the distance. How dare she ride out of the park alone after he'd forbidden her not to, and how dare she take that horse out of the stable when there wasn't a lad employed by him who was willing to ride out on the animal? On the other hand, he thought with increasing fury as his long legs descended the stairs in leaping strides, that defiant, conniving, dark-eyed witch would dare anything.

Jenkins waylaid Alex in the hall. He shot him an impatient look. 'What is it?' he demanded brusquely.

'I was just coming to inform you that Sir Nathan Beresford and his wife Lady Verity arrived a few minutes ago, my lord. They are with Lady Fortesque in her room.'

'Thank you, Jenkins,' Alex replied. Brushing past the butler he stalked towards the door. 'I have an urgent matter to attend to at the stables. Apologise for my absence and tell them I will be along directly.'

On reaching the stables he cornered one of the lads. 'Who gave Miss Hamilton permission to ride Forest Shadow?' he demanded.

'I don't know, milord. She just appeared—saying she was

going to ride him. We thought you must have told her she could. She wasn't afraid to ride him, milord.'

'No, I don't imagine for one minute that she was,' he seethed.

'Miss Hamilton's good with the horses. Seems to have taken a special fancy to the Shadow—and the Shadow to Miss Hamilton. She understands him. She seems to have a natural communication with him.'

'Indeed!'

'Yes, milord. At first, though, when she mounted him, we thought he was going to throw her, but the oddest thing was that when she talked to him—quiet like, into his ear—he seemed to know what she wanted him to do and settled down.'

'And didn't anyone think to go with her?'

'Yes, milord. But she refused the offer of a groom. Will you be wanting Lancer saddled?' the lad asked, hoping not, having just finished rubbing the stallion down and giving him his feed after returning from St Albans with his lordship. He considered it prudent to keep to himself the stir the young American miss had created by appearing at the stables in breeches—breeches that had seen better days, by the look of them—and of how she had grasped a handful of the Shadow's mane and leapt on to his back with the casual grace of a well-trained acrobat.

'No,' Alex snapped, striding out of the stables like a raging hurricane. He could see no point in riding all over the estate looking for the pesky wench when he knew damn well that she'd come back of her own accord anyway, and when she did he'd teach her obedience if he had to beat it into her.

Walking quickly back to the house, Alex knew a wrath that was beyond anything he had ever felt in his life. That was the moment he encountered Nathan, who had left Verity chatting to her mother and come to look for him. After greeting each other Nathan fell into step beside him.

'Patience tells me your uncle is in Cornwall,' said Nathan.

'He's visiting a sick friend.'

'Convenient, don't you think,' he remarked, observing his friend thoughtfully, 'leaving you and Patience to care for Miss Hamilton?'

'Absolutely,' Alex growled.

Nathan sensed that Alex was definitely put out about something, and he suspected the cause of it might be about to appear out of the woods on which Alex's eyes were fixed. Rather than wait for an explanation, he plunged straight in.

'At the risk of intruding into your thoughts, Alex, might I ask why you are wearing such a formidable frown? Your thoughts appear to be damnably unpleasant—in fact, you look fit to commit murder.'

'I am,' Alex ground out.

Nathan smiled. 'So you have not found the peace at Arlington you sought when you left London.'

'Peace? I cannot envisage any peace with someone like the American chit around. Never did I realise that when I quit London for Arlington—where peace and quiet has reigned supreme for centuries—that it would lead to such frustration and aggravation. But then I never could have imagined a girl quite like Angelina Hamilton either.'

'I think this business with your uncle's ward is preying too much on your mind.'

'I seldom think of her—if it can be avoided.' Which was true—but impossible. It seemed that whenever he thought of Angelina his thoughts became angrily chaotic. She was like some dancing, irrepressible shadow imbedded in his mind.

Nathan gave him a laughing, sidelong look. 'So you would have me think. But I did notice before you left London that your conversations were often sprinkled with varied references to Miss Hamilton.'

Alex threw him a black look. 'Really?' he growled with a hint of mockery. 'I didn't realise you were being so observant, Nathan—but since you are, you will have noticed that the only references I have made to that pesky wench have been unfavourable.'

'And nothing has changed now you have got to know her a little better?' he inquired.

'No—in fact, they have taken a turn for the worse.'

'Patience told me you were beginning to get on rather well.'

'We were, until she decided to take one of my best stallions for a ride to God knows where—without an escort or my permission.'

'Which one?'

'Forest Shadow.'

Nathan's blue eyes widened with astonishment. 'What? You mean that magnificent sorrel you bought at Newmarket recently?'

'The same.'

'Good Lord. He's a peppery beast at the best of times. Much too powerful for a young woman to handle.'

'One thing I have learned about Miss Hamilton, Nathan, is that she is no ordinary young woman—as you will discover very soon. She is also more trouble than I need right now.'

'Shouldn't you go after her?'

'No. The pesky young whelp is only happy when she's courting danger and annoying me. If she chooses to test her skills against that restless, high-stepping beast, then so be it.'

Nathan's chuckling merriment could not be restrained and he laughed out loud. 'Pesky she may be, Alex, but Patience tells me she has been blessed with the most incredible looks. Considering your reputation as a rake of the first order, you cannot have failed to notice.'

Alex's frown was formidable. 'It depends on one's taste— which is something we never did agree upon. The girl is a menace and has wreaked havoc in my life from the day I met her. She is everything I expected—a savage—and temperamental. She brings out the worst and everything that is alien to my nature. She also has the infuriating ability to rouse all that is evil in me, and she has a tongue that would flay the skin off a man's back better than any cat.' Yes, he thought, everything about her annoyed him, everything except her courage, which was a quality he could not help but admire.

'Perhaps if you were not so hard on her—if you tried to be more understanding towards her—you might find her more amenable,' Nathan said, blithely ignoring the simmering rage emanating from his friend. 'Give way a little. Try a softer, more gentle approach. Smooth her feathers and you'll soon have her purring like a kitten. I'm sure if you do you'll discover a more docile and agreeable young woman.'

Alex stopped and looked at his friend as though he'd taken leave of his senses. 'God in heaven, Nathan! There is nothing docile or agreeable about her. She has no respect for authority—and the only feline she resembles is a hellcat. That girl's the biggest stumbling block my temper has ever known. Try a softer approach, you say! The only softness about her I would like to make contact with right now would be laying the flat of my hand firmly on her derrière. The girl needs a sound thrashing that will leave her unable to sit down for a month. I will not be defied and dictated to in my own home by an eighteen-year-old chit of a girl.'

'Or anywhere else for that matter,' chuckled Nathan. It was clear that, where Angelina Hamilton was concerned, Alex's patience was wearing thin and he was in no mood to negotiate a better relationship with her.

Alex's mouth tightened. 'Her defiance cannot be overlooked. She resolved to be difficult from the start. With each day that dawns I wonder what kind of uproar she will cause next. The other day she went shooting rabbits for my dinner, and this very morning I caught her making use of my bathing chamber—and now the brazen wench has ridden off on a high-spirited, excitable horse without my permission.'

Nathan's brows shot up in astonishment. 'Do you mean to say she actually shot a rabbit?'

'She did,' Alex replied icily, 'and she very nearly shot me in the process.'

Stupefied, Nathan stared at him, thoroughly amused. It was unbelievable that Alex, who always had absolute control over his emotions, who treated women with a combination of indifference, amused tolerance and indulgence, could have been driven to such an uncharacteristic outburst of feelings by an eighteen-year-old girl.

'Miss Hamilton has a way with her, I've been told. Your uncle is enslaved, and she has your entire staff eating out of her delectable hands. According to Patience, every one of the grooms down to the youngest stable lad are all in love with her. She's even managed to charm old Jenkins. God help you if she uses it on you, Alex. You may well be lost. There will be no escape—and I very much doubt you will wish to.'

Alex glared at him. 'Don't count on it.'

Nathan directed his gaze towards the house, knowing there would be no reasoning with his friend until he had severely chastised Miss Hamilton. 'I am already feeling sorry for Miss Hamilton. The look on your face tells me you are going for blood, no less.'

'You're right,' Alex replied, lengthening his stride. 'And after the run-ins we've had in the past, she doesn't have very much left to lose.'

Having ridden further than she intended on the brave, fast horse, Angelina found herself enveloped in a shadowy world of muted sounds, where damp and decay rose from the undergrowth and assailed her nostrils, and squirrels skittered in the upper branches of the trees. Without the sun a bitter chill had fallen on this twilight world.

A feeling of unreality crept over her and she shuddered, glad when she saw an opening in the trees ahead where sunlight slanted through. Riding towards the light, she reined in beneath a canopy of oaks. The scent of wood smoke hung heavy in the air. Experiencing a prickling sensation at the nape of her neck and an eerie, familiar feeling, her head snapped up like an animal scenting danger.

She had emerged into some sort of encampment with an assortment of brightly painted caravans and carts, all of which had a shabby appearance. Dogs roamed and several piebald ponies grazed nearby. Men, women and children prowled about furtively in their garishly coloured attire, and some older people sat around a fire where ribbons of smoke spiralled upwards out of the embers.

Angelina knew instinctively that these people were the gypsies Alex had told her about, the gypsies he had told to move on. She sensed that every eye had become fixed on her. Two men with gold rings in their ears and brightly coloured scarves tied loosely around their necks rose from where they were sitting on the wooden steps of the caravan nearest to her. She swallowed nervously as they stood quite still, watching her.

They looked foreign—their skin swarthy and their hair hanging loose, lank and shiny black. Distrust and resentment lurked in their fathomless, totally unrevealing dark eyes. Her heart almost ceased to beat when her eyes were drawn to a knife sheathed at one of the men's waists, and when she met his gaze she felt a sudden chill, as if a shadow had passed in front of the sun, robbing her of its warmth.

No one made any attempt to speak to her, but the air was charged with an ugly tension, menace bristling all around her, the very silence an enemy. She shuddered, feeling extremely vulnerable and afraid. Through a veil of confusion and fear, what she now saw was a scene from her past. She glimpsed the dark, shadowy images creeping with stealth out of the locked doors of her mind, and she was sure they were catching up with her. All her deepest, darkest nightmares lay among the ghosts these gypsies resurrected, and with her emotions heightened to fever pitch, she feared she was about to be attacked again.

Whirling Forest Shadow about, she kicked him into a gallop. Trembling with fear she was borne homeward, unaware as Forest Shadow's iron-shod hooves struck the cobbles in the stable yard with ringing tones that her low state was about to be brought even lower.

Chapter Seven

Angelina's distress on coming face to face with the gypsies had lessened a little when she entered the house, but the threat they posed to her peace of mind was not forgotten.

Hoping to reach her room without encountering anyone, she was disappointed to find Jenkins waiting for her in the hall. When he saw her his body froze and he seemed to lose control of his expression as his gaze swept over her attire. His thick eyebrows rose up his forehead, and Angelina was sure she saw a little smile tug at the corners to the stern line of his mouth. But apart from this he was too respectful to show any other reaction. When he spoke, his voice was perfectly calm and controlled.

'Lord Montgomery has asked to see you the minute you return from your ride, Miss Hamilton.'

Angelina's stomach plummeted to the bottom of her boots with dismay. 'I'll go up and change first. I can't possibly face Lord Montgomery looking like a ragamuffin.'

At that moment a door across the hall was flung open and Alex materialised. 'Angelina.'

Her head shot round. 'Yes.'

'A word, if you please.'

Angelina bristled, not caring for the tone of his voice. 'And if I don't please?'

'Then I shall say what I have to say right here.'

'But—I was just—'

'I'm waiting.'

Angelina could see that Alex was furious. The glacial look in his silver eyes and the stern set of his features sent shivers down her spine. There was certainly nothing soft or lover-like in his tone, as there had been when she had left him in his rooms earlier. On a sigh she frowned. Casting a weary glance at Jenkins, she saw sympathy in his eyes.

'Oh, dear, Jenkins,' she breathed softly, 'I think I'm for it.'

'Chin up, Miss Hamilton, and you'll be all right,' he murmured, with his back to his ill-tempered master and with all the skill of a ventriloquist, for Angelina was certain his lips never moved.

She doubted the conviction of Jenkins's words as she turned and walked across the hall. There was not a single trace of reason in Alex's expression, only an undeniable aura of restrained fury gathering pace inside him, waiting to be unleashed on her.

He stood at the door to the sitting room like a soldier on sentry duty, waiting for her to pass—which she did, tilting her chin in a haughty manner.

Just through the doorway Angelina stopped. The ominous thud of the door behind her was too much for her lacerated nerves. Turning to face him, she was vaguely aware of two people seated at the opposite end of the long room, but she and Alex might as well have been alone—in fact, they should be, and she was angry that he had not chosen to chastise her in private. Her blood froze at the anger burning in his eyes. He had savaged her emotions once already today and it would seem he was about to do it again, but instead of seducing her into submission, she strongly suspected that this time he was about to go to the other extreme.

With her hands thrust deep into the pockets of her breeches, in a state of grinding tension, for what seemed an eternity she stood perfectly still, glaring at him mutinously, watching as his mercurial mood took a turn for the worst. As his eyes raked over her they opened wide, his sleek black eyebrows climbing higher and higher. Slowly he began walking round her, and she could only surmise that he was contemplating her shapeless flannel shirt and deerskin trousers. She thought to escape and her eyes shot to the door. He saw her intention.

'Don't try it,' he said, his silken voice almost turning Angelina's blood to ice as he continued to walk round her.

Alex kept his mercurial gaze levelled on her, a nerve jerking at the side of his rigid jaw. Undaunted, she lifted her chin with a small but stubborn toss of her head. It was a gesture of open defiance. Stopping in front of her, he moved closer, the silver eyes boring down into hers. When he could finally bring himself to speak his voice was ice cold.

'I have hired scullery maids better garbed than you. I do not know the meaning of this, Angelina, but you have a propensity to wilfully defy me at every turn. How dare you take a horse out of my stable without my permission and without the animal being approved by me first? Nor you did not take just any horse, but Forest Shadow, the most dangerous horse in my stable.'

'Were you worried about my welfare?'

'Don't flatter yourself,' he growled, demolishing the sudden flickering of hope he saw in her eyes. 'Forest Shadow is also my most valuable horse.' This was not entirely true. Forest Shadow was his most prized horse, but he'd been worried as hell about her on that powerful beast. However, he would not give her the satisfaction of telling her so.

'You need not have worried,' she said, with infuriating calm and no hint of an apology for taking the horse without his permission. 'I took good care of him. I do ride extremely well, you know.'

'So my uncle went to great pains to point out before he went to Cornwall,' Alex mocked. 'I have no doubt that he did not exaggerate about the excellence of your prowess. But until I have seen your *exceptional* skills for myself, the stables are out of bounds. Is that clear?' he seethed, his blistering gaze sliding over her face.

Angelina's reply was to glower at him.

'And another thing I want you to remember, I consider stallions to be unsuitable mounts for females to ride.'

'Why—you conceited, pig-headed beast,' she gasped. 'I am just as capable of riding stallions as any man.'

'Be that as it may, but not at Arlington. Now, you will go to your room and remove those outrageous clothes and appear dressed in normal attire. I will see you before me in precisely ten minutes. Is that understood?'

Angelina glowered at him with stubborn, unyielding pride, her chin pert, her hands balled into tight fists by her sides, sorely tempted to tell him to go to hell. 'Who do you think you are? I will wear what I please and do what I please.'

With his hands fixed firmly on his hips, Alex thrust his face close to hers, his eyes glittering with a fire that burned her raw and his eyebrows drawn close, giving him an air of fiendish intensity. 'I know who I am, Angelina. What bothers me is who you are. While you live in this house—*my* house—and until my uncle returns from Cornwall, you are under my care. You will do well to remember that and the sooner you accept it the better it will be for us all. You will be accountable to me for your actions. Is that understood?'

Angelina didn't even recoil from the blazing violence as she took the full force of his volcanic rage. Fury rose up like flames licking inside her, her face as uncompromisingly challenging as his. 'You can go to hell, Alex Montgomery, and the sooner the better. I own no man my superior—and least of all you. Ever since I left Ohio I have never been accountable to anyone for my actions. I do not intend to start now.'

'Yes, you will. Someone should have taught you some sense and beat that wilful pride out of you years ago,' he said, anger pouring through his veins like acid, his fury making him carelessly cruel. 'I am not daunted by your defiance.'

'You wouldn't be daunted by a pit of rattlesnakes,' she spat. In her fury Angelina forgot the man and woman watching them with astonishment and a good deal of interest from across the room.

Nathan and Verity found it hard to believe that Alex, a man so self-assured and masterful when in the presence of some of the most powerful men in England, had been stripped of his composure and was being baited with such boldness by an eighteen-year-old girl. They were taken aback by the quite unexpected heated altercation between these two. They were such a combustible combination, and it was evident that Angelina, who looked magnificent, glorious and indestructible as she faced the master of Arlington despite the shabbiness of her garb, had a will every bit as strong and stubborn as Alex's own.

'Go to your room,' Alex gritted. 'I will not have you behaving in this disgraceful manner in front of my friends and relatives.'

'Friends!' she scoffed, breathing hard. 'You don't have friends—you have subjects who bow and scrape at your feet. Tell me, does everyone always march to your orders?'

'Always.'

'Not me, Alex Montgomery,' Angelina flung back. 'I shall match you stride for stride and be damned to your orders.'

'You little baggage. If you continue to flout my authority and do anything else to inconvenience my staff or myself while you live in my house, I will personally make your life a living hell. Is that understood?'

'Why—what will you do? Beat me?' she scoffed.

'Out of respect for your sex, I will curb my temptation to resort to physical violence. But if you brazenly defy me one more time, do not depend on my ability to exercise similar restraint. More of this and you will find yourself on your knees begging my forgiveness. You are outrageous, outspoken, as obstinate as a thousand mules and your manners are deplorable—and look at you. You don't even look like a female and you certainly don't act like one. You will make a laughing stock of us all if you continue in this disgraceful manner. It is unacceptable. If you think you can go traipsing around my estate dressed like a gypsy, then you would do well to think again. I know females younger than you who are married—but who in God's name would marry you looking as you do, like a savage?'

Mentally adding his words to the list of insults thrown at her by him over the past weeks, like a cat Angelina slowly moved towards him, a feral gleam lighting up her eyes as she faced him in blinding anger, so close that she could feel his hot breath on her face.

'How easily that word trips off your tongue, my lord,' she seethed, each word clearly enunciated, 'and how ready you are to insult me. How do you know what a savage looks like? Have you ever seen one—a true savage, an uncivilised being marked by brutality and deprivation—in this privileged, cocooned world of genteel drawing rooms you inhabit? I do all manner of unladylike things you disapprove of, don't I? And if being outspoken, outrageous and unfeminine makes me a savage in your eyes then you are right. I am a savage.'

There was something close to murder in Alex's blazing eyes. As she turned from him, pushed beyond reason he reached out and grasped her shoulder, his fingers biting into her like knives. Like lightning and acting purely on instinct, Angelina flung her head round like an enraged lioness and violently thrust his hand away, accidentally catching his flesh with her nail. The unexpected action stunned Alex into momentary inaction, then he regained his senses and quickly took a step back.

'You witch,' he said in a savage snarl, white faced with fury, all his former admiration for her beauty, her strength of mind and courage instantly demolished as spots of bright red blood began to seep out of the small puncture mark on his skin. 'If you were a man, I'd run you through for that.'

'If I were a man, I'd have done the same to you the instant we met. Don't you ever touch me again,' she hissed through her teeth, standing with her legs braced and her fists clenched by her sides. Transfigured with fury, rigid with accumulated pride and rebelliousness, she dominated the situation as much as he. Her eyes were shining assertively, alive with the hidden mysteries of a rare jewel, her breasts rising and falling with suppressed fury as she struggled with the furious sensation burning through her veins. 'I killed the last man who dared do that. Is it not enough that you insult and degrade me without laying your hands on me? Keep them to yourself and perhaps we'll get on better.'

'That won't be difficult.'

'You are a loathsome, overbearing, despicable monster, Alex Montgomery—'

'I think I have the picture,' he drawled.

'Good. Then I needn't go on—but how I wish I'd never come here. I wish I'd never come to England and met you. I want to be free of you. I didn't want any of this. I didn't ask for it. It was thrust on me against my will.' She breathed as if she couldn't inhale enough air. 'Don't you understand that I hate you?'

Alex looked at the proud beauty that was glaring at him like an enraged angel of retribution and realized that she was on the brink of tears. He felt a twinge of conscience, which he quickly thrust away. 'I know you do,' he said coldly. 'And you will hate me a good deal more before I'm through. Now go to your room. I said ten minutes. It's now eight. Go and change—and if you disobey me, by God I shall come and remove those infernal breeches myself and render a certain part of your anatomy incapable of sitting down for a week. Is that clear?'

Angelina glared at him, her vow to murder this illustrious nobleman renewing itself in her mind. She would like to rend his heart to pieces. She would like to do so much damage to this mocking, sardonic man that it would prove irreparable. She would like to see him on his knees begging her for her favours, to grovel, and then she would spurn him. Turning from him, she walked away.

Alex watched the door close behind her, standing perfectly still, unable to believe the tempestuous, brave young woman who had stood and faced his wrath. His anger gave way to a reluctant admiration at her magnificent show of courage in admitting that she had once killed a man. He was stunned and deeply troubled by her confession, which, in her fury, she hadn't seemed to realise she had made. Remembering her stormy eyes shining with unshed tears, he felt a consuming, unquenchable need to know more about her past—but for the present he was determined not to let what he considered to be a childish act of defiance pass.

With Nathan and Verity sitting quietly in the background, Alex's fury had been reduced to a dangerous calm as he watched the door. He sat and waited, his jaw hardened with resolve, mentally crossing off the minutes and the seconds as Angelina's time ran out, his fingers tapping on the arm of the chair in a clear indication of his impatience. When her eight minutes were up he rose.

'Damned wench,' he muttered. He reached for the doorknob at the same moment that it swung open and Angelina swept in, dressed in her daffodil yellow gown. Tipping her head, she met his eyes with a smile of pure innocence—unchastened and unrepentant.

'Dear me, Alex. You do look vexed. You should be careful. It really is not good for anyone to get so worked up.' She smiled demurely and walked past him, with no trace of her previous anger or the mental exhaustion that had engulfed her when she had entered her room following his severe chastisement. She had seriously considered defying him and not returning to the sitting room, but the overriding fear that she would have to deal with his wrath once more put paid to such meanderings of the mind. She knew that Alex Montgomery was a force to be reckoned with, and that when he had told her he would come to her room and remove her clothes himself it had been no idle threat. But she had loathed him with each discarded garment for making her do it.

'Aren't you going to introduce me to your guests?' she asked, trying to crush the apprehension that was stirring restlessly inside her on being introduced to the tall, fair-haired gentleman and Aunt Patience's daughter.

Alex was rendered speechless. How was it he'd started out as the conqueror and ended up feeling like the vanquished? Neither threat nor punishment would oblige Angelina Hamilton to bow to a higher authority. At that moment he wanted to stride across the room, take hold of that impudent madam, and shake her. His eyes met Nathan's in a 'now do you understand' way. Nathan was visibly and infuriatingly amused.

Eager to be introduced to the tantalising young American girl who had turned his friend's world upside down and inside out in the matter of just a few short weeks, Nathan came towards her. As he reached for her hand, his handsome, boyish face broke into a brilliant, reassuring smile and his blue eyes twinkled with delight.

'Your servant, Miss Hamilton,' he said, bending over and pressing a gallant kiss on the back of her hand. 'And may I say I am truly delighted to meet you at last—having heard all about you from Alex,' he said meaningfully, casting his friend a mocking, lopsided grin.

'I'm sure you have—and nothing pleasant, I'll wager,' Angelina quipped brightly without looking at Alex. She liked Nathan Beresford at once, and for the life of her she could not understand how such a charming and amiable man could possibly be the friend of her antagonist. 'But please—you must call me Angelina. Everyone does.'

'Thank you—and you must call me Nathan—and this is Verity, my wife,' he said, taking Verity's hand and drawing her forward. 'No doubt her dear mama, Lady Fortesque, has told you all about her and how she keeps us all on the straight and narrow,' he said on a teasing note, casting his wife a fond look.

Angelina looked at him obliquely. Aware that Alex was hovering behind her like a dark threatening thunder cloud, her smile did not falter. 'An unenviable task, if I may say,' she replied softly, leaving no one in any doubt that she was referring to Alex.

She looked at the slender young woman dressed in a fashionable high-waisted gown of emerald green and smiled, wishing she had paid more attention to her own appearance instead of dragging on the first dress her hands had come into contact with. Verity was a pretty brunette, with a delicately arched nose and winged brows over friendly blue eyes. Her hair was gathered in glossy curls about her ears, a braided coil sitting prettily at her crown.

'I'm so glad to meet you at last, Angelina,' Verity said, her tone warm with obvious sincerity. 'I must welcome you to the family. Mama has been singing your praises for the past hour— telling me how patient and considerate you've been to her during her illness. I really must thank you. I had no idea she was so ill, otherwise I would have come to Arlington sooner.'

'She has been quite poorly, but as you will have seen for yourself she is a good deal better and hopes to grace us with her presence at dinner this evening.'

'I must offer you my deep apologies, Angelina. Alex should

not have subjected you to that rude display of ill temper earlier,' Verity said, throwing her cousin a glance of severe displeasure. 'He can be so overbearing at times.'

'My sentiments exactly,' Angelina agreed, feeling a fresh surge of anger against Alex for chastising her in front of these two, which he must have known would humiliate her. Her confrontation with Alex had been so distressing and unsettling to her peace of mind however, she remained silent, wanting to put the unpleasant incident behind her.

Alex had no intention of letting her off the hook lightly. He moved to take a dominant, indolent stance by the fireplace, one arm braced on the mantelpiece. His jaw was set hard, his eyes intense as he slanted a look at Angelina.

'By taking Forest Shadow out of the stables without my permission, what else did you expect from me? To ask if you'd had a pleasant ride?' he asked, the ghost of an ironic smile suddenly touching his mouth as his manner began to soften towards her at last. 'I am a reasonable man, Angelina, and I am perfectly willing to allow you as much freedom as you wish, but that does not mean for you to act brazenly and irresponsibly—and taking the Shadow was an exceedingly irresponsible act on your part.'

'Pay no attention to my ill-tempered cousin,' Verity said, casting Alex a slightly imperious though smiling look in an attempt to ward off further argument. 'I must express my admiration for your courage. You have my profound sympathy for what you must have endured—having to put up with him at Arlington all alone whilst Mama has been indisposed. It cannot have been easy for you.'

'No—but I've found myself in far worse situations than trying to keep on the right side of an irate lord.'

Verity laughed, a pleasant, warm sound, which went a long way to relieving the tension in the quiet room. 'Come and sit by me and we will have a quiet gossip together without being overheard by these tiresome men. I'm sure they'll have plenty to converse about without us. I want to hear all about America. There is a breath of adventure and excitement about it I find fascinating. We hear such varied and colourful tales that I would simply adore to go there myself.'

'You would?' Nathan remarked, somewhat astonished. 'First I've heard of it.'

'That's because you can see no further than Europe and what's happening in France, my love,' his wife said with sudden playfulness, which was so much a part of her charming nature. 'My husband's interest in politics exceeds everything else, Angelina. Whenever France and that upstart Napoleon are mentioned, he immediately becomes embroiled in a serious debate. I'm afraid that the Duke of Wellington and the progress of the war in the Peninsula eclipses all else.'

'As it does in all who are politically minded,' Nathan stated.

With a deep sigh Verity gave Angelina a long suffering 'now do you see what I mean' look. 'My dear husband eats, sleeps and breathes politics. You really should consider being a Member of Parliament, Nathan, and then you could air your views openly in the House of Commons—where, hopefully, you would wear yourself out in debate and be happy to come home to me. We could then converse on more agreeable matters that interest us both.'

Taking Angelina's hand, Verity moved away from them and drew her down beside her on a sofa. 'I'm so glad we're going to be friends, Angelina.'

'So am I. When I returned to Boston from Ohio I had so much to do and so many responsibilities. I had no true female friends.'

Verity saw a strange brooding look darken the brilliant eyes. 'Then we shall rectify that as soon as you return to London,' she said gently. 'We shall go shopping together and drive daily through the park—and there will be parties to attend and the theatre. We shall have such fun together. Although I must warn you that London in winter can be a cold and dreary place, so I shall steal you from Uncle Henry. You must come to Hanover Square and stay with us.'

'I would like that.'

'I was truly sorry to hear of your mother's recent death, Angelina. Pray accept my deepest sympathies.'

'Thank you. Uncle Henry has been very kind to me. I am so looking forward to seeing Mowbray Park. While I'm there I hope to persuade Uncle Henry to take me to Kent so that I might see where my mother lived.'

Verity merely smiled and nodded, taken aback by what she said, wondering if Uncle Henry and Alex knew what she intended. Like everyone else, Verity was aware that Angelina's maternal grandmother was still alive. She had no idea why Uncle Henry wanted it kept from his young ward, and her natural curiosity had been roused, but, not being the sort of man to indulge in subterfuge without good reason, she would respect his wishes and remain silent on the matter.

Angelina was unaware when Alex left the room and returned after just a few minutes' absence. She would have been surprised and angry to learn that he had gone directly to her room, startling a bemused Pauline, who watched in rigid, terrified silence as he strode into the dressing room and snatched Angelina's discarded trousers and shirt off the floor where she had left them in a heap. Alex thrust the garments into her arms.

'Drinkwater, the gardener, is burning some rubbish in the kitchen gardens. Take them and burn before your mistress returns,' he ordered.

When he returned, Angelina caught the smug, self-satisfied look he threw her way but thought nothing of it just then. It would be some time before she missed her breeches and shirt, and when she did they would have ceased to matter.

Sleep, chased by a thousand images, eluded Angelina. Dark shadows darted eerily into the corners of the room, transforming them into secret places hiding a hundred ghosts. Scrambling out of bed, she went to the window. Suddenly a brilliant cobalt blue streak of lightning flashed in a sudden spurt of brilliance across the sky, quickly followed by a rolling rumble of thunder. Rain began lashing at the glass panes and the wind rose to a fierce pitch, bending and twisting the trees in the garden so that they resembled grotesque, tortured beings, their huge shadows moving on the ground like furtive, creeping—what? Indians? Gypsies?

They were like the fairytale monsters of her childhood that had waited somewhere beyond the bed in the dark. Something terrifying pierced the raw centre of her soul, tearing open old wounds and clawing at her with savage, dirty fingers. Quickly she ran back to bed and buried her head beneath the covers, telling herself not to be silly and forcing herself to concentrate on sleep, willing the past to go away. But it refused. It whispered in the air about her, creeping closer still. A branch was beating on the window like the rhythmic beat of a drum, growing stronger and stronger as the wind increased in strength.

Eventually she fell into a fitful sleep invaded by hideous memories and her nightmare returned for the first time since she had left Boston. Cold and shivering, suddenly she was fifteen again and her terrors engulfed her—cold and implacable, real. A mist swirled around her, cloying, choking. The figure of the Shawnee materialised out of the shadows, out of the dark, and she was screaming and struggling with this creature who had killed her father and injured her mother, who was now trying to kill her. She was clawing at the face, watching bright red blood spurt from where her fingernails had raked his skin. She had to kill him—but where was the knife? Oh, dear God. Where was the knife? She must find the knife.

After sharing a few late-hour brandies in front of the fire with Nathan when the ladies had retired, Alex bade him goodnight. Walking past Angelina's room, he paused, straining his ears, hearing faint sounds coming from within. Believing the noise he'd heard to be the night storm, he was about to move on, but the sound came again. Someone was crying, whimpering, he was certain of it. Remembering how pale and anxious Angelina had been before going to bed, he became concerned. Unable to quell his curiosity or stem the need to comfort her, he went inside.

Closing the door behind him, he stood for a moment as his eyes adjusted to the gloom. Angelina's broken crying and muttering came from the bed. Wondering what could have happened to bring her to such wretchedness, he went to her, thankful when the moon chose that moment to appear from behind the clouds and to wash the bed in its silver glow. Looking down at her, the state of the tumbled bedclothes told him she had been thrashing about for some time. Perspiration glistened on her forehead and she was flinging her head from side to side, her fingers clawing at the covers and hitting out at some imaginary object.

'Angelina,' Alex murmured in alarm, about to reach out and gather the distressed girl in his arms. But he stopped when suddenly her eyes snapped open and she stared in abject terror at the dark figure bending over her, a figure looming larger that life.

With a strangled cry, like lightning she scrambled out from beneath the covers and huddled at the head of the bed like a terrified animal, clutching her nightdress about her knees, visibly trembling. Her eyes, black and enormous, burned with the fever of unspeakable agony.

'Get away,' she hissed. 'Don't touch me.'

Alex could see she was in extreme distress, confused and disorientated. 'Angelina—it's me—Alex,' he murmured gently, longing to reach out and take her in his arms and soothe her as he would a frightened child who was having a bad dream. But he could see her nerves were stretched tight, and that any sudden strain might cause them to break and fling her into a state of hysteria. 'I'm not going to hurt you.'

Looking at him for a long moment, every nerve vibrating, his voice slowly penetrated the inner sanctum of her mind. 'Alex?' she whispered. 'Oh, Alex.' Quite suddenly her features crumpled. She closed her eyes and shuddered violently, clasping her arms tight around her chest and beginning to rock back and forth as if in some terrible grief.

'Angelina—don't. Please don't.' The painful, unfamiliar constriction in Alex's chest made his hand tremble slightly as he reached out for her, but she jerked away, screwing her eyes tight shut, as if to blot out some intolerable sight, hitting out at him wildly, as though she imagined herself to be in the grip of an enemy.

'Don't. Please don't touch me.' Her voice was a hollow whisper. She began to cry silently, huge tears spilling over her lashes and coursing down her cheeks, her eyes begging him not to come near. 'Don't. Don't,' she repeated. 'Please…' She backed away against the head of the bed, unable to go any further.

It was an agony for Alex to watch her anguish, raised from the vast reservoir of despair threatening to drown her. He was unable to know how to deal with her. He couldn't leave her like this, because if he did he felt he would be failing her. Nor could he go for help without raising eyebrows about what he was doing in her room at this hour of the night.

Lighting the taper beside her bed, he looked at her pathetic huddled figure illuminated by its glow, weeping silently, wretchedly, shrouded in a thick curtain of long silken hair. The forlorn droop of her head went straight to his heart. Caught totally unprepared by her fierce display of emotion, he felt reason and control swept away. Sitting on the edge of the bed, with aching tenderness he reached out and took firm hold of her, pulling her close and fastening his arms around her like a vice.

At first she resisted and struggled, lashing out at his restraining grip, but then she grew still and grimly endured his touch. Through the material of her nightdress Alex could feel the alert tension of all her body. Her tears had ceased and her breathing was rapid. The warmth of the room wrapped itself around them so that it seemed that they were alone in a world without substance or reality.

'It's all right, Angelina. I'm not going to hurt you,' Alex breathed, his lips against her hair on the top of her head. 'I don't know what has frightened you and I am not going to leave you until you are all right. Try to relax.'

As if awakening from a deep trance, Angelina began to do just that. The storm of tears had ceased, and with its passing some of her tension had been washed away. Having dealt with tragedy and adversity for three years, she was too weak to fight Alex when he was being kind and understanding—and besides, he felt so warm and strong, his arms comforting and his voice soothing. His mere presence gave her a sense of security and safety. Alex was both surprised and touched when she nestled closer and turned her face into his chest. It was as if she wanted to hide herself in his embrace.

'Tell me, Angelina,' he said at length, 'have you experienced anything like this before?'

She nodded.

'And this nightmare you keep having, is it always the same one?'

'Yes,' she mumbled.

Releasing his hold, Alex turned her face up to his, stroking her hair from her damp face. 'What happened to you in Ohio, Angelina?' he asked, cradling her face in his hands and tracing her cheekbones with his thumbs. 'What are you afraid of?'

Fresh tears collected in her eyes and spilled hot moisture over his fingers. He brushed them away gently, feeling her give a convulsive shudder. 'Don't. Please don't,' she whispered, feebly trying to push him away to evade his touch, but Alex was having none of that now he had succeeded in subduing her and drew her firmly against him, placing her head on his chest once more and stroking her hair.

'Tell me about Ohio, Angelina,' he asked again. 'What happened to you there on the night the Indians came?'

White faced, she shuddered. 'No. I will not tell you,' she answered in a voice that was a raw whisper, her whole body rigid with anger in his arms—whether anger against himself for asking or her memories Alex didn't know, but to his relief she made no attempt to remove herself. 'Don't ever ask me, because I won't tell you. I try never to think about it.'

'But you do, don't you? And I can see that it pains you.'

'Yes—yes, it pains me,' she said in a torrent of anguished words, gulping on her sobs and pressing her face to his chest in an attempt to shut out the memory. Drawing a deep, quivering breath she tried to still her trembling limbs, trying to gain control of her rioting emotions. 'Damn you for mentioning it. Damn you, Alex Montgomery. It was vile and ugly—and I don't want to remember.'

'I can see that,' he said softly. 'But whatever happened to you, Angelina, you cannot go on carrying it around inside you like this. Have you never spoken of it to anyone?'

She shook her head fiercely.

'Perhaps talking about it will finally exorcise it from your mind.'

'It won't. It won't, I tell you.' No, she thought, not after keeping it to herself for so long. It would be like sharing her soul. Pride and shame had prevented her from speaking openly—even to Will. But Alex! No. Never to Alex.

Not wishing to cause her further distress, Alex decided not to press her on the matter just then. 'What was it that brought this on?' he asked, gentling his voice. 'Was it because I upset you earlier—or the storm?'

'No,' she mumbled through her sobs. 'Neither. It was the gypsies.'

Alex frowned. 'The gypsies?'

She nodded against him. 'I saw them when I was riding. I came upon their encampment on the other side of the woods.'

Alex stiffened and held her away from him, forcing her to look at him. 'Angelina, did they hurt you?'

She shook her head. 'I thought they were going to attack me. Seeing them—they—they reminded me—'

'Of the Shawnee,' Alex finished for her, understanding how the swarthy-skinned gypsies, with their dark eyes and black hair, would resemble the red-skinned Indians of America. Silently he cursed the gypsies and his bailiff for failing to get rid of them as he had ordered him to do. First thing in the morning he would ride out to their encampment and order them to move on himself.

He pulled Angelina back into his embrace and, his strong arms tightened about her. With her face pressed into the curve of his shoulder she seemed so small, so utterly female, warm, fragile and vulnerable. His heart ached with the fear of what the Shawnee might have done to her. Not even in his mind could he bring himself to voice his suspicions, but they were there, thrusting through his brain like knives. He couldn't say it. He couldn't even think it. The thought of Angelina knowing a moment's terror was too agonising for him to deal with.

Murmuring soothing words of comfort, he held her tightly, tenderly, as she wept, soaking his shirt front with her warm tears; racking sobs that shook her slender body with such violence that Alex was afraid they would tear her apart. They remained like that until her sobbing turned to quiet whimpering, and finally she grew silent and still.

'Do you feel better now?' he asked.

She raised her face to his, giving him a teary smile. 'I'm sorry. It—it's just that I didn't think it would happen again after I left America.'

'These things have a habit of recurring when you least expect them.'

Angelina felt the strength of his arms and the warmth of his masculine body. Slowly the fear began to recede, but she made no effort to free herself from that tight circle of arms—and Alex had no intention of letting her go while she was content to remain there. She could feel the hard muscles of his broad chest and smell his maleness and the spicy scent of his cologne. A tautness began in her breast, a delicious ache that was like a languorous, honeyed warmth.

As he sensed the change in her Alex's arms slackened. His senses were invaded by the smell of her. It was the soft fragrance of her hair—the sweet scent of roses mingled with a musky female scent—that made his body burn. Curling his long masculine fingers round her chin, he tilted her face up to his. She was calmer now, her eyes large, black and soft, her eyelashes moist and glistening. Gently he brushed the remaining tears from her cheeks, his fingers infinitely gentle.

It seemed a lifetime passed as they gazed at each other. In that lifetime each lived through a range of deep, tender emotions new to them both, exquisite emotions that neither of them could put into words. As though in slow motion, unable to resist the temptation Angelina's mouth offered, slowly Alex's own moved inexorably closer. His gaze was gentle and compelling, when, in a sweet, mesmeric sensation, his mouth found hers. Angelina melted into him. The kiss was long and lingeringly slow.

Raising his head, Alex gazed down at her in wonder. Her magnificent eyes were naked and defenceless. 'My God, Angel,' he whispered, his voice hoarse, 'you are so sweet. The next time you disobey me, instead of lashing you into submission with threats of physical punishment, in future I can see I shall have to change my tactics.'

'Oh?'

'All I have to do is kiss you into compliance.'

Angelina was full of remorse and regret for that unpleasant

incident earlier. 'I did behave badly, didn't I?' she whispered, her words filled with shame and a hundred other things Alex could not identify. 'I'm so sorry I hit out at you, Alex.' A knot of tenderness swelled in his chest as he watched her take his hand in both her own and press her trembling lips gently to the place where she had accidentally caught it with her nail. 'I should not have scratched you—I didn't mean to. It was unforgivable of me.'

Deeply touched, he smiled down at the incredibly desirable young woman who was setting his body on fire with her innocent gesture. Her beautiful profile was solemn. 'You may feel free to scratch me whenever you wish, providing you kiss it better afterwards.'

'It was wrong of me to take Forest Shadow without your permission. I know that now.'

Alex sighed, placing a kiss lightly on the soft curve of her cheek. 'Yes, it was. I was almost driven out of my mind when I discovered you'd taken him. He is barely broke to the saddle and still a bit wild and hard to handle—even for me.'

Angelina's heart jumped with elation. 'So you were concerned about me?'

'I told you. I was out of my mind with worry. That was why I was so angry.'

His expression was touching, his words so sincere, that Angelina forced down a lump forming in her throat. 'I—I didn't mean what I said.'

'What didn't you mean?' he murmured, nibbling her ear.

'When I said I hated you. I don't.'

'I know,' he answered, gently drawing the curtain of hair from her face and draping it over her shoulder.

'You do?'

His eyes fastened on her lips once more. 'Your lips have just told me so.'

With her heart pounding turbulently Angelina saw his eyes

translucent in the ghostly candlelight, his lean features starkly etched. 'Oh?'

'Another kiss I would have, Angel—to confirm what your lips first told me,' he murmured.

She shook her head in feeble protest. The insistent pressure of his body, those feral eyes glittering with power and primeval hunger, washed away any measure of comfort she might have left. A strange, alien feeling fluttered within her breast and she was halted for a brief passage of time when she found her lips entrapped with his once more, and though they were soft and tender, they burned with a fire that scorched her. Closing her eyes, she yielded to it, melting against him.

Alex tasted the sweet, honeyed softness of her mouth, finding himself once more at the mercy of his emotions, when reason and intelligence were powerless. Savouring each intoxicating pleasure he gloried in her innocence, her purity, painfully aware of the trembling weakness in her scantily clad body pressed against his own.

Alex's conscience, which he had assumed was long since dead, chose that moment to resurrect itself. Expelling a ragged breath and out of sheer self-preservation, he flung himself away, raking fingers of angry self-disgust through his hair as he fought to reassemble his senses and bring his desire under control. Devil take it, he cursed silently as he fought to tame his body's fierce, frustrating urges, what the hell was happening to him? He was using Angelina as he would one of his sexually experienced mistresses. But she was not like them. She was uncompromised and untainted. Compared to them, she was a gullible child.

Kissed and caressed into almost unconscious sensibility, a moment passed before Angelina realised something was wrong, that there was an unexpected lull in their kiss. She opened her eyes in a daze of suspended yearning, newly awakened passion glowing in the velvety depths of her eyes. 'Alex?' she murmured, reaching out and lightly touching his bare forearm, feeling empty and unable to understand why he had stopped kissing her.

Turning his head, he looked at her, his gaze smouldering, his breathing ragged, the throbbing ache in his loins reminding him how much he wanted to make love to her, how close he had come to taking her. With her hair tumbling around her in a glorious silken mass, she lay like a beautiful, pagan goddess among the ruins of her bed. He stilled her fingers tracing up his arm. It was a provocative movement and she was too innocent and inexperienced to be aware of the devastating effect it was having on his already ravaged self-control. Riven with guilt, he raised her hand to his lips and pressed them to the soft centre of her palm.

'We must stop now, Angel, before things go too far for us to draw back.' His voice was tight. He was unable to believe this innocent temptress had surrendered in his arms, returning his passion with such intoxicating sweetness that had almost shattered his self-control. Unwittingly he had released the raw sensuousness he had known all along lurked beneath her veneer of prim respectability.

Alex wanted Angelina more than he'd wanted anything in his life…more than he could believe possible. The weeks of being around her, of self-denial and frustration, the tension and explosive emotions her nearness elicited by her stubborn refusal to be dominated, had been hell. Like a siren in Greek mythology whose singing was believed to lure sailors to destruction on the rocks, Angelina's weeping had lured him into her room, and her vulnerability had finally broken all bounds of his restraint.

'This shouldn't have happened. It was a mistake. When my uncle left you in my charge I agreed to take care of you until he returns. I will not break that agreement by seducing you. Not only would I be failing in my duty to my uncle if I did that—

but I would also despise myself. I should not be here alone with you,' he said, getting off the bed.

Angelina drew the covers around her. 'Thank you for coming, Alex,' she whispered, reason beginning to return.

'I heard you crying. I couldn't walk by your room. Will you be all right?' His face, like an ancient warrior prince, was set in determined lines.

She nodded, wanting to conceal how deeply she was affected by what had just happened between them. 'Yes.'

He reached out and let his fingers lightly brush her cheek, then he turned. Her eyes followed him out of the room. Not until then did her mind come together from the far reaches of her senses where it had fled the instant Alex had taken her in his arms, and realise the full impact of what she had done. She, Angelina Hamilton, the woman who had been so sure in what she wanted, who had vowed never to yield to a man's embrace, had almost brazenly given herself to the one man she had every reason to despise.

Chapter Eight

As Pauline was about to pull back the curtains Angelina grimaced, in no condition to endure the brightness of daylight, feeling as tired and ill as she did.

'Please don't pull the curtains back, Pauline. My head aches so.'

Pauline stopped when she observed her mistress's pale face in the dim light. Her wan face and puffy eyes surrounded by mauve shadows bore mute evidence of her sleepless night.

'Oh, Miss Angelina, you do look poorly. You stay right where you are. I'll go down to the kitchen and have Mrs Hall make you up a breakfast tray.'

Angelina's eyelids, feeling like lead weights, closed, and when she opened them again it was to find Verity beside the bed. Trying to clear the fog from her mind, she struggled to sit up, but Verity put out a hand and pressed her back into the pillows.

'Don't get up,' she said softly. 'You're not well.'

Angelina sighed, unresisting, amazed at how weak she felt. 'It's nothing, Verity. Truly. I'm just tired, that's all.'

'Does your head still ache?'

'No—at least not like it did earlier. I'll get up shortly. Alex's guests are arriving today.'

'You're not to think about getting up. With rest you'll be as right as rain in no time.'

Alex's head snapped up and alarm brought him to his feet when Verity told him that Angelina was indisposed. His face taut, his eyes narrowed, he sharply demanded to know what was wrong with her, his reaction causing everyone round the table to look at him in amazement.

Ever since he had left Angelina's room in the early hours, Alex had tried not to think of her and to concentrate on the arrival of his guests, but now he became consumed with anxiety and unable to think of anything other than Angelina.

After a full night's sleep Angelina awakened, feeling much better. Wrapping herself in a warm cloak, she ventured outside to walk in the deserted gardens. Reluctant to bump into any of Alex's guests, she left the house by one of the many passageways.

The air was cold, the heavy clouds loitering overhead heralding more rain. From the terrace she was about to descend a flight of steps when quite unexpectedly she came face to face with Alex. She was aware of the elegant presence of the woman by his side, but in that moment of meeting there was no room in her vision, her heart or her mind for anyone else but Alex.

As surprised by her appearance as Angelina was by his, a world of feelings flashed for an instant across Alex's set features when their eyes locked, but it was the expression of immense concern she saw that touched Angelina the most, replaced at once by one of polite inquiry.

Tenderness welled in her heart as she remembered how he had comforted her in her moment of need, and she remembered how desolate she had felt when he'd left her.

'Angelina,' he said with polite formality, giving no indication how her pale features and the mauve shadows beneath her eyes wrenched his heart. He stood beside Lavinia Howard with all the tenderness of a lover, but his eyes never once left Angelina's. 'You are recovered, I hope?'

'Thank you, yes. I am much better. Feeling the need for some fresh air, I thought I'd take a turn around the garden before it comes on to rain.'

Alex turned to the haughty woman by his side. 'Lavinia, allow me to introduce Angelina Hamilton—my uncle…the Duke of Mowbray's ward. She is staying at Arlington until he returns from Cornwall, where he's visiting a friend.'

Lavinia's austere gaze settled on Angelina in a cool and exacting way. Impersonally her eyes raked her from head to foot in a single withering glance. She had heard all about the Duke of Mowbray's ward—gossip travelled like a forest fire among the *ton*—and it was rumoured that this untutored American girl was nothing but a poor relation and had no social credentials to recommend her. Nevertheless, having sensed that she might have a rival for Alex, she resented the American girl's presence here at Arlington. With a practised smile she looked at Angelina.

'Why, Miss Hamilton, how delighted I am that you are able to join us at last. How do you like Arlington?'

Protected from the cold by an immaculately cut, full-length dark green coat with a black fur trim, Miss Howard was a striking looking woman, secure in her own strength and sure of her own incomparable worth. Sadly, Lavinia Howard's appearance at Arlington on Alex's arm had stepped in to shatter Angelina's newfound happiness. Angelina smiled, seemingly oblivious to Lavinia's animosity, and because it was so elegantly done, and because Alex was looking at Angelina, he appeared not to notice.

'I like it very well,' Angelina said in reply to Lavinia's question. 'It is so very different from my own home.'

'You are American, I believe,' Lavinia said, her tone lightly contemptuous. She touched a perfumed handkerchief to her nostrils and sniffed delicately, as if Angelina carried a bad smell. Angelina felt her hackles rise and a faint surge of anger momentarily diverted her thoughts from her own disappointment at seeing her with Alex, her kid-gloved hand placed in a possessive manner on his arm.

'Yes—although my parents were from England,' Angelina informed her, in full possession of herself, the hard light of battle gleaming in her eyes. She had taken an instant dislike to Lavinia Howard and had no intention of letting the woman bait her. She pulled the hood of her cloak over her head to protect her from the cold, the fur trim brushing her cheeks and framing her exquisite face in the most charming manner. 'If you will excuse me, I will continue on my walk. It is far too cold to be standing about.'

Smiling frostily, Lavinia stepped aside to let her pass. 'Shall we have the pleasure of your company at dinner this evening, Miss Hamilton?'

'Yes, you will,' Angelina answered, having no intention of hiding herself away in her room any longer. She had decided that she would show all the Lavinia Howards of fashionable London society what being an American girl was all about.

'Verity, I have decided not to hide myself away any longer,' Angelina announced when Verity came to her room later. 'I shall have some fun for a change.'

Verity was pleasantly astounded, though cautious, as she asked, 'And a Season?'

'That too.'

'Oh, Angelina, I am absolutely delighted—and I know Mama will be over the moon. As for Uncle Henry—well—it is what he wants, for you to become a proper lady and take your place in society, which was what your mother wanted too.'

'I know, although I am certain I shall encounter many difficulties.'

'You are bound to—and you cannot be blamed if you get it wrong occasionally, for you cannot assume a way of life utterly foreign to you overnight. But you are clever and will learn quickly. I have not known you very long, but I do know you have the strength of character that will survive in any kind of society.

'And now,' she said, holding Angelina at arm's length, 'we have the important task of making sure you look your best for dinner this evening. I swear you will not recognise yourself by the time I have finished.'

The forty or so guests assembled in the hall were about to go into dinner. With Lavinia by his side Alex was talking to Lord Asquith, an old friend, who was bemoaning his poor harvest, but when Angelina appeared on the stairs he heard not a word. For the first time in his life Alex was rendered speechless as his eyes fastened on the young woman wearing a high-waisted white gauze dress flecked with gold descending the stairs. Her lustrous hair was drawn from her face with a thin strand of white ribbon, leaving the heavy tresses to tumble freely down her back to her waist. Angelina possessed the grace and beauty of a Grecian goddess and the regal bearing of a queen. Her presence reacted on everyone assembled like a rare sunburst.

In a shifting blur of people, of colour and flashing jewels that moved beneath her eyes, Angelina saw Alex. Magnificent in an olive green coat and white breeches, he was striding towards the stairs to meet her. Angelina's gaze went to the woman he had left standing, and she saw a face ice cold, the eyes glowering up at her. Steeling herself, she looked nonchalantly away.

When she reached the bottom step Alex took her hand. There was a twinkle in his eyes, and a slow, appreciative smile worked its way across his face as his eyes leisurely roamed over her body. The unspoken compliment made her blood run warm.

'You look entrancing,' he said in a quiet voice. 'I'm delighted you were able to join us—if tardily.'

'I'm sorry. Am I late?' The look she gave him was one of unadulterated innocence.

'You know you are. What were you trying to do? Hold out to make a grand entrance?'

'What? Me? Really, Alex—you know me better than that,' she murmured quietly, meaningfully.

He glanced down at her with a hooded gaze. 'Do I?'

She smiled impishly. 'No one knows me better,' she breathed.

'Minx,' he replied. 'Come and meet my guests before you say something that might embarrass us both.'

'You, my lord? Embarrassed? Never.'

Blind to the satisfied, conspiratorial smiles Patience and Verity exchanged, Alex's manner was that of pride as he calmly presented Angelina to his house guests—a polite, friendly gathering, and some of the more sedate members of London's *haut monde*.

Lavinia, who cleverly contrived to place herself on Alex's right-hand side at the end of the long dining table, gave Angelina a cool glance and then directed all her attention on their host.

Seated at the head of the table, Alex found his eyes drawn to Angelina like a magnet, where she sat halfway down the table, sandwiched between Nathan and Lord Asquith. She lit up the room simply by being present. Looking for unease on her face, he found nothing but calm and the soft glow of light in her velvet-dark eyes. Despite her inexperience in social repartee, she was extremely popular. She became lively, amiable, a laughing, beautiful young woman in possession of a natural wit and intelligence.

The following morning found a large complement of guests out for the ride into Arlington village. The stable yard was a hive of colourful activity, the atmosphere jovial and relaxed as people mounted Alex's splendid horses—some having brought their own, all champing at their bits, eager for the ride.

Looking extremely fetching in a ruby-red riding dress, with a matching hat cocked at an impudent angle atop bunches of delectable ringlets that bounced delightfully when she moved her head, Angelina appeared among them. With his noble head leaning over the stable door, Forest Shadow whickered on seeing her, stretching out its nose and shaking its mane vigorously.

'Poor thing,' she whispered, removing her glove and rubbing his velvety nose affectionately. 'What an infuriating tyrant your master is. How awful for you having to stay behind while all your friends ride out without you.'

At that moment Alex appeared by her side. 'Tyrant I may be, lady, but that horse is staying here.' Taking her elbow, he propelled her away towards a snowy white mare Trimble was holding. 'Let me introduce you to Sheba. Sheba is to be your mount for today.' He scowled when he saw her cast a regretful glance over her shoulder at Forest Shadow. 'Forget it, Angelina,' he said firmly, taking the reins from Trimble and leading Sheba to a quiet corner of the yard.

Angelina followed, looking at Alex admiringly, thinking how attractive he was, with his darkly handsome face and the breeze lightly ruffling his shiny black hair. He was resplendent in an impeccably tailored dark-brown riding coat. His gleaming white neckcloth was perfectly tied, and snug-fitting buckskin breeches disappeared into highly polished tan riding boots. But there was still an aggressive virility about him, an uncompromising authority and infuriating arrogance that was not to her liking.

When he brought the horse to a halt he turned, the heat of his gaze travelling the full length of her in a slow, appreciative perusal, before making a leisurely inspection of her face upturned to his.

'I'm pleased to see you are appropriately dressed for the ride.'

'Why—did you think I wouldn't be?' she asked, smiling provocatively at him out of the corners of her eyes.

'Thank God you didn't decide to wear those disgusting

breeches. I half-expected you to turn up in them just to antagonise me,' he remarked, curious as to whether her maid had told her he'd ordered her to burn them—and knowing how she would react when she realised he had. Her reply told him she hadn't.

'Why, Alex! As if I would,' she gasped, feigning innocence, but inwardly goaded by the mocking amusement in his eyes. Then her cheeks dimpled as her lips suddenly curved in a vengeful smile. 'Although I must confess that I did consider it. However, to save you from embarrassment and disgrace, not to mention the scandal it would cause, I decided against it.'

'Then I suppose I must be thankful for small mercies,' Alex jibed lightly. 'Now—give me your opinion of Sheba.'

'I'll be able to do that better when I've ridden her.' The mare rubbed her head against her, her soft dark eyes alive with intelligence. Angelina wrinkled her nose at the saddle with distaste, having forgotten she would be required to ride side-saddle. 'How on earth can anyone be expected to communicate with the horse on that contraption—let alone stay on! I shall probably become unseated at the first obstacle and break my neck—which I am sure will fill your lordship with morbid delight,' she retorted tartly.

Alex grinned. 'Heaven forbid! All the other ladies seem to manage it. You do ride side-saddle, I hope?'

'Not since I was a girl—and I didn't like it then. I love to ride, but this stupid saddle will take all the pleasure out of it. Still...' she sighed out loud '...it's a serious handicap, I confess, but because I have no wish to drive you to murderous fury today by insisting that the saddle be changed, I suppose I have no alternative but to get used to it.'

'Very sensible. I'm happy that you are beginning to see things my way,' Alex said with a wicked grin.

'Don't count on it.'

'If you're afraid to ride Sheba side-saddle—if it's more than you can handle—simply say so,' he suggested generously, a lazy, challenging, taunting smile tugging at his firm lips.

Angelina merely glowered at him, affronted that he should dare suggest such a thing.

'No lady rides like I saw you riding Forest Shadow the other day. Had anyone seen you, you would be ostracised from society before you've had a chance to enter it.'

Running her hand over Sheba's glossy flank, Angelina tossed her head, indifferent to his words. 'That doesn't concern me in the slightest.'

'No,' he chuckled, 'I did not imagine for one moment that it would.'

'Does Sheba have any peculiarities that I should know about before I risk life and limb?'

Alex lifted one eyebrow lazily. 'She's as docile as a lamb.'

'Not too docile, I hope. Although, should the horse balk, I shall be straight over her head.' She scowled at Alex. 'If I am, no doubt you will blame my poor horsemanship and not the saddle. I know that it would please you enormously if I were to make a spectacle of myself, my lord, but I am determined not to gratify your wish to see me take an undignified tumble—so come, help me into this monstrous instrument of torture before I change my mind and retire to one of the carriages.'

Placing his hands on her waist, Alex lifted her effortlessly into the offending saddle, watching as she hooked one knee around the pommel and placed her foot in the stirrup before settling her skirts. 'Take her out into the park and have a trot round. Get used to her before we set off.'

Taking the reins as Sheba moved restlessly, Angelina controlled the horse effortlessly and slanted Alex a querying glance. 'I don't see Miss Howard here. Shouldn't you go and find her and ensure she is properly mounted?'

'Lavinia isn't riding. She dislikes horses and has no fondness for riding. She is to follow on in one of the curricles with some of the other ladies. We'll meet up with them at the Wild Boar in the village.'

Angelina smiled inwardly, secretly suspecting this was because Miss Howard was an indifferent horsewoman and had no wish to be shown up, but she prudently kept her suspicion to herself.

Alex's expression suddenly became serious. 'There is one thing I should mention before we depart, Angelina. We won't be riding to Arlington directly and will more than likely pass the place on the other side of the woods where you encountered the gypsies.'

Angelina paled, her eyes locked on his.

'Don't be alarmed,' he told her gently. 'They moved on yesterday so you are in no danger of confronting them again.'

She nodded, her relief evident, glad that they had gone and were no longer a threat to her peace of mind. But how long would it be before something else came along to remind her?

When the party set off a biting wind had risen. Out in the park whips cracked and they were off at full gallop down the hill towards the lake. Angelina was happy that Sheba turned out to be a spirited little horse, certainly less docile than she had first thought. Several hounds bounded on ahead. Followed by a sea of horses—Alex and Nathan out in front setting the route—they poured over the land with a fluidity reminiscent of a river in full flow.

After a time they slowed their horses to a leisurely walk. Turning in his saddle, Alex looked back at Angelina, reining in his horse to wait for her to draw level.

'My compliments, Angelina. I know few men who ride as well as you,' he told her, falling in beside her. 'I am certain that the huntress Diana could not rival you.'

'That is a compliment indeed—coming from you.' The genuine warmth and admiration in his voice and in his eyes flooded her heart with joy.

'Is Sheba to your liking?'

'She most certainly is, but she does not perform as well as Forest Shadow. She's an ambler in comparison—but we get on well enough.' She laughed, leaning forward and stroking Sheba's neck when she saw the mare prick her ears back, as if aware of what she was saying. 'She's a beautiful horse.'

'I'm glad you like her. She's yours.'

Angelina stared at him, almost speechless with pleasure. 'Mine? Oh, Alex. No one has ever given me such a wonderful gift. I can't possibly accept it.'

'Yes, you can—unless you wish to offend me.'

She smiled a little shyly. 'I wouldn't dare. I don't know what to say.'

'Thank you will do.' He'd decided to make her a gift of the horse days ago, but because of her disobedience over Forest Shadow and the arrival of his guests, somehow he'd never got around to it.

'Thank you. But what will happen to her when I return to London? Will I have to leave her here?'

'You can take her with you if you like.'

'Really? Oh, that would be wonderful.'

Alex studied her in silence for a moment before saying, 'You're a strange young woman, Angelina Hamilton. Has there been no young man in your life? Before you came to England.'

Angelina sighed, a wistfulness entering her eyes. 'There was once,' she confessed, remembering Stuart Thackery, her child-hood sweetheart.

'Tell me about him?'

'There's nothing to tell really.'

'Was he handsome?'

'Oh, yes—very. To my romantic imagination he was Apollo and Lancelot all rolled into one—a thousand times more won-derful than all the knights of King Arthur's Round Table. No legendary hero could compare.'

Alex found himself resenting and thinking jealously of that

young man. 'He sounds like the answer to every maiden's prayer. And what happened to this prince among men?' he asked carelessly, unaware how deeply his cruel sarcasm hurt Angelina.

The question seemed to discomfit her. As if stalling for time she looked straight ahead, fighting a sudden mistiness in her eyes. She waited a moment before answering, and when she did her voice was low, almost a whisper. 'He—he was killed by the Shawnee.' Suddenly she urged her horse on.

Alex cursed his thoughtlessness. With a heavy guilt and his words eating away at him, he rode after her, catching Sheba's rein and bringing her to a halt. Angelina's expression was so wretched that it drove a piercing pain through his heart. At that moment he wanted all the other riders to disappear into thin air so he could drag her from her horse on to his own and kiss away her pain. She averted her eyes, looking anywhere but at him.

'Angelina, I apologise for my thoughtlessness.' Leaning across, he tipped her chin. 'Look at me and tell me you forgive my insensitive, thoughtless blunder.'

Her face broke in a teary smile and she looked directly into his eyes, seeing they were soft and yearning as they rested on her. 'Of course I do. How could you know anything about Stuart when I've never mentioned him? Along with many other things, I have several reasons for not wanting to talk about him.'

'I think there are a lot of things you don't speak of. Maybe you should. Quite often when one talks of what is troubling them, it helps relieve inner pain.'

'I can't. I will not confide in you or anyone else to share my misery.'

Alex looked into the moist depths of her eyes for a lengthy moment before nodding slowly, hesitant to press her further on an issue that clearly caused her extreme distress. 'I won't mention it again. Now, dry your eyes and we'll join the others.' Taking a handkerchief from his pocket, he handed it to her, realising how far they had lagged behind the rest when he looked ahead. 'We are in danger of being left behind and becoming the subject of a good deal of senseless gossip and conjecture.'

Angelina wiped her eyes and handed the handkerchief back to him.

'Are you ready to ride on?'

She nodded, a faint smile on her lips.

'Good girl,' he murmured, angry with himself for hurting her, and grateful to her for accepting his apology so graciously.

It was a merry group that arrived back at Arlington in the late afternoon. Everyone dispersed to their respective rooms to make themselves presentable for dinner. Jenkins approached Alex, slightly agitated.

'There is someone to see you, my lord.'

'Who is it?'

'A gentleman by the name of Mr Monkton. He arrived just a few minutes ago and has been shown into the library. He has come from Spain.'

Alex's face hardened, his gaze shifting from the butler's face to the closed library door. Angelina saw his jaw clench and his hands ball into tight fists as, in frigid silence, he strode towards the library and went inside. Her instinct told her that Mr Monkton's arrival boded ill.

She was proved right. Her aunt's expression was grim as they went in to dinner.

'Alex's mother has died, Angelina—some kind of seizure, I believe. Her death followed that of her husband, who died of his wounds following a military engagement in July.'

Not having known Alex's mother, Angelina had no feelings on the matter, her only concern being how Alex was affected by this news. 'Have you seen Alex?'

'Yes—an hour ago.'

'How has he taken it?'

'Very much as I expected he would. He is unmoved, coldly indifferent and without any emotion. I told you Margaret had a zest for hurting people—especially Alex. The damage that woman did to him makes me furious.' She sighed, distressed by all that had happened. 'I don't know why Alex's attitude should upset me, but it does.'

Throughout dinner Alex presided over the meal with his usual calm composure. He was politely courteous and attentive to his guests, giving no hint of his feelings.

Afterwards, guests found their way up to the long gallery, where they gathered in intimate little groups to amuse themselves. Angelina heard Alex excuse himself to Lavinia, telling her he was to join a group of gentlemen to play a game of billiards.

It was to the music room that Angelina was drawn, but not before she had observed Alex walk the length of the long gallery, bypassing the billiard room, and disappear through a door that led to the east wing. In the music room Patience was already ensconced on a sofa. The older woman's face brightened when she saw her and she patted the space beside her invitingly.

'Sit by me, Angelina. Miss Asquith is about to play for us on the pianoforte.'

Angelina excused herself on the pretext that she was to fetch her fan. Reaching Alex's suite of rooms, she knocked gently on the door she knew opened into a small anteroom that led into his office, without the visitor having to pass through his bedroom. When there was no response, she opened it and stepped inside, moving slowly towards the open study door.

Having removed his coat and rolled up his shirt sleeves, Alex was standing by the window, a drink in his hand. Angelina's heart twisted with remorse when she saw the pain etched on his unguarded face. He sensed her presence his shoulders stiffened and he turned, his expression stony and preoccupied.

'If you want me to go away, I will, Alex. You only have to say.' She was relieved when she saw his granite features relax a little.

'No—please stay.'

Angelina moved towards him, feeling momentarily at a loss to know what to say, how to comfort this suffering man.

'What made you seek me out?'

'I saw you leave. I was worried...'

His sudden sweeping smile was disarming and confounded her. 'What better way to lure you into my chamber.'

She gasped, thinking how absolutely unpredictable he was. 'I thought you were upset—because of the news Mr Monkton brought you...'

His smile faded abruptly and his expression became guarded, his eyes as brittle and cold as glass. Moving away from her towards the fire, he braced his foot on the brass fender. Leaning his shoulder against the mantelpiece, he folded his arms over his chest and looked at her coldly. 'So, you know about that?'

'Yes. Aunt Patience told me.'

'What did she tell you? How much?' he demanded tightly.

Drawing a long breath, Angelina knew she had come too far to stop now. 'That your mother has died and—'

'How my father shot himself?'

She did not lower her gaze. 'Yes. That too. Alex, what happened is no secret. Aunt Patience did not betray a confidence. When I came to see you, I hoped that you would have had time to come to terms with the news and I—thought—'

'What? That now my fury has abated I would be crying into my cups?' His lips twisted with irony. 'If you thought that, you do not know me.'

'No. I don't think I do,' she said quietly, refusing to back away from this hard, cynical man. 'Does anyone?'

'No. That's the way I like it. Angelina, I appreciate your concern, but do not involve yourself in something you know nothing about. I'm dealing with this in my own way. I don't need your help.'

Angelina stiffened, but she managed to keep the hurt out of her voice. 'That's all right. You don't have to accept it. I don't mind.' She looked towards the door and turned away. 'I'm sorry. I shouldn't have come.'

Alex reached out and placed a restraining hand on her arm. 'Stay. I admire you for having the courage to seek me out at this time. But as you see, you were correct in assuming I've had time to come to terms with the news Mr Monkton brought me. I never loved my mother—I loved neither her inconstancy nor her heartlessness.'

Angelina looked at his proud, lean face, moved by the pain that edged his voice. 'And you are still tortured by what she did to you, I can see that.'

'That woman inspired me with nothing but disgust and loathing. As long as I live I shall never forget that day when I watched my father kill himself—the horror-sickening shock, the feeling of helplessness, the overwhelming despair, betrayal—and the hatred I felt when I realized that my mother alone was responsible. My father was weak—some might have called him spineless—and my mother, who considered male superiority a myth, mocked him for it. She should never have married him. It was Uncle Henry she wanted—but he—' Aware of who it was he was talking to Alex suddenly stopped and looked at Angelina. 'I'm sorry. I shouldn't be telling you this.'

'I think you were about to say that Uncle Henry wouldn't marry her because he was in love with someone else. Is that not so?'

He nodded slowly, meeting her candid gaze, wondering just how much Angelina knew about the feelings Uncle Henry cherished for her mother to this day. 'Yes.'

'Did your father do nothing to stand up to her?'

'His continual submissiveness to her amoral behaviour was

something I was never able to understand. It infuriated me when he tried to make excuses for her. I wanted him to berate her, to stand up for himself. She humiliated him, spurned and shamed him before his friends, flaunting her lovers in front of him— and instead of teaching her a lesson, my father sought oblivion in drink before shooting himself.'

'And you still carry your hurt and bitterness around your neck like a millstone.'

Alex's smile was one of cynicism. 'Does it show all that much?'

'Sometimes.'

'There are some things, Angelina, that cannot easily be put aside. You, more than any other person I know, should understand that.' He stopped his pacing and looked down at her. 'You said you came because you were worried. About me?'

She nodded.

'So, you came—even though you knew I might send you away.'

'I anticipated that—and I must confess to feeling how Daniel must have felt when he entered the lion's den.'

'Were you not afraid of my anger?'

'I don't fear you, Alex,' she replied, calmly looking into his clear eyes. 'You should know that by now. Among the many emotions you must be feeling I knew you would be angry and hurt, but seeing you at dinner, so composed, so…'

'Anaesthetised,' Alex suggested wryly when she hesitated for want of an appropriate word.

'If you like.'

Alex's gaze searched her face with something like wonder in his silver eyes. There were depths to Angelina that every other woman he knew lacked, and she never ceased to amaze him. 'You confound me—do you know that? You try my patience like no other, you shoot rabbits like a barbarian and ride a horse like a gypsy, and yet what an amazingly sensitive, perceptive, wise little thing you've become, Angelina Hamilton.'

'If I were wise, I would have come to terms with everything that happened to me in Ohio and put it behind me, but I can't. That is still a millstone around my neck I have to bear. I, too, was fifteen when I saw my father die—brutally—so I know how you must have felt when you witnessed your father's suicide. I also saw my mother run to his side only to be brought down by an Indian's knife thrust into her back. I laid their ghosts to rest before I came to England. Perhaps you will be able to do the same now you know your mother is dead.'

Alex picked up a decanter from his desk to replenish his glass. Finding it devoid of liquor, he uttered a soft curse and strode towards the door to his bedroom. Holding it open with his arm, he indicated that she follow. 'Come, you already know your way around my apartment,' he grinned. 'Will you join me in a glass of wine?'

Seeing her hesitate, he said, 'You can't leave. You came to comfort me in my hour of need. Remember? I'm still in need.' He smiled lazily when she jerked her head in alarm. 'Why—you're not afraid to enter my bedroom, are you, Angelina?' he murmured with a sardonic tilt to his dark brows, his eyes compelling, flashing with that particularly silver light that was a herald to trouble.

Angelina was amazed at his ability to push his worries into the background so effortlessly. 'Yes—no, of course not.'

'You were brave enough to enter it on a previous occasion as I recall. Remember?'

His voice held a quiet challenge, and when she saw he would not take no for an answer, she relented. 'Well—perhaps just for a minute. I told Aunt Patience I was going to my room to fetch my fan. I also told her I would not be long,' she said, throwing him a meaningful glance.

'I'm sure Aunt Patience will not mind if you don't return immediately. Before I left, I observed her settling down in the music room to listen to Miss Asquith perform on the pianoforte.

She may not even notice your absence,' he said, standing aside to let her sweep past. 'Welcome to my parlour.'

'Said the spider to the fly,' Angelina couldn't help retorting drily.

Alex grinned. 'In no way do you resemble a fly, Angelina. You are far too nimble and sensible to become entrapped in any kind of web—especially one of my weaving.'

Chapter Nine

'Allow me to congratulate you.' A lazy, devastating smile passed over Alex's features, his eyes doing a slow sweep of her body so that Angelina could almost feel him disrobing her. 'It appears the engaging young girl I first knew has become a gorgeous young woman of exotic beauty. In the space of twenty-four hours you have endeared yourself to every one of my guests—especially the gentlemen. No doubt when you return to London you will slay the lot of them.'

'Alex, please don't exaggerate.' Angelina moved closer to the fire to hide her confusion, aware of the magnetic charm he was exuding, and beginning to wish she had left when she had said what she had come to say.

'I don't. You will bowl them over and down they will fall like skittles. No doubt they will all turn poets overnight to express their love for this bright new star in their heaven.'

'Really?' She smiled, her eyes slanted and quietly teasing, feeling a treacherous warmth seep through her. 'And will you pen one yourself, my lord?'

He grinned. 'Haven't you broken enough hearts among my guests without wanting mine? So, tell me. What is your opinion of Miss Howard?'

Angelina was completely taken aback by the question and her head snapped up. 'We are not acquainted—but—she seems—quite nice,' she answered hesitantly.

'Liar,' Alex said, amused at the way she tried to equivocate. 'You cannot stand her.'

Angelina's cheeks flamed. 'Then if you know my opinion, why did you ask me?' she retorted crossly. Not for a moment did it enter her head to deny it. She moved to step past him in the direction of the door, but his hand shot out, capturing her elbow.

'You're not leaving.'

'I think I must.'

'No, you're not. You are going to stay here and have a glass of wine with me.' Striding to a small carved table, he poured two glasses of red wine and handed one to her. She took it reluctantly.

'You are neglecting your guests, Alex. Don't you think it's time you returned to them?'

'No—not when I find myself in such enchanting company.'

'Why did you invite all these people if all you want to do is escape?' The answer dawned in her eyes when a slow smile curved his firm lips. 'Oh—I'm sorry. I forgot. It was to assess Miss Howard as a possible wife without appearing too obvious. Am I right?'

'Absolutely.' He chuckled. 'But it isn't difficult. Lavinia is the kind of woman any man would enjoy having as his wife. She is accomplished in many things and will preside over Arlington Hall and Mowbray Park with grace and poise. She will not be daunted by the many duties she will find thrust upon her, and she is also sophisticated and clever.'

'And cold and dispassionate and difficult to please,' Angelina concluded drily. 'I wish you joy in her. Good luck, Alex. You will certainly need it. But if I did not know any different, I would think it is a woman who has just applied for the position as your housekeeper you speak of—not the woman you intend making your wife. All of a sudden I am beginning to feel pity for Miss Howard. You seem to have considered marriage to her with the same dispassionate reasoning that marks everything you do in life.'

Alex disregarded the sardonic edge to her voice and cocked a sleek black brow at her, his eyes shining with suppressed humour. 'Jealous?'

Angelina looked at him, her eyes steady and her expression serious. 'No, Alex. I am not jealous. I have no reason to be. Besides, jealousy is an emotion I have never experienced in my life.'

Alex was immediately contrite and wished he'd never asked the stupid question. 'I know, Angel,' he said softly, reaching out and lightly touching her cheek. 'I'm sorry. So, you are of the same opinion as Uncle Henry and Aunt Patience. You don't think I should marry Miss Howard either.'

'It's just that I have no wish to see you made unhappy,' she answered quietly, reaching up and placing her glass of untouched wine on the mantelpiece.

Alex was moved by the sincerity of her words and a constricting knot of tenderness formed in his throat. 'And if I marry Lavinia, you think I will be?'

'Undoubtedly.'

For a moment Alex considered her in thoughtful silence. 'I'm touched. I didn't realise you cared.'

'I do care, Alex—otherwise I wouldn't be here. Miss Howard is cold and hard, and when she's fifty she'll look just like her mother.'

Unable to contain his mirth, Alex was laughing now with real amusement, his teeth flashing white from between his parted lips.

'Good Lord, I do believe you're right,' he said, composing his features once more. 'And is there a danger that I'll become like Lord Howard?'

'No—you're not in the least like Lord Howard. He never opens his mouth unless Lady Howard gives him permission to do so.'

'Nevertheless, Lavinia does have some good points.'

'I know. I feel like a pincushion already,' Angelina told him, her lips curving with humour. She looked at him a little quizzically. 'Do you realise that whenever you mention marriage to Miss Howard, you become tight lipped and your expression goes all serious—in fact, you become positively grim?'

Alex's mouth grew hard and he looked annoyed by her question, but he answered it. 'No. As a matter of fact I don't.'

'Well, you do. And there,' she accused, 'you're doing it again. Have you given her reason to believe you care for her? Have you kissed her?' Her head cocked slightly on one side as she looked at him, knowing she shouldn't ask so personal a question, but unable to stem her female curiosity.

His eyebrows shot up in sardonic amusement. 'Your question is impertinent, but, to appease your curiosity, the answer is yes.'

'Oh.' Angelina was unprepared for the rush of disappointment she felt, and was surprised by it, for why she should care whether he had kissed Miss Howard or not bemused her.

Alex's smile was merciless. 'Are you wondering how you compare?'

Two high spots of angry colour mounted Angelina's cheeks. 'Of course I'm not—and please don't be crude, Alex. You must forgive me if I appear stupid—but I am confused, you see. By you. I never know quite what to expect. Will you tell me why you kissed me when you came to my room? A man of your experience—you knew exactly what you were doing. I'm not used to that sort of thing, you see. I don't go around kissing people.'

'I hope not.' His lips quirked with wry amusement at her naïvety, and then, raking his fingers through his hair, he sighed, no longer in any mood for the light banter that had laced their conversation so far. 'I'm sorry, Angel. I never meant for it to happen. It was wrong of me to take advantage of you. You must forget it happened.'

But I can't, Angelina almost shouted at him. That's the trouble. The memory of that night lingered far too strongly for her to discount its effect on her. 'So,' she said, 'your intentions weren't honourable when you entered my room and took advantage of me in my weakened state.'

She tried to sound light and flippant when she spoke, but somehow it didn't sound like that to Alex. When he heard the tell-tale catch of hurt in her voice, it was so touching and tragic that he was moved in spite of himself. In a blinding flash it dawned on him that she might expect him to say he loved her, and if so he must put a crushing end to it before she had time to nurture the idea.

'I entered your room because I heard you were distressed. I wanted to comfort you—and it should have stopped at that. In time you will learn that kissing does not bring commitment. Understand this, Angelina. For a moment I may have lost my head, but I am not going to make any undying declarations of love. I don't need any woman—and I don't need the added guilt and responsibility of a naïve eighteen-year-old girl. The ritualistic proposal that usually follows such encounters will not come from me.'

His words sounded so final, so insulting, that Angelina felt as though she had been slapped. An icy numbness crept over her body, shattering all her tender feelings for him. Deeply regretting the impulse that had brought her to his rooms to offer words of comfort, she now realised she should have stayed away, for he did not deserve either sympathy or understanding from her. She expelled her breath in a rush of tempestuous fury as the fragile unity they had shared moments ago was shattered and the battle that constantly simmered beneath the surface between them was resumed.

'How dare you mock my feelings. What a callous, self-opinionated, loathsome blackguard you are.'

He arched an eyebrow, his tone one of irony when he spoke.

'Yes, I am all those things. What did you expect—some infallible being?'

'No, not that. How excruciatingly naïve you must find me. Just to set the record straight, my lord, I do not expect a proposal. It never entered my head.'

'It didn't?' He seemed genuinely surprised.

'Why, you conceited ass,' she flared. 'Cast your mind back to my arrival at your house in London. I told you then that I have no intention of marrying—nor will I become any man's light-of-love, fawned over today and forgotten tomorrow. I meant it then and I mean it now. Matrimony is not for me. I will not sacrifice myself on that particular altar for any man.

'But should I change my mind, my lord,' she seethed, planting her hands firmly on either side of her tiny waist and thrusting her angry face closer to his, her eyes sparking with ire, 'if you were the last man on earth I would never marry you. I find the whole idea of us forming any kind of relationship quite ludicrous.'

'I agree,' Alex snapped rudely, his cold, threatening gaze impaling Angelina to the spot as he moved closer to where she stood. 'You, my pet, would make an exceedingly poor wife.'

'And you, my lord, would make an exceedingly poor husband,' Angelina countered furiously, humiliated to the core of her being by his unkindness. 'However, one thing has changed since last we spoke. I have told Verity that I will concede to everyone's wish and be introduced into society at the next Season.'

'What! With all the glitz and ostentation?' He smiled wryly. 'God help all those unsuspecting males when you descend on them. But do you realise that when you make your début you will be making yourself available to every unattached male in the country?'

'That does not mean to say I have to accept any of them. I value my freedom and independence too highly to give it up.'

Alex's face could have been carved from a block of granite. 'So, unlike others of your sex, you harbour no ambition to snare a wealthy husband.'

'Material wealth does not interest me. But if I did marry, I would marry the meanest pauper if I loved him and he returned that love. But what of you? Don't any of the ladies of your acquaintance fall in love with you? Oh, I'm sorry,' she exclaimed heatedly, glowering at the man before her and tossing her head back haughtily, the curls on either side of her face doing a frenzied dance. 'What a stupid thing to ask you of all people, when half the female population in England must have been in love with Alex Montgomery at one time or another. But what do they love about you, Alex? Your wealth? Your title? What you can give them? Don't any of them love you for just yourself? Oh, I pity you. What a lonely, bitter old man you will be in years to come.'

Alex's jaw hardened. 'I told you I do not need any woman's love. I certainly do not want it. If my mother taught me anything at all, it is that love is more destroying than hate.'

'That is not true. Love is what is essential to make a marriage work. Money has no place when it comes to happiness.'

'That is the kind of sentimental drivel spoken only by romantic young girls and idiots,' Alex uttered with biting scorn.

'Which is precisely what I am.'

'And is only for the naïve,' he mocked cruelly.

'Then I am also naïve.'

'I know that, too.'

'Oh, my, Alex,' Angelina remarked, her tone heavily laced with sarcasm. 'Your notion of love is nothing more substantial than mere indulgence. The only kind you seem to know about is the kind made between the sheets. You really are so insecure and disenchanted with life that I find myself feeling almost sorry for you.'

He fixed his cold eyes on her. 'Don't. Men in my position must marry to beget an heir, and after fulfilling that requirement—'

'Don't tell me. They are then free to enjoy their mistresses,' she flung at him derisively, her fiery, angry spirit giving her a radiance that reminded Alex of all the female attributes that stood just within his reach, a radiance that was drawing him towards her with increasing power. 'What a degenerate black-guard you are, Alex Montgomery, with mistresses strewn all over London town. That's what you like, isn't it? Pedigree ladies who look good. Ladies who don't make you feel too much. But where is the decency in that, pray? Have you no con-science—no sense of honour?'

'Apparently not,' he answered, torn between anger, amuse-ment and desire as he looked down at her proud beauty. 'I will not change the way I live my life, and I make no apologies for it either. But I do not recall you complaining when I kissed you,' he said on a softer note, moving closer, his gaze devouring her face.

Suddenly the walls seemed to close in on them, making each aware of the closeness of the other, of the warmth, the intimacy. The pull of Alex's eyes was far harder for Angelina to resist at that moment than the frantic beat of her heart.

'Don't you dare touch me,' she warned, unable to move towards the door because he blocked her way. 'I swear that if your hand comes anywhere near me I'll shred it to the bone, you vile, despicable knave.'

His laugh was merciless, his eyes unrelenting. 'I'll risk it.'

She was about to spring past him, but iron-thewed arms went around her with stunning force and drew her against a broad, hard chest. 'Get off me. How dare you?' she objected furiously, struggling against him. His face was so close that she had no difficulty defining every detail, and the lazy smile awoke disturbing memories. 'Let me go. Must I remind you of my virtue—and that you are almost a married man?'

'A fact that weighs more heavily on your mind than it does on mine, Angel,' he murmured, chuckling softly. 'Damn it all, your virtue is the greatest stumbling block I have ever encountered. Were you not my uncle's ward, I would have demolished it long since.'

'Please let me go, Alex,' she whispered, overcome with an irrational fear, primitive and instinctive. Never had he looked so tall, so powerful, so coldly frightening as he did at that moment. She saw the burning light in his eyes, and deep within her she felt the answering stirring of longing she'd felt when he'd held her in his arms once before and kissed her. 'Do you forget so soon your promise not to repeat what happened between us the other night?'

'I have a hankering to repeat the offence—especially when I look at you,' he said huskily, turning the full force of his gaze on the young woman he was reluctant to let go. His conscience was making a damned nuisance of itself again and telling him he should end what he had started, but his body was sending out messages of a different kind.

Because Angelina was not the kind of sophisticated, worldly woman he usually made love to it made her more alluring, more desirable. She was nothing like the glamorous, experienced women who knew how to please him, women who were mercenary and hell-bent on self-gratification, whose beds he sought only to leave the moment his ardour was spent.

Reading the sudden glow in his eyes, Angelina was alarmed. 'Please don't—you can't do this to me.'

Deaf to her pleas, Alex's arms tightened, his gaze focusing on her lips. 'But I can. I am a degenerate bastard,' he said, calmly repeating the accusation she had flung at him earlier, 'with no moral principles, honour or conscience, so I can do anything I please.'

'Not with me.' He was so close that Angelina could feel the heat of him. 'Release me,' she ordered, infuriated by his obvious intention to weaken her resolve.

'Not a chance,' Alex whispered, as touched by her fear as he was by her innocence and inexperience. This time there was no burst of conscience as he gazed at those soft pink lips quivering close to his own. 'What I want, Angelina, is the same thing I want every time I look at you.' All he could think of was shattering her demureness and reserve and laying bare the woman of passion. His mouth covered hers, and, forcing her lips apart, he began kissing her with fervency, determined to make her respond.

Angelina's determination not to yield was as strong as his determination to make her. She knew that he wanted her full co-operation, and that if she gave it, it would be more damaging to her pride than anything else. Tears gathered under her eyelids and the world seemed to tilt around her and retreat. She fought the weakness, not wanting to be completely at his mercy, but her body was already beginning to respond with a gross miscalculation of her will. She wasn't made of stone. She was flesh and blood, and her blood was on fire.

The moment she leaned into him and opened her mouth in response, Alex's arms tightened round her. With the swell of her breasts pressed against his chest, he kissed her deep, drawing her tongue into his mouth and caressing it with his own. The sheer wonder of it sent exhilarating sensations darting and tingling to the far extremities of Angelina's body.

Knowing he must stop before he went too far, raising his head, his eyes hooded and dark with passion, Alex looked down into her upturned face. 'Good Lord, Angelina! What have you done to me? What might you do to me if I let you?' he whispered hoarsely, standing there with her in his arms in an agony of lust, wondering how someone as innocent, as pure and devoid of guile as she, could drive him half-mad with desire. Slowly he released her and stepped back.

Still trapped in the throes of passion, Angelina felt a tightening in her throat as she met his gaze. His eyes were hooded and moody, and his frown made a deep furrow over the bridge of his nose. Why? Why did he look like that?

'Alex—what is it? What is wrong? Is—is it like the last time—and you regret kissing me?'

'Yes. It was a mistake—my mistake,' he said, his voice strained. 'You must have cast a spell on me, for I do not seem to have the strength or the inclination to resist you. However, deflowering a properly reared virgin—and one who happens to be my uncle's ward—violates even my code of honour where women are concerned, no matter how degenerate you consider me to be.'

Picking up his coat, he thrust his arms into the sleeves and straightened his cravat. 'I'm sorry, Angelina. I take full blame for what happened.' He glanced towards the door. 'I think you'd better go while you still can.'

In the tearing, agonising hurt that enfolded her, Angelina was ashamed at how easy it had been for him, following all her harsh words, to expose the proof of her vulnerability. Tears blinded her vision. Lowering her head, she moved towards the door, silently weeping for her lack of will and with a fear of her feelings for Alex she seemed unable to control.

As Alex watched her go, he wasn't to know that what had just passed between them had been the second most humbling event of her young life. Her head was bent forward, her steps slow, and he thought he saw her shoulders shake. She looked so young, so small and vulnerable, he felt disgusted with himself and his conscience wrenched. Unable to watch her leave after she had sought him out to offer words of comfort, he was about to go after her, but at that moment her head lifted and she squared her shoulders. She turned once more. He stiffened, feeling reluctant admiration for her stubborn, unyielding refusal to cower before him.

In her fury and ravaged pride, looking like an enraged angel of retribution, Angelina dashed away her tears and looked once more at the granite profile of the man who had just kissed her into mindless oblivion, whose face had taken on a judicial look.

'You conceited, supremely amoral beast. How dare you take

liberties with me and then try placating me with a lame attempt at an apology? Weren't you satisfied with the humiliation you inflicted on me two nights ago without doing that? I'll never forgive you for what you've just done, Alex. Ever. If you ever touch me again...' she told him with a quiet firmness, 'I will fight you with my dying breath.'

Her words scorched Alex's soul with its fierce, despairing passion. 'You won't fight me, Angel. I know you. I know how you feel.'

'No, you don't,' she cried, her cheeks and eyes blazing hot, fists tightly clenched as she struggled to contain her rioting emotions. 'No one knows how or what I feel. No one. When you asked my opinion of Miss Howard, I told you she was heartless and cold. The same applies to you, Alex. Should you decide to make her your wife, I wish you joy with her. You deserve each other.'

Alex was disgusted with himself, disgusted and contrite. Angelina was right. He was cold and callous for ridiculing her, for mocking her feelings. His passion for her was torn asunder by guilt. It had to end. In the past hard logic and cold reason had always conquered his lust—with Angelina it was different. He had to purge her out of his mind before he was completely beaten and went insane—and if she continued living in the same house he would lose the battle. He was in danger of losing his heart to her, and he would not permit that. The stakes were too high.

He had no choice but to send her away.

When the last of the guests had left, in thoughtful and determined mood Alex joined Patience, Verity and Nathan in the sitting room.

'I have come to the decision that it would be best for all concerned if Angelina returned to London with you,' he stated without preamble.

Three pairs of eyes became glued to him. 'What?' they uttered, simultaneously.

'You will have to go with her, of course, Aunt. She can stay with either you at Richmond or Nathan and Verity in Hanover Square for the time being. It really doesn't matter which. Notify Bramwell at my house in Brook Street, and when Uncle Henry returns from Cornwall he'll naturally know not to come to Arlington. He'll understand why I had to do this.'

'Will he!' Verity exclaimed, not at all pleased with what her cousin had decided. 'Well, we don't.'

'It is time she went, Verity—she—she's too much of a disruption.'

Verity gasped, unable to believe what she was hearing. 'That's an excuse and quite ridiculous, Alex, and you know it. The only disruptions Angelina has caused are inside you. Angelina is a nuisance only in upsetting the precarious balance of your temper.' Alex threw her a withering look, but she was not deterred. 'Goodness. You can't send her away. She's just beginning to settle down. Have you any idea how much Arlington has come to mean to her?'

'She can visit. She'll settle down just as well in London. I don't want her here,' Alex said with icy finality.

Wearily Patience sighed, determined to fight for Angelina. 'Please don't do this to her. Do not forget so soon that when Henry brought her to England she had lost everything. You are familiar with death and the loss of a parent, Alex—or have you forgotten that?' Patience reminded him.

Her words hit their target with such force Alex tensed, his jaw tightened and his hands clenched. Patience pressed her advantage, but she knew as she spoke that Alex's mind was made up and nothing would change it. 'Angelina is still very young, Alex, and she has come to love and trust us, to see us as her family. Try to remember how it was for you when you found yourself alone. You were in the same situation as Angelina. Please do not make her feel unwanted by sending her away.'

Alex could not be swayed. 'My mind is made up. She goes

to London.' His gaze slid to his cousin, sitting ramrod straight beside her mother. Verity was incensed and he knew it. 'What's on your mind, Verity?' he demanded. 'I can see you're in high dudgeon about this.'

Verity's eyes snapped to his. 'Yes, I am.'

'I know.' His eyes appealed to Nathan, who had moved away to take a natural stance by the window. 'Nathan, can you not exert your husbandly influence and persuade your wife to guard her tongue?'

Nathan smiled wryly. 'I'm afraid not, Alex. She's too much like you in that,' he reminded him.

'Not entirely,' Verity objected, shooting her husband a look of annoyance.

'Well, perhaps not quite,' Nathan conceded.

Verity rose to face Alex, and they stood in the centre of the room, their gazes clashing—cousins, with the same unyielding Montgomery blood in their veins. 'I always thought you took your responsibilities seriously.'

'I do.'

'No, you don't,' she contradicted angrily, as she prepared to do battle on Angelina's behalf with the hardened cynic. 'Uncle Henry placed Angelina in your care, and after just three weeks you've had enough and have decided to pack her off back to London. You're heartless, Alex. Do you know that?'

He grimaced. 'I have been accused of being so on occasion.'

'And unjust.'

Glaring down at her from his superior height, Alex's eyes turned to shards of ice. 'You go too far, Verity.'

'It's about time someone did. I am extremely tired of watching everyone pussyfoot around you in fear of offending or annoying you. It's little enough to ask you to let Angelina stay at Arlington until Uncle Henry returns from Cornwall.'

Alex was quickly beginning to lose his temper. 'No. Angelina goes to London,' he said flatly. 'Verity, whatever you may think of me, I am no fool—and I know Uncle Henry better than he thinks. However, I never thought I would see the day when he would play Cupid. Do you think I don't know why he went to Cornwall, leaving Angelina in my care—that I cannot see what you are all trying to do that you have some idiotic romantic notion of bringing us together? Can you deny it?'

Confronted with the truth, with guilt written all over her face, Verity didn't reply, but she had the grace to look contrite and some of the anger drained from her face

'It won't work, Verity. Forget it. You too, Aunt Patience,' Alex said on a gentler note when he addressed his aunt. 'I know you are capable of setting a town alight when you put your heads together—and Uncle Henry is an interfering old rogue. He has played an important role in my life, and the gratitude and love I feel for him is immeasurable. But I will not marry Angelina out of mere sentimentality. I know both you and my uncle mean well, Aunt. But you don't always know what's best for me. I will not be influenced or manipulated by anyone over this.'

In a desperate attempt to soothe the situation before it erupted into open warfare, Patience stepped in. 'You are right. Henry is an old rogue, but his interference—if that is what it is—is kindly meant. He is of the opinion that the best way of restoring your zest for life is to revive your appetite for love.'

'Good God, Aunt Patience!' Alex expostulated, astounded to hear his aunt utter such drivel. 'To hear such talk from you I can only assume there must be a decline in your reading standards. I have repeatedly condemned such trivial and uninstructive reading flooding the market and always thought you above such rubbish. Contrary to what my uncle thinks there is nothing wrong with my "zest for life". And as for reviving my "appetite for love"—how can something be revived that was never there in the first place?'

Patience refused to let go of the argument. 'But Angelina is a rare treasure, Alex. Any man would be proud to have her as his wife.'

'I agree. But not me. You seem to have forgotten that I am on the brink of offering for Lavinia Howard.'

'You are?'

'I am considering it. But whatever I decide, I am not marrying Angelina and that is final.'

After pinning all their hopes on a union between them, Alex's harsh words doused all Patience's and Verity's expectations. Alex ignored their despondency, knowing he'd dashed their scheme, but it had needed saying.

'Take Angelina to London,' he went on. 'Give her a Season and find her a husband—which shouldn't be difficult, given the fact that every male I invited to Arlington this weekend went away singing her praises and all more than halfway to being in love with her.'

'Have you forgotten that Angelina has stressed time and again that she has no intention of marrying?' Patience reminded him.

'No. But I recall her saying that she did not want a Season, either—and she changed her mind pretty quickly about that. She'll change her mind about marriage soon enough when she gets to London and has every rake in town sniffing after her. Uncle Henry won't have long to wait before he has her off her hands,' he said unkindly.

'Alex! Do not speak like that. Why are you deliberately trying to be cruel?' Patience reproached harshly. 'I know you aren't as unfeeling as you sound. And who's going to tell her?'

'I'll save you all the trouble,' came a quiet voice from the doorway.

Every eye turned towards the door to see Angelina standing there, unable to believe what she had heard—Alex was sending her away.

Her world tilted crazily. There was no room in her sights for anyone except Alex. She beheld the faint widening of his eyes as they turned on her, but his expression was as inscrutable as a marble mask. She found it difficult to endure his gaze, but she did, his words sounding inside her head like a death knell.

Displaying a calm she did not feel, as she crossed the room she managed with a painful effort to dominate her disappointment and accept the slap fate had dealt her. She must blot from her mind the events of last night, the exquisite sweetness of Alex's kiss. Jerking her mind from such weakening thoughts her eyes encompassed the other three, having decided not to make an uncomfortable scene.

'Would you mind if I spoke to Alex alone?'

With a pained expression Patience moved to her side and gently squeezed her hand. 'Of course not, my dear. I think it's as well that you do,' she said, bestowing on her nephew a cross, disapproving look.

'Angelina, I am so sorry,' Verity said, looking extremely concerned.

She managed a faint smile. 'It's all right, Verity. Truly. I always knew I would have to leave some time.'

When they were alone, Alex raised one brow in arrogant inquiry, knowing she had heard his remark and unprepared to refute it—which was no consolation for Angelina. Why did he adopt this cold, remote, almost hostile attitude to her? Was it possible he was ashamed of the way he had behaved towards her, or was his hunger for her so great that he couldn't bear to be close to her? She hoped it was the latter, but the way he was looking at her made her discount it. Her eyes met his proudly.

'So! You really think that, do you, Alex? That as soon as the rakes and fops in London begin paying me attention and whispering sweet nonsense in my ear, I am so silly and weak that I will be unable to resist them and reverse my decision not to wed?'

'Why not?' His mouth curled with irony. 'You were eager enough to yield to me when I held you in my arms.'

His cutting tone and the injustice of his words increased Angelina's anger. But it was the way he retained his arrogant superiority that was hard for her to take. 'I don't know why you are being deliberately cruel to me, Alex, but as I recall, you gave me little choice. I did not invite you to kiss me. In fact, if you will cast your mind back, you will recall that I begged you not to.'

'I admit that I behaved in a manner for which I am ashamed and regretful,' he said, his voice curt, thinking when he looked at her how hard it was going to be sending her away.

'You? Ashamed? Are you quite sure you know the meaning of the word?' she scoffed. Drawing herself up proudly, she showed him that she too could be hard and cold. He would never know how much he had hurt her. 'And if Uncle Henry really wanted me off his hands, he would not have encumbered himself with me in the first place. He is warm and generous— unlike you, a man whose heart is encased in ice.'

Angelina expected the words she flung at him to get a reaction, but, except for a glacial hardening of his eyes and a muscle that began to twitch in his jaw, there was none.

'Do you mind telling why you are dismissing me as though I were an untouchable?' she asked. She knew the answer, but wanted to hear him say it. 'What have I done that makes you treat me so despicably?'

Everything, Alex thought wretchedly. She was too much of a threat to his sanity. He couldn't live in the same house with her any longer if he was to have any peace. Everywhere he turned she seemed to be there, ready to ensnare him, and when she was absent his need to see her made him seek her out. He was furious with himself for feeling like this—for wanting her. He'd never realised that sexual desire for her would become a complication. Better that she was away from him altogether, before she disrupted his whole life.

'Nothing,' he said. 'At least, not intentionally. You will stay with Aunt Patience until Uncle Henry gets back from Cornwall. Now you have decided to be launched into society, you can begin preparing for it. According to Verity it's time consuming, so you cannot begin too soon.'

Angelina could hear the absolute finality in his voice that told her it would be futile to argue. 'Then there is nothing more to be said. I thank you for your hospitality, Alex,' she said with the polite cordiality of one of his guests who had just departed. 'I have enjoyed my stay at Arlington, and I am now ready to return to London.' Her words were of resignation, not defiance.

Suddenly Alex looked at her with unexpected softness. Surprised by the change in his expression, she opened her mouth to speak, but he stopped her and, taking a deep breath, continued, 'You have to go, Angelina. You must. I want you to go. There are some things you cannot understand.'

Angelina's face was a pale, emotionless mask as she turned from him and crossed to the door. Her heart and mind felt empty, and she was chilled to the marrow, and even now, when she was desperate with the thought of leaving him, she had to ask herself why it should hurt so much, and to question what was in her heart.

Chapter Ten

It was decided that Angelina would stay with Nathan and Verity in Hanover Square, and that Patience would delay returning to her own home at Richmond for the time being. Angelina became firmly fixed under Aunt Patience's wing as the elderly lady arranged her vast wardrobe for her début, employing modistes who enjoyed her own and Verity's patronage.

There followed many long weeks of intensive instruction in perfecting the intricate steps of the minuet and the quadrille—a dance, like the waltz, which was considered 'fast' by some and only danced at informal affairs and in private. She learned how to curtsy without wobbling, deportment, and how to utilise her femininity by learning the art of the correct use of the fan—how to hold it, how to close it—which almost drove her to distraction.

To alleviate the tedium they often drove through Hyde Park, which was a rendezvous for fashion and beauty, with splendid, shining carriages and high-stepping horses. Angelina was a new distraction, drawing the admiring, hopeful eyes of several dashing young males displaying their prowess on high-spirited horses. Under the watchful eye of Nathan, she was introduced to several, promising to dance with each and every one of them at her début ball.

Under Verity and Patience's instruction, Angelina blossomed into an extremely attractive and desirable young woman, who was refreshingly unselfconscious of her beauty. The furore she was causing delighted them, and they were secure in Angelina's certain victory before the Season got under way. Before too long she would have London at her feet.

There were few people in the elevated circles of society who hadn't heard of the Duke of Mowbray's American ward, and all the unattached males clamoured to be introduced. It was not just her beauty that drew them to her, or the mystery of her American background and the fact that she had, until recently, been staying at the home of London's most notorious and sought-after rake, Lord Montgomery, but also the huge dowry the Duke of Mowbray would be certain to settle on her.

On Henry's return to London, Patience told him everything that had transpired at Arlington and the reason why they had returned to London earlier than intended. Henry was disappointed and yet unperturbed to learn that Alex had made it plain that marriage to Angelina was out of the question. From what he knew of their highly volatile relationship, he suspected that Alex was sorely missing Angelina and when Patience told him Alex was to come to London two weeks hence—stressing he had to attend important business meetings—Henry's instinct told him that it was an excuse to see Angelina again.

In the beginning it had been Henry's intention to throw the two of them together, but now he would do exactly the opposite. In an act of pure mischief he whisked Angelina off to Mowbray Park for Christmas.

When Angelina wasn't in London waiting to receive him, Alex knew a disappointment and fury that was beyond anything he had ever felt in his life. Despite his belief to the contrary, when she had left Arlington he had found it no easy matter thrusting her out of his mind. He threw himself into his work, but it was Angelina he saw in his mind, Angelina who stole his thoughts away from important matters at hand.

When she'd been with him he'd had difficulty keeping his eyes off her, and at times he'd been unable to keep his hands off her. And now she was gone he couldn't keep his mind off her. Who was she with? What was she doing? Were suitors already lining up, waiting for the Season to begin so they could offer for her? He could hardly contain his jealousy at the thought of any other man touching her.

Cursing himself for behaving like a love-smitten youth, he tried to divert his irrational thoughts away from her, but it became an internal battle—one he began to lose a little more with each passing day. He couldn't eat, he couldn't sleep, and he spent most of the night pouring brandy down his throat and pacing up and down his room so that he almost wore a path in the carpet. That was when the need to see her became paramount to all else.

But that was before he arrived in London and read his uncle's letter informing him that he had taken Angelina, Nathan, Verity and Aunt Patience to Mowbray Park for Christmas. Alex knew a fury like he'd never known. He knew that this was his wily old uncle's way of trying to manipulate him. Not for one moment did he consider going after them. He'd meant what he'd said to Aunt Patience, that he would not be coerced or lured into marriage. But on returning to Arlington and finding no peace without Angelina, he reached the most momentous decision of his life—he would return to London in time for Angelina's début ball.

On the day itself, with her thoughts on what lay ahead and the many difficulties she may encounter during the evening, Angelina stood while Pauline fastened her in her ball gown, feeling extremely nervous now the moment had arrived. When she was pulling on her gloves Verity, resplendent in pale blue satin, came to tell her that Uncle Henry had arrived.

'My dear Angelina. You look wonderful,' she enthused.

Beholding her reflection in the mirror, Angelina knew Verity was not exaggerating. Her fashionable, high-waisted gown of white satin, with an overskirt of white tulle, was intricately embroidered and decorated with seed pearls. The sleeves were elbow length, with a flow of delicate Brussels lace caressing her forearms. The French hairdresser had skilfully entwined a slender necklace of diamonds through the heavy curls at her crown so that, every time she moved, her head glittered and sparkled.

Henry watched her descend the stairs, his expression one of admiration and calm. Taking her hand, wonderingly he shook his head. 'You look enchanting. How I wish your dear mother could see you now. She would be so proud—as I shall be when I walk into Romney House with the most beautiful débutante in the whole of London on my arm,' he said, not mentioning the unexpected guest who would be making his appearance at the ball later.

The streets in Piccadilly were congested with carriages depositing the cream of London society outside the open doors of Romney House. Inside, footmen in powdered wigs and crimson-and-gold livery lined the stairs up to the ballroom. The head footman announced the Duke of Mowbray and his party in a stentorian voice, and there was much fluttering of fans, bobbing of curtsies and bowing of elegant heads. Guests were arriving all the time—débutantes in gorgeous pale-coloured gowns accompanied by their chaperons, and young men dressed in black, with brightly coloured waistcoats and pristine white cravats.

They were greeted by Lord and Lady Romney in the foyer and then climbed the stairs to the grand ballroom, with its highly polished parquet floor, Venetian mirrors and crystal chandeliers, to be announced again. Between the long French windows opening on to a balcony were huge urns on pedestals, bursting with a profusion of flowers, and elegant gilt chairs were placed at intervals along the walls.

Angelina was dazzled and confused by this impeccable *ton*-ish company, recognising several faces from her drives through the park and visits to private drawing rooms. She felt a sudden shyness combined with a curious reluctance to join these distinguished, sophisticated members of society—this gay, rakish and exclusive set who graced 'The Regent's Clique'. Looking like a vision from heaven, she entered the ballroom on Henry's arm.

Every influential head turned to the new arrivals and conversation became hushed as eyes strained to have a look at the Duke of Mowbray's American ward.

Henry gently squeezed Angelina's hand in the crook of his arm, sensing her nervousness. 'Don't be nervous, my dear. Within half an hour your card will be full. But make sure you save a dance for me. This is going to be the most enjoyable evening I've had in a long time.'

Within minutes there was a near riot to see who could get to her for the first dance. Laughter and frivolity surrounded her, and she found herself responding to it automatically. The first two dances of the evening went to young men she recalled meeting in the park, one of them a dashing and flamboyant young lord called Duncan Aylard.

'I'm delighted to see you again, Miss Hamilton,' he said with a sardonic grin as he swept her a deep bow. 'You haven't forgotten me, I hope—or that you promised me a dance.'

'No.' She laughed, warming to his natural charm and easy manner. 'I do remember you, Lord Aylard—and, yes, I shall be delighted to save a dance for you.'

His grin was impudent as he subjected her to a long, lingering gaze. 'And the next and the one after—and perhaps you will permit me to take you into supper later.'

'More than two dances would be quite improper and commented upon,' she chided teasingly, amused and flattered by his persistent manner, 'and I have arranged to have supper with my uncle. Do you forget that this is my début, Lord Aylard, and I have my reputation to uphold?'

'I would not dream of doing anything to damage that—so I shall have to be content with two…waltzes,' he insisted with a grin, preferring the darting flurry of the waltz to the minuet. The waltz was considered by some to denote a general decline in moral standards, but Lord Aylard thoroughly approved of the dance and would not consider partnering the staggeringly beautiful Miss Hamilton in any other.

He proved to be a superb dancer and Angelina happily abandoned herself to his encircling arm as he twirled her about the floor. Unashamedly he flirted and flattered her and made her laugh, but their entertaining conversation came to an end when someone caught his attention. He stiffened. 'Good Lord! Did you know he was to attend the ball? I had no idea he was back in London.'

'Who?'

'Lord Montgomery.'

Angelina felt her heart slam into her ribs. She froze for an instant, her thoughts scattered. She could feel Alex's presence with every fibre of her being, and, despite the shock of seeing him again after so long, an increasing comforting warmth suffused her. A strange sensation of security, of knowing he was close at hand, pleased her. But the memory of their parting, of the pain and the hurt he had caused her, was still present.

Over the heads of the crowd Angelina saw him standing with Nathan, even more powerfully masculine and attractive than she remembered. For a second their eyes met, then he looked away, seemingly without interest. Praying Lord Aylard had not taken note of her discomposure, she studied Alex surreptitiously.

His commanding presence was awesome, drawing the eye of everyone in the room. A group of people moved to speak to him, and she noticed how everyone was hanging on his every word, doe-eyed young débutantes gazing at him dreamily, and that there was a tension about the group that seemed to begin and end with him.

When he had arrived a short while ago with Nathan, Alex had paused in the action of kissing the hand of an acquaintance's wife and quickly glanced up to see Angelina taking to the floor with young Aylard. Nothing had prepared him for his first sight of her after months of absence. His heart wrenched when he looked on her unforgettable face—so poised, so beautiful that he ached to hold her.

Never had he seen her look so provocatively lovely, so regal, glamorous and bewitching—and he wanted her to belong to him entirely, to take her in his arms and send her persistent suitors packing. He was not noted for his patience. His yearning was like an obsession in his blood.

His gaze shifted to Aylard, who was looking down at her upturned face like a hungry fox looking into a hen coop. Of all the males in London, why did she have to draw the attention of Aylard—a young man with the potential to earn a reputation to rival his own? He could not bear to see other men vying with each other with infuriating persistence to dance with her, coveting her, to watch the admiration and appreciation in their eyes as they followed and devoured her every move. He guessed their thoughts were not so very different from his own, and he despised them for it. For the first time in his life he experienced an acute feeling of irrepressible jealousy that twisted his gut and caught him completely off guard.

The dance over, Lord Aylard escorted Angelina back to her uncle. Unfortunately he couldn't do that without passing Lord Montgomery. Good manners dictated that he stop and offer polite words of greeting, which he did, bowing with a grand, sweeping gesture.

'Lord Montgomery, it's good to see you again.'

Alex did not deem to pay Aylard the same homage. Looking the younger man over with a haughtily cocked brow, he nodded, his eyes cold and ungracious. 'Likewise.'

Angelina stood by Lord Aylard's side and looked at Alex. After a parting of five months, it was like coming face to face with a stranger. That well-remembered silver gaze slid from Lord Aylard to her. She had not forgotten how brilliant and clear his eyes were—how cold they could be.

'Hello, Alex,' she said quietly. 'I had no idea you were in London.'

Smiling pleasantly, Lord Aylard turned to look at Angelina. 'If you will excuse me, I will leave you now. Should you find you have another dance free, I shall be more than happy to oblige.' Passing his appreciative eyes over her exquisite features, he was unheedful of Alex's face hardening as he witnessed the perusal.

'I don't think so,' Alex said stonily, the cold grey eyes considering the other without a hint of expression, then with slow deliberation. 'Miss Hamilton's dance card is full. However, should any over-eager young swain on her card have the misfortune to fall over in their rush to get to her and break a leg, I shall oblige.'

Uncertainty flickered across Lord Aylard's face, cutting through his easy, friendly demeanour. Angelina felt her ire rising at Alex's deliberate rudeness, having no reason to think it stemmed from jealously.

'Why, Alex! Since when did you care a fig for my reputation?' she flared.

Before Alex could reply, Lord Aylard gave Angelina a brief nod of farewell, and left the ballroom in search of strong liquid sustenance, feeling unusually put out.

Angelina watched him go and then turned to Alex, incensed. 'You beast. How could you be so rude to Lord Aylard?'

He cocked a brow and regarded her with a tolerantly amused smile. 'Was I?'

'Inexcusably so and you know it. He has done nothing wrong and did not deserve such a cruel set-down. I will not tolerate your interference in matters that are none of your concern. And should one of my partners have the misfortune to fall and break a leg, there are others already waiting to oblige.'

Alex grinned in the face of her rage, meeting her stormy eyes. 'Then take my advice and choose your partners with more care. Aylard's a veritable tulip who floats around the edges of the Carlton House set. The man's a rake of the first order.'

'Which you should know all about, Alex,' Angelina was quick to remind him, 'having the reputation of a rake yourself.'

'Be that as it may, but I may not be around to save you the next time.'

'I sincerely hope not.'

Alex noted that the angry exchange was not going unnoticed by those close by. 'Do you mind not looking at me as if you are about to run me through, my pet? Do not make a spectacle and try smiling. People are staring at us.' His voice was soft, though his smile was knowingly reproachful.

Angelina forced her face into more subdued lines, but when she spoke her voice shook with quiet fury. 'How dare you call me your pet after the way you treated me at Arlington? I am not your pet and people can stare all they like. Excuse me. I'm going to find Uncle Henry.' Turning on her heel, with her head held high and two angry red flags of colour burning her cheeks, she stalked away, longing to bring that arrogant, insufferable man down a peg.

Chuckling softly and watching Angelina's retreating figure with admiration, Nathan moved to his side. 'My word, Alex. Methinks the lady is extremely vexed. Her aversion to you will not easily be appeased—and who can blame her, considering the way you sent her away from Arlington.

Alex watched the tempestuous beauty rejoin his uncle and Aunt Patience. Her beauty fed his gaze, stirring a sweet, hungering ache deep inside that could not easily be put aside with anything less than what he desired.

'With a little tender persuasion I am certain I can overcome that problem. However, I can see that, despite all the teachings in etiquette she has received since I last saw her, her spirit remains intact.'

'Would you have it any other way?'

Alex shook his head. 'I intend to marry her, Nathan, to gentle her, to make her complaisant to my demands, but God help me if I do anything to change what is inside her. She is quite unique.'

Nathan was astounded by his declaration. 'So, the renowned libertine and despoiler of women has decided to call it a day and settle down to domestic bliss. Have a care, Alex. Angelina has a strong will, and it's a courageous woman who will pit her will against yours.'

'In that, as in everything else, I intend to have the upper hand. She'll soon come to realise that.' He spoke with supreme confidence. Lounging back against a pillar, his arms across his chest, a dangerous light entered his narrowed eyes and a smile tempted his lips.

Nathan saw that look, and if he'd had to tell Angelina what it foretold, his explanation would have angered her far more than she already was. Alex looked exactly like a marauder who was about to invade a particularly challenging and desirable country and claim it for his own—and refused to be deterred by any fight from the opposition.

Now Alex had made up his mind that he was going to marry Angelina, he began to enjoy the ball and was in fine spirits for the rest of the evening—enjoying it all the more when Aunt Patience suddenly complained of feeling unwell. After making her excuses to Lord and Lady Romney, Alex saw her out to her carriage—Uncle Henry too, for he was so overly concerned about the onset of his sister's sudden weakness that he refused to allow her to go home alone. Of course, he made Alex promise to remain with Verity and make quite certain that Angelina was properly chaperoned and to see her home.

Alex wasn't fooled and knew *exactly* why his aunt had suddenly decided to feel unwell. He was convinced that she was perfectly well and that her sudden weakness was nothing more than part of the scheme concocted by her and Uncle Henry to throw Angelina in his path. He chuckled with humour. This time he wasn't complaining. He was content to follow the course his uncle had been plotting from the beginning.

He found Angelina in conversation with Verity, looking quite bemused by what she was telling her. She looked at Alex anxiously when he appeared by their side.

'Verity tells me that Aunt Patience has been taken ill,' she said, her eyes filled with concern. 'Perhaps we should all leave.'

Alex smiled imperturbably. 'I am sure Verity has told you that her dear mama has nothing more serious than a headache, which I strongly suspect is feeling much better already. Don't you agree, Verity?' he queried with humour, giving his cousin a look that clearly stated that he fully understood the situation.

Verity flushed with embarrassment at being caught out. 'Yes, I'm sure you are right—as always, Alex,' she replied drily.

Alex turned his attention to Angelina, and there was something subtle in the way his expression changed that made her uneasy.

'Uncle Henry has left you in my very capable hands, Angelina—to make quite sure you enjoy what is left of the evening and are returned home unmolested.'

'I find it hard to believe that Uncle Henry would trust you

to protect and uphold my virtue. It's rather like a wolf being left in charge of a flock of sheep,' she quipped.

Alex's answer was a slow, impudent grin. 'My uncle's skill with weapons is as sharp as it was thirty years ago, and I do not doubt for one minute that he would take up arms against me should I fail in my duty.'

Angelina regarded him sceptically. 'And I can dance with whom I like?'

'Providing I approve of your choice of partner,' he prevaricated.

'I do not need you to check out my dancing partners, Alex. I am not a child.'

'That's the first sensible thing I've heard you say all evening. I agree with you absolutely.'

His remark and taunting grin brought a bright hue creeping into Angelina's cheeks, and made her realise the folly in baiting him.

'I believe this next dance should have been Uncle Henry's,' he said, slipping a hand beneath her arm to escort her onto the floor as the orchestra struck up the next waltz. 'Come. I would have this dance before you are swept away by yet another devoted, over-zealous swain.'

'My feet ache. I think I prefer to sit this one out,' Angelina said, resisting by pulling back.

'No, you won't. I insist,' he said, tightening his hold on her elbow.

Without more ado he headed towards the dance floor. A group of young bloods with flirtatious grins standing on the periphery raised their glasses in a salute as Angelina drew level, and Alex fumed when he saw her acknowledge their homage with one of her bright, generous smiles.

'Do you have to smile at every man you come into contact with?' he seethed between his teeth.

'Why not?' she replied, her look one of complete innocence. 'I was only being polite.'

'Forward to the point of being fast is how I would describe it. You smile and flutter your lashes like an accomplished flirt.'

'As I understand it, flirting is an accepted, highly desirable mode of social behaviour,' Angelina argued quietly.

Angelina abandoned her waist to his encircling arm. It was as steady and firm as a rock. Alex was a superb dancer. As he whirled her into the dance she seemed to soar with the melody. It was as if they were one being, their movements perfectly in tune.

'My uncle informs me that the evening has been a resounding success for you,' Alex remarked at length.

'That depends upon what you mean by a resounding success. For myself I am enjoying every moment of it. What brought you to London, Alex? Business?

His hooded eyes captured hers. 'That was one of the reasons.'

'I'm surprised you decided to attend a ball with nothing more interesting to amuse you that a host of silly débutantes.'

'Don't be. The company at White's tonight was exceedingly dull. I came here to please Aunt Patience and Uncle Henry— and to see you.' She stared up at him, searching his eyes for the truth behind his words. 'I am quite serious,' he assured her softly in answer to her unspoken question. 'You look enchanting, by the way.'

'Thank you. Did Uncle Henry know you were coming to London?'

'Yes. I wrote and told him several days ago.'

'Then why didn't he tell me?'

'My uncle moves in mysterious and devious ways. Perhaps you should ask him—and while you're about it, ask him why he whisked you off to Mowbray Park on the eve of my coming to London before Christmas.'

Angelina gasped, her eyes opening wide. 'You mean Uncle Henry knew you were coming and didn't wait to see you?'

'Exactly.'

'But why?'

'You'll have to ask him,' he replied drily, twirling her round. Making a quick sweep of the room, Alex was not unaware of the attention they created. 'We've become something of a curiosity among the gossips, my pet,' he said softly, his palm firm against the small of her back, his breath warm and smelling pleasantly of brandy on her cheek. 'Nathan tells me you have become extremely popular—the darling of the debutantes, I heard someone comment at White's earlier.'

'I'm glad of the opportunity to show them I'm not a red-skinned savage with feathers in my hair,' Angelina responded, laughing merrily with a light-hearted toss of her head.

'Don't get carried away, Angelina,' Alex murmured with a note of caution, smiling nevertheless. 'It's true there have been rumours drifting about town about the Duke of Mowbray's American ward for some time now, and most people who have not had the opportunity of seeing you have dealt with a wild, rather plain young woman who wears buckskins and her hair in a pigtail. Nothing has prepared them for how you look tonight.' His eyes rested warmly on her face. 'You dance divinely, by the way.'

'So every one of my partners has told me.'

'Saucy minx,' he murmured, smiling.

'And you dance better than most.'

'Praise indeed,' he quipped, sweeping her into another dizzying whirl.

Content to let the music carry them along they fell silent, unaware of the passing moments. Angelina stared up at Alex's achingly handsome face and into his bold, hypnotic eyes, lost in her own thoughts, before she realised that his gaze had dropped to her lips and his arm tightened around her waist, drawing her against the hard rack of his chest.

'Have you missed me, Angel?' he asked.

'Yes—a little,' she confessed awkwardly, feeling his warm breath fan her cheek. In truth, she had missed him more than she could have imagined.

'Only a little?' Alex watched the reaction to his question play across her expressive face, correctly interpreting it.

'I thought you were still angry with me.'

'Why? Should I be?'

'I don't know. I was so confused when I left Arlington. We both said things—'

'Forget them. Everyone says things they don't always mean in the heat of the moment—and as I recall,' he murmured, a spark of laughter in his eyes, 'the temperature was definitely heated on the occasions when I kissed you.'

Angelina's cheeks burned and her heart began to throb in deep, aching beats. The reminder of his kiss, his touch, had been branded on her memory with a clarity that set her body aflame. She raised her eyes to his, seeing them darken and his expression gentle.

'You, my pet, are blushing.'

'Any female would blush when you say the things you do and look at them like that. Please stop it, Alex. People are watching.'

'Then let's go somewhere more private.'

Before Angelina knew what he was about, he'd waltzed her through the glass doors and out on to the deserted balcony. His arm slipped about her waist and tightened, bringing her full against his hardened frame.

'Alex,' she protested, 'this is most improper.'

'To hell with proprieties. I will not stand by and watch every male in London ogle you.'

'Why, Alex—are you jealous, by any chance?'

With his lips close to her cheek his voice was husky and warm, his eyes devouring her with a ravenous hunger. 'I am jealous of your every word, thought and feeling that is not about me. I want you. It is my dearest wish to make you mine. Don't waste yourself on the likes of that young cockscomb Aylard. They're not worth it.'

Trying to ignore what she saw in his eyes, his lips hovering just above her own, Angelina tried to still her rapidly beating heart. 'And what of you, Alex?' she asked, breathing heavily. 'Are you worth it? You say you want me. If I were to yield myself to you, would you honour me?'

'Until death,' he breathed, brushing the round softness of her cheek with his burning lips, one of his hands sliding beneath her hair, his fingers caressing her nape. 'Since you left Arlington you have been for ever in my thoughts, plaguing me, torturing me. Dear Lord, Angelina. You sorely test my restraint. Don't you know how much of a temptation you are to me?'

Her mind reeling over the shock of what he was saying, Angelina could only stare at him as a torrent of emotions overwhelmed her.

'I want you, Angel,' he murmured, raising his hand and tracing the gentle curve of her cheek with his fingertip. 'There is a chemistry between us—has been from the start.'

She shook her head in an attempt to regain her sanity. 'What I am afraid of is how many other women you share your chemistry with, Alex.'

'You listen to the gossips too much.'

'It's difficult not to where you are concerned.'

'What if I were to tell you that I need you?'

'I would say you don't. You collect things. Women in particular.'

A look of exasperation crossed his face. 'Angelina, stop it. All that is over.'

'No, it isn't. You're a rake.'

'I'll reform. Does my reputation worry you?'

'Not in the slightest.'

Alex grinned suddenly, lifting an impudent brow. 'There is a saying that reformed rakes make the best husbands.'

'They do?'

'Yes.'

'Who said it?'

'I did.'

Suddenly, something he'd said snapped Angelina's eyes to his. 'Why did you say that?'

'What?'

She swallowed. 'About husbands.'

'Because, princess, I want to marry you—to make you my wife.'

Understanding dawned with his meaningful gaze. In the deafening silence that engulfed them, neither of them moved. Angelina breathed at last, staring at him in confused shock as she understood the truth of what he was asking of her.

'I want to marry you,' he repeated, watching her closely.

The entire colour drained from her face and her body became tense. Raising her clenched fist to her mouth, she pulled away from him, seeking to be alone so she could think clearly.

After a moment Alex came slowly towards her. 'Angelina, look at me.'

Reluctantly she raised her eyes to his and looked at him in desperate appeal. What Alex saw in their innermost depths— a confusion of anger, pain and fear—almost took his breath.

'Angelina, what is it?'

'I cannot believe that you want this. I have certainly not encouraged it.'

'Unconsciously you have encouraged it every time we have been together. Have you any objections to me as a husband?'

'All I know is that I don't want to marry anyone. You know that. Besides, what sort of marriage would it be when you treat love lightly?'

Placing his hand under her chin, he tilted her face to his, wanting more than anything else to eradicate the reluctance oozing out of her.

'You are wrong. I confess that I know nothing about the kind of love you speak of, but what I do know is that when you left Arlington you were never far from my deepest thoughts. You suit me better than any other woman I have known or am likely to. You anger, amuse, delight and frustrate me to the point where I don't know whether to throttle you or make love to you. You test my patience and my sanity beyond the limits of my endurance. And yet, despite all this, I still want you for my wife. I've had mistresses, yes—but it is to *you* that I offer marriage. No other woman has been able to get that close. So, what do you say? Will you do me the honour of accepting my proposal—and become my wife?'

Angelina looked directly into his face just above her own, feeling herself respond to the dark intimacy in his voice. His expression was gentle, understanding, soft as she had never before seen it. And there, plain for her to see, was the sincerity of his words.

'Have you spoken to Uncle Henry about your intentions?'

'Not yet, but for us to marry is his dearest wish. Uncle Henry is as crafty as an old fox and it has been his intention to bring us together from the start.'

Her lips trembled into a little smile. 'Yes, I can see that there has been a real conspiracy going on—and that Uncle Henry has been aided and abetted by Aunt Patience and Verity.'

'I was determined not to be lured or coerced into marriage by anyone—which was one of the reasons why I sent you away from Arlington and why I did not follow you to Mowbray Park, which, I might add, was part of Uncle Henry's plan.'

Confusion clouded Angelina's eyes. 'But—how? Surely if he wanted to draw us together, the last thing he should have done was take me away from London when you were expected.'

'One thing I learned from an early age is that there is always method in our uncle's thinking, my sweet. When he saw his little scheme had failed to bring us together at Arlington, he decided on a different approach—that absence inclines to deepen the affection.'

'And did it?'

Alex grinned, having no wish to deny the truth. 'I confess it did. For once in his life that cunning old man got it right.'

'And when did you realise you wanted to marry me?'

'When I came to London, expecting to see you, only to find Uncle Henry had whisked you away. I missed you like hell when you were no longer there, but my pride refused to capitulate to Uncle Henry's scheming. But things have changed, so don't disappoint everyone by refusing my suit. Uncle Henry will be mortified.'

'I wouldn't intentionally do anything to hurt Uncle Henry. I love him dearly and would sooner die than cause him pain. I am grateful for all he has done for me. At a time when I had nothing he gave me a home and his protection.'

'I gave you my protection too when you needed it at Arlington,' Alex reminded her with an impudent grin.

'Now you're trying to make me feel beholden to you.'

'That's because the more indebted you feel towards me, the more compliant you will feel when you consider your answer to my proposal. If you refuse me, another suitor will take my place tomorrow or the next day.'

'I don't have to marry any of them.'

'I shall try to persuade you to consider my suit. Since you have just listed my many shortcomings, allow me to convince you of my merits. As you know, I come from a long line of noble forebears, and I have titles and wealth envied by many—which I would like to share with you. I am not unattractive to look at— at least, so I've been told,' he said with an arrogant quirk to his lips, 'and which you can determine for yourself.'

Angelina looked at him obliquely, a smile tugging at the corners of her mouth. 'You're passable, I suppose.'

He grinned. 'Come now, Angelina. Admit it. You find me more than passable.'

'If I do, I see no sense in giving you a bigger head than you have already by telling you so. If you desire compliments

from me, then you are going to have to work extremely hard
to get them.'

'I intend to.' He laughed, unable to stem his mirth. 'Now,
where did I get to? As I was saying—we know each other well
enough and share common interests as well as family. Further-
more,' he murmured, his eyes rapturous, 'we have a shared
passion. I know you are not indifferent to me. So don't fight me,
my sweet. Face the truth of what I've said.'

'I thought you had decided to live your life in unemotional
objectivity. Marriage to me will bring you a wealth of strife.'

'I don't doubt that every day you will pit your will against
mine—but do not forget that, in a conflict of wills, man has
force on his side. I am certain that you will flout my wishes and
drive me to distraction with your disobedience, but it will be
stimulating. You and I will never be bored.'

'Nevertheless, it is arrogant of you to assume I might prefer
you to any of my other suitors.'

One dark eyebrow rose in a measuring look. 'I won't change
my mind. I know exactly what I want.'

'You're so sure of yourself, aren't you, Alex? I hate it
when you are.'

'I know you do. But that is something you will have to learn
to live with. Will you accept my proposal?'

After he had treated her so badly at Arlington, Angelina
was reluctant to make any kind of commitment to him. Besides,
his conceited assumption that she would accept without demur
tempted her to decline his suit out of hand. But then, she
thought with quiet mischief, might it not be both interesting and
satisfying to keep this arrogant lord dangling for her favours?

'Marriage is important and serious and not something to be
undertaken lightly—especially for me,' she said, facing him
squarely. 'Forgive me, Alex, but I'm reluctant to commit myself
to you or anyone else just now. Everyone has gone to a great
deal of trouble in making me a débutante and I want to savour

the opportunity to enjoy the Season. I would also like to take the opportunity to look over other eligible suitors before I settle on a husband.' She smiled up at him obliquely. 'But don't be too despondent, Alex. I promise to consider your proposal—along with any other I may receive.'

Alex sensed victory slipping away and, momentarily thwarted, his expression hardened. 'I'm not noted for my patience, Angelina—as you well know.' Cupping her chin in his hand, he gently kissed her lips before raising his head and looking at her with that all-absorbing attention Angelina had come to know. 'The die is cast, Angel. You will be mine in the end.'

For the rest of the evening, without a qualm Angelina happily used all her untapped ability at flirtation. She smiled happily at the gentlemen who flocked around her, allowing first one and then another to lead her into the dance, clinging on to their arms and hanging on to their every word. Alex stood watching from the sidelines, his face a veneer of bland sophistication, while inside he was seething. With the wisdom born of years of experience with the female sex, he knew what Angelina was playing at, and no matter what game she played, he did not doubt his own ability to lure her into marriage to him.

Henry's expression was one of calm speculation as he regarded Alex. He quirked a brow in amused inquiry, waiting for him to speak.

Alex looked directly into his uncle's eyes, his expression unreadable, neither warm nor cold. 'I believe I have to ask your permission to marry Angelina?' he asked, having no intention of beating about the bush.

Henry beamed, scarcely able to conceal the rush of joyous satisfaction. His plans had advanced even further than he had hoped. Here he was, offering for her like an impatient, lovesick swain on the eve of her début, rushing in before the competition got a foot in the door.

'As her guardian it is the correct thing for you to ask me. I was wondering how long it would take you to get round to it.'

'My compliments to you, Uncle. You and Aunt Patience from the beginning have planned this very carefully. You can congratulate yourselves on the outcome.

'I am so glad you have come to realise what a dear, sweet girl Angelina is.'

'I would not describe Angelina as sweet,' Alex replied, his tone impervious, irritated because his uncle looked like he was enjoying his predicament enormously. 'It has taken me five months to appreciate that that high-minded little madam is the most exasperating female I have known in my entire life. She is also the woman I want for my wife.'

'Pardon me, Alex, but I have to say that you do not look in the least like a man in the full flush of love.'

'I am not.'

'After weeks spent brooding on your regret for sending Angelina away from Arlington, during her absence I realise how anxious you have been to see her again—and the more disagreeable and difficult you have become.'

'I am not disagreeable.' Alex's patience was being strained.

'If you say so,' Henry said, smiling, the taut expression on his nephew's face belying his words. 'Tell me, Alex, why do you want to marry Angelina? Have you come to care for her?'

'Of course I care for her—more than I have ever cared for any other woman, which is why I want her to be my wife,' Alex replied, annoyed when he saw his uncle's victorious smile widen on hearing his confession. 'I want to marry her as soon as it can be arranged.'

'That will not be appropriate. You will marry her after a decent interval of courtship, Alex, and not before.'

Alex stared at him in frigid silence, unable to believe all his carefully thought-out plans were about to be demolished. The last thing he had expected from his uncle, after all his machinations to bring himself and Angelina together, was opposition. The two men looked at each other, both stubborn and tenacious, both unyielding, but this time one of them would have to retract, and it had to be Alex.

'How long?' he asked tautly.

'July.'

'July?' Alex exploded with disgust. 'Do you mean I have to endure weeks of letting the *ton* gawp at her and other suitors call on her before I can make her my wife? Good Lord, Uncle! July is three months away. I can't wait that long.'

'You'll have to, Alex. You will just have to curb your impatience—and your lust,' Henry told him with a mocking grin, knowing that his nephew was caught in something he had not bargained on, something he could not control and could not be easily cooled. When he saw his nephew's impervious expression begin to waver, his eyes became amused. 'Besides, you haven't asked her yet so how do you know she will accept your suit?'

'I have asked her—and—she's thinking about it.'

'Has it not occurred to you that she might very well turn you down?'

'No. If she does, I am confident she can be persuaded,' Alex replied, with a steely determination that he would succeed in doing just that. He had some knowledge and experience of Angelina, and he knew he could seduce her into insensibility in a matter of moments.

Henry saw the tell-tale gleam in his nephew's eyes and knew exactly along which path his thoughts were travelling. 'Angelina is not one of your mistresses to be tumbled and then tossed aside, Alex,' he admonished sternly. 'She is innocent and guileless and unused to the irresponsible ways of men. She must be treated with the respect she deserves. Where women are concerned you are quite ruthless. The world and its neigh-

bours know you are no saint—that you have nothing to boast
about in your dealings with the female sex—but all that must
change if you are to marry Angelina. Your reputation for pro-
fligacy must be a thing of the past.' His chuckle was rich and
deep as he quirked a brow. 'Who knows—perhaps you might
be redeemed by a good marriage?'

'Maybe I will, if I'm allowed to get on with it,' Alex
replied with a low grunt of derision. 'I can see I can get no
sympathy from you.'

'You're correct—you won't. I know your pride has taken a
hammering over this, that you have tried to fight your feelings
for her but to no avail. But that will mend. You will have to
dispose of your current mistress, you understand.'

'I've already eliminated that problem.'

'I'm glad to hear it. Considering Angelina's aversion to
marriage, I insist that you woo her first, Alex—gently. We must
observe *all* proprieties. If you go rushing in with your usual impatience, you'll be bound to intimidate her. Let people see you
together before you announce your betrothal. When it's announced, I have no doubt it will be received with dismay among
the ladies of society and relief among the bachelors, glad that you
are out of the way at last and they no longer have to compete.'

Alex stared into those grey eyes so like his own and struggled to contain his exasperation with this wily old uncle of his,
whose expression was a combination of infuriating satisfaction
and sublime innocence. 'I have the distinct impression that you
are both for me and against me on this, Uncle,' he said,
watching an inexplicable smile trace its way across the older
man's face.

'Am I? Explain what you mean, dear boy.'

'From all that confusion I can draw no argument,' Alex
conceded.

'Fine. Now that's out of the way, I think a toast is in order,'
Henry said, getting to his feet and pouring them each a large

brandy and handing one to Alex, already thinking what wonderful great-nephews and great-nieces they would produce to continue the illustrious Montgomery line. 'I am delighted things have turned out this way. I could not be happier.'

'Good,' Alex said, suddenly thinking that his uncle looked ten years younger. He tossed his brandy back before fixing him with a hard stare, humour tugging at the corner of his mouth. 'Now we have established that Angelina is to be my wife, there is just one small matter we need to discuss.'

'And what is that, pray?'

'Her dowry.'

Alex had the satisfaction of watching his uncle almost choke on his brandy. 'Dowry?'

'Dowry,' Alex repeated, a wicked, calculating gleam lighting his eyes. 'You must have thought about it. It is usual for a bride to bring a dowry to her husband on marriage, and, as her guardian, that is for you to take care of.'

'But of course—and I did say it would be generous. But—'

'Don't think you're going to escape settling a dowry on her because she is marrying your nephew,' Alex warned, scarcely able to conceal his mirth when he sensed his uncle was about to try to evade the issue. 'Now,' he said, handing him his empty glass and settling comfortably into a chair as he prepared himself for a long and interesting discussion on the issue of his future wife's dowry, 'pour me another splash of brandy and we will sit and discuss how generous you are going to be.'

Chapter Eleven

⚬⚭⚬

After Angelina's first ball the house in Hanover Square was deluged with callers, and there followed an intense round of social functions. Escorted to all the stylish gatherings by family members, there were regular visits to a play at the theatre at Covent Garden or Drury Lane, or the opera at the King's Theatre in the Haymarket. Occasionally they visited the gardens at Marylebone where they drank tea, or visited the Pleasure Gardens at Ranelagh.

Like a bird set free Angelina was surprised to find herself revelling in the fun of it, and most of all she was happy because Alex was nearly always present, attentive, considerate—conspicuously so—and she knew this was to frighten off prospective suitors, which quietly amused her. His proposal was never mentioned between them, but his eyes were ever watchful, showing nothing of his frustration as he watched her suitors come and go. Aylard was the most persistent, and Alex was sure she encouraged that young coxcomb merely to put his back up.

But this period was not all fun and games—Angelina went through a great deal of deliberation and heart searching, before deciding that, for better or worse, she would become Alex's wife. She could hardly believe how deep her feelings were running, and the joy coursing through her body melted the very core of her heart. She loved Alex. She knew that now, and that perfect certainty filled her heart and stilled any anxiety she might otherwise have had.

The feeling was so strong there was no room for anything else. Ever since their first meeting they had moved towards this end, and now there was no doubt in her heart. Nothing could change it. Nothing could touch it—neither now nor in the future. She gave him her answer to his proposal when they were walking in the garden at his house in Brook Street.

An unbearable sense of joy leaped in Alex's heart. The yielding softness in her eyes, the gentle flush that bespoke her untainted innocence and youth, brought faint stirrings of an emotion he thought long since dead. Reaching out, he cupped her chin in his fingers, tilting her face to his and softly placing his lips on hers.

'Thank you,' he murmured. 'If at times I have seemed brutal in my behaviour, it is because I found it difficult coming to terms with how I feel about you. But, Angel, what I want you to know is that I shall never force you into anything. I want you to accept me of your own free will.'

His words gave Angelina reason to hope. 'Do you promise?'

'I never say anything I don't mean.' He smiled suddenly, a warm gleam entering his eyes. 'I think I can still see a shadow of doubt in those glorious eyes of yours, which I intend to eradicate. You have just become betrothed to me and I intend sealing the bond by kissing you senseless.'

'You wouldn't.'

'Watch me.' He let his eyes drop once more to her lips, moist, soft, beckoning his own. 'I am afraid, Angel, that we need to reach a better understanding before we commit ourselves at the altar. I want to make quite sure I am not bringing a frigid, unwilling bride to my bed. You have no idea what I will do to you when we have said our vows, my pet,' he warned hoarsely. 'I cannot look at you without wanting you.'

Lowering his head, he placed his lips on the soft curve of her cheek, moving gently, exquisitely, assaulting her defences, his eyelids lowered in anticipation of what was to come, so he did not see the fear cloud her eyes, could have no idea of the cold tremor of dread that passed through her at the mention of his bed and what he would expect of her when she was in it. Angelina told herself that he could have no idea what he was threatening, that she must trust him, and when his lips claimed her own she told herself that she would do just that.

Everyone was delighted at the way things had turned out.

'Now, where will the happy event take place?' asked Patience, already mentally making out the invitation list, who to include and who not to.

'We'll be married at St George's Church here in Hanover Square,' Alex stated. 'It will be more convenient than Arlington for most of the guests, who tend to remain in town after the end of the Season anyway. We shall be wed as soon as the banns have been called for the ritual three weeks—the week after, in fact.'

'A month? But that's too soon,' Patience gasped. 'Alex, you cannot possibly mean that.'

'I do.'

'But—why—there's so much to do—not to mention Angelina's bridal gown. A guest list has to be drawn up before the wedding invitations can be sent out, and there are the menu and the flowers to be taken care of. Oh, really, Alex! It's obvious you have never been married, otherwise you would know it is virtually impossible to arrange a wedding on a scale that befits the ward of the Duke of Mowbray in four weeks. And do not forget that we have bridesmaids to find and dresses to be made.'

'I don't see why that should be a problem. There are children in abundance on your husband's side of the family to choose from. And then there are the two Asquith girls.'

'I still think a little more time is needed,' Patience said.

'My dear aunt,' Alex said, not in the slightest perturbed by his aunt's objections. 'You and Verity are two of the most competent and capable women I know. I have every confidence that you will be able to arrange the bridesmaids, the food and the flowers in time.'

'But we can't possibly.'

Alex grinned, casually propping one booted foot on the opposite knee and gently stroking the palm of Angelina's hand with his thumb in the folds of her skirt, knowing how susceptible she was to his caress when he heard her breath catch in her throat and saw a pink hue mantle her cheeks. 'Yes, you can. Four weeks,' he insisted implacably, trying to maintain his straining patience and his own escalating pulse rate caused by the closeness of the adorable young woman by his side. 'A long delay seems pointless. You must approach my secretary. He will assist you in the preparations and knows how to go about getting things done.'

'Very well,' Patience conceded, knowing her nephew's mind was made up and there was no point arguing.

When the betrothal the Duke of Mowbray's ward to the Earl of Arlington was officially announced in the *Post*, it was received with considerable surprise, although, since the Earl of Arlington's attentiveness towards the American girl at all the stylish gatherings had been duly noted, word was already getting out that she had won the heart of London's most eligible bachelor.

When Lavinia Howard was told, furious and humiliated to the core, she discreetly removed herself to the Howard ancestral home in the country.

When Angelina walked slowly down the aisle with her hand resting on the Duke of Mowbray's arm in the candlelit church and bearing a spray of white lilies, all the radiance in the world was shining from her large amethyst eyes, which were drawn irresistibly to the man who was waiting for her at the front of the church, overwhelming in stature, his ebony hair smoothly brushed and gleaming. His plum-coloured coat, dove grey trousers hugging his long legs, matching silk waistcoat and crisp white cravat were simple but impeccably cut.

Unable to contain his desire to look upon Angelina, Alex turned. The vision of almost ethereal loveliness he beheld, her face as serene as the Madonna's, her body slender, breakable, snatched his breath away. Something like terror moved through his heart. Dear Lord, he prayed, make me cherish and protect her all the days of my life, and give her the joy and happiness she deserves. With Nathan by his side he stepped out and took his place in front of the priest, waiting for her in watchful silence.

Angelina's eyes were irresistibly drawn to him, clinging to him, and she met his gaze over the distance without a tremor, surprised to find she felt perfectly calm, her mind wiped clean of everything but the moment. She was unaware of all the eyes focused upon her, the many faces belonging to people of social prominence on either side of her a blur. There was a faint smile on Alex's firm lips, and her heart warmed as if it felt his touch.

When Angelina reached him, she looked up into his piercing grey eyes, and the gentle yielding he saw in those liquid depths almost sent him to his knees. Still smiling, he took her hand, his long fingers closing firmly over hers. She responded to his smile—in that moment of complete accord, her marriage to Alex seemed right. Together, side by side, they faced the priest to speak their marriage vows, unaware of Patience and Verity dabbing away their tears of happiness and Henry looking proudly on.

When at last they were pronounced man and wife, Alex bent his head and gently kissed his bride on the lips, unable to believe this wonderful creature belonged to him at last.

The wedding breakfast was a truly opulent and impressive

affair, with course after course of exquisite, mouth-watering dishes served with all the pomp and splendour expected at the Earl of Arlington's table.

Alex leaned close to his wife, the sweet, elusive fragrance of her setting his senses alive. 'What are you thinking?' he asked quietly.

She turned and looked at him, her face lively and bright. 'Oh—about all this—our wedding. I never believed it possible that this could happen.' A cloud crossed her eyes and a note of regret entered her voice. 'My only regret is that my parents are not with us.'

Alex squeezed her hand comfortingly under the table. 'They are not far away. I am certain that they are watching you from that mysterious place where we all go to one day.'

'Do you really think so?'

'Yes. Perhaps our children will produce their likeness,' he said softly, his eyes gleaming into hers, lazy and seductive, feeling a driving surge of desire at the sultriness of her soft mouth and the liquid depths of her eyes.

Angelina stared at him, unaware that she had paled. 'Children?' A lump of nameless emotion constricted her throat. Alex's casual reference to any future offspring they might produce reminded her of what would come later.

'At least half a dozen,' Alex replied, laughter rumbling in his chest. 'But you have to promise me one thing.'

'What is that?'

He stretched his arm possessively across the back of her chair without taking his eyes off her, slowly running his fingers along the back of her neck. 'At least one of them must look like you.'

She smiled, enjoying his caress. 'I'll do my best.'

Later, when the orchestra struck up and began to play the first dance—a waltz—Alex proudly led his wife into the centre of the floor and took her in his arms. Gazing down into her upturned face, he whirled her around to the delight of everyone, their bodies falling gracefully into the rhythm of the music.

They were the only couple dancing, the others being content to watch and admire. The desire that leapt between the groom and his beautiful bride was like nothing they had witnessed before. They watched transfixed as Alex's long fingers splayed across the small of his bride's back. All the while he was looking at her, and she at him, as if there was no one else present, and everyone was bewitched by the mystery that seemed to lie behind the highly charged communication of their eyes.

The revelry at its height, few people noticed when they slipped away. Angelina was halfway up the stairs when the full impact of what was about to happen hit her. Panic engulfed her, but she managed to cling to her composure with strength and fortitude as if it were a shield with which she could protect herself from Alex.

Pauline was waiting to remove her wedding finery. The girl was noticeably quiet as she proceeded with the ritual, which Angelina welcomed. After slipping the white satin nightdress over her mistress's head and letting it fall in a swirl about her feet, in numb silence Angelina watched as she snuffed out the candles, leaving just one burning close to the bed, its covers turned down. Pauline went out, leaving Angelina to her fate.

For what seemed an eternity she stood perfectly still, trembling with apprehension. Her eyes fixed on the connecting door, she saw a sliver of light beneath it, and a shadow passing to and fro. When at last it opened her heart slammed into her ribs. She took a step back as though to escape.

From the doorway Alex was looking at her in a way he had never looked at her before. He was implacably calm, but now he positively emanated a ruthless determination. Taking refuge inside herself seemed to Angelina the safest, most natural thing to do, and with revulsion and denial starting to heave in her chest, she felt herself shrinking back into the person she thought she would never be again.

Nothing Alex could say or do could make her climb into that bed with him, feeling as she did at that moment. Her decision made, there was a sour feel to her mouth and her throat was dry. She watched him close the door and move slowly further into the room, his robe falling open to the waist, revealing his firm, well-muscled chest covered with a mat of dark hair.

He paused, his eyes devouring her as she stood so very still close to the bed. Her nightdress gleamed, outlining the womanly shape of her: the soft swell of her breasts, her tiny waist, rounded hips and long, slender legs. In that strange pattern of candlelight she looked almost ethereal.

Suddenly he paused, and Angelina knew it must be the tortured expression and the way she was looking at him with numb paralysis that had brought him to a halt.

'Angelina? Is anything the matter?'

'Alex—I—I want to talk to you,' she said, shrinking at the presumptuously possessive gaze he swept over her, her self-control teetering very close to the edge.

'To talk is not what I have in mind,' he gently mocked.

Swallowing nervously, she saw in his eyes a need that would not be denied. 'Please don't look at me like that.' Her voice was scarcely above a whisper.

'How am I looking at you?' he asked cautiously. A hard line settled disquietingly between his black brows. 'A man is entitled to look at his wife any way he chooses.'

'Not when she doesn't want him to,' she whispered, her words ragged, his look prompting her to seek the protection of her robe. Thrusting her arms into the sleeves, she wrapped it around her with a protective tightness.

'Angelina, what is this?' Alex asked with an ominous quietness. 'I am not a monster ready to spring at you.' Not having expected to encounter resistance, Alex was both puzzled and annoyed by her behaviour. He sensed that all was not well with her, that the past had reasserted itself, and in the hope of finding out what it was, he made a supreme effort to overcome his impatience. 'Why don't you tell me what is wrong?' he asked quietly.

Angelina turned from him and moved away from his threatening presence to stand by the window, gripping the sill. Her eyes burned and her throat ached, as if her heart was being pushed up into her mouth, but she was determined not to cry. Alex came up behind her, his fingers closing around her shoulders, feeling a shudder pass through her entire body at his touch.

'Angelina,' he asked gently. 'Are you so frightened of letting me make love to you?'

Shrugging herself out of his grip as if it scorched her flesh, she moved to the centre of the room, averting her eyes.

Her silence chafed, and when Alex spoke his voice was edged with anger. 'If you are thinking of what happened to you in Ohio, I ask you to forget it. It is in the past. You must put it behind you.'

Her eyes darted to his and flamed. 'Is it?' she said fiercely. 'The ugliness of what happened is still between us. My memory is still clear. No matter how hard I try, I cannot forget.'

'Angelina, listen to me. I don't know what happened to you and I swore I would put no pressure on you to tell me, hoping that you would eventually. Lacerating yourself with memories will only deepen the pain, so don't you think it would be easier and sensible to tell me your secret so its power will be less potent? The past will always be with you. It is almost impossible to forget. But you must put it behind you. I know it hurts to hear that, but you're young and it's the only way.'

'But I can't,' she cried, 'and nor can I speak of it.'

'Good Lord, Angelina!' he said, raising his voice in exasperation. 'You behave as if you have some terminal disease.'

His eyes taunted her and Angelina felt the heat rise to her cheeks. 'That's how it feels—to me.'

Alex moved closer but she backed away.

'Don't come near me, Alex. I don't want this.' All the blood drained out of her face, leaving it ashen.

Alex's firm jaw tensed and his fists clenched. 'Do you mind telling me what has got in to you? His eyes were penetrating, searching, and he was no longer able to stem the question that had been uppermost in his mind ever since he had found her in the grip of her nightmare. He tried to prepare himself for the answer she might give him, dreading it with every fibre of his being. 'Angelina, did those savages rape you?'

Looking down in abject misery, she shook her head. 'No.'

The word was spoken so softly that Alex almost didn't hear it, but when he saw her lips form the word relief and thankfulness tore through him. 'Thank God,' he murmured, exhaling long and deep.

'But they might as well have. They have taken away my sense of worth, and I loathe myself with all the passion of my being.'

When at last she looked up it was as though a mask had dropped over her exquisite face, leaving it remote and expressionless. Her eyes were lifeless and dull, as if something inside her had died. Never before had Alex seen her like this. He was tempted to ignore what she was telling him and draw her into his arms, but a sixth sense warned him not to move too close.

'Have you been hurt so badly that you recoil from the touch of another human being—from me?'

'No. Please don't think that.' She wanted to tell him that she loved him, and that whatever he did to her she would bear the pain of it to make him happy. But it wasn't the pain that worried her. It was something else, something dark and insidious she could not put a name to.

'Then forgive me if I appear stupid,' Alex ground out, trying hard to fight his feeling of inadequacy and his inability to break through the invisible barrier she had erected around herself. Raking his fingers impatiently through his hair, he began pacing up and down. When he had walked into her room he hadn't known what to expect—but rejection? Never. Suddenly he came towards her and stopped, hands on hips, his elbows bowed outward.

'I admit to being confused, for whenever I have kissed you you have raised no objection and returned my kisses with an ardour equal to my own.' He fell silent, for he remembered that at those times he had been tender, gentle with her. 'Angelina, you knew what to expect when you agreed to become my wife.'

'Yes—I did. For some time my subconscious has been urging me to face the things I am afraid of, to question my weakness, and until the ball tonight I had every intention of being a dutiful wife. I thought I could, but—'

'Then what happened?'

'I don't know. I only know the closer it came to retiring, my fear increased. It's not you, Alex. It's me.' She drew a long shuddering breath, drawing from an inner strength the courage she needed for what she was about to ask him. 'Please—will you agree to wait—give me time?'

Apart from a tightening of the lines around his mouth his face was expressionless. 'You do realise that what you ask is highly irregular?'

'Yes.'

'And if I refuse to do as you ask?' His voice was dangerously quiet.

Her soft mouth trembled as she stared like an animal wounded unto death into those fiery silver eyes that rested on her. 'Alex, I am begging you. You must. I'm not ready. I thought I was, but I'm not. You would not force me to submit to you?'

One black brow rose as he gave her a long, cool look. 'I find your choice of word distasteful, Angelina. When I eventually take my wife to bed, I hope she does not find it necessary to prepare herself mentally before she will let me touch her. I do not expect her to yield or surrender to my will or authority—to subject herself to me as if it is some form of punishment for wrongdoing.'

To Alex at that moment Angelina looked both beautiful and tragic. Not wishing to drive her to the precipice of hysteria, cursing silently he turned away in angry frustration. For the first time in his life he found himself confronted by a wall he could not breach. 'Before God, Angelina, I will not force you. I want to make love to you, not fight you.'

'All I am asking is for you to give me a little time—a delay, that is all.'

Alex moved closer, anger ripping through him when she visibly shrank from him. With a quivering finger he pointed to the bed. 'Either you get into that bed with me now, or I shall walk through that door—and it will remain between us until *you* decide to come to *me*. But I will not allow it to remain between us for ever.' He regarded her with a terrifying firmness. 'The choice is yours.'

The temptation to give in, to cast herself into his arms, was so powerful to be almost irresistible. She needed him so much, his warmth, his strength. Yet fear restrained her on the very verge of yielding and it chilled her heart. Naked pain slashed across her face and she looked at him, not knowing what to say. In the end, she lowered her eyes and shook her head. 'I'm sorry, Alex,' she whispered.

His fury erupted and his eyes flashed a dangerous steely silver as he made as if to go to her, but checked himself. 'When you have the courage to become my wife in every sense, you know where I am. Out of consideration for your anxiety and fear and my ignorance as to what did happen to you in that accursed land, I will make concessions and agree to wait. But be warned. My patience is not inexhaustible. You cannot evade the issue indefinitely.'

Crossing the room in long swift strides, he opened the door, where he paused and turned back to her. 'To keep your memories of that time in Ohio is not good. It's like running away, and whatever you run away from will always come to find you.'

'Is that what happened to you when you saw your father kill himself?'

'Yes, so I do understand some of what you are going through. Has it never occurred to you that a thing feared and dreaded is better done and put behind you—that to combat a fear one must meet it head on?'

She shook her head, wanting to believe his assurances and surrender to hope. But she had lived so long with pain and grief that she was unable to do so just then.

Angelina's suffering was so near the surface, it was plain for Alex to see. Unable to be so dismissive about what had happened to her, something moved in the region of his heart. His expression softened as he looked at her with aching gentleness. 'I will not give up, Angelina. Whatever it was those savages did to you and your family—that made you feel inadequate as a woman—I know they did not break you. I believe the image of what happened is more vivid because you have made it so.'

'Do you hate me?' she whispered brokenly.

'I hate this demon that's consuming you. Fight it, Angelina. Beat it.'

'I can't.'

'Yes, you can. Let me love you. Do not forget that I have felt the way you surrender in my arms—that you return my kisses with equal passion. Whatever I set out to do I achieve, and a woman whose desire for me is as great as mine is for her will not defeat me. I want you, Angelina, and I mean to have you—but on terms that are agreeable to us both. Will you promise me to think about this seriously and accustom yourself to marriage?'

'Yes, of course I do.'

'Thank you. Having no wish to bring ridicule to me or my name, I must insist that this sorry state of affairs remains between ourselves.'

'Of course it will. I would not embarrass you by speaking of it to anyone,' she replied. He had always said he didn't give a damn to what people thought of him, but he did after all.

He nodded and left her then, closing the door firmly behind him. That was the moment when Angelina knew the true meaning of heartbreak.

Back in the splendour of his lonely room, intending to drown himself in drink, Alex poured himself a generous brandy and tossed the fiery liquid back, immediately pouring himself another, knowing he would get no sleep that night. With the woman—his wife—he wanted more than any other in his bed just behind the door, he intended getting well and truly foxed to stop himself thinking about her, to keep his mind from riveting upon the way she had looked today as his bride.

He paced the carpet, and with each footstep he swore violently under his breath, and each time he turned he threw a virulent look at the closed connecting door. He found it incredible that he—the future Duke of Mowbray, courted for his favour by men and women alike, a man who with cold logic could override his emotions whenever he wished, should find himself in this intolerable situation. Good Lord, this was his wedding night and his wife had denied him her bed—and what was worse, much worse, was the fact that he had allowed her to do it.

The weather was fair, the sun adding warmth to the day when Alex and Angelina returned to Arlington. Their marriage was the cause of much celebration in the surrounding districts. It was a time for gaiety and dancing, when villagers, tenant farmers and their families, servants and lords and ladies alike joined in the merrymaking. Angelina was happy to be back at Arlington, to reacquaint herself with the staff; however, it soon became obvious to them all that things weren't as they should be between the Earl and his new wife.

Feelings between Angelina and Alex were strained and tension ran high. At first they tried being amiable to each other, but they were both guarded, and it was impossible to sustain empty pleasantries indefinitely. In public they put on a cheerful front, seeming to be loving and agreeable, but in private it was a different matter. All Angelina's attempts to engage her husband in amicable conversation yielded nothing but cold, uninterested responses.

Alex went about his work with his usual single-minded determination and efficiency, but he had withdrawn from Angelina as if those tender, happy moments they had shared in the weeks prior to their wedding had never been. He became a stranger to her, cold and unapproachable.

After three weeks the situation became intolerable. Each avoided the other, and when they did meet, usually at dinner, Alex was so imperiously polite that Angelina wanted to hit him. The Alex she had come to know and love was no longer there in the new role he had created for himself.

One morning, after taking her early morning ride, she was returning to her suite of rooms in the east wing adjoining her husband's when, passing his door, she halted her steps when she saw his valet and a servant carrying a large trunk out on to the landing. Slowly she moved inside, looking at them in alarm.

'Where are you going with that? Is my husband going somewhere?'

'Your husband, madam, is leaving for London,' came a cold voice from behind her.

Angelina spun round with disbelieving eyes when Alex emerged from his dressing room, fastening his waistcoat. His valet and the servant made a hasty retreat on to the landing, closing the door behind them.

'London! Oh, I see,' she said quietly, feeling her heart almost grind to a halt when she looked at his hard, handsome face, seeing that his mercurial mood she had been living with since their marriage had taken a bewildering turn for the worse. 'Am I to go with you?'

'No,' he replied, trying not to notice how ravishing and invigorated she looked after her ride, dressed in her scarlet riding clothes, her cheeks adorably pink and her eyes sparkling. Fastening a gold pin in his cravat, he strode past her without giving her so much as a glance, disappearing into his office. 'You are to remain at Arlington,' he said to her through the open door. 'No doubt you will find plenty to occupy your time.' He emerged, carrying official papers and correspondence and thrusting them into a large leather bag on the bed, his long fingers threading the straps through buckles to secure it.

Angelina stood watching him in tearful silence, hurt and disappointment tearing her in two. 'May I ask why you have suddenly decided to go away?'

His face was unyielding and impassive, with no sign of the passionate, sensual side to his nature, and when he turned his gaze on her she felt the full blast of his contempt. 'I would have thought that was obvious.'

Angelina's cheeks burned from the cruelty of the remark, and she was swamped with guilt. In silent, helpless protest she stared into his icy, metallic eyes, feeling as if something had shattered inside her. He was dismissing her as someone he considered unworthy to be his wife. He wanted to leave her—to be rid of her. She could feel it. And why shouldn't he, something inside her cried accusingly, when he had saddled himself with a wife who had spurned him on their wedding night? Any other man would have got rid of her before now, or forced her to comply.

'When will you be back?' she asked, clutching her riding crop with her gloved hands in front of her, wishing she hadn't asked when she beheld the cold glitter of his eyes and the rigid hardness of his jaw.

Taking his jacket from a chair and thrusting his arms into the sleeves, he met her gaze directly. 'I can't say. I have important business matters to take care of. My stewards will see that things run smoothly at Arlington while I am away.'

'You're always busy, Alex. You do too much.'

His eyes snapped to hers, his mouth curving into a humourless half-smile. 'Meaning?'

'That I—I see so little of you,' she murmured hesitantly, desperate for him not to go, thinking wildly of some way to reach him.

'Are you complaining?'

She became flustered, cautious. 'No, of course not. Can't your business transactions be taken care of here?'

'I can only do that in London. It may have escaped your notice, Angelina, but owing to the war in both Europe and America, there is an economic crisis. If I am not in London to discuss matters at first hand with my business managers and bankers, the implications could prove disastrous. I also think it would be best if we were apart for a while.'

Angelina flinched. 'I see.' She stared at him as he strode around the room, picking things up and throwing them on to the bed for his valet to pack into bags, fighting to control the mistiness that suddenly affected her vision. She drew a shaking breath. 'Alex. Are—are you leaving me?' she asked quietly, overwhelmed with emotions and the fear that this might be so.

He stiffened, and when he turned and looked at her she could almost feel the effort he was exerting to keep his temper under control. 'What in God's name gives you that idea?'

'I—I thought that because—we—don't—'

'What? Sleep together? You are quite wrong,' he snapped. 'I renounced my freedom for you. You belong to me as I belong to you. I do not admit defeat so easily. There will be no separation between us, no matter how much you desire it.'

'But I don't,' she cried.

'I meant what I said. I have important business commitments that need my personal attention, and I shall return to Arlington as soon as they are settled—in which time I hope you will give serious thought to what we discussed before we left London.'

'I will. Alex, I am not doing this to hurt you. The fault is entirely mine—I accept that, and you can't possibly blame me more that I blame myself.'

He gazed down into her pain-shadowed eyes, fighting the simultaneous impulse to shake her for her stubborn refusal to be a proper wife to him, and the stronger urge to clasp her to him, carry her to bed and lose himself in her. She was very lovely, this obstinate young woman he had married. So lovely, in fact, that he would forgive her the past three weeks and the insult she had offered him night after night with her firmly closed bedroom door, and postpone going to London if tonight she would come to him willingly.

'I'm not blaming you.'

'Going away won't solve anything.'

'For me it will.' He strode back into his office.

'That seems like an easy way out of a difficult situation,' she said, following him, standing in the doorway whilst he collected the documents from the top of his desk and began thrusting them in drawers.

'It is not easy. I have to do something to quench the fury of not being able to make love to my wife,' Alex retaliated coldly.

He was going away because, having become hopelessly entangled in his desire, he couldn't help himself. Every night he fought against it to go to her. He thought he was stronger, but she had bewitched him. He was obsessed by her and if he didn't put some distance between them he was afraid of what he might do—that he would force himself on her and she would hate him for ever more, and they would set about destroying each other like mortal enemies. Emerging from his office, he stopped what he was doing and came to stand before her, his awesome presence filling the room, his face austere, his voice calm and authoritative.

'I do not think you realise what this enforced abstinence is doing to me, Angelina. It is both unacceptable and intolerable. Like every other man, I have needs.'

'And these needs you speak of are the kind that you go to London to satisfy? How excruciatingly naïve and stupid you must find me, Alex,' she said scathingly

Alex's eyes narrowed dangerously as he fixed her with a piercing stare. 'Are you accusing me of seeking my pleasure elsewhere?'

'What else am I to think?'

'I agree. There are numerous beds in London with willing occupants.'

'And when I recall your reputation as being London's most infamous libertine, no doubt you are familiar with every one of them.' she accused coldly, two high spots of indignation highlighting the flush on her cheeks.

'Some of them,' he admitted. 'And I shall not fail to avail myself of one of them if I so wish. I feel more like a man considering holy orders than someone who has recently married. Do you expect me to live the life of a monk?'

The threatening quality of his behaviour sparked Angelina's anger. She suddenly felt weary before this display of selfish rage on the part of her frustrated husband. How could he ignore all she had told him—her sufferings and fears, her grief? None of that interested him. The only thing he cared about was sating his lust. She had to summon all her patience to stop herself bursting out in fury.

'My, you are feeling sorry for yourself, aren't you, Alex?' she said, her words heavily laden with sarcasm. 'There are other worthier ways of finding forgetfulness for yourself than in the women who will willingly fall into your arms. You are being quite unreasonable.'

'Don't push me, Angelina,' he snapped coldly, his eyes glittering like shards of ice, his tone promising terrible consequences. 'By denying me your bed you have already reached your limit. In my present "unreasonable" mood, nothing would give me greater pleasure than to throw you on to that bed and spend the rest of the day showing you what is expected of a wife and how attentive a husband I can be. The very thought of you, the sight of you here in my room, having you close, wrenches my insides in a painful knot and begs to release the desire you have aroused in me. I have been patient long enough. I shall give you ample time to come to terms and prepare yourself for what I shall expect of you when I return.'

'Which is?'

'I don't think I need to spell it out. Do not forget that you are bound by your word and I expect you to fulfil the vows you made to me in church.'

'I intend to—'

'So, I am to live in hope, am I?' he cut in with bitter irony.

'Yes, of course. But how dare you remind me of what I promised when you are considering breaking your own?' Angelina went on recklessly, the colour heightening on her cheeks as she glared at him with bitter accusation, heedless of his mounting rage.

'Am I not being driven to it my own wife? Are you still afraid of the prospect of lying with me?'

'I—I don't know,' she answered truthfully.

'If you would allow me, I think I could remedy that.'

He was standing so close and was looking at her so intently, that Angelina's eyes moved involuntarily to his mouth. On impulse she backed away. 'Don't, Alex.'

His arms reached out and caught her, bringing her slamming against his chest. She gasped, thinking he was going to kiss her when his head lowered slightly, but he continued to look at her with a humourless smile, his warm breath fanning her lips. 'Don't threaten me, Angelina. It is not in my nature to rape an unprepared innocent. But you are my wife—

and, by God, when I return from London you will be my wife in truth. My patience is at an end. There will be no more childishness.'

'If you bully me, it will avail you nothing.'

'I advise you to think very carefully if you intend continuing with this charade, because if you do you will regret it, I promise you. I will decide which course our future will take, and I do not intend spending our lives together sleeping apart. Do I make myself clear?'

'Perfectly,' she answered, flinching from the sharpness of his tone, hearing determination in every word.

'Good,' he said, releasing her as abruptly as he had taken hold of her. 'I'm glad we understand each other.'

'No, Alex,' she flared, her face scorching. 'I understand you but you do not understand me. Your own conduct where I am concerned cannot be faulted, I suppose? Has it not occurred to you that I would have found it easier to adjust to my new, awesome position as your wife if, since coming to Arlington, you had not been so ill tempered and treated me with callous indifference? You are manipulative, stubborn and extremely selfish. Let me remind you that as your wife I am equal in all things—not your possession or your chattel, to be told what I will and will not do.'

Alex gave her a long, speculative look. 'Will you not?'

'No,' she snapped, throwing back her head and raising her chin mutinously. He was playing the role of a husband whose honour has been smirched a little too well. 'And it is really too much for you to start laying down rules in this lordly fashion. If you insist on being disagreeable, I suggest you make haste and leave for London—and do not feel that you have to hurry back.' With that she turned and walked across the room so he wouldn't see her tears of humiliation.

Not until her hand touched the handle did his cold, ominous voice slice across the chasm that separated them. 'Angelina!'

Despite herself she stiffened and half-turned back to him, eyeing him suspiciously as she waited for him to speak, recognising that the stern set of his face and the thin line of his lips did not suggest much tolerance. He came to stand in front of her, and when his eyes peered into hers, she could sense the menace behind them.

'I meant what I said. I do not see why I should have to go to the inconvenience of travelling to London to avail myself of a mistress when I have a wife who shares my money and my name living under the same roof. When I return, you will not deny me. Is that understood?'

Bravely she tried to smile, hoping her voice wouldn't break and trying to hold on to her shattered pride. He made his feelings plain in the one inimical glance. 'What you mean is that I must learn my place. Yes, I understand you perfectly.' Feeling her control collapsing, she went out, hot tears burning her eyes, the lump in her throat almost choking her.

Alex watched her go, tempted to go after her, but he remained motionless. Having made her understand what he expected of her when he returned from London, he was certain she would give it serious thought and obey him. The idea that he would allow her to go on as they were, living together but sleeping apart, was unthinkable.

When Alex had left for London, never had Angelina felt so bereft. Her conscience smote her and she was sick with dread that he might have returned to the arms of one of his former mistresses—and she had sent him there. She tried telling herself that he would not do that to her, but her tortured imaginings almost drove her crazy.

What had she done? Alex was the most precious thing in her life. Without him it meant nothing. Alex might not love her, but he liked her enough to want her, to want to make their marriage work. He could not be faulted. After one whole week of self-condemnation and missing him so much it was driving her to distraction, she told Pauline to pack her trunk and arrange for the carriage to take her to London.

Chapter Twelve

The streets were congested when Angelina arrived in London. During an enforced halt her attention wandered to the carriage next to her own, an open barouche, its occupant an elderly lady. She was conversing with a gentleman on horseback whom Angelina recognised as Duncan Aylard—graceful and indolent and decked out in the very height of fashion. On seeing her, he nudged his horse closer to her carriage and, true to form, proceeded to charm and flatter her before turning to the lady in the carriage and introducing them.

Lady Broadhurst, a kindly widow, was in London to attend Lord and Lady Unsworth's party that evening and was to return to Kent tomorrow. Eager to chat, she said how pleased she was to meet Lady Anne Adams's granddaughter and how disappointed Lady Anne had been when she had been unable to attend the wedding, due to a recent accident.

Lady Broadhurst's words drifted off somewhere into the bright afternoon sunshine. Angelina could hear her, but her words made no sense. She felt her face drain of colour and her body felt ice cold in this dreamlike world that had come upon her so suddenly. Giving no sign of the blow Lady Broadhurst's words had dealt her, she cleared her throat painfully and continued to make polite conversation, gleaning as much as she could about her grandmother—the woman she had always believed was dead—before moving on.

Travelling to Brook Street Angelina could feel only anger. Everything her mother and Uncle Henry had told her about her grandparents being dead had been a lie, and what hurt more than anything else was that Alex had colluded with them. He knew—had known all along—and he hadn't told her. It was wicked and cruel, deceitful and underhanded. When the coach stopped outside the house and a footman opened the door, her rage was contained in a deadly calm.

Fully prepared for a confrontation, Angelina marched past Bramwell and made her way to Alex's study. Not bothering to knock, she walked straight in, halting in the doorway. Having removed his jacket, her husband was seated at his desk. As she looked up his body became rigid, but then very calmly and deliberately he pushed back his chair and stood up. His jaw was set with implacable determination, and he seemed to emanate the restrained, unyielding authority Angelina had come to know and dread. But she felt no fear as he moved towards where she stood, undeterred by the deadly menace she saw in his eyes.

'Angelina, what are you doing here?'

'If I had any hope that you might be pleased to see me, your question has told me you are not,' she said tightly.

'That is beside the point. How dare you disobey me?'

Angelina glared her defiance, refusing to lower her eyes beneath that terrible silver gaze. 'Disobey you? What are you talking about?'

'I specifically told you to remain at Arlington until I returned—and yet, not one week after my departure, here you are. Well? I am waiting. What is it that is so important you wish to speak to me about?'

Angelina's eyes locked on his. There was no warmth in her

fine-textured skin and her eyes were like shards of frosted glass beneath the long sweep of her lashes as she spoke, enunciating each word. 'Why was I told that my grandmother was dead?'

Stunned as much from the icy tone of her voice as the words, it took Alex a moment to react. At last he said cautiously, 'Who told you?'

'That is not important. It is true, I take it?'

They faced one another, the truth standing between them like an open door.

'Yes, it's true.' Alex said in a calm, flat voice, leaning his hips on the edge of his desk and folding his arms across his chest, closely watching the irate young woman in front of him.

'I knew it,' she hissed, her anger beginning to mount. 'Of all the treacherous, deceitful—'

'Angelina,' he interrupted with irritating calm. 'Please remember that I was not the one who told you your grandmother was dead.'

'Nevertheless, you were a party to it,' she argued, standing her ground, determined to have the satisfaction of hearing his explanation, disappointment and betrayal spinning inside her. 'I trusted you. I expected better from you than that.'

'If you must know, I was against it. I have always been of the opinion that you should be told the truth, but I promised Uncle Henry that I would abide by his wishes.'

'Why?' she demanded, her voice shaking with angry emotion. 'Why did you keep it from me? What is so terrible about my grandmother being alive that Uncle Henry has made you pledge not to reveal to me?'

'You must ask Uncle Henry.'

'I am asking you,' she fumed. 'You knew, Alex—and yet you let me go on believing my grandmother was dead, that I had no family of my own. How could you? How could you of all people deceive me like this? It was unspeakably cruel.'

Alex relinquished his perch and moved towards her. Despite

her haughty stance and the fact that her eyes were hurling knives at him, he sensed that she was deeply hurt by what she had learned about her grandmother, and rightly so.

'I can neither defend nor condemn Uncle Henry's actions for keeping it from you. I agree that you should have been told, but then again, Uncle Henry had no choice but to respect your mother's wishes.'

'Why did my mother tell me my grandmother was dead?' she persisted. 'Why did she want to keep it from me? What happened to make her reject her own mother? And why did she make Uncle Henry my guardian instead of my grandmother?'

'You ask questions that I am not at liberty to answer.'

Angelina moved to stand close to him, looking deep into his eyes as she steeled herself to ask the question that had lain dormant since Uncle Henry had made her his ward, knowing that if she disturbed it there was every possibility that it would crucify her.

'Will you tell me something, Alex?'

'That depends on what it is.'

'Was Uncle Henry the reason why my mother married my father and went with him to America? Was that the reason for the rift between her and my grandparents?'

Alex's heart wrenched at the way she was looking at him, recognising her attempt to control her fear on being told the truth. 'I can neither confirm nor deny what you ask. That is something you must take up with Uncle Henry. What I will say is that his guilt has been torturing him. He's been tempted to tell you about your grandmother many times—especially before the wedding, when he knew how much you wanted kin of your own to see you married. But he promised your mother he wouldn't. He begged her to make amends and write to your grandmother, but she told him it was too late. It came as a cruel blow to your mother when your grandfather wrote and told her he was severing all ties between them, that he had no daughter. After that as far as she was concerned she had no mother, you no grandmother, and that was the way she wanted it to remain.'

'Well, I am not my mother and I think that it's up to me to decide whether or not I want to see my grandmother.'

Alex frowned when he saw a thoughtful, determined gleam implant itself in his wife's eyes. He had long since learned to be wary of such a look. 'Angelina, you are not thinking of going to see her?' His voice held a quiet warning.

Angelina regarded her husband with disturbing calmness. 'Yes. I have every right to see her if I want to.'

'You are not going anywhere while you are thinking irrationally.'

'Don't try and stop me, Alex. Perhaps she will be more forthcoming about what really happened all those years ago,' she flung at him bitterly.

'To have a granddaughter turn up on her doorstep…a granddaughter whose existence she would have known nothing about until you were made the Duke of Mowbray's ward and she saw your name splashed all over the newspapers—in all probability the shock may cause the poor woman to suffer a seizure.'

'If she knows who I am, then why hasn't she tried to contact me?'

To Alex at that moment, Angelina looked so unbearably beautiful, young and vulnerable, facing him so courageously in this outrageous defiance, that if the situation weren't so serious, he would have smiled. 'Hasn't it entered that stubborn head of yours that she might not want to? Just as your mother chose to keep it from you that your grandmother was alive, she too may have her reasons for remaining silent. Perhaps you should respect that.'

'But I can't,' Angelina cried, trying to control the wrenching anguish in her chest when she recalled Lady Broadhurst's words—that it would have given Lady Anne such joy to see her granddaughter wed. To Angelina, this implied that her grandmother would be happy to see her granddaughter. Her face became intensely passionate in her determination. 'I'm going to see her at once.'

Alex was adamant. 'Don't be ridiculous. You are not going to Kent until you have spoken to Uncle Henry. Perhaps when he's explained everything, you will understand.'

'My grandmother will explain it all to me.'

'Angelina, you are going nowhere.' His voice was implacable and as cold as steel.

She stared at him with growing anger. 'Yes, I am.'

'No, you are not. Remember that no one but myself has the ordering of my coaches. This is my house and my servants and you are my wife. I do not choose to risk the life and limb of man or beast in some harebrained scheme of yours to go tearing off to Kent at this hour of the day. So, in case you have some crazy idea of doing just that, I shall instruct the driver to block any such move.'

Her eyes dashed fiery venom over him. 'You wouldn't.'

'Try me.'

'Are you forbidding me to go?'

'Most definitely—until you have spoken to Uncle Henry.'

'But it could be weeks before I see him.'

'Why the hurry?'

'My grandmother is ill and I wish to see her,' she answered, turning towards the door.

'Then I will write to Uncle Henry and ask him to return to London. Or, if you prefer and to save time, we could journey to Mowbray Park together.'

'That will take too long. I shall walk to Kent if I have to,' she flared furiously, turning back to him.

Her wilful defiance ignited a blaze of fury on her husband's hard features. 'Angelina! You are going nowhere. Now, let that be enough.' Turning from her, he went back to his desk, his manner telling her the matter was closed. 'I have been invited to an important party at Lord and Lady Unsworth's house on the Strand tonight. Now you are here, you might as well accompany me. Who knows—you might even enjoy yourself. We mustn't stay too late. I have an important appointment at nine o'clock in the morning.'

'Blast you, Alex Montgomery. Go by yourself. I am in no mood for partying.'

'Angelina!'

About to open the door, she spun round, her anger in no way diminished. 'What?'

'Just one thing piques my curiosity. How did you find out about your grandmother? How do you know she is ill?'

'Lady Broadhurst told me. She is my grandmother's neighbour.'

He looked at her with narrowed, questioning eyes. 'I didn't know you were acquainted with Lady Broadhurst. When did you meet?'

'When I was on my way here. There was a snarl up in the traffic and Lord Aylard—' She stopped...too late. A cold, sinking fear gripped her and she groaned inwardly, wishing she could cut out her tongue for mentioning Lord Aylard's name, for it never failed to ignite Alex's wrath. Alex advanced on her with the predatory grace of a stalking Indian. His threatening manner almost made Angelina back away, but with the door behind her she was forced to remain where she was. He loomed over her, his eyes gleaming oddly. 'So, you have been speaking to Aylard.' His voice was ominously quiet.

'I happened to see him when the coach was stopped. He was speaking to Lady Broadhurst and he introduced us.'

'I see.' One black eyebrow went up as he bent a long, cool look at her.

Angelina watched her husband turn away as the demon

jealousy that took hold of him whenever Lord Aylard's name was mentioned in connection with his wife began to relax its grip.

'Go to your room. Since you have no wish to accompany me tonight, I will see you in the morning.'

Not until he was alone did Alex frown and cast a puzzled glance at the closed door. He recalled the intense feeling of joy that had shot through him when he had raised his eyes and seen Angelina, hoping her reason for following him to London was because she had been missing him, only to have his hopes dashed when she had challenged him about her grandmother. But then, he mused, lounging back in his chair, when she had left Arlington she had not known about her grandmother—and so, what had brought her to London?

Angelina realised that the answer to her dilemma was staring her in the face. Unsworth! She distinctly recalled Lady Broadhurst telling her that she was to attend their party and that she was to leave for Kent in the morning. Angelina was certain the good lady could be persuaded to let her accompany her. Alex had an engagement at nine o'clock so he wouldn't discover she was missing until she was halfway to Tonbridge.

Unfortunately, by the time she sent Pauline to inform her husband that she would go with him to the party, he had already left. He was to dine at his club with friends and go on to the party later. Angelina had no alternative but to order one of the carriages to take her. At first the driver was reluctant to comply, having been ordered by his lordship not to take his wife out of London under any circumstances, but when told she was going to join her husband, he agreed.

It was late when Angelina arrived at the house along the Strand to attend the party—a truly magnificent affair, with only the cream of London society invited. The large ballroom was filled to capacity, a festive air prevailing. Standing alone at the top of the steps leading down to the ballroom, she looked about her, seeing several familiar faces, but not that of Lady Broadhurst. Lady Unsworth came to welcome her.

'Good evening, Lady Montgomery. How nice of you to honour us with your company. I'm so delighted you were able to attend our party after all.'

'My husband has arrived?'

'Just a few minutes ago.'

From where he stood conversing with a group of friends, like everyone else Alex was aware of a distraction. Absently his eyes did a quick sweep of the ballroom. He saw Lady Unsworth descending the stairs with one of her female guests, but paid scant attention, then something in the way the woman moved and the rich vibrancy of her hair brought his eyes snapping back.

'I say, Alex,' said Lord Asquith beside him. 'Isn't that your wife?'

Alex stared at Angelina, whose whole presence seemed to blaze across the ballroom at him, eliminating all else. His whole manner was calm and composed, while inside he was seething. How dare she embarrass him like this by arriving late and unescorted? But as he kept her within his sights he could not deny that, clad in the deepest pink chiffon gown with a scooped neckline, lower than any he had seen her wear before, her neck and shoulders and the soft swell of her breasts aglow, she looked sensational.

Angelina watched the tall, daunting, devastatingly handsome man, attired in an exquisitely tailored claret jacket and pristine white cravat, cut a pathway through the throng with a feeling of impending disaster.

Lady Unsworth was full of smiles as she received him with lighthearted repartee, but Alex, impatient to have Angelina to himself and take her to task, bowed his head respectfully as he excused himself.

Beneath his icy calm, such was the force of his fury that

Angelina flinched. His long fingers closed on her elbow like a vice as he walked with her towards the dance floor, where the orchestra was striking up the next waltz.

'You needn't hold my arm so tightly, Alex. I'm not going to run away.'

'Shut up,' he seethed, increasing the pressure on her elbow.

When he took her in his arms his face was so close to hers that she could see the ice-cold satanic glitter in his eyes. He didn't speak, and to Angelina his silence was both unbearable and insulting.

'Why did you drag me out here if you can find nothing to say to me?' she said at length.

'I can find plenty to say. It's knowing where to begin.'

Angelina smiled, a trace of irony on her lips. 'Why, Alex, I never thought to see you lost for words.'

'Does your rebelliousness know no bounds?' he ground out, incensed, keeping his voice low so as not to be overheard by others. 'What the devil are you trying to do? See how far you can provoke me?'

'What? More than I have already, you mean?'

'Don't be flippant and smile, damn it,' he said through gritted teeth when she glowered up at him. 'We are the object of every pair of eyes in this ballroom. Rumours are already being bandied about that there is a rift between us.'

Angelina's eyes opened wide with genuine astonishment, and she experienced a sharp pang of regret. 'Alex, is this true? But that's ridiculous.'

'Is it?'

'Well—maybe you have yourself to blame for that,' she said quietly.

His eyes impaled hers. 'What the devil are you talking about?'

'Perhaps you shouldn't have returned to London alone so soon after our marriage. That alone must have fuelled the rumours.'

'Your own actions tonight won't have helped matters. Was

it your intention to make me a laughing stock—to embarrass and publicly humiliate me by coming to the party alone?'

'No, Alex. I wouldn't do that. And anyway, I didn't think you cared a hoot for what people think of you.'

'I don't,' he said, aware of the lingering and lascivious looks from raffish young bloods that Angelina was inviting by sporting an outrageous décolletage. His eyes were like shards of ice as they insolently dropped to the daring display of her creamy expanse of bosom—giving no indication how his hands ached to touch and feel that soft skin next to his own, a desire so great that it was driving him insane. 'What I do mind is my wife making a public exhibition of herself by choosing to wear a gown that I consider indecent in its exposure. It gives me no satisfaction to see other men coveting you.'

The insult brought Angelina's head snapping back and her eyes flying to his in anger. 'On the contrary, Alex. I think I am very *à la mode*. And if the glances I am receiving from some of the other gentlemen are an indication of how I look, then I would say that you are alone in your opinion. I expose no more than any other woman here tonight and you know it,' she flared, surprised how quickly she had overcome her own unease when she had donned the gown. 'Just because I haven't chosen to wear a gown so revealing before now is entirely my own affair.'

The modest cut of her gowns had not gone unnoticed by Alex, and, sensing her reluctance to expose herself—as other women delighted in doing—had something to do with her past, he had tactfully not mentioned it. 'Then why did you choose to do so tonight?'

'For no other reason than that I thought the gown would look nice on me.' His blunt criticism of her beautiful gown caught her between hurt and the urge to kick him in the shin.

When Alex saw the disappointment in her eyes, her pursed lips and angry frown, some of his imperious expression began to waver. 'What made you decide to come to the party?'

'I simply wanted to sample a little enjoyment myself, that is all. Unfortunately, by the time I decided, you'd already left for your club. I did not think you would mind if I came alone—and I foolishly believed you would be pleased to see me,' she said quietly, pulling back an inch, her eyes unwavering as she met his gaze. 'I also thought you would like my dress.'

'I would like it a lot more if there was more of it,' he said drily.

'If you insist on being disagreeable for the entire evening, Alex, when the dance has finished I suggest you return to your friends and let me reacquaint myself with some of the ladies I recognised when I came in.'

His arm tightened around her, drawing her closer to his chest. 'Not a chance,' he said, his lips close to her ear. 'Until it is time for us to leave you will remain cleaved to my side.' His mood softened. It felt good to hold her again, to have her close, to smell the elusive scent of her flesh. A slow, lazy smile spread across his features as he gazed down at her alluring face, and when he spoke his voice was low and seductive.

'I am pleased that you decided to come, Angel, and, despite the fact that it displays your charms with a wantonness I and every other man present find hard to resist, I do like your gown.'

Her eyes widened until they were huge amethyst orbs. 'You do?' He nodded slowly. 'I've never worn anything quite like it, and I confess to feeling a trifle awkward and over-exposed.'

Alex was determined to continue the seduction. He dropped his eyes, bold and admiring, taking another look at those tantalising orbs swelling out of the bodice of her gown and feeling his blood run hot. 'Think yourself lucky that you are in the middle of a dance floor with an audience, my love. It is the only thing that keeps you safe from me—but not for long.' He grinned, aware of her unease. 'So, am I to understand that you are no longer angry with me for deceiving you about your grandmother?'

Her face became grave. 'Yes. I apologise for what I said to

you earlier. It was wrong of me to take it out on you. I know none of it is your fault, and that you were bound by your word to Uncle Henry.'

'Angelina…when are you going to tell me why you came to London?'

She looked up at him. His eyes were intense. 'You mean I haven't?'

He shook his head, holding her gaze, waiting for her to tell him.

In panic her eyes darted away from his. 'I didn't like it at Arlington on my own,' she confessed. 'I was upset when you left so abruptly. You were so angry. I wanted to settle the argument between us.'

'You did?'

'Yes.'

'How?'

'By saying I'm sorry.'

'You are?' Alex looked down at her dubiously, noticing the soft light in her eyes.

Angelina nodded. 'Yes.'

'What a chaste little thing you are,' he murmured.

Her flush was one of pure innocence. 'I—I know I must appear that way to you and I—I told you I was—'

'A virgin, I know. But it's curable. It is my dearest wish to have done with it. I want to show you how to love in the tenderest way I can. Whatever happened to you in the past, I will make you forget—and I know you will be an avid pupil.'

True to his word, Alex did not leave his wife's side for a moment, but all the while Angelina's eyes searched the throng for Lady Broadhurst. Her inattention did not go unnoticed by her husband. His brows drew together with displeasure.

'Your attention seems to be wandering, my love. If you are looking for Aylard, he has just arrived—and by the look of him he's disgustingly foxed and making a damn fool of himself.'

'As a matter of fact I wasn't looking for Lord Aylard. I have seen him and he does look rather worse for wear,' she remarked, observing the man in question amidst a circle of his friends, each and every one of them flushed and whooping with unrestrained merriment. She was unable to resist a little smile when she saw Lord Aylard sway slightly as he leaned forward to plant a huge kiss on Lady Unsworth's cheek.

'Then who is it your eyes are searching for?'

'If you must know, I am looking for Lady Broadhurst. She happened to mention that she would be here tonight.'

Alex threw her a look of annoyance. 'This must stop, Angelina,' he said harshly. 'Nothing can be achieved by it. There must be no more questions about your grandmother until you see Uncle Henry. Is that understood?'

Though Angelina's chin was tilted a notch too high for comfort, to Alex's relief she remained silent, but as he turned away to speak to a gentleman on a political matter, so engrossed did he become in the issue that he was unaware of the moment his wife left his side when she saw Lady Broadhurst at the bottom of the stairs saying goodbye to their hosts.

Lady Broadhurst told Angelina that she would be delighted to share her coach with her. It would make the journey to Kent more pleasurable having someone to talk to.

Her mission accomplished, Angelina uttered a sigh of relief—which was not without trepidation. Alex would be absolutely furious when he found her gone, but she refused to think about that just now lest it weakened her resolve.

Suddenly a satin-garbed gentleman appeared by her side and seized her attention, astounded at his good fortune to find the adorable Angelina Montgomery at the party—without her husband lurking behind her like some damned guard on sentry duty.

Positively glowing with robust health and champagne, his face almost as red as a cock's comb, he made a sweeping bow, swaying in the process and almost falling over. 'My dear Countess! You are simply ravishing,' he complimented enthusiastically, making small effort to subdue the admiration that shone in his mischievous blue eyes.

Unable to resist Lord Aylard's ebullient mood, Angelina laughed. 'Why, Lord Aylard! You have arrived at last, I see. And here was I thinking you were avoiding me.'

'Not you, sweet Angelina. Never that. 'Tis your glowering, pompous husband I avoid. Where is he, by the way?' He looked over her shoulder, as if expecting to find him lurking behind her back.

'He's talking to an acquaintance.'

'Remiss of him to let you out of his sight.'

'Alex doesn't watch over me every minute of the day.'

'Seems like that to me. Whenever he and I meet, I swear he would like nothing better than to slay me on the spot.'

Angelina was suddenly surrounded by a boisterous pack of Lord Aylard's friends. A footman passing by with a tray of brimming champagne glasses was accosted and divested of his load amidst a rousing burst of laughter.

'Come, Countess.' Lord Aylard grinned as he attempted to extricate a glass of champagne from one of his friends. 'I'm having a high old time. You must have a glass of champagne with me to celebrate my good fortune at the tables this evening.'

'No, thank you. And I think you are awash with it already,' Angelina commented, looking for a way through the throng of surrounding males, confident she could manage to fend them off without making a scene. 'You must excuse me.'

Lord Aylard was persistent. In no hurry to let her go he took her arm and looked deep into her eyes, having to blink to try and keep his own in focus. His face was lethargic and sleepy looking now he had stopped grinning for the moment. 'I think you are wonderful. Do you know that every man in this room is madly in love with you?'

Gerald Buckley, one of his more sober friends, seeing Angelina throw him a look of helpless appeal, came to her aid. 'Steady on, old man. You'll end up making an ass of yourself. As you can see, Countess, my friend isn't himself right now. Since his luck at the tables tonight he's imbibed too much.'

Angelina gave him a smile of tolerant understanding as Lord Aylard waved him away dismissively.

'Go away, Gerald,' he snorted. 'The Countess and I are going to dance. You do want to dance with me, don't you Countess?'

'No—really…' Angelina laughed, resisting his arms, which seemed to be all over the place. 'If I dance with you in your present state, I fear we are both in danger of ending up in a heap on the floor—and then where will my dignity be? You have drunk far too many glasses of champagne.'

'That's because I am celebrating my colossal win at tables.'

'I know. Why, your face is almost the same colour as your waistcoat.'

Lord Aylard looked down at his flamboyant scarlet-and-gold waistcoat with pride, puffing out his chest. 'It is rather splendid, isn't it?'

'It—certainly catches the eye.'

He grinned. 'Gerald here doesn't like it,' he said, turning his back on his friend, who was hovering close in case Angelina should have need of his protection. 'Says it's much too brash—but I think it's rather elegant.'

'You certainly have distinctive taste. Now, please excuse me. I simply must return to my husband.'

'I have a plan,' Lord Aylard said, catching her arm and half-lowering his eyelid in a conspiratorial wink. 'Why don't you ditch that devilishly handsome husband of yours and run off with me?'

'I wouldn't dare. I value my life too much.'

'You are absolutely divine. Have I told you?'

'You do have a habit of repeating yourself.' Had it been anyone else behaving so outrageously, Angelina's sensitivity would have been offended, but she liked Lord Aylard too much to be cross with him.

He swayed, and it was no straight line he walked before he plonked himself down into a chair. Angelina gave a couple of quick little steps to avoid his hand as it reached out for her, but catching her heel in the train of her skirt, she tripped and lost her balance, unable to prevent herself from falling in an undignified heap in Lord Aylard's lap.

'Good Lord!' he exclaimed, his arm snaking round Angelina's waist. 'You are incredible, Countess. You really should run away with me, you know.'

'I think not,' Alex said.

Everyone, not least Angelina, was suddenly aware of a tall male presence. Alex had moved across the room with such speed and the silence of a panther that no one had seen him come. At a stroke amusement fled from the florid faces. Angelina froze. Her eyes were wide open, her expression incredulous. Their eyes met, Alex's glacial, his mouth drawn into a ruthless, forbidding line.

He glared down at Aylard. 'You, sir, forget yourself.' His voice was like steel. Tempted to commit murder, he restrained himself, but it was an effort.

Lord Aylard's friends stood back with the wary disbelief of the innocent and uninvolved. Quickly Angelina sprang up from Lord Aylard's lap, but he remained sprawled out in the chair, his senses and his body too anaesthetised by champagne to be concerned by the threatening menace emanating from the formidable Earl of Arlington. Making no attempt to rise, he grinned inanely up at Alex—seeing double.

'Hello, Montgomery. Would you care to join us for a glass of champagne—or is it to be pistols at dawn?'

Alex subjected him to a look of severe distaste and chilling contempt. 'You're drunk, Aylard, and not worth the shot.' His eyes sliced to his wife. 'If you are ready, Angelina, we will say goodnight to our hosts.'

* * *

With a mask of feral rage, on reaching the house Alex marched Angelina into her bedchamber. His eyes sliced to Pauline. 'You may go to bed. Your mistress will not be needing you tonight.'

After Pauline had wordlessly made a hasty retreat, Angelina waited for the onslaught of her husband's fury. She deeply regretted the unfortunate incident that had occurred. Alex was a proud man and she had foolishly made him an object of public ridicule. It would be no simple matter placating him.

Drawing a quick breath, she tried to swallow her mounting alarm by saying, 'Really, Alex. If you are going to be difficult, might I suggest you go to bed.'

His look cut through her. The anger and rage were gone from him. What there was instead was ice. 'I intend to. With you. But I have a matter to settle with you first, lady.'

'I thought you might.'

'Damn it,' he snapped, raking his fingers through his hair and pacing the room with angry, frustrated strides. 'Are you so simple that you didn't know what you were doing? Have you forgotten so soon that you are a lady and my wife? The incident with Aylard would not have happened if you had done as you were told and stayed with me.'

'And how could I know that?' she flared. 'I am not some trained pet to do as it's told. You were engaged in conversation with someone else—and I saw someone I wished to speak to, so I left.'

'And when I next saw you you were cavorting with Aylard on his knee. How dare you play and flirt with that man so shamelessly?' he accused, his anger making him unreasonable, for he had seen her trying to distance herself from Aylard before she had tripped and overbalanced into his lap. 'I will not stand by and watch you parade and flaunt yourself brazenly before Aylard and his friends as though it pleases you to make me a laughing stock.'

Angelina gasped. 'Alex! That's not fair. I think you forget yourself.'

'Oh, no, lady. It's you who forget yourself. It's you who plays the strumpet with Aylard.'

Stung by his insult Angelina clenched her fists by her sides and her cheeks flamed. 'I object to that. How dare you say that to me? I tripped and accidentally fell on to his knee. And I am not a strumpet.'

'Then why were you behaving like one?'

'Oh, you mule-headed oaf. I was not. You make too much of it. Lord Aylard was—'

'Drunk out of his skull,' Alex shouted, throwing his arms in the air in exasperation.

'And are you always so very civilised and proper?' she mocked.

'My own behaviour is not the issue.'

'Had it been anyone else's lap I'd fallen into, you wouldn't have turned a hair. The mere presence of Lord Aylard at the party was cause enough to tweak your nose. When will it penetrate that thick skull of yours that you have nothing to be jealous of? He accosted me when I had been speaking to an acquaintance.'

Alex stopped pacing the carpet, his eyes snapping to hers. 'What acquaintance?'

Realising her mistake too late, Angelina remained silent. Her husband's brows knit together.

'What's this?' he seethed savagely, moving closer, his eyes, refusing to relinquish their hold on hers, a terrifying gleam visible and deadly in their depths. 'More secrets? Don't dig the hole deeper for yourself, Angelina. What is needed in this marriage is less secrets—not more.'

'What do you mean by that?'

'You went to speak to Lady Broadhurst, didn't you?'

Angelina raised her chin, trying to look scornful and proud, despite the trembling in her limbs. 'Yes, I did.'

'Dear Lord. My patience as a husband is fast running out.'

'Then perhaps you shouldn't have married me in the first place. Perhaps I chose the wrong husband,' she flared daringly.

Alex's eyes narrowed and he moved closer still, so close that Angelina could feel his hot breath fanning her face. 'If you had chosen anyone else, lady, one thing you can be sure of is that he would not have been as considerate as I have been. He would not have spent his wedding night alone and the subsequent four weeks. Now, get your clothes off and get into bed,' he ordered coldly, his eyes looking directly into hers, leaving her in no doubt as to his meaning and intention. 'This is one night I will not sleep alone.'

'Whose bed, my lord?' Angelina asked, as he was about to go to his own rooms to undress. With her elbows akimbo and her fingers drumming on her hips, her manner mocked him. It bore the submissive tones one might expect of a chattel. 'Shall I get into my own bed to await your pleasure, or yours?'

Alex ignored her overstated humility. An almost lecherous smile tempted his lips as his eyes swept her bed. 'Which bed do you prefer?'

'Neither.'

'Angelina,' he said softly. The warning in his narrowed eyes and in his voice was unmistakable.

For a moment she shrank from him, her tender eyes darkening in fear. But then her soft lips tightened and her chin came up proudly. 'Very well, then. Considering I've never seen your bed—let it be my own.'

'The fact that you have never seen my bed is not my fault. Now get undressed. I'll be back in a minute,' he said, striding to the connecting door and opening it, his long fingers forcefully unfastening his cravat as he went.

'And what if I have no desire to sleep with you, Alex?' Angelina persisted, knowing she was provoking his anger to dangerous heights, but she would do anything to stave off the moment when she would have no choice but to get into that huge bed with her husband in his present mood. 'I would remind you of the promise you made.'

Without warning he exploded. Slamming the door, he bore down on her relentlessly. Grabbing her by the shoulders, he gripped her with a violence that ripped the breath from her lungs as his fingers bruised her flesh.

'Until you tell me what happened to you in Ohio, you will not mention that time to me again. If you do—so help me God I swear you will regret it,' he said, speaking through clenched teeth. His fingers did not relinquish their brutal grip as he thrust his enraged face close to hers. His eyes were narrowed, the silver orbs burning ruthlessly down into her own, his anger surmounted by growing passion. 'I am heartily sick of it. I will not stand aside and watch you sacrifice our whole future because you cannot bring yourself to speak of it or forget. I refuse to let you go on moping, of seeing it haunt you. I'm damned if I will allow this situation to continue.'

He thrust her from him roughly. 'Take off those bloody clothes and prepare yourself—and let there be no tears, no virginal platitudes, no outraged modesty or cries of shame. Love me or hate me, Angelina, I will have my own way—especially in my bedroom. Whether you consider it a duty or a pleasure—one way or another it will be done. If you do not remove your clothes, I shall personally remove them myself.'

Her chest heaving, her cheeks aflame, Angelina glared at him. 'You wouldn't dare.'

His dark brows rose. 'Try me. You have precisely the time it takes me to remove my own to find out.'

Chapter Thirteen

When Alex strode back into the room two minutes later in a maroon velvet robe and saw her still fully clothed, her eyes blazing defiantly, his own were a fierce white hot heat. Slowly he moved towards her.

'Perhaps I did not make myself clear before.'

'You made yourself perfectly clear, my lord.'

'Well?'

'It is simply that since you took it upon yourself to dismiss my maid, I cannot reach to unfasten the buttons down the back of my dress.'

'Then allow me.'

Angelina turned her back, standing perfectly still while his fingers quickly released the row of innumerable tiny buttons from their loops.

'I can tell you have done this before,' she commented drily.

'Correct.' Task complete, he stood back.

Turning to face him, Angelina kept her eyes fixed on his, taking strength from her anger. Slipping her gown off her shoulders, she pushed it down over her petticoat and stepped out of it, kicking it to one side and making no attempt to go any further.

Hands on hips, Alex quirked a questioning brow. 'Do you prefer to remove the rest yourself, or would you like me to oblige.'

Angelina struck a mountain of stubbornness as great as his, and with one glorious movement she drew her petticoat over her head and flung it on to the floor. Although no word passed her lips, the look in her eyes as she silently met his gaze was one of pure mutiny.

'I will die before I let you touch me,' she hissed.

A crooked smile accompanied his reply. 'Then die, lady, because I am not leaving. Pray continue.'

'Go to hell,' she breathed, the flush of anger deepening over the delicate softness of her cheeks, knowing that without her clothes she would have no protection against those probing eyes.

Her gaze was scornful, as challenging as his own. But Alex was determined. When he moved closer Angelina did not flinch as his fingers gently shoved the thin straps off her shoulders and down her arms, slowly peeling the bodice down and exposing her pert, soft young breasts.

With outraged modesty she had an urge to cover herself with her arms, but with a superhuman effort she managed to conquer her fear and refrain from doing so. As she held his gaze her anger overrode the shock of finding herself almost naked. She allowed his hands to do what she had vowed she would never let happen to her again—to touch her bare flesh, to cup the gentle swell of her breast—and Alex, suspecting what was going through her mind, thanked God for her spirit, for it had given her what she needed to exorcise her fear of what inevitably must happen between them.

Compassion flashed across his features as he caught a fleeting glimpse of the naked pain in the translucent depths of her eyes, and at the sight the demon anger relaxed its grip on him at last. But then his jaw tightened. For some obscure reason he wanted her to maintain her anger, for it would help sustain her over the coming moments until her desire was aroused, and to do that he must remain firm.

It was a difficult moment for Angelina. She wanted to keep an air of cold disdain, to face her husband in calm defiance, but her mauled pride and aching memory of the past assailed her senses. Momentarily a rush of tears blinded her, and she was furious with herself that she should display such weakness. When she saw his gaze resting on her with something akin to pity, it was too much for her to bear. It came to her mind that the time had come to consummate their marriage, and desperately she sought to delay that moment.

'Alex, let me go.'

'Not a chance.'

An iron-thewed arm snaked around her waist and his mouth swooped down on to hers. Like a tigress Angelina struggled violently against him, but she was no match against the power of his arms, imbued with even greater strength by the charged passion overwhelming him. When his lips left hers she breathed deeply, feeling the rising pleasure, the kindling of desire that threatened to smother her reason. Suddenly it was all too much. She shook her head, drawing back in his arms.

'Don't. Please don't,' she begged. 'Please don't make me.'

'Why not?' Alex murmured, dragging his lips down the slender curve of her neck. 'Are you as cold as you would have me think?'

She tried to shove away from him, but his arms tightened around her. 'Oh, no, my angel, my little tease. You have flouted my authority and tormented my senses for long enough. Now I have you—now your reckoning is upon you.'

Angelina arched her back as he held her, pressing her body close to his, his lips caressing and burning her bare skin like fire as he lowered his head to her breasts. To Angelina he seemed larger, more powerful than she had ever seen him, and, strain as she did, she couldn't break free.

Suddenly some protective barriers snapped inside Alex and he scooped her up into his arms.

Angelina's breath came in heated spasms. 'Please don't. Oh, please. I loathe you—I hate you.'

Her words came on a breath and without conviction. Alex's grin was almost fiendish. 'I know, my pet, and you can hate and loathe me to your heart's content—in bed.'

Suddenly she felt the downy softness of the bed beneath her back. In desperation she resumed her struggle, but somehow Alex managed to tear away what remained of her garments and strip off his robe.

She gasped, her eyes widening at the sight of her husband towering over her, his body eternally masculine and primeval in its naked power. Her shocked reaction to his nakedness brought a smile to his lips and a low chuckled sounded in the back of his throat.

'So, my love, I have your full attention now.'

In an attempt to cover her own nakedness she reached for the covers, but he tore them from her grasp and snatched her to him, his eyes capturing hers, challenging.

'No, Angel,' he said, his eyes telling her there would be no denial as there had been in the past. He would not be turned away with this craving hunger eating away at the pit of his belly. 'There will be no more barriers between us. I will look at my wife, as is my right. Now and always.'

The softness in his tone and the tender, compelling light in his eyes reassured and calmed her. Fighting him was futile. Besides, physical resistance would be useless against his unswerving seduction. She waited for the screaming denial to come from that dark corner of her mind she had kept locked for so long, determined to ban its intrusion. But there was nothing, only a strange, empty silence. She lowered her hands that had risen to push Alex away, one of them covering part of the flesh from her naval to her groin whilst the other reached up and brushed her fingertips against his warm, sensual lips with a tenderness that astounded him, her eyes silently telling him that she had no thought of holding back or refusing him.

'Then look, Alex,' she said softly, 'and tell me what you see.'

His lean, handsome features were starkly etched above her. As she watched his eyes course down the supple curves of her body, over the proud swell of her breasts and narrow waist, to the beckoning curves and soft, secret hollows and shadows of her hips, she tried not to remember the agony of the last time her body had been laid bare for other eyes to look at, when, in shame and humiliation, she had wanted to die. But this time it was Alex looking at her, not a stranger but her husband, and she loved him with all her heart and soul.

Angelina's voluptuous bloom of womanhood evoked in Alex a strong stirring of desire. He could not believe how much he wanted her, that the body his own had so fiercely craved for so long lay alongside him. His hand reached out and gently traced the outline of her hip, his fingers moving over her slender waist and on to her breast, cupping its fullness.

'Have you any idea how lovely you are, Angel—how adorable, or how much I want you?' he murmured huskily. Her hair had come loose from its pins in the struggle and lay in luxuriant, tangled disarray around her head like a vibrant halo. Alex's eyes were hungry and dark with passion, and, unable to resist her a moment longer, he leaned over, covering her mouth with his own, snatching her breath away, teasing her lips when they opened to his. Her lips were warm, eager and sweet as sweet could be.

Slowly his hand slipped about her waist as he drew her body against his so that they were touching full length, while he kissed her in a passionate frenzy, amazed and intrigued by the mixture of innocence, boldness and fear which fired this woman. At first he had intended to take her swiftly, but now he had no such haste in mind. One thing he was sure of—he would not stop until he had achieved what he intended and sealed their vows securely in a physical knot of passion. Nothing short of an earthquake would prevent him making love to her now he'd started. He would make her body sing with rapture before he was done.

Angelina could not believe the pain of ecstasy increasing within her. Where his hand had gone before, so his lips followed. He would have gone further still, but a straight silver scar running from just below her waist to her groin caught his eye. Her arm had concealed it earlier, which was the reason why he had not seen it.

Momentarily he paused. His whole being silently screamed when he saw the evidence of what he knew those savages had done to her, the pain they must have put her through. Please God, let that be all they had done to her, that, despite telling him her virtue was still intact, she had not been violated. He clenched his eyes until the screaming had stopped, feeling her hands as they sought him, wondering why his caresses had stopped—and then she knew. He brought his face on a level with her own, his expression hard, his eyes filled with an intensity and something else that she could not define.

'Alex—please don't look like that.'

'Did those savages do that to you?'

She nodded, her eyes bright with unshed tears, her face tormented.

Alex scooped her into his arms, cradling her head in the hollow of his shoulder, burying his face in her tumbling, sweet scented hair and feeling a deep surge of compassion and grieving. 'God above, how you must have suffered—how they must have hurt you. Little wonder you hated being touched.'

Angelina raised her head and looked at him. 'Don't. Please don't make me remember—not now. You told me you could make me forget, Alex. Please try. Kiss me,' she murmured, her lips close to his own.

Alex needed no prompting as he captured her mouth in an all-consuming kiss, rousing her sensations and persuading her heart to beat in a frantic rhythm. His hands stroked downwards over the curve of her hips and then upwards along the velvet softness inside her thighs. She gasped, reflexively tensing her muscles and clamping her legs together. Alex felt her resistance and groaned.

'Angelina, please, my love,' he said huskily, his face taut with restraint. 'Trust me. Relax, my darling.'

Above her Angelina could see his face was hard, his eyes dark with passion, and yet there was so much tenderness in their depths that her heart ached. But it was the desperate need she heard in his voice that made her respond.

His blood spilling through his veins like molten lava, Alex rose above her and lowered his hips between her thighs, seeing fear and sudden panic in her wide eyes when she felt the probing, burning heat of his maleness intruding into her delicate softness.

'I'm sorry, Angel,' he whispered, his hands moving behind her and raising her hips. 'I'm going to hurt you.'

With a faint sob Angelina wrapped her arms around his neck, pressing her face against the base of his throat when she felt the unrelenting pressure against her tight, resisting flesh, feeling his rigid hardness inch its way into her soft warmth. Her body jerked and she gasped when he breached the barrier and buried himself deep inside her, a burning pain exploding in her loins. She clung to him, digging her nails into his back, but he seemed not to notice.

Waiting for the pain of his intrusion to subside, Alex found her lips and kissed her with a long, leisurely thoroughness that soon turned her pain into a hungering, throbbing ache. He filled her fully, touching all of her. It was incredible, and as she slowly began to move as he moved, beauty and something wonderful began to happen to her body.

Fury of a moment ago had become raw hunger, her fears

burnt beneath the scorching heat of their mutual desires as they were merged into one being, husband and wife, wrapped in the absolute bliss of their union. The awakened fires, the bittersweet ache of desire so long restrained, overwhelmed them both. They were two beings fused together in a spinning eddy of passion. And then ecstasy as they came closer still, and Angelina felt his seed erupt, spilling into her, their lives merging. She gasped and cried out, unable to stop the words that sprung naturally to her lips as she was torn into a thousand shimmering pieces.

'I love you.' Whether Alex heard or not she had no way of knowing.

Holding her close with his lips against hers, he waited until the flame that had ignited them both subsided and they relaxed. Sated, a fine film of perspiration glistening on his body, his hair damp, his breathing deep, he moved his weight from her and pulled her into his arms as he came down from the unparalleled heights of passion she had just sent him to. In all his years of amorous liaisons, not once had he ever come close to the shattering ecstasy he'd just experienced. His wife was innocence and wantonness, passionate and sweet.

Angelina sighed and melted into her husband's embrace, unable to believe that she could feel such joyous elation quivering inside. She was overjoyed that she had been able to give Alex what he had desired and sought from her since making her his wife, and her only regret was that she had made him wait so long—that she had denied them both the pleasure they were able to give each other. If only she had known it could be like this. Now she did, Alex would find her an eager, willing wife.

'Are you still angry with me?' she whispered, her dark eyes awash with tears of happiness, lingering passion and innocence.

Alex reached out and gently smoothed her tumbled locks from her face, tracing his finger down the soft curve of her cheek. He gazed at her with something akin to awe and reverence, feeling humbled by her beauty and her unselfish ardour and uninhibited giving of herself.

'On the contrary, Angel. How do you feel?' he asked, his voice gentle, his gaze so tender that Angelina's heart contracted.

'Like your wife,' she murmured, placing her lips gently on his chest.

'Then why do you weep?'

'It's happiness that makes me weep,' she reassured him. 'Happiness and freedom—and the final shattering of a door I have kept locked and bolted in my mind for far too long. Oh, Alex,' she said, trailing her arm over his lean waist and sighing against him, reflecting on their love-making, 'thank you for being so understanding and patient with me. But now I know what I've been missing I wish you hadn't.'

'So do I, sweetheart. So do I,' he chuckled softly.

'You could have forced me.'

'I could. But I was not willing to gamble with so precious a prize. I had no wish for you to hate me for ever more. But you were well worth the wait.'

'And did you wait?' she whispered, feeling uncomfortable as she asked the question, but she had to know.

Alex frowned, lowering his head better to see her face. 'What do you mean, Angelina? What are you asking?'

Suddenly she wished she hadn't spoken. 'Oh, it—it doesn't matter. Forget I asked.'

Taking her shoulders, Alex forced her to look at him. 'Yes, it does matter,' he said quietly. 'You wouldn't have asked otherwise. So ask me.'

'When you left Arlington—you—you led me to believe that you—you were coming to London to—'

'Avail myself of a mistress,' he finished for her. Drawing her into his arms, he silently cursed, loathing himself for causing her pain. 'No, my love. I've been an idiot. I was angry when I left Arlington and I wanted to punish you for refusing me your bed. Since I returned to London my mind has been too full with thoughts of you to think about seeking another woman to relieve my lusts. I know I implied that I would and that was a mistake. My regret is that I hurt you. Condemn me for saying it if you must, but I can be pardoned for not doing so. Besides, you're the one I want. No other.'

A warmness stole over Angelina, bringing a smile to her lips. 'I'm glad. Thank you, Alex.'

'My pleasure,' he murmured, smiling tenderly into her upturned face and bending his head to caress her lips lightly with his own. When his mouth left hers his hooded eyes smouldered with renewed desire as they moved with leisured thoroughness over her delicately hued curves, his loins already hardening in demanding response to her nearness. 'Now, speaking of pleasure…'

Angelina's mouth curved in a sublime smile while her eyes grew dark and sultry. The heat of his gaze set her blood on fire and set her heart racing with sweet anticipation. 'Yes?'

'There's more,' he told her, nuzzling her ear.

Her eyes opened wide. 'There is?'

'I'm afraid so. I don't think I can blame Aylard for coveting you, Angel. What man could be indifferent to a woman like you? I find myself completely enamoured with this beautiful sprite that came into my life with such panache. There is something about you that makes a man commit the wildest follies. Oh, Angel, my sweet. You have the power to make my life hell. One must either love you to distraction or strangle you.'

Drawing back from his lips, which were about to descend upon hers once more, Angelina eyed him closely. 'And what would you choose, Alex? You haven't strangled me yet—so can I assume you—?'

Realising the folly of his words and what she was about to ask him, Alex placed a finger on her lips, silencing her. 'Not now, Angel. There is much, much more I have to teach you in the way of pleasing me.'

Angelina was hurt by his reply, but did not show it. 'Then teach me,' she murmured, her sensual lips quirking in a half-smile, a rosy blush covering her soft cheeks. 'It would seem I have some catching up to do, so I think we should begin my lessons right away.'

Alex's happiness shattered the moment he read Angelina's note. Incapable of any kind of rational thought, what he felt at that moment was raw, red-hot anger. As he prepared to leave for Kent, his volcanic anger grew, and it wasn't until he left London that it began to abate and he realised that he may have been too hard and insensitive to her desire to see her grandmother.

On a sigh and a whimsical smile tugging at the corners of his mouth, he admitted the truth of it. At twenty-nine years old and more women than it was decent to confess to, he had fallen victim to a beautiful, courageous, nineteen-year-old innocent, who was in possession of an undesirable streak of fiery rebellion, who constantly taunted, mocked and incurred his displeasure at every turn. He felt his body tense as the unfamiliar emotion drove into him like a physical force, becoming aware that his reticence had been eroded by that stifling, most destructive of all emotions, making the paradox of his passions and conflicting needs difficult to control.

Despite everything, he was now in no doubt that he loved Angelina, that what they had together was real and transcended anything else. It filled him with a sense of wonder, want and hunger—an ultimate love that can only be understood by the two people involved.

When Lady Broadhurst had left, Angelina waited for the housekeeper to tell Lady Anne of her arrival. The house was quiet, its walls exuding something of the old days that was stable and unchanging. The sound of her mother's laughter drifted through her mind, while the face of her father passed ghostlike through her memory. Tears pricked her eyes and sadness claimed her heart. They had been happy as a family, which was nothing now but a vacant shadow in her memory.

Her gaze came to rest on a picture over the mantelpiece. It was of a young woman in a blue gown, her hair arranged in exquisite curls around a heart-shaped face. Her smile was enigmatic, and the warm intensity of her eyes gazed back at her with eyes that were extraordinarily alive.

It was her mother.

Angelina's heart wrenched, her gaze clinging to that achingly familiar face, as if, by dint of will, she could hold on to remembrances of her life in Ohio with her mother and father before the Shawnee had come. The woman she saw in the picture was a woman she had never known. It touched her deeply.

When she was admitted to her grandmother's room, there was a lump in Angelina's throat and tears pricked the backs of her eyes as she moved slowly towards a small, frail old lady. There was a calm serenity about her features. She was dressed in a beribboned pale pink robe covering her nightdress and a blanket was tucked around her legs.

Angelina could only stand and look at the woman on the sofa, all the questions dammed up in her mouth. Sensing her discomfort, Lady Anne, who had absorbed every detail of this lovely young woman, smiled reassuringly and stretched out her hand, indicating that Angelina should sit in the chair close by her.

'So, you are my granddaughter,' she said softly. 'You are so like your mother. You have her eyes.'

'Yes,' Angelina replied, sitting down. 'Although I have my father's colouring. I am sorry that I come here as a stranger.'

'You are not a stranger to me, my dear. And it is not natural for those who are so close to be strangers to each other. But I have an unfair advantage. You see, I have known of your existence since your arrival in England. The papers have been full of the Duke of Mowbray's beautiful young American ward—

Angelina Hamilton. Of course, I realised you had to be Lydia's daughter—and that my lovely Lydia must have died and placed you in the care of her cousin, Henry Montgomery. I also read about your recent marriage to the Earl of Arlington—which was very grand, by all accounts.'

'My only regret is that you weren't there to share it with me. It would have made my wedding complete. Why didn't you write to me?'

'Because I suspected your mother would have told you I was dead. Am I right?' she asked, arching a quizzical brow.

Angelina bowed her head as a deep sadness crept over her. 'Yes.'

'I did not know how you would feel if I wrote to you, that perhaps you would bear some resentment.'

'Of course I wouldn't. It wasn't until yesterday that I discovered you were not dead after all.'

'How did you find out that I wasn't?'

'I met Lady Broadhurst. I was shocked when she told me.'

'And you came directly,' Lady Anne murmured, touched by Angelina's eagerness to meet her.

'Lady Broadhurst was returning to Kent and she very kindly let me accompany her.'

'I see. And your husband? He did not come with you?'

'No.'

'He does know you're here?'

'Oh, yes. I—I left him a note.'

'A note? Dear me. From what I know of him, I believe the Earl of Arlington is renowned for his formidable temper. Was it wise to leave London without telling him?'

'No, not really. Alex does have the devil's own temper, and I know he will be absolutely livid. But I couldn't wait to meet you—and I was so concerned when Lady Broadhurst told me about your accident that I wanted to come at once. How are you feeling now?'

'Much better. My legs don't always do what they should, but I make a point of going downstairs during the afternoon and coming back upstairs after dinner.'

'I'm so glad I came. I knew that if I didn't leave with Lady Broadhurst, it might have been weeks—or even months—before Alex allowed me to come.'

'Am I to understand that he does not approve of you visiting me?'

'No—I mean—yes. But not until I had written to you and spoken to Uncle Henry first.'

Lady Anne looked at her intently. 'I can understand that. So, should we expect a visit from your husband?'

'It's very likely. In any case, he'll have to come to fetch me home.'

Lady Anne smiled, a smile so amazingly young and mischievous that Angelina was astonished, and she saw in her eyes a restless vitality that had been her mother's. 'Then I shall look forward to meeting him—and we must prepare ourselves as best we can to placate him. I—believe he bears a strong resemblance to his uncle.'

'They are very alike. Poor Alex. I led him a merry dance when I first came to England—America was so very different and to him I was just an awkward, ill-bred girl from the backwoods. I'm grateful to Aunt Patience and her daughter Verity, who helped and supported me enormously.'

'Patience is my niece, but we haven't seen one another for years,' Lady Anne replied with a note of regret. 'You would have found out about me in time, you know. This house and everything else I own will be yours one day.'

This had not even entered Angelina's head and the knowledge of it astounded her. 'Will it? But—but I didn't—oh, Grandmother!' she gasped, horrified that her grandmother might think she had come to stake her claim on her inheritance. 'Please don't think I came because of that.'

She smiled and patted her hand. 'I don't think you came for anything other than to see a sad and lonely old lady.'

Angelina suddenly realized how she had addressed the older woman—that she had called her 'Grandmother'. It was only a word and it had tripped off her tongue naturally, but there was a world of feeling in it, and Angelina sensed that there was a need in them both for some of the familiarity and warmth of kinship. 'Are you really sad and lonely?'

'I missed your mother so much when she married your father and went to live in America—more so when Jonathan, your grandfather, died.'

'What went wrong between you and my mother? Why did you never write to her?'

'In the beginning I wrote to her many times, but—but the letters were never posted,' she confessed. 'Your grandfather was not an easy man to get on with—and Lydia was not of a submissive nature. Things happened that were extremely upsetting at the time and are not easy to explain. They are wounds best not reopened, my dear,' she said quietly, and there was something in the tone of her voice and the expression in her eyes that told Angelina not to question further. 'Tell me—was she happy?'

'Yes, she was.'

'And—and was Henry with her at the end?'

'Yes.'

'I'm glad,' Lady Anne said after a prolonged silence. 'Now I know that my darling Lydia would have died happy.' Smiling at Angelina and taking her hand, she held it affectionately. 'There is so much I want to tell you about Lydia as a child, Angelina. You will stay with me for a few days, won't you?'

'If I may. I will leave you to rest now, Grandmother. I can see you're tiring.' After placing a gentle kiss on the old woman's cheek, she moved to the door.

'Angelina?'

She turned and looked back. Their eyes met with an intensity that was far beyond words.

'I'm so glad you came.'

Angelina smiled. 'So am I. Now we have met we shall not lose each other.'

The following afternoon when Angelina entered her mother's old room, the first thing that she became aware of was the familiar, subtle smell of jasmine. In that room she felt close to her mother and she loved her in death as she had in life, with a pure and filial love devoid of selfish need. Lovingly she touched the silver-backed mirror and hairbrush on the dressing table, seeing that strands of her mother's hair still clung to the bristles. Unable to stem the tears and the tide of grief, she lay prostrate on the bed, too wretched to move.

When she arose at last, all cried out, she sat on the window seat, drawing her knees up to her chin and wrapping her arms round her legs as she gazed out over the well-kept garden to the green meadows and woods beyond. Everything was serene and dappled with sunshine, and she wondered how many times her mother had sat on the same seat, looking out as she did now, and what her dreams had been.

This was how Alex found her.

When he came in, Angelina stared at him, feeling her heart give a joyful leap. Gradually life began to flow back into her body. Placing her feet on the floor she stood up, watching him nervously as she waited for him to speak.

His face was inscrutable, and after a long moment he said, 'Darling, come here.'

His arms were open, and like a sleepwalker Angelina's legs moved to obey his summons, but, unable to wait, Alex met her halfway and pulled her against him, wrapping his arms around her. Angelina was startled. She had expected cold rage, for him to chastise her for disobeying him, not this. Never had she known a man who was so perplexing.

'You're not angry with me for coming here without asking you?' She tilted her head and stared into his fathomless silver gaze while his soft voice caressed her.

'It was not my intention to come in here and berate you, my love. I know this was your mother's room, and I am not so insensitive that I don't know what you must be going through. There are things to be said—matters to be settled between us— but they can wait until later.'

'Have you seen my grandmother?'

'Yes. We talked.'

'What about?'

His lips quirked in a wry smile. 'You,' he said, reaching up and tracing the curve of her cheek with his fingertips. 'She told me you were up here. When you didn't come down I didn't think you would mind if I came to find you.'

'No, I don't mind,' Angelina murmured. 'I'm glad you've come, Alex. Can—can I stay with my grandmother for a while?'

'If that's what you want.'

'And will you stay with me?'

He smiled down into her upturned face, his arms tightening about her slender body, feeling her breasts pressed against his chest and unable to suppress the exquisite sensation that passed through him. 'Try to stop me.'

Angelina gave him a wayward smile. 'After disappearing the way I did, you appear remarkably calm, my lord.'

'I wasn't, and for a man who has neither eaten nor slept since you took off from London like that, it's nothing short of a miracle that I am now. After reading your note, if I could have got to you within the hour I would happily have murdered you. You can thank your lucky stars you had a head start.' Taking her hand, he sat down on the window seat, pulling her down beside him. 'We'll stay here three or four days and then go on to Mowbray Park. Feel free to come and see your grand-mother whenever you wish, but don't stay too long, my love, because I really don't think I can do without you. And I would not want my wife to forget about me altogether when she is away from home.'

'I could never forget you,' she whispered after a moment, an aching lump beginning to swell in her throat. Without looking at him she raised his hand and solemnly placed her lips against his fingers. 'I love you, Alex. I love you as much as it is possible for a woman to love a man. I have loved you for so long, ever since you caught me taking a bath in your tub and you told me that you wanted me. And when I had my night-mare and you heard me crying, when you kissed me it sealed what I felt for you in my heart.' Raising her eyes, she looked at him, and the gentle yielding and the love in their melting dark depths defeated him. 'I hope you don't mind.'

'Mind?' The heartrending tenderness of her words sent a jolting tremor down Alex's spine. With a groan he snatched her into his arms, crushing her to him, and with a raw ache in his voice he said, 'Bless you, my darling. I don't deserve you.' Combing the hair from her face with his fingers, he tilted her head and kissed her lips tenderly, all the love that had been ac-cumulating over the months he had known her contained in that kiss. 'I love you,' he murmured, his breath warm against her lips. 'Though I would have been the last to admit it, I think I loved you even before that day I found you making use of my bathtub.'

Catching her breath, Angelina raised her brows in amaze-ment, silently questioning, hoping.

'I have come to realise just how much you mean to me,' he went on. 'When I sent you away from Arlington all those months ago, I went dead inside. You spoke the truth that night when you sought me out in my room. You accused me of being insecure and disenchanted with life. I remember how cruelly I mocked you for saying it, but you were right. I told you I did not need any woman's love—that I did not want it. But I can see now that I was wrong. I want your love, Angelina. All of it.

'So you see, my darling, you have caught me in the tenderest trap of all.' On a sigh and a whimsical smile tugging at the corners of his mouth, he admitted the truth of it. 'What we have transcends all else. You are a rare being, Angelina Hamilton, and I love you.'

'Montgomery,' she corrected with a teasing smile. 'My name is Montgomery now.' She kissed him gently. 'Thank you, Alex. That's the nicest, most wonderful thing you've ever said to me. I hope you mean it, because now that you've said it, I couldn't bear it if you didn't.'

'I'll never lie to you,' he promised quietly, and she believed him.

Chapter Fourteen

After dinner—during which Lady Anne gave them an insight into her daughter's life as she had been growing up, which Angelina listened to avidly—when they retired for the night Angelina knelt in front of the fire in the room she was to share with Alex. Clad in only her nightshift, she waited in a state of nervous anticipation for him to emerge from the dressing room.

When he appeared, attired in his robe, his face was inscrutable. Sensing he had something on his mind, she reached up and took his hand.

'What is it, Alex?'

He sat beside her, one leg propped up and an arm resting lightly on top of it, thinking how sensational she looked kneeling in front of him, with the glow from the fire shining on her, warming the amber and gold lights in her hair.

'Earlier I said that there were things to be said, matters to be settled between us.'

'I know. But does it have to be now?'

'I'm afraid so.' Slipping his arm about her shoulders, he could feel her soft flesh beneath the thin material of her nightshift. He was eager to take her to bed and make love to her, but that must wait. They had to talk. The one remaining barrier that stood between them had to be demolished.

'Do you miss America very much, Angelina?'

'I miss Boston and my friends.' Her eyes softened as she gazed into the glowing embers of the fire, thinking poignantly of Will. 'They were people who were like me, ordinary and poor, but they were blessed with a special kind of happiness most English people will never know. They will never have kicked off their shoes to wade in the rivers to fish, to swim in those same crystal-clear waters, to ride the high mountains and low meadows, through forests, with nothing to depend on but your senses, the horse beneath you, and your rifle.'

'You make it sound wonderful, but I suspect it is anything but to those who aren't born to it,' he murmured, watching her with pride.

'It was wonderful to me. But now I am here and I have you. That is compensation enough.'

'I would like to see it one day.'

'You would?' Hope abounded in her heart.

'When the war between our countries is over, I'll take you back for a visit. Would that please you?'

Her eyes lit up joyously. 'Oh, yes. And shall we go to Boston?'

He laughed, planting a kiss on her shoulder. 'Anything my lady desires.'

'Oh, Alex. That would be wonderful.'

'On one condition.'

'Oh?'

'You will introduce me to your Will and Mr Boone.'

She kissed him. 'Done. Now, what do you want to say to me that is so important it must take precedence over you taking me to bed?'

Taking her chin between his long fingers, Alex forced her to look at him, the expression in his eyes suddenly grave. 'It's about secrets,' he said quietly.

'Secrets?' Angelina looked bemused, but then light dawned on her. 'No, Alex. Don't spoil it. Don't bring that up now. It doesn't matter any more.'

'It does matter,' he said with gentle firmness. 'Didn't your parents tell you that a trouble shared is a trouble halved—that two can bear a cross more easily than one?'

'Yes, but I don't want to go over it. Can't you understand that?'

Alex noticed a marked change in her mood. Despite the indications that she was likely to fly into a temper, his conscience and his need to shatter that final door in her mind forced him to press on. 'You may not want to tell me, Angelina, but can't you see that *I*, as your husband, need to know. Not knowing what happened to you is torturing me.'

Angelina's heart almost broke as she stared at him. It had never occurred to her that what had happened to her would affect him so deeply.

'All I want to do is to keep from losing my mind. To speak of it will be like reliving it.'

Angelina worried Alex with her last statement and the supplicant way in which she looked at him. It was like a frightened child pleading for help. He decided to push on. 'I will not let the matter rest until you tell me, Angelina.'

'I appreciate your worry about me, but you mustn't,' she said vehemently. Tears were forming in her eyes. 'I want to forget it.'

'It can't be done. It will always be there.'

'It isn't your problem.'

'Yes, it is. It became my problem when you married me. Share it with me, Angelina.'

Conscious of his scrutiny, suddenly agitated she got to her feet. 'How can you be so sure that telling you will make me feel better—that it will resolve everything?'

'I'm not saying that. But it will make me feel a damn sight better,' he said, standing up.

With tears spilling over her lashes, Angelina looked at him

long and hard before turning away, wrapping her arms around her waist as if to contain the horrors behind that locked door in her mind. Hysteria threatened her, and she put her hands on either side of her head, as if to relieve her over-burdened mind. No matter how she tried to push the memories from her, they returned, lapping inside her mind like an ascending sea. Still she hesitated, but she was beginning to realise that it was important for Alex to know. In the end she turned to confront him, and a flicker of sanity lit the chaos of her thoughts.

'I know you are right, Alex but—but—Oh, God…'

When Alex saw the tears and the fear steal into her eyes, he suddenly pulled her to him and held her very tight. Gently he brushed the hair from her face. Her lovely, luminous eyes were saturated when at last she drew back and looked at him, but, knowing what he was asking of her, she covered her face with her hands.

'I can't tell you the things they did to me.'

Alex removed her hands. 'Yes, you can.'

Shaking her head, she was gasping for breath, and Alex could only guess at the torment the Shawnee had inflicted on her, and he loathed himself for adding to it by forcing it out of her. As she turned away from him her thoughts were in chaos, her eyes registering horror as she realised that the door, kept closed and locked at such great cost for so long, was wide open, and she was about to let the horrors spill forth. Very slowly she took hold of her emotions, rigidly controlling herself as she turned once more to face him.

'You are right. I should tell you everything. I owe you that, at least.' She held his eyes a moment, and then her gaze slid away. Drawing a deep breath, she let it out harshly. 'It's difficult to know where to begin.'

Alex settled himself into a chair, crossing his legs, watching her calmly, his heart going out to her. 'When the Shawnee came would be as good a place as any,' he suggested quietly. 'It is clear the people and your parents living in the settlement were unprepared for the attack.'

'There is only so much people can do to prepare themselves for an attack on the scale the Shawnee launched on us that night.'

She paused, and, although Alex appeared calm, he waited in a state of nervous tension for her to go on, relieved when she did, but she wasn't looking at him, she was looking into the flames, as if the images of the past were marching with each dancing flame.

'I was asleep—it was the middle of the night. That's when they always came, furtively, usually to steal our livestock—but that night they came to kill and burn.' She wrapped her arms around her body and hugged herself as she remembered. 'Our cabin was away from the settlement, across the river. The settlement was on fire and I went to wake my parents, but they were already up and dressed. They told me to get dressed and stay in my room until it was safe to come out. Safe!'

Wringing her hands in front of her, she turned away and hugged herself again. She turned towards him, her brows knitting together. Watching her, Alex clenched his hands into fists, having to struggle to stop himself going to her and cradling her in his arms. Her voice tore through him, her face was ravaged, but he couldn't make it easier for her. He had to let her go on.

'I did as they bade me. I stood at my window and watched a lone Indian ride towards the cabin—and my father...' She faltered and began gnawing at her bottom lip. 'My—my father went out to him, and—and the Indian...'

'Did the Indian kill your father, Angelina?' Alex asked gently.

Tears sprang to her eyes and she nodded, swallowing hard and looking down at her hands. 'My father was a gentle man—not forceful or violent, and he—he never even raised his gun when the Indian swooped on him and split his head in two like he would an apple. Mother ran out of the cabin to help him and—and the Indian stabbed her in the back. She fell beside my father and I thought she was dead too.'

Her pain and anguish tore at Alex. Her body shook violently. He reached out his hand to comfort, to make the telling easier for her, but she jerked away.

'No, Alex. Don't touch me,' she cried in her wretchedness. 'If you do, I won't be able to tell you the rest of it—and I must. I hid in my room, in a corner, hoping the Indian wouldn't find me. But he did. When I heard him come in I was so frightened I thought I would die. I wanted to. I prayed for God to let me— but he didn't hear me. When the Indian saw me he—he dragged me out of the corner—and I fought him, Alex. I tried to get away from him, but he wouldn't let me,' she said, her words pouring out of her with such unmistakable pain. 'He was too strong for me, too big. And then he rolled me in a blanket and he—he hit me. Everything went black, and the next thing I knew I was in an encampment and it was still dark.'

She fell to her knees in front of her husband, reaching out and gripping his hands, as if she needed something to hold on to, as if by doing so some of his strength would pass to her, giving her added courage for what would come next.

'I was in a tepee and there were a lot of Indians. They—they ripped away my clothes—until—until—' she swallowed, her dark eyes huge, her voice barely above a whisper '—I didn't have any on at all. That was when one of them cut me with his knife—but I didn't feel the pain at first—not until later.'

Having seen the wound with his own eyes, Alex's face became taut and grim, his grip on her hands tightening, but she wasn't aware of it.

'I didn't know what they wanted, what they were doing— when they—when they— Oh, Alex—they—they touched me,' she cried brokenly and with so much wretchedness that his heart wrenched. 'They hurt me so much—and I was so ashamed and humiliated. I cried and begged them not to do it—but they wouldn't listen. Then they tied me up and left me alone while they went to drink the liquor they had taken from the settlement. I was bleeding so much, and I prayed to God to let me bleed to death so they couldn't hurt me any more.'

Something black and formless began to uncurl inside Alex. He had known something terrible had happened to her, thinking in his ignorance that it might be the manner in which her mother and father had been struck down before her eyes—that it might have been her mother who had been violated that haunted her— but not this. Never this. How alone she must have felt, how terrified. The full reality of what had happened to her came to him in that silent moment. But they hadn't raped her, thank God. But they might as well have raped her, for that's how it must have felt to an innocent, fifteen-year-old girl on the brink of womanhood.

As the full implication of what she was telling him began to sink in, he saw the truth at last, along with all the horror locked away inside her since that night. It made what had happened to him when he had been fifteen years old—when he had seen his own father blow out his brains—pale into insignificance. There was small wonder she had been afraid of being touched.

'Eventually the Indian who had captured me came back,' she went on, her voice controlled as she looked at a space beyond Alex. 'When he severed my bonds I scrambled away from him. But I slipped and fell to my knees. He clamped his hands around my throat and I thought he was going to strangle me. When he finally let me go he threw me down on to the blankets where I lay choking, gasping for breath. Somehow I managed to struggle to my knees but he grabbed hold of me, hauling and bruising me, shoving me back down.'

She fell silent, bowing her head over Alex's hands still gripping her own until she was able to go on. 'The Indian grabbed my arm and pulled me towards him. He fondled me, Alex, and tried to cover me with his vile body—laughing at me when I tried to wriggle free. I screamed, but my screams brought only laughter from the Indians outside.' With her head still bowed, silent tears of misery rolled down her cheeks onto Alex's hands. 'In desperation I fought him, but I was overpowered by his size and strength. He pinned my arms above my head and my terrified impulse was to submit to whatever it was he wanted to do to me, anything to stop him hurting me, but I knew that beyond that point something terrible awaited me—something vile and sinful.

'When the Indian released my arms and wedged a knee between my thighs, fearing I was about to be cast down into hell—I knew there could be no yielding. He had taken everything from me that I loved. I would not let him have more. I wasn't sure what he would do to me that he hadn't already done, but something inside my head told me there was more. That was when I reached out onto the ground and retrieved the knife he'd used to sever my bonds. It was all over in the blink of an eye—just as he was about to—to—violate me...' she whispered, avoiding Alex's eyes, unable to go on. Sitting back on her heels, she shuddered violently and covered her face with her hands.

Alex raised her up off her knees and dragged her to his chest, cradling her on his lap and wrapping his arms around her tightly, as if he would never let her go. 'You killed him,' he stated quietly.

She nodded, sobbing out her wretchedness. 'Do you hate me?'

'Hate you? Never that, my love. Don't you remember when I berated you for taking Forest Shadow from his stable, how you told me then that you had once killed a man for daring to lay his hands on you the way I did that day?'

Angelina gasped. 'Did I? I don't remember.'

'You were angry, and rightly so.'

'Then why do I feel so ashamed?' she wept.

'Don't. You brave, brave girl. What you did was for your own preservation. You cannot be blamed.'

Angelina's head shot back, and Alex was surprised at the pure cold hatred etched in every line of her lovely face as she remembered the look on the Shawnee's face, how, for a split second, he had seemed mesmerised by the very poise with which she held the knife, waiting for the inevitable thrust.

'What I remember is how I felt, Alex. At the time I was glad—glad the Indian was dead. Glad that I had killed him. I found it strange that I was no longer trembling. I raised my hand and stabbed at his heart and felt nothing when the blade sank into his flesh. He looked at me with surprise. Mercifully he uttered no sound as his whole weight fell on top of me. I shoved him off. Sitting up, I threw the knife on to the blankets, and for a short time I knew no pain, no fear. But it soon passed when I realised what I had done.

'I was glad he was dead, but I could not believe that I had killed him. Until then I had never raised a hand against another human being, but at that moment it felt no different to when I shot a rabbit or speared a fish in the river. Besides, I thought, it was no better than he deserved for killing my mother and father and abusing me. In that moment I forgot my parents' teachings—that it was a mortal sin to take a life, even in defence of one's own. All I could feel at that moment was an enormous relief.'

Tenderly Alex wiped away the strands of hair clinging to her wet face and tucked them behind her ears. 'What you did was no more than an act of personal survival—something anyone quick thinking and courageous would have done, faced with the same situation. How did you escape?'

'Will found me. He'd seen the Indian ride away with me from the settlement and followed. He cut his way into the tepee and helped me to escape. By that time the Shawnee were too drunk to notice. Will took me back to the settlement where he had left my mother. I couldn't believe she was still alive. After that we made our way back East, but for weeks afterwards we lived in fear that the Shawnee would catch up with us and exact their revenge for what I had done.'

Having emptied her heart, Angelina could not stem the grief and anguish that burst from her in a sea of tears and emotion. Slowly she crumpled down on to the carpet as if her weight and the weight of her anguish she could not sustain. Alex let her weep, hoping that by doing so she would cleanse her soul of all the ugliness that had defiled it for so long.

When her weeping subsided, she rose. Alex was standing beside the bed and the pull of his gaze was too strong for her to resist. It was as though he were looking into the very depths of her heart and soul. She felt the touch of his empathy like healing fingers touching and soothing her pain like a balm. She had seen in his eyes the reflection of her torment, and now, as though he were God's own advocate, he was offering her redemption.

Like a celestial being she moved towards him. She lay on the bed and Alex knelt beside her in reverence. Her fear was like a cutting edge and yet sublime, and when it left her she was wide open to a flood of wondrous new emotions. When she tasted the warmth of his lips, she felt all the love, the compassion and respect he carried for her in his heart, and when he finally took her the pleasure transcended anything she had known before.

Later, little remained of the girl who had been a victim of the Shawnee. She was a creature of the past. The mysterious alchemy of her inner self, mixed with elements inside Alex, had worked the miracle of transformation. The change in her was clear, and for the first time in three years Angelina felt at peace with herself.

Alex wrote to Henry from Tonbridge to inform him of their arrival. He also thought it best to warn him that Angelina had discovered that her grandmother was alive and had insisted on paying her a visit.

'You will not be too hard on Uncle Henry, will you, Angelina?' Alex said as they journeyed to Mowbray Park. 'I do not want this subterfuge on his part to cause a family rift. After all, he was only abiding by your mother's wishes.'

Angelina met her husband's eyes calmly. 'I am not angry, Alex. I am more concerned about how Uncle Henry feels now he knows I have found out that he lied to me. I do realise he was honour bound to my mother to keep the promise he made before she died. Did you know that he was in love with my mother?'

'Yes. But I did not find out from Uncle Henry.'

'Then who?'

A coldness entered Alex's eyes and his jaw tightened. 'My mother.'

'But—I don't understand?' After she had spoken Angelina suddenly recalled a conversation she'd had with Aunt Patience at Arlington, and that she had told her that Alex's mother had been in love with Uncle Henry. Alex's next words confirmed this.

'My mother had her sights set on Uncle Henry from an early age. Whether she had any deep, abiding affection for him or merely had her eyes set on his ducal title we will never know. Uncle Henry did not reciprocate her feelings and she took his rejection badly. To spite him she married my father, and went out of her way to punish him for Uncle Henry's rejection. In those days it would seem Uncle Henry had eyes for your mother and no other. However, both sets of parents considered the relationship incestuous, which was why they parted, but the fact that Uncle Henry never married tells me he never got over losing her.'

'It seems that one way or another we have both been touched—and damaged—by the love my mother and Uncle Henry bore each other.'

'That must have hurt you, knowing how much your father loved your mother.'

'It did. Deeply. My mother's and Uncle Henry's hearts and

minds were so clearly entwined, even after all the years in between. I sensed it when Uncle Henry came to America. It was as if I had stumbled on a secret, but I didn't want to think about it, because to do so would, in some peculiar way, be a betrayal to my father.'

'Didn't your grandmother tell you anything about what happened to cause the rift?'

'No—and I could see it was all too painful for her to remember. I believe it all stemmed from my grandfather being unforgiving in his attitude towards my mother's determination to thwart his authority. Grandmother told me that he strongly disapproved of my father—he had neither breeding nor substance, you see. My grandfather severed all ties with my mother—even though it broke my grandmother's heart. When she asked me if Uncle Henry was with my mother when she died and I told her he was, in a way she seemed relieved, as if a great burden had been lifted from her heart.' A sadness touched her eyes and she sighed. 'I'm rather glad I didn't know my grandfather. I don't think I would have liked him very much.'

'I think it wise that when you speak to Uncle Henry you don't probe into the past, Angelina. Let it be over.'

She looked at him, her eyes soft with love. 'Of course. That's what I want.'

After receiving them both, Henry faced Angelina, encouraged by the fact that she looked relaxed and was smiling her usual sweet smile.

'I'm sorry you had to find out about your grandmother like this, Angelina. Believe me when I tell you that I did not want to keep it from you, but your mother left me with no choice. I gave her my word, you see. I'm sorry if I hurt you.'

He held out his hand to her, his face pleading for her understanding. She took it in both her own, and she felt her heart go out to him.

'I don't blame you, Uncle Henry. I do understand why you didn't tell me. You couldn't break your word.'

Henry wondered how much she knew, how much her grandmother had told her. Did she know that the abiding love he and Lydia had felt for each other had been an affair doomed from the start, but while it lasted was filled with exquisite joy for the two lovers involved, who knew it was to end in heartbreak?

'Angelina, if you knew—'

'No, Uncle Henry,' she said quickly. 'You don't have tell me anything.' Reaching up, she tenderly placed a kiss on his cheek. 'I love you.'

They looked at one another, and smiled. Angelina's was one of love and understanding, Henry's one of gratitude.

Basking in naked splendour after a glorious night of love on their first night back at Arlington, nestling in the crook of her husband's arm, Angelina glanced up at him adoringly. With his head against the pillows and his tousled black hair falling over his brow, she could not believe how handsome he was. Sated and relaxed, he was the epitome of absolute, masculine contentment. Her heart abounded with love. When she placed a kiss on his chest he opened his eyes and let his silver gaze rest lovingly on her upturned face.

'What's this?' he whispered. 'Have I not tired you out, Angel?'

'Not quite,' she murmured, nestling her head against his shoulder and letting her hand wander over his chest in a leisurely caress. 'I feel too happy to go to sleep.' With a sigh she tipped her chin up so that she could gaze into his eyes. 'Have I told you how much I love you, Alex Montgomery?'

A lump of emotion swelled in Alex's chest and his heart lurched, as it never failed to do when she said those words to him. For the first time in his life he was filled with a sense of well being. She was the first woman to tell him that she loved him and mean it, and it filled him with wonder, gratitude and love.

'I have heard you mention it, and I don't want you to ever stop saying it,' he murmured in the gentlest voice Angelina had ever heard. 'I want to hear you say it every minute of your life. I can only count myself fortunate that you share my life and will continue to do so for many years to come.'

'It is my most heartfelt wish,' she whispered achingly.

'I love you too, my darling, and since you are the one who has shown me how to, no one has a better claim to it than you.'

Angelina sighed deeply, pressing her lips against his chest, her sweet-scented hair spilling over him. 'And I have triumphed against all the odds. I have you to thank for unlocking the door to my past. Now I am free.'

'No, you're not.' Alex raised her up and placed a hand on each side of her face, forcing her to look directly at him, looking at her with a combination of awe and reverence. 'You, my love, belong to me now—as I belong to you. We are pledged to each other—you and I—body and soul. We are partners for life, bound together for good or ill.'

For Angelina the world seemed to tilt when his mouth, hot and hungry, claimed her own. 'I would have it no other way, Alex,' she whispered against his lips, knowing the truth of it.

* * * * *

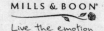

THE STEEPWOOD

Scandals

*Regency drama, intrigue, mischief...
and marriage*

VOLUME FOUR

An Unreasonable Match by Sylvia Andrew

Hester has learnt the hard way that men look for pretty
faces, not stirring debate. Accepting of her life as a
spinster, the last thing Hester wants is to accompany her
family to London for another Season.

❧

An Unconventional Duenna by Paula Marshall

Athene Filmer seizes the opportunity to act as a
companion to her decidedly timid friend when she
enters the *ton*. Could this be Athene's chance to
make a rich marriage?

On sale 2nd February 2007

*Available at WHSmith, Tesco, ASDA,
and all good bookshops*

M&B

A young woman disappears.
A husband is suspected of murder.
Stirring times for all the neighbourhood in

THE STEEPWOOD

Scandals

Volume 1 – November 2006
Lord Ravensden's Marriage by Anne Herries
An Innocent Miss by Elizabeth Bailey

Volume 2 – December 2006
The Reluctant Bride by Meg Alexander
A Companion of Quality by Nicola Cornick

Volume 3 – January 2007
A Most Improper Proposal by Gail Whitiker
A Noble Man by Anne Ashley

Volume 4 – February 2007
An Unreasonable Match by Sylvia Andrew
An Unconventional Duenna by Paula Marshall

Also available from M&B™ by
New York Times bestselling author
Stephanie Laurens

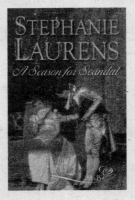

A superb 2-in-1 anthology of linked Regency stories

Featuring

Tangled Reins

Miss Dorothea Darent has no intention of ever getting married, but the disreputable Marquis of Hazelmere is captivated when they meet – and determined to win her heart…

Fair Juno

The Earl of Merton's days as a notorious rake are numbered when he finds himself rescuing a damsel in distress. But the lady flees the scene without revealing her name, leaving the Earl in pursuit of his mysterious *fair Juno.*

M&B

An enchantingly romantic Regency romp
from *New York Times* bestselling author
Stephanie Laurens

After the death of her father, Georgiana Hartley
returns home to England – only to be confronted with
the boorish advances of her cousin. Fleeing to the
neighbouring estate of Dominic Ridgely, Viscount
Alton of Candlewick, Georgiana finds herself sent
to London for a Season under the patronage of the
Viscount's sister.

Suddenly Georgiana is transformed into a lady,
charming the *ton* and cultivating a bevy of suitors.
Everything is unfolding according to Dominic's plan...
until he realises that he desires Georgiana for his own.

On sale 15th December 2006

*Available at WHSmith, Tesco, ASDA, Borders, Eason, Sainsbury's
and all good paperback bookshops*

2 FREE

BOOKS AND A SURPRISE GIFT!

We would like to take this opportunity to thank you for reading this Mills & Boon® book by offering you the chance to take TWO more specially selected titles from the Historical Romance™ series absolutely FREE! We're also making this offer to introduce you to the benefits of the Milss & Boon ® Reader Service™—

- ★ FREE home delivery
- ★ FREE gifts and competitions
- ★ FREE monthly Newsletter
- ★ Exclusive Reader Service offers
- ★ Books available before they're in the shops

Accepting these FREE books and gift places you under no obligation to buy, you may cancel at any time, even after receiving your free shipment. Simply complete your details below and return the entire page to the address below. You don't even need a stamp!

YES! Please send me 2 free Historical Romance books and a surprise gift. I understand that unless you hear from me, I will receive 4 superb new titles every month for just £3.69 each, postage and packing free. I am under no obligation to purchase any books and may cancel my subscription at any time. The free books and gift will be mine to keep in any case.

H7ZED

Ms/Mrs/Miss/Mr .... Initials ....

BLOCK CAPITALS PLEASE

Surname ....

Address ....

....

.... Postcode ....

Send this whole page to:
UK: FREEPOST CN8I, Croydon, CR9 3WZ